I08183333

# Compass

**Copyright © 2023 Amanda Cale**

**All rights reserved.**

**No part of this book may be reproduced in any form or by any electronic or mechanical means including information storage and retrieval systems, without permission in writing from the author. The only exception is by a reviewer, who may quote short excerpts in a review.**

**This book is a work of fiction. Names, characters, places, and incidents either are products of the author's imagination or are used fictitiously. Any resemblance to actual persons, living or dead, events, or locales is entirely coincidental.**

**ISBN-13: 978-0-9895211-3-0**

**For Pippa**

# Chapter 1

The trampoline moved a little as I tensed up in the presence of the wasp drifting by. The insect bobbed ten feet away before it made its way to the underside of the gutters on the back of the house.

The heavy summer heat warmed the trampoline's surface, but I was sitting still and not sweating yet. A warm breeze suddenly gave a strong gust as I gazed at the woods. Trying to ignore the burning ache in my side, I resisted the urge to touch the stitches. I hadn't dared let that part of my skin show since we'd come home. I hadn't even looked at it myself since we'd left Trenavell.

As I shifted, a small twinge shot up my side. If I had my friends here to ask whether I should jump on the trampoline, Noam would offer his solemn advice, Matt had a good chance of telling me not to, and Meris wouldn't care what I did. I got to my feet, seeing the healing marks of animal claws on one of my ankles. Liberal application of antibacterial ointment and aloe vera gel since the night we'd gotten home, plus the low light of my house in the evening, had kept those more or less hidden.

Socks helped, too.

Not wanting to start jumping too fast, I eased into a bounce, tightening my stomach as I felt another twinge spidering along the scar. As I pushed down and up, the black stitches tugged and pulled. It hurt, but with each bound upward into the humid summer air, exhilaration started to overtake discomfort.

The sound of Matt's back door opening drew me to turn, but as I twisted too fast, a hard jolt ran through my side.

"Ow!" jerked out of my mouth, and I slowed to a stop before plopping onto the black surface of the trampoline. I lay back and closed my eyes against the sunlight, hearing Matt's feet shuffle across the grass.

His voice came from behind the top of my head. "Why were you jumping?"

Sweat, more than I thought there'd been, trickled down my temples. "Because I wanted to?" I cracked my eyes open and squinted at him. His hair was damp.

He moved out of my line of sight to another part of the trampoline and climbed on. The surface under me bucked gently. "Should you?"

I pushed up slowly, the burn steady, and a trickle on my side got my attention. "Probably not." I tugged the right edge of my t-shirt up so Matt could see the stitches. "Everything good?"

He peered at it and looked up at me, not answering, but giving me that dry "of course it's not good" look.

"Matt, did I pop a stitch open?"

"No. Probably because it's been long enough for that to heal, but honestly, you need to ask Noam." He paused. "Or a doctor here."

"I can't ask a doctor here." I rolled my t-shirt back down, smoothing it gently, trying not to accidentally touch the bumps along my side.

Matt glanced toward the woods. "I'd guess they need to come out by now."

"Yeah." We'd been home for a week, and I'd spent that time trying to hide the stitches and be normal, and pretend we hadn't done anything more than being in the woods too long for Mrs. Dobken's comfort. My clothes had fit a little more loosely when we'd gotten home, but even that was starting to change the longer I had regular food to eat.

How we'd locate our friends once we did return to Trenavell, I didn't know, nor was I sure how to tell Meris what we'd heard: that she'd gotten something wrong. That me and Matt activating the device wasn't necessarily what the kingdom wanted. That people in Salt's Creek had an interest in it. That my own best friend's parents had known secrets that we'd randomly stumbled upon.

At least the stitches weren't infected.

Matt leaned back on his hands, his eyes on me, and tilted his head. "Do you want to try today?"

A wave of nerves rolled through my body, and my stomach dropped in dread. "We should." Maybe we'd find Noam and Meris, but how were we supposed to get back into the castle at all? Would the soldiers even let us in?

Somewhere behind me, an engine rumbled. I glanced over my shoulder as a mail truck moved past Matt's house and disappeared in front of mine with a squeal of brakes.

Slowly, I moved to the edge of the trampoline to hop off. As Matt stood, I grabbed the curved rail and swung down. My feet thumped onto the ground hard, and I hissed as the impact ran up through my side.

Matt swung off and approached me, his eyebrows raised.

Heat bloomed in my face, a contrast to the grass cooling the soles of my feet. "I'm gonna get the mail."

We walked silently to my mailbox. The humidity hung thick in the air, the mid-nineties temperature making almost a cook surface out of the concrete driveway. Down the street, the squeal of the mail truck's brakes sounded at short intervals, growing softer as it drove farther from my house.

The stack inside the box was short. "I don't have my key," I told Matt. "We have to go in the back door."

As we climbed onto the deck, I flipped through the mail. In the middle was a thin envelope from Ravenbook Academy, addressed to me.

Wrinkling my nose, I held it up so Matt could see. "Didn't we just get out of school?"

He looked at it. "I probably got one, too."

After glancing around to make sure that the wasp from earlier had gone somewhere else and wouldn't try to get in the house, I pushed the back door open and led the way into my air-conditioned living room. I'd been outside for long enough, and had warmed up enough, that the cool air raised goosebumps all over, including a fiery patch around the stitches. With a toss that thankfully kept the stack of mail together on the table, I filled a glass with water and sat back down.

Matt settled in the kitchen chair to my right, a glass in his hand.

My envelope wasn't thick, but it also couldn't be a tuition bill if it was addressed to me. I tore it open and pulled the single piece of paper out.

"Dear Ravenbook Academy senior,

I trust that you are enjoying your summer vacation. I'm looking forward to leading your class this year through some of our best traditions.

Orientation, as you are likely aware, will be held Friday, August 29, at 7:00 PM. The first day of school will be the day after Labor Day. At Orientation, we will host all senior parents for a reception, and the senior class is traditionally responsible for the setup of this event. We will plan to have a selection of refreshments, which the school will provide. If you wish to participate in setting up the reception, please arrive no later than 5:30 PM, in your school uniform, with appropriate footwear. No flip-flops, please.

Traditionally, the senior class also leads organization and preparation for Homecoming activities in October. While each class contributes and participates in Spirit Week festivities, our class will be responsible for the organization of game-time events, including the Homecoming parade and the Homecoming court ceremony, as well as the Homecoming dance. Class meetings will be held on the first Friday of the school year, at which time you will be choosing student leaders who will serve as representatives of your class.

This year, we will also be raising funds for a senior outing to the North Carolina Zoo, as well as a longer senior trip, both of which we will begin discussing at the first class meeting. Traditional fundraising methods include bake sales, car washes, and concession sales throughout the year.

I look forward to seeing you at the end of August, and to working with you for a successful senior year.

Have a great summer!

Joanna Whitley."

The nerves along my scar prickled, and I rubbed the itch absently, wincing at both the burn and the texture of the bumps there. I read the letter again, going through all those normal words. Summer vacation, refreshments, school uniform, homecoming. Bake sales.

Just regular stuff. We'd come home. This was life. If nothing else, we had to navigate it, and that wouldn't be that weird if we hadn't listened in on Matt's parents and Mr. Simpson.

*That conversation would have taken place whether or not you were there to hear it.*

Playing with the corner of the letter, I caught Matt's gaze shooting from my right hand up to my face. Pushing down the irritation, I pressed my teeth together for a second before speaking. "So…bake sales."

Matt's eyes focused on the letter again. "Yeah."

The itch returned. I resisted it.

"We can work together for that." Mom had to have some recipes, and failing that, I could buy cookie dough or cake mix at the grocery store.

Matt nodded. "Okay."

After another few quiet moments, I met Matt's gaze. "What do you think Meris is going to say?"

His eyes narrowed. "About what?"

"When we tell her that there are people here who knew about the device." Mr. Simpson had told Mr. and Mrs. Dobken that he and others were not aware of the existence of something. He had meant the gate in the Dupree house. But he'd also mentioned Mrs. Barnes and her daughter.

Why had he told Matt's parents that no one knew the gate existed? Who did he mean by "we"? "All that stuff Mr. Simpson said, about Mrs. Barnes and the gates and stuff."

Plus, based on how Mr. Simpson had answered a question from Mrs. Dobken, Matt's parents even knew about the gates.

Matt's eyes hardened for a second, clear anger shooting through them. "Good question."

With another long drink of water, I finished the glass. "Mr. Simpson said they didn't know the Dupree gate existed before." I knew hesitation bloomed over my face.

"You don't think he was telling the truth," Matt said.

Wincing, I answered. "Who'd he mean by 'we'?"

The hardness in Matt's eyes turned to confusion. "I assumed Trenavell, since Meris and Noam didn't know it was there."

"But he's not Trenavellan, and he knew about the gate network."

Matt was quiet, his eyes focused on the table. "Why would he lie about that specifically, especially if my parents knew about the gates?"

The itch spiked in my side, and I curled my toes, not wanting to scratch it again, not in front of Matt. My spine tensed with frustration. "I don't know." Matt's assumption about Trenavell not knowing about the gate could be wrong. "But...Dupree was supposed to be a friend of Trenavell, remember?"

He frowned a little. "Yeah, but...he could have just used a different gate, right? If there were a whole bunch of them?"

It made sense. If he was a friend of Trenavell, and if no one had known about the gate, then there probably was an official gate he used. "Then where was it?"

Matt shook his head. "No way to know."

We'd have to tell Meris and Noam. We'd have to tell them that Matt's parents had been instructed to keep an eye on us.

And the map. I hadn't told Matt about the map, and I hadn't looked at the letters since the mysterious drop-off on my porch.

Another itch traveled over the stitches. "So…if we're going to go, I need to change." My stomach dropped, and my heart lurched.

"Me too."

I set my glass by the sink. "I'll meet you by the trampoline in ten minutes."

"Yeah." Matt got up. "See you then."

After he left, I hurried to my room, nerves roiling in my stomach, my heart beating faster.

*Calm down.*

Once I'd pulled on my jeans, I rushed to get my socks and shoes on, and I must have twisted too much. A sharp pain shot through my side, jerking a cry from my mouth, making me freeze as the initial pain moved on, leaving a steady burn behind. My hands shook as I tied my shoelaces, and I stood slowly, reaching under my t-shirt to feel the healing wound. As I touched the flaw in my skin, the burn lit up.

At some point, I'd actually have to look at it myself. At least, if Noam could take them out today, the dark threads would be gone. It would just be a scar.

With my sweatshirt draped over my arm and a small flashlight in my pocket, I headed down the hall, my feet pounding on the stairs, each impact sending a smaller jolt through my side, but not as painful.

The sense of something bearing down on me was worse. We'd left Trenavell safely, under good circumstances and on good terms, but I knew that could change fast in wartime. They'd retaken the capital city, but if conflict heated up again, Compass Hill could have easily changed hands.

What if a year had passed there? After all, we'd spent weeks in Trenavell while only a few hours had passed on Earth. In all of our Earth days, Trenavell could have lost the war, and going back at all could be dangerous for me and Matt.

A single thought intruded.

Meris and Noam could be dead.

Rushing out the back door, I let it slam behind me, nearly ran down the deck steps, and leaned against the trampoline, wishing my heart would stop hammering and slow down, trying to convince myself that our friends were okay and still there somewhere. Matt would be out here soon. We'd know, I hoped.

As the humidity pressed on me, and the panicky sensations faded, the burn still persisted on my side. I had jarred my body by jumping, bending, twisting, and running. Now all that was just overtaking the anxious adrenaline. Maybe it would ground me, as it allowed me the illusion of outrunning my own thoughts.

The sound of Matt's back door echoed across his backyard. I pushed away from the trampoline. It was hot and I'd normally be sweating anyway, so maybe I wouldn't look too weird, but I tried to get my face to appear normal, in case it still betrayed fear. As I shifted, so did my sweatshirt, sliding along my arm a little. I put my other hand on it to stop it from sliding off, and my fingers found the edge of the rip that I still hadn't sewn up. Once I put it on, it would more or less line up with the stitches.

*Please let Noam be there.*

The brush under our feet crunched, loud in the woods. We could probably talk about something quietly. The map I'd found in the strange garage was still something I kept secret, and for now, that was probably best, in case someone was back here in the woods. But I could bring up the letters.

"I still haven't looked at those letters." They waited in the top drawer of my dresser, hidden under stuff.

"Who do you think dropped them off?" Matt asked.

"No idea." The car had been pulling off by the time I'd gotten to the door. "They were driving a burgundy car, but that was all I saw."

The side of the Dupree house appeared, the window and vine-covered porch drawing my gaze. Mrs. Barnes knew we came here, and likely more about what went on and what was hidden in the depths of the house, especially if she'd lived here.

Mr. Simpson hadn't known about the gate, but why did the person who owned the brown car know about it?

"Make sure that car's not here," I told Matt softly, stepping behind the big tree.

He nodded as I pressed myself against the trunk.

As he crept around the back of the house, I watched the part of the dirt driveway that was visible, hoping that I wouldn't see the dust of an approaching car.

Matt reappeared a few seconds later. "We're good."

We rushed into the house together. My tennis shoes scuffed softly as I stepped off the new planks of the steps and onto the old ones of the porch. They didn't creak, but how long until the wood began to rot and fall apart? As deserted as the house had been, the porch really should have fallen apart by now. Maybe it had, long before the steps were repaired. The porch could have been replaced long enough ago to be weathered, but not worn out.

Picking our way over the broken door that no one had moved from where it had fallen across the threshold, we moved into the shadows of the house. Quickly, I edged in front of Matt, but he didn't slow down to give me space. The back of my neck prickled as I remembered, vividly, leaning up against him while Noam wound bandages around the dressing on my side. Then I stopped, and Matt smacked into me.

"Why are you on my heels?" I snapped, jerking away from him and whirling around.

"Why did you stop?"

Gritting my teeth together, I glared at him. "Quit trying to walk on the back of my shoes."

"Sorry." He glared back at me. "Can you just let me walk in front?"

Aggravation flooded through me. *Calm down.* "Don't try to push past me."

"So let me go first?"

"Why?" But I knew why.

He held my gaze. "Because." And for a split second, again, his hazel eyes flicked down to my side.

My foot slipped a little on the floor's dust as I spun to face the kitchen and away from him. "You can't be my bodyguard."

He followed. "I'm not trying to."

The kitchen wall hung open a quarter inch, and I pulled it wide enough to slip into the dark cellar, then stopped to wait at the bottom of the steps. My eyes adjusted to the golden light from the top of the stairs on the opposite side of the room as Matt pulled the wall back closed as far as he could and stepped down into the dark beside me. For a moment, his eyes caught the glow of the moss lamps that grew along the stairs.

"Stop trying to get in front of me," I told him.

He didn't soften. "I'm going first this time."

"Sure. You're like a flashlight."

Matt rolled his eyes and led the way across the cellar and up the winding stone staircase.

At the top, sharp daylight shone around the edges of the door, and in the softer light from the moss lamps, I could just see that it was still barred. Was there really no one using it?

For a few long seconds, I stared at it. This gate hadn't been sealed like the others. Lukas Simpson and the "we" he'd mentioned hadn't known it existed, but he was aware of the gates being sealed. And Rebecca, Mrs. Barnes' daughter, was wanting to get something done, something involving the device. Why had activating it been such a surprise?

If Dupree had been a friend of Trenavell, what was the point of the device at all?

As smoothly as I could in the little space, trying not to twist too much, I pulled my sweatshirt on. Matt pulled the bar up and pushed slowly on the door.

Cold air filled the top of the staircase. We stepped out onto the mountain road together, alone as far as I could see.

"Where do we go?" Matt asked, his voice quiet.

The first time we'd met them, Meris and Noam had been in a cave, hiding, waiting to go down into the city. The thought of entering Compass Hill itself made my stomach drop again. "Do you remember how to get to the cave?"

"Yeah." Matt's questioning tone came through in his simple answer. "Should we try that?"

Unless years had passed, or disaster had struck, I doubted that Noam and Meris had left the city. I just didn't want to go there.

Then again, Meris had had to be summoned by her dad to a meeting once Trenavell had retaken the city, and I could imagine that there was a scolding in that. Maybe, if Meris and Noam had found themselves under the direction of adults again, they'd decided to return to the cave where they'd sheltered before. "We can go to the cave first."

Our footsteps sounded impossibly loud in the near-silent forest, and a chill crept over me. "Weren't there guards when we left?"

"There were." Matt kept his answer quiet.

My heart ticked a little faster. Why were the woods so empty now? Wouldn't Trenavell want to keep at least a patrol here? The thought that this war, even after Compass Hill had been retaken, might have had some terrible turn rushed through my head, inviting more thoughts that our friends could have been killed. Or maybe a hundred years had passed here, and everyone we'd known was dead regardless of the direction the war went in, because there was no Naolon presence here, either. Maybe the war wasn't part of anyone's living memory. Maybe it was just a history lesson now.

I kept my voice low. "At least we won't get caught."

As we approached the cave, I tried to see if there were any tell-tale flickers from a fire that they might have lit inside, but the pale sunlight shone too bright. Matt moved in front of me to approach the entrance. If there was a fire, he'd be able to see it earlier than I could. If there wasn't, the light from the sun might let him see well enough to tell what was in the cave. He ducked inside.

*If they're gone, what would we even find in here?*

The cave held nothing but a deep chill, with no warm glow of a fire. They probably hadn't been in it, at least not today.

Matt stood quietly. My eyes slowly adjusted. It still held the remains of a fire, so clearly they or someone had sheltered in the cave somewhat recently.

*That could be left from the last time we were all here.*

"Why would they bother with coming here?" Matt asked suddenly.

He knew Meris. "If Meris wanted to get away from her parents, then she knows this cave has been useful before, and if no one else knows about her and Noam sheltering here…"

Matt turned to me. "Assuming she can get away, or that they're letting anyone out."

There wasn't a single part of me that was ready to check Compass Hill. My hesitation wasn't logical. I had to have the stitches out, and I needed Noam for that, so we had to find him. With a deep breath, I leaned back against the cave wall. "Short of going into Compass Hill and trying to get into the palace, how in the world are we supposed to get ahold of them?" The tickle in my side started up, taking a couple seconds to become a full-on itch, and I rubbed at it. My fingers caught in the rip in my sweatshirt. For a few seconds, the skin burned where I'd touched it through my t-shirt.

Matt let out a breath. "I don't know." He eyed me.

"We'll have to go there," I conceded, trying to swallow the nerves in my gut. "Do you remember how long it takes?" It wasn't hard to find the city, but it also wasn't a short walk from the gate.

"It takes a while," Matt said. "Maybe half an hour?"

We might get detained if we tried going into the castle by ourselves. It wasn't like we were heroes, and clearly what we'd done hadn't been applauded. If anything, it had confused and inconvenienced people. "We could leave a message with Miriam." My stomach took another dive as I remembered Ira's ax rushing toward me.

Matt looked down the mountainside. "I think we should go home right now."

It had taken us a bit to climb up to the cave, and it would definitely take a while to walk to Compass Hill. But maybe we'd be let in. Meris could have made that possible, even if we weren't heroes. "I think we should try to get to Compass Hill." I didn't particularly want to, but the stitches had to come out. It was early in the day at home. We had time, and if no one was around, that probably meant that Naolon wasn't around.

Matt's mouth quirked. "Do you really want to?"

"I need to."

With a slow nod, he stepped back out fully into the sun. "Let's try, then."

We made our way back down to where the gate was. The way to Compass Hill was something I did remember a little more clearly, plus the open expanse of land made it pretty clear what direction it lay in, and I could even see it, not far away and set as a dot on the horizon, but close. It would still take a while, since we were walking, but a half hour wouldn't be too bad.

The clouds passing over Trenavell's sun waxed and waned. The sky stayed bright white and gray over the empty road. When we'd departed the city to find the train, we'd gone north, and I wondered what lay south of Compass Hill.

Matt cleared his throat as I scanned the land around us. "How are you really?"

We hadn't talked in depth about everything that had happened to us. I'd given myself the week to breathe and eat and sleep and heal, stuffing Trenavell into a box somewhere in my mind. One of the things that wouldn't stay in that box was the image of Matt's hazel eyes, rimmed in red.

Hoping my face didn't itself turn red at that memory, I kept my eyes on the landscape. "Okay."

He smiled a little. "We found a portal to another world or planet or whatever."

"I know." A breeze blew past. "I mean, right now we're here, and it doesn't seem all that weird." I'd stuffed Trenavell into a mental box because it was too big to think about when we weren't actually here. The wound and the stitches also didn't send me into an existential spiral. That was a daily thing to deal with. That was concrete. Trenavell was tangible the last time I was here, and it was again. Sandwiched in between that could be thoughts of barriers between realities and outer space and how time worked and what the gates might be, and those were things too hard to think of. "It's a lot otherwise." Flickers of movement far off caught my eye for a minute.

Matt's face turned solemn again. "Yeah."

The road continued to be empty as we got closer to the city, and quiet reigned. Was that weird? Shouldn't the city have been louder? There were plenty of people in it; there always had been. Compass Hill did have walls, though. That could keep sound in.

"The gates are closed," Matt observed.

That would definitely keep plenty of sound in, and us out. "So…do we knock?"

Matt snorted. "Maybe."

No one guarded the gate. No one patrolled. We halted ten feet away. No one called down or stopped us.

Eyeing the solidly closed-off city, I thought of the way we'd gone in the last time, the day of the battle. "Remember the other way we got in?" I asked quietly.

Matt looked at me. "Yeah, but…"

"What?" With a deep breath, I tried to calm the irritation at my friend.

"Considering that it's really tightly closed off, sneaking in might not be a great idea," Matt said.

With a step towards where I remembered the hole in the wall being, I answered, "It's worth trying, especially considering why we're even trying to get in right now." My footsteps shuffled over the ground, the sound bouncing a little off the wall in a goosebump-inducing echo that exacerbated the heavy silence of Compass Hill. Matt followed me.

The hole wasn't too far from the gate, maybe a quarter of the way around the city.

But this entry point had changed. Instead of an easily-moved section of wall, boards stretched across the opening.

"They fixed it," I said, puzzled.

"Wouldn't they want to?"

Studying the repair, I stepped closer. "How hard do you think it would be to get these off?"

Matt's mouth opened. "That would probably be pretty loud."

"Who do you think is around to hear it?" There were streets on the other side. This entrance, I knew, wasn't too far from Miriam's house.

"Plenty of people," Matt told me.

"Plenty who care?" I tugged on one of the boards. It moved outward enough for me to wedge my fingers between it and the wall, the nail scraping softly through the wood, the board itself giving off a creak.

Without much more resistance, it gave way, and I stumbled backwards, the plank in my hands.

But on the other side was another layer of boards on the inside of the wall.

*Maybe I can push those out.*

"It's a weak spot," Matt said, taking the board from me and pushing it back into place.

A tickle ran along the scar. "It is." With a sigh, I looked up at the top of the wall. "I doubt it's like Skyrren inside, though."

"Probably not."

Turning, I headed back for the main gate, Matt beside me.

"We could knock," I offered.

He shrugged. "It's worth a try."

At the gate, I raised my hand and rapped my knuckles against the wood, loud enough for someone to hear, for sure.

No one came, and after another minute, I knocked again.

And no one answered.

How was I supposed to get the stitches out if I couldn't find Noam? Backing away from the gate, I took a deep breath and turned to go back up the road. Another far-off movement to my left pulled my gaze there, offering nothing more to see as we went back to the woods. The Trenavellan sky turned more gray than white.

"We can try tomorrow," Matt said. "But if we can't get in, the stitches still need to come out."

"I know."

As we crossed into the trees, the wind picked up, blowing heavy clouds across the sky. I shivered, the moisture in the air becoming evident. As we climbed up to the mountain road, raindrops began to smack the ground around us. We hurried for the gate, and as we ducked inside, the rain clattered down in a rush, muffled by the door as I closed it behind me.

We stood in the golden light for a minute, my eyes adjusting quickly.

“Wanna hang out?” I asked Matt. Normal stuff. The door could be the lid for the box I kept Trenavell in. “We can watch TV or something.”

“Okay,” Matt answered.

The Salt’s Creek summer day would seem much hotter now that we’d been in the fall weather of Trenavell.

But was it fall? It had been when we’d been there before, but had the seasons changed over to winter? Did Trenavell have mild winters, or was it even far enough north to be that cold at all? The temperature rose as we crossed the cellar and climbed into the kitchen. As the heavy air made me immediately start sweating, I pulled my sweatshirt off, trying not to twist.

We parted at the edge of my yard, Matt heading to his house to change. I couldn’t wait to get my shoes off, and I wished I had them off now as I walked across the grass. Rubbing the stinging itch in my side, I knew I’d have to actually look at it myself.

As my foot landed on the bottom step of the deck, a flash of brown at the corner of my left eye tugged my gaze in that direction, my nerves jolting. A car, but this one green, drove by to the left and disappeared down the street. Somewhere else, kids yelled and the noise of cicadas covered up the sounds of tires on asphalt.

Rushing inside, I told myself that there were plenty of brown cars in the world.

***

That night, I stood in front of the mirror in my bathroom, my side freshly burning. My heart rate ticked up fast until it pounded on the inside of my ribcage, near painfully, as I reluctantly prepared to look at the threads that had held my skin together.

Closing my eyes tight, I took a deep breath and rolled the hem of my t-shirt up slowly, cringing at the brush of fabric against the scar. The tip of one of my unsteady fingers caught in a thread for a moment. Flinching, I kept rolling until the cool air flowed across my skin. Then, with an exhale and another deep breath, I looked into the mirror.

The black threads made stark lines against my skin. The wound had healed and left dots of yellow and green bruise remnants from the ax's impact. The threads pulled taut across raised red knots. Looking down, gazing directly at it for the first time since we'd left Trenavell, I touched one of the bumps, gently. It burned.

There was no way that could be good.

It wasn't like I could really go alone to a clinic here in town. I didn't want to try taking them out myself, but I knew I might have to.

A flash of Matt's red-rimmed eyes came to mind.

I reached for the antibiotic ointment, wondering for a second what the point would be now. It was healed, even if it was inflamed. It probably just wouldn't feel normal for a long time, if ever, considering how bad the wound had been. I didn't want to entertain the thought of infection, but the truth was that the threads were foreign objects that had probably overstayed their welcome. After smearing a glob of ointment across the scar, I rolled my shirt back down. The fabric stuck for a moment. Suppressing a gag, I left the bathroom, hoping we'd find Noam and Meris soon.

# Chapter 2

We peered out of the gate, hesitating. The weather was the same as it had been when we'd come the day before, and though the road looked wet, it wasn't currently raining.

"We'll try again with the city," Matt said.

"Yeah." Maybe we could access the hole in the side of the wall with another try. "Think the rest of the boards would come away from the hole?"

"They might."

That was a satisfying enough answer.

We left footprints on the road to the city, though it didn't seem like there was anyone to follow them. They'd probably follow the prints back, if they wanted to. But Trenavell knew about the gate. Whoever hadn't known about it before did now.

Somewhere in the distance, I saw movement again. Flickers of something, almost like a fish splashing in water. "What do you think that is?" I asked Matt, pointing.

He watched, frowning. "Not sure."

Maybe the weather was why everything was so quiet. More rain making its way to this part of the mountains could be reason enough for people to take shelter. The weird thing was how much of a standstill Compass Hill stood at. We spent a couple of minutes at the gate, knocking to no answer. Not a sound came through the wall. It was possible that the type of wood the gates and the wall were made of didn't really allow for sound to travel all that well, but the absence of the guards wasn't normal.

"Let's go try the other part," I told Matt.

When we reached the boards, the one I'd pried off looked unchanged. Matt had put it back in place, but without a hammer, he could only do so much.

It came away easily when I tugged, revealing the one on the other side.

"Are you gonna get the next one down?" Matt asked in a whisper.

With narrowed eyes, I studied it. "I think I should try and push the one on the other side first and see how hard it is to get that one off."

"What if someone sees you?"

“We can run.” Half-crouching, I placed both hands on the other board and pushed.

This one moved some, a tiny fraction of an inch, before meeting resistance that I didn’t think was the nails keeping it in place. Something on the other side had stopped the board from moving.

“I think they took plenty of precautions with this wall.” Straightening, I turned to Matt, at a loss. “How…I mean, we’ve tried knocking on the gate twice and the only thing I can think of is making another hole like this one somewhere else.” The scar itched. How was I supposed to get the stitches out?

Matt’s eyes softened. “We can figure it out. It’s not an emergency yet.”

*Yet.*

He kept going. “Let’s head back home.”

“Yeah.” Part of me wanted to kick the wall, as if that would help anything.

The eerie stillness of the road and the woods increased my worry that either something bad had happened to our friends, and Trenavell as a whole, or that somehow centuries had passed and all of them were long gone. The latter wasn’t the most rational line of thinking, but considering how time worked between our two worlds, it was a remote possibility.

We kept quiet until we were back inside the mountain and on our way down the stairs. I tugged my sweatshirt off, careful not to twist too much as I stepped into the kitchen and froze.

"Uh-oh."

"What?" Matt asked as he closed the wall.

"The light's different," I said. "Really different."

He looked around at the longer beams of sunlight that filled the kitchen. "Oh."

"I didn't think we were there that long."

"We weren't. Not on that side." He swallowed.

"What if it's been a whole day here?" I asked, rushing for the hallway.

"It might not have been." Matt followed me, and in his voice, I could hear his effort at trying to be optimistic and reassuring.

"Well, it's been a few hours for sure." It didn't exactly seem like late afternoon, but it also wasn't still just after noon like it had been when we'd left my backyard. Matt had said his mom might be off work early today, and that we would definitely need to beat her home. But, though I had been so sure that we would, time had done that thing again, and now there was no telling what day it even was.

"My mom's probably definitely home," Matt said, sounding way too amused to my ears.

"Yeah, it'd be real cool if she's got my parents in a conference in our living room again." A twinge of guilt at yelling at him when he didn't deserve it welled up inside as we made our way through the woods. We got to the trampoline just as Matt's mom was getting out of her car. Her gaze landed on us, her face still. As we approached, her eyes moved back and forth between us. After a few seconds, she smiled, stepping into my yard.

"Hey, Anya," she called. Was there a falter, an awkwardness, in her smile? Something in her face didn't look too thrilled to find us exiting the woods together.

"Hi, Mrs. Dobken." She knew all about all of this. She wouldn't speak a word about it, but she knew.

Her smile dropped as she turned to Matt. "Matt, I need you to come help me with something, please." Her words had an edge. She turned the tight smile at me again. "We'll see you later, Anya."

*Okay...* I nodded. "See you later."

Matt gave me a weird look as he stepped away. "'Bye."

As he followed his mom into their house, I made my way to my porch, trying not to take it personally that she suddenly had some mysterious task for Matt. But why had her face looked like that? Did she not want me to hang out with him?

After all, she'd been the one to keep all that stuff from him, and she seemed to be completely aware that I had dragged him into something she'd apparently tried to escape. Matt hadn't been real happy with her or Danny's mom for what the two had hidden from him. Based on what he'd said, though, it was clear his Aunt Della was the one that was less interested in hiding things. After all, Danny seemed to be some kind of messenger for Trenavell, or maybe even a spy. It was hard to know, and neither of us had heard from him since the day we'd come back home. I'd always been welcomed by Matt's parents, but Mrs. Dobken didn't want to involve him in this stuff, and I'd undermined that.

***

Mom made her way down the hallway and leaned into my bedroom, still wearing her scrubs.

"Hey Mom," I said. My side itched, but I didn't dare scratch it in front of her.

"Hey." She cleared her throat. "I have a favor to ask for one of the ladies I work with."

"Okay." Why would her coworker have a question for me?

"Melissa Tomlinson needs someone to watch her twins in the morning, the day after tomorrow. She lives a couple streets over from us, on Peach. The kids are nine." Mom raised her eyebrows. "It would be good for some extra money."

"How long would she need me for?" I asked. I did need to save up some money.

"Couple hours. She'll need you to be there around nine-thirty."

"Okay."

Mom leaned away. "I'll text her. Thanks."

"You're welcome."

She smiled and left my room, her footsteps shuffling down the hallway.

Money. I guessed I could put it towards textbooks for college, assuming this all ended by then.

Another itch worked its way along my side. I rubbed it, careful not to press too hard. It stung.

I eyed the top drawer of my dresser. The letters needed to be read. Who'd brought them back? Why had they brought them back? How had they known to, or where to bring them? Goosebumps blossomed slowly over my skin.

Who was watching?

***

It was well after ten o'clock when the usual tapping started on my window. One single two-word text had arrived from Matt after supper. *Talk later.*

I tossed my book down on my bed and got up too fast, pain knifing across my side at the sudden movement.

"Erk." Staying still for a few seconds let the nerves calm down, and I took slower steps to the window before yanking the blinds open and pushing the window up.

Matt leaned on his windowsill, the lamplight behind him golden, his eyes catching the glow of the streetlight. "This is literally the first free time I've had all day."

"What did you have to do?"

"Mostly hauling boxes of stuff down from the attic so Mom can donate it. And I had to clean my bedroom. And vacuum the upstairs hallway." He stretched. "And we ate supper."

"Oh."

He shrugged. "I guess it all needed to be done, but…" He frowned.

Accusing Matt's mom of keeping us apart wasn't something I wanted to do, even if she had acted weird, so I just waited for him to speak.

He shook his head. "I found out that Danny's going to college here in the fall."

There was no reason for me to be frustrated at him not finishing his other thought. *Calm down.* "Cool. Where? And why?"

"I don't know why, but ECU, apparently."

We'd left Danny in Trenavell, because he'd chosen to stay. But beyond that, when had he decided to go to college in North Carolina? It couldn't have been a last-minute decision. It had to have been made before we ever stepped foot into the Dupree house. The goosebumps raced over my scar.

*What is going on?* "Do you think he's seen Meris and Noam?"

"No idea."

It sounded like Danny had possibly made it back home safely, which meant that if anything bad had happened in Trenavell, it hadn't been when Danny was there.

*Or he escaped something.*

The timing confused me. "How long was the college thing planned?" He could have heard back from ECU before stepping through whatever gate he used.

Matt's chin rose at his realization. "I…don't know." He tilted his head, eyes widening, staring at a point in space. "He had to have planned it ahead of time."

"Yeah." Why here? "Wouldn't a school in Michigan be easier and a lot cheaper?"

"It would be."

It struck me that he might have been using a now-sealed gate, and was trapped in Trenavell. If that was the case, his only route to North Carolina could be the Kings Road gate.

Matt started speaking again. "Maybe Aunt Della wants him to keep an eye on us."

She'd sent that note in the cave, or she'd been there herself to leave it, speared into the remains of the fire on the end of a dull knife. But the school year was pretty far off. Wouldn't Danny come now, if keeping an eye on us was the purpose of him going to ECU? Any immediacy that his mom felt would make it pointless for him to wait until school started.

And wouldn't he tell Matt if his mom wanted to have us watched?

Matt yawned. "I'm gonna play a game for a while."

"Okay." With a glance back into my room, I remembered the map that I still hadn't shown Matt. It was probably not a good idea to yell across at his house about it. "I was reading. Do you want to come over tomorrow?"

"Yeah."

"Okay." Reaching up for the window, trying not to stretch, I pulled it down an inch. "See you then."

"See you," Matt answered, stepping back into the golden lamplight and shutting his window.

I wished he'd finished his incomplete sentence as I wondered if Mrs. Dobken did have something against me.

# Chapter 3

The stitches were definitely warm. Maybe it was friction from how I'd been scratching them all morning.

The doorbell rang, and I jumped, every nerve alive, before remembering that Matt was supposed to be on his way over. With a sigh, I made my way downstairs and opened the front door.

He smiled "'Morning."

"Good morning." A wasp hovered under the corner of the porch, and I instinctively grabbed Matt's arm and forcefully pulled him inside, letting the glass door slam.

"What?" Matt asked, whirling to look out the door.

"Wasp."

"Oh."

"Come upstairs," I told him, closing the wooden door. The jumpy nerves I'd activated twice in a short span of time suddenly made the itch ten times worse. As we climbed the stairs, I reached under my t-shirt to scratch the skin. It hurt when my fingers met the warm bumps there. I knew the warmth wasn't good, and knew it was bad that a brief tug on a knot hurt so much.

Maybe I *would* have to go to a doctor here. The alternative was looking up a way to remove stitches and doing that myself. We had to find Noam and Meris.

Matt followed me to my room, waiting as I went to my dresser. In the top drawer hid the map and box of letters, the former underneath the latter. We needed to look at the letters, but Matt knew about those. I hadn't told anyone about the map.

Carefully unfolding it, I brought it over to Matt and held it out.

He took it and sat on my bed. After a glance at the parchment, his eyes lingering on the signature at the bottom, he looked back up at me. "Where'd it come from?"

"That garage in New Mexico." My desk chair squeaked as I sat. "Under some stuff on a table."

His eyes roved over the parchment again. "Remember the sign for Moon-eye?"

"Do you think the name of the town means what it sounds like it means?"

"Probably." He leaned forward. "Do you think Meris and Noam would want to see this?"

"Maybe." My glance down the hall was pointless. No one was home. "The gate on Kings Road is on there, but it's not on the map Noam had." That lined up with Mr. Simpson saying they didn't know the Dupree house gate existed. "Remember how Meris and Noam were surprised that we came through it?"

He studied the parchment again. "I'd find a way to protect it before you bring it." He handed it back to me.

I took it and hopped out of my desk chair, moving too fast, and choking off a squeak of pain as I crossed to the dresser.

"Does it hurt that bad?" Matt asked.

"I wasn't expecting it right then." The map slipped easily back under the still-buried shoebox, and I closed the dresser and turned to Matt.

"Anya." His gaze fixed hard on me. "We haven't been able to find Noam. You need to go to a doctor."

"We haven't tried today." We could do that. "I need to change, though."

The worry on his face bloomed. "You want to go soon?"

"Yes."

"Then I can meet you outside in a few minutes."

"Good."

He stood and walked into the hallway, me following him to the top of the stairs, watching as he descended to the front hall, headed out the door, and pulled it tight behind him. We hadn't even taken a peek at the letters. What would those have in them?

What would Meris and Noam want to do with the map, if anything? Was it safe to take it to Trenavell at all? Was it even useful? There had to be a reason someone had hidden it in a garage by a highway.

The map was small and folded easily, so I could stick it into a zip bag if I needed to, if I was careful. If the Kings Road gate was on there, then where did the other ones go?

***

At least the sun was out, the sky faintly striped with slender clouds as we walked down the road to the city.

"Should we bother?" I asked Matt, gesturing at Compass Hill as we got close enough to see the closed city gates. Some movement flickered in the corner of my eye, in the same place as it had before. What was that? Matt followed my gaze as clumps of dirt flung up a foot into the air, and we stopped together to watch it, a chill creeping over my skin. Farther away, a shadow moved smoothly, fluidly, out of the ground.

Matt turned fully to face the shadow as it turned and slithered away from us, toward the far mountain landscape.

"What's that?" The words slid out of my mouth, a moan on a wave of dread.

"It's leaving," Matt said, doubt dripping from his words.

"For now." Even if it didn't bother us on the way to the city, whatever the thing was, it could wander back toward us.

"I don't think it cares about us either way," Matt remarked. "It…looks like a burrow beast."

"But slow." The one we'd seen before had been a lot faster. What if there were a bunch more?

Matt glanced at me. "We have to find Noam."

"Do you really think we will?" I snapped. "We can't get into the city, there's no one around to help us, and there's a dirt whale hanging around over there that could completely undermine the ground under our feet."

Matt had cracked a smile at "dirt whale."

That made me relax. "I'm…we need to figure out how to find the other two." Desperation filled me up. "I just want to go home right now, though, please. We can figure something out." I hesitated. "You could try and text Danny. Or call your aunt and see if you can get ahold of him."

"I could." His eyes narrowed, clearly calculating. "Do you think she'd tell my mom?"

"Do *you* think she would?"

Slowly, he shook his head. "No."

The creature in the distance moved, its direction indeterminate, clumps of dirts flying up again from another spot. "Then let's go and try to figure something out. You don't have to call your aunt or anything, but…" I turned back to face the woods.

"Do you want to get something to eat, then?" Matt asked. "Whitley's?"

"Sure."

***

The cool front porch steps made a contrast with the hot afternoon. The air conditioning in Matt's truck would be so welcome.

His front door opened, and I watched him close it behind himself before I got up and walked to his yard. My forehead broke out in sweat in the minute it took to get there.

Matt unlocked the truck. Carefully, I climbed in, glad for the air conditioning as it gusted out of the vents when Matt cranked the ignition. For some reason, my skin had been more sensitive since we'd gotten home. I had the same t-shirt on, but even the brush of it, on top of the persistent burn, irritated the red bumps.

Matt backed out of the driveway. "Are you nervous or something?"

"No," I answered, shifting.

"You're sweating."

My face grew warm. "It's hot."

"I know, but…"

"Hush."

Whitley's stood nearly at the edge of downtown, almost the last building there. Salt's Creek Bank and Trust, across from the library, formed something like an entryway to this wilted part of town. A block past them, city hall stood with the police station and sheriff's office on each side of it, all three facing the courthouse. We passed an empty storefront on my right, the words "Gertrude's Bridals and Formals" painted on a window, a backdrop of yellowed paper stuck to the inside of the glass, falling down in one corner. Next to it, another closed business had boards on the windows. Nothing remained to indicate what it had been at one point. Whitley's closest neighbors were the train station next door, and across the street, an empty house, long in disrepair. The house's yard held a faded wooden sign, paint cracked, that had been there for as long as I could remember, which read "Future Project of the Salt's Creek Restoration Society." Beside the house, a street led back into a historic neighborhood. The homes that I could see from the truck were a mixed bag of fresh paint and steady porches beside chipped siding and the slouching edges of roofs.

Matt pulled into the cracked asphalt parking lot of Whitley's. The parking space lines had long ago mostly faded away, leaving only ghosts and suggestions behind in flecks of white paint. Matt parked between two line remnants and turned the truck off.

It wasn't too crowded inside. Most of the people in Whitley's looked like they were on lunch break from whatever workplace was nearby. Fishing in my shorts pocket for my wallet, I let Matt go ahead of me, and stopped short when I bumped into him. He was still three feet from the counter, with no one in front.

I stepped around him. "Want me to go first?"

He nodded, and I turned to the cashier.

Samantha, the girl from school he'd once said had been stalking him, stood behind the register, her face polite and neutral.

"What can I get for you?" she asked.

"Cheeseburger, fries, and a drink," I said, trying to hold down the bubble of laughter that wanted to pop up.

She punched my order into the register. "Anything else?"

"That's it."

"Five dollars and thirty-three cents."

I handed over a ten dollar bill.

Samantha handed me back my change and a cup. "Yours is order number thirteen."

"Thanks," I said, and moved away, heading for the drink fountain and letting Matt step forward.

"How about you?" I heard her ask. Their exchange faded as I reached the drink fountain and the big canisters of tea, sweet and unsweet, beside it. As I filled up my cup with sweet tea, I glanced back. Matt's face was solemn as he stepped away from the counter, and a weird, unexpected sense of satisfaction went through me.

*Her conversation skills sure didn't work on him.*

Where in the world had that come from? *He's not yours. He doesn't belong to you.* She'd been perfectly nice.

Matt's head tilted as he reached me. "What's wrong?"

My face got hot. "Nothing."

He filled his cup with ice. "Okay, well, I'm pretty sure you're not sunburned."

"I'm gonna find a table." The random one in the middle of the restaurant would be fine, and I rushed to it, willing my face to cool off and return to normal.

"Order thirteen!"

I stopped, sighed, changed direction, grabbed my tray from the counter, and went back toward the table, picking a seat that faced the door. A swallow of iced tea cooled me off as I waited. The same voice called out order fourteen, and Matt showed up at the table soon after, settling down across from me as the restaurant door opened.

Brandon's girlfriend Sara entered Whitley's and waved at Samantha before making her way to the counter.

Matt glanced over his shoulder. "That's Brandon's girlfriend, right?"

"Yeah." The memory of Brandon meeting my eyes in Compass Hill played clearly in my mind. "Where do you think he's at?"

Matt shook his head.

I couldn't guess what might have happened to him.

Sara turned away from the counter and her gaze fell on us. Her face brightened as she made her way over.

*At least* she's *friendly.*

"Hey, y'all," she said, smiling as she stopped at the edge of the table.

"Hey," I answered.

"Have y'all seen Brandon?" The question was sudden.

*Not on Earth lately.* "Not for a week or so…"

Sara's shoulders slumped. "I was hoping you might have. Samantha hasn't seen him, either."

Was he okay? I winced. "Sorry."

She smiled, waving her hand and dismissing my apology. "That's fine. I know he's friends with y'all, so I thought I'd ask."

Matt set his cup down. "If we see him, we'll let him know you asked about him."

"Thank you. MeeMaw needs her grass cut, and he said he would, so…" Sara smiled and shrugged. "I'll see y'all around!" She rushed out of the restaurant.

I still didn't know why I'd seen Brandon in Trenavell. "So… do you think there's a bad reason she can't get in touch with Brandon?"

"I didn't see him with…you know." Matt ate a cluster of fries. "The other people."

Prisoners. "I didn't, either, but what if we didn't see all of them?"

Matt's broke a single fry in half. "Maybe he shouldn't have been with them, then."

Brandon still didn't really deserve to die, and I hoped he hadn't. "Matt…"

When he looked up at me, his eyes softened. "Sorry."

"It's fine." As I chewed a bite of my burger, I realized that I didn't exactly know what I'd do whenever I did see Brandon. Him not being here, and the uncertainty of what might have happened to him, could make him a better person in my eyes, at least until we met again.

"Anya?" The woman's voice accompanied a light shadow falling across us.

Our teacher Miss Whitley stood at the edge of our table, smiling.

My spine straightened, for some reason, as I set my food down. "Hi, Miss Whitley."

"How's your summer going?"

"Good."

"You, Matt?"

He'd set his burger down. "Yes, ma'am."

"Excellent." She paused, looking around. "My brother's sure happy that everybody still loves this place."

I'd never once put it together. Whitley's.

She kept talking. "Anya, while you're here, I wanted to ask you something."

"Sure."

She smiled, cringing a little. "This might be a little awkward, but I heard from a neighbor of mine, Melissa Tomlinson, that you might be available to babysit some this summer."

I had a referral even though I hadn't even been to the Tomlinsons' house yet. "I am." I wasn't working anywhere else, and Trenavell wasn't all that open to us.

"Excellent." She glanced at her phone. "Could you do it this Friday?"

My nod made her break out in a grin.

"Awesome. I live on Peach Street, at 2806. If you can come by a little before six o'clock, that would be perfect."

"Okay." At least neither job was all that far. Peach Street was close enough that I could take my bike.

"Thanks!" She pocketed her phone. "I'll have dinner for you and Jimmy to eat. Probably a frozen pizza or something, if that's okay."

"That's fine."

She seemed amused for a second. "One more question, and that's just if I can have a phone number to contact you at, in case there are any changes?"

"Sure."

Once I'd given her my phone number, Miss Whitley stepped back. "Great. Oh, and I'm teaching an advanced North Carolina history class in the fall. You two might find it pretty interesting if you need a senior elective."

"Okay." That probably would be interesting. "Thanks."

She smiled warmly. "See you two later!" she called, and left.

Matt dumped the rest of his fries onto his burger wrapper as I finished my food. "What's it going to be like babysitting for one of our teachers?"

"I don't know, but more money for college, I guess." It would be weird if it was a regular thing to babysit for Miss Whitley, but maybe it was just this one time.

When we were done and had gone outside, I quietly climbed into Matt's truck, flinching at the stretch in my side, telling myself I didn't care if Matt saw. I looked over at him and opened my mouth.

He cut me off. "I saw that."

Okay, I did care. "Look, it was a pretty big wound, so even when I get the stitches out, it's still gonna hurt a little because it's big and there's scar tissue and severed nerves and everything. It's not gonna feel good all the time and I have no idea how long that's gonna be true for." My voice had risen in volume before I stopped to take a break, anger heating my face. "So please stop talking about it."

Matt stared at me for a long moment, his face tense. "I'm not—" His lips pressed together, and his ears turned pink. "I'm not gonna stop worrying." He turned the key in the ignition, backed out of the space, and drove toward the street.

"You can't be my bodyguard." Why had his ears turned pink? "You can't just push or jump in front of me. You can't go back in time and get between me and Ira." Sunlight flashed off a distant windshield. "I know I'm human and you have some issues with your mom's family being extraterrestrials and with how they didn't tell you all this stuff, but you can't always be in front of me." It wasn't as strong a finish as I'd wanted.

Matt sighed, glanced each way, and pulled out into the road. "Why don't you want me to?"

With no idea what to tell him, I squirmed, because I couldn't really articulate what I was actually thinking. Flashes of memory of that day, of pain and Matt yelling at Noam and Matt's hazel eyes rimmed in red, came rushing back, along with the one of Matt running across the chapel and falling, and me thinking he might have been shot.

I settled for a jerky shrug. "I don't know." Why would it make me uncomfortable? Matt was just being a good friend.

"Fair enough." He was quiet, and the county passed by as we drove home.

As Matt pulled onto Willow Drive, the tension felt for all the world like a fight. When he stopped in his driveway, I got out and walked in front of the truck.

Matt stared at me. "You really do need to get them out."

A single bitter laugh jerked out of my mouth. "Don't I know it."

"Go take a look at them," he said. "Seriously."

"I will."

Maybe I would have to go to a doctor here. The alternative, if I couldn't get to Noam, was to look up a way to remove them and do it myself.

"We have to try again tomorrow," Matt said.

"I'm babysitting earlier in the day."

"We'll go after."

"Yeah." The humidity draped heavily over me, and I started sweating again as we stood outside. "Right now I'm going inside, though."

"Okay." He turned to his house. "Maybe I'll see you later?"

"Of course."

We parted ways. No wasps hung around the porch, but I still hurried as fast as I could inside.

***

The smell of pizza found its way up into my room with the sound of my parents' voices.

"Anya, pizza!" my mom called.

The distant buzz of discomfort sharpened as I stood, with a harsh note accompanying the brush of my t-shirt against the scar. It would be all night and part of the morning before we could even try to head to Trenavell.

The crunchy pop of a soft drink can being opened snapped through the front hallway as I made my way to the kitchen. My parents stood by the stove, putting pizza slices on paper plates.

"Pizza from the new place," Mom said. "It's a supreme."

"Sounds good." The can being opened had sounded even better. I put two slices of pizza on my plate, and grabbed one of the two cans of store-brand colas from the shelf in the refrigerator before following my parents into the living room.

Dad flipped through the channels on the cable guide and settled on a World War II documentary.

I bit into the pizza. The cheese and sauce and toppings and chewy crust were good. Hopefully this place would stick around longer than the last pizza place, which was some chain that didn't last in Salt's Creek, closing when I was eight years old.

"Jen Dobken told me her nephew's going to ECU in the fall," Mom said, taking a drink.

"That's what Matt said." I picked at a pepperoni.

“Sounds like Danny had been considering it for a while.” Mom took a bite of pizza.

We hadn’t talked to Danny frequently enough for his college choice to be a topic of conversation, but still. If he’d considered it, applied, and been accepted…why keep that from us?

Maybe Danny really was being sent here to keep an eye on us. It was cool that he was going to college nearby, but if we were going to be spied on, that wasn’t so great.

Footage of D-Day played as I stood up out of my chair. “I’m gonna go upstairs.”

“Okay,” Mom answered.

I threw my plate and can away, then headed down the hall. A shadow of movement and headlights from the street, visible through the blinds, told me that a car was turning into the driveway next door.

I didn’t have anything good for throwing across the gap, so I reached for my phone and sent a text.

*Hey, whenever you can, I want to talk.*

Getting comfortable on my bed wasn’t the easiest thing. Reaching under the hem of my shirt, I carefully felt the stitches there. The skin poked up around the string, swollen and burning, nerves raw like an open wound. Jumping into the story of the book on my bed also wasn’t that easy, with the persistent burn in my side and the wait to hear from Matt.

Something hit the window with a quiet *tick*. With a careful roll off my bed, I moved to the window, flinching, and tugged on the blind cord.

A figure sat silhouetted against the golden lamplight in Matt's bedroom. Careful not to touch the edge of the window with my side once it was open, I leaned out a little, my elbows resting on the windowsill, part of me twisted awkwardly away.

"Hey." After glancing behind me, though I knew no one had followed me upstairs, I winced. "We definitely need to take care of this soon."

Matt's face dipped into a frown. "How bad is it now?"

"There's some swelling."

"Swelling?" Matt's voice had an edge that made it sound louder.

"Shh!" My face reddened. "Just around the threads."

"Are you feeling all right otherwise?"

"Sure."

He still frowned. "Wanna come over?"

"I could." Matt's mom had acted pretty weird the other day, though. "Or you could come over here."

"I'll come over there."

"Cool." I reached up for the window to pull it down. "See you in a minute."

It sent a twinge through my skin to pull the window down. Not a bad one, but it was there, fading as I made my way downstairs. The night was humid, but maybe we could sit on the porch. My parents had always allowed Matt in my room, as long as the door was open, but I also didn't want them to hear too much of anything.

Matt's front door opened and closed, and I watched him cross the yard, his eyes glowing for a few moments as he approached the glow of the porch light.

"Inside or out here?" I asked.

With the flick of a frown, he answered "Inside."

"Okay." Inside, it wasn't humid.

Matt took the glass door from me and followed me up the stairs. When I was halfway up, I heard him greet my parents, and looked back down. He was leaning into the living room, speaking to my parents before backing up and following me. Scratching my side gingerly, I kept going up.

"Door open, Anya." Mom's voice came up the stairs from the living room as we reached the landing.

"Yes ma'am," I called back, my face warming for some reason. We continued down the hall to my room, and I took a seat in my desk chair while Matt sat on my bed.

"So how bad are they really?" Matt asked, his voice low.

I gripped the hem of my t-shirt and rolled it up enough to show him.

His mouth dropped open. "Wow."

"Yeah." The fabric brushed a bump as I rolled the shirt back down.

"We need to find Noam tomorrow."

"After I babysit." With a deep breath, I met Matt's eyes. "Should we…take anything in case we do find them?"

"Like what?"

"Food. Supplies."

His face tightened for just a second. "No more quests."

I scoffed. "I just want to be prepared."

"Good point."

But I wasn't optimistic at all that we wouldn't just have to turn around and come back again.

# Chapter 4

I pedaled onto a driveway on Peach Street, eyeing the "2807" on the mailbox post, a jolt going through me as I hit an uneven part of the concrete. Wincing, I braked my bike and climbed off, unsure where it was supposed to go. The Tomlinsons had a garage, but it was closed up for now.

*I'll ask if my bike can go in there.*

The doorbell echoed enough for me to hear it on the porch, and the loud bay of a dog rang out right after, getting louder as it approached the door. A shuffle of nails on wood preceded footsteps, and the wooden door opened.

The woman on the other side smiled brightly at me, a beagle circling her feet in a frantic and joyful orbit, his movements punctuated by more baying. Mrs. Tomlinson pushed the glass door open with one hand, bent, and scooped the dog up with the other hand.

"Come on in," she said. "Anya, right?"

"Yes, ma'am." I stepped into the cool hallway, the sound of happy panting filling the space.

Mrs. Tomlinson scratched the dog's head with her free hand. "Sorry, Bubba gets excited to see just about everyone."

He was a cute dog. "That's okay." A clatter of plastic on plastic came from the living room. "May I put my bike in your garage?"

"Sure! I'll open the door for you."

"Thanks."

Mrs. Tomlinson set Bubba down and headed for the kitchen as I went back out the door. The garage door ground open, and I quickly pushed my bike to the back of it and headed back to the door. Somewhere nearby, a car idled, the sound overtaken by the start of a lawnmower down the street. I rushed back inside, and Mrs. Tomlinson waved me into the living room.

"I plan on giving them lunch when I get back," she told me. "If they want a snack, there's some applesauce on the second shelf in the fridge, or cheese sticks if they want that instead. Help yourself to something, if you'd like." With a smile, she added, "These two can get pretty focused on a project, so they might not want anything."

"Okay."

The kids sat among a pile of plastic bricks at the far end of the room. Thankfully, they didn't seem to want to play tag or hide and seek or anything to do with running outside. Bubba's wagging tail brushed my leg as he trotted past me.

"Lily, Ian, this is Anya," said their mom.

"Hey," they answered absently, but in unison.

"Hi." I approached them. "What are y'all working on?"

Lily's mouth quirked as she focused on me, considering. "Something big." Bubba settled next to her.

"A skyscraper?" I suggested. Mrs. Tomlinson headed back towards the door.

"'Bye, y'all, I'll be back!" Mrs. Tomlinson called from the door.

"'Bye, Mom," came the two voices again. I waved at Mrs. Tomlinson and lowered myself to my knees carefully. The door shut.

"How tall do we build it?" Lily continued.

Ian narrowed his eyes and turned to me, appraising. "How tall are you?"

"Five feet and nine inches," I answered.

He glanced at the bricks on the floor and jumped up. "I'm gonna go get the baby blocks." He tore off to the hallway.

Lily hopped up and began corralling the blocks onto the floor into a pile as Ian's feet pounded on the staircase, and with my help, had them together by the time Ian returned with what he'd called the baby blocks. He dumped them out and inspected the pile.

"I think we need to make it real skinny," Lily told him.

He gave a single determined nod, and the twins went to work, with me and Bubba watching.

They worked intently on their skyscraper, declining snacks and drinks, though I did get a glass of water myself. At some point, Bubba settled beside me, content in letting me pet his smooth coat. By the time their mom got home, Lily and Ian's skyscraper had been successfully constructed, and the swaying plastic brick tower stood as tall as me, like they'd wanted. I'd helped them a little with the base, but it didn't take them long to be intent enough on the tower that I could just sit and watch them and not move around too much. They had made me stand up as close as I could beside it when they were done to check that it met their standards, and the key sounded in the lock as I stepped away from it.

As I left, Mrs. Tomlinson handed me money, her other arm clutching Bubba. "Thank you so much, Anya."

"Thank you, as well," I said. As I leaned back into the living room, the clash of falling plastic filled the air. "'Bye, guys!" I called.

"'Bye, Anya!" they both said, not looking up from the confetti of bricks on the floor.

"Can I schedule you for four weeks from now?" Mrs. Tomlinson asked at the door. "Same day of the week, same time?"

I nodded. "That works."

She smiled again. "Thanks. I'll give you a call before then. The garage door is still open so you can get your bike."

With a nod, I stepped onto the porch. "Thanks."

Mrs. Tomlinson smiled and waved again as I went down the steps and made my way to the garage. The door to the house closed as I wheeled to the driveway. As the garage door ground shut, I carefully climbed onto my bike and pushed off.

Within a hundred feet, it was clear that there was something wrong and unbalanced about my bike. It took more effort to push the pedals, and it moved less smoothly than it had when I'd ridden it over before. After braking, I hauled it onto the grass of someone's yard, wincing at the shot of pain up my side.

My back tire was flat.

"You've got to be kidding me," I muttered. Crouching slowly, I turned the wheel, searching for a hole or a slit. The rubber was whole and unbroken.

But the valve cap was loose, halfway threaded onto the stem. How long had it been like this? I hadn't put any air into the tire at home, and everything had been fine on the ride over. I knew that for a fact. The back of my neck prickled.

I'd have to walk my bike home. It wasn't that far, but I couldn't ride on a flat tire. Pulling it back up, I started walking at a brisk pace. Now that I didn't have the wind rushing in my ears, I could hear the faint flapping sound of the tire on the pavement. Distant voices of kids echoed from a backyard. A sprinkler hissed to life across the street from me.

It wouldn't take too long to get home, but walking fast like this in my flip-flops wound a tightness up my shins, the impact of my feet exacerbating the burn in my side. Sweat trickled inside my t-shirt, and a tickling pulse of nerves ran along the scar. I rubbed at it with my shirt, hissing.

At first, I didn't really pay much attention to the crawl of tires on asphalt behind me, and didn't turn to face the car. Maybe the driver was being cautious because I was a pedestrian, and since there weren't other vehicles, they'd pass me.

But they didn't, and they weren't speeding up.

*Maybe they're lost or don't live here.*

I turned.

In one quick glance, I took in the unmistakable shape of the brown car that had slammed into Matt's truck.

Why were they following so closely and so slowly? I hadn't been walking that fast. The engine got just a hair louder. Were they speeding up in response?

Home was still a street away. As I walked faster, all reason narrowed into focused terror.

I was going to ruin the rim of my bike wheel, but I didn't care. I could get a new one. I swung my leg over the seat and took off, cringing for a second at how the back wheel felt. The metal grinding into the asphalt was probably my imagination, but I was undeniably slower, the hard flatness of wheel on road jolting me and irritating my side.

Over the wind in my ears, I could hear the car's engine. Something squealed. Not daring to look back and slow myself down, I pushed harder.

Willow Drive. The turn on the bad tire wasn't smooth, and the bike wobbled hard. From where I was now, I could see Matt walking to the Dobken's porch. The engine behind me got louder.

I swept into the Dobken's driveway, my heart racing, and got off the bike, stumbling to the concrete, pain from the impact of the fall rushing up my side. As I got to my feet, the skin below my ribcage on fire, the brown car continued on past at a leisurely pace.

A scream of rage tore from me, and I suddenly found myself darting forward, wanting to somehow grab the car and do something, not even sure what.

A hand closed down on my arm, and I twisted around, my fist extended, the stitches raging in my skin.

Matt jumped back and let go of me. "Were you really gonna chase after the car?"

"He followed me," I said, my voice too loud. "He followed me from near the Tomlinson's house to here." The brown car had gotten to the end of the street, its turn signal blinking, and I aimed another shriek at it.

"What happened to your bike?" Matt asked.

"The tire's flat." I swallowed. "It…the valve cap was loose when I checked it, and I didn't feel it until I was on my way back and I didn't even touch the valve cap at all before I went over there and it was fine on the way." With a deep breath, a paranoid idea started to form in my head. That someone, somehow, while I'd been at the Tomlinsons' house, would have let the air out of my tire.

*Why?*

My hands shook, and my left leg stung where I'd scraped it. The abrasion went from the side of my calf near my knee almost to my ankle, but there wasn't too much blood at all. The stitches burned.

"Are you okay?" Matt asked. I liked to think the fear in his wide eyes was from my reaction.

*And if he hadn't been here….*

"Yeah." My voice hitched as I leaned over and jerked my bike up, flinching.

"You rode on the rim."

"I know." Another breath, in and out. "After I figured out something was was wrong, I started walking home, but whoever that was showed up behind me and I'm pretty sure they started speeding up when I noticed them. I had to get on the bike."

Matt followed me to the shed. "We should go to Trenavell."

Under the sweat of fear and exertion, everything burned. My side. The scrape. Terror and anger.

"I'm gonna take them out myself." The flame in my side flashed as I lifted the bike up into the shed.

"Please don't." Matt stared at me, his eyes desperate. "Not yourself."

"Then help me." I shut the shed door and made my way to the back deck, Matt following.

"How am I supposed to do that?" His voice rose as I opened the back door.

"You can hold the scissors." My hands shook as I made my way to the stairs. The back door closed, and Matt caught up with me.

"You don't even know how to do it."

"I can look it up." The air conditioning started up with a gust that nudged the string on the attic door. Our first aid kit was under the counter in my bathroom, and I knew it was well-stocked. I grabbed it out of the cabinet and snagged two washcloths, then turned the sink on, plunging one into the cold water and sudsing it up with hand soap.

"Please don't," Matt pleaded again.

I wiped the cool, soapy washcloth down the scrape on my leg. "They have to come out sometime, and I'm not all that sure we're gonna find Noam before it gets really bad."

Matt's hands hung at his sides.

In a flash I remembered the red around his eyes that day. "Can you make sure the scissors are clean?"

He nodded and picked them up.

I rolled the side of my t-shirt up and knotted it so it would stay out of my way. The contrast of how hot I'd been outside with how cold in was in here hurt. The red bumps stood out, stark against my skin, an unpleasant accessory to the black knots. I suppressed a shudder. "I need to see if there's a video online or something that shows how to take stitches out." I washed my hands, keeping my eyes on the strings and seeing each knot that Noam had tied.

"Clean it first," Matt said, his eyes fixed on the black and pink on my side.

"Yeah." I grabbed a cotton ball from the jar on the counter, and got the other washcloth. "I'm gonna wash it and use alcohol."

Matt nodded.

I gave him the bottle of rubbing alcohol, remembering the one I'd found in that garage in New Mexico, how Noam had used it. Matt quietly cleaned the short blade of the scissors.

"So…did Noam just…sew it up, or…" My jaw tightened.

Matt's face stiffened for a second, souring. "Yeah." He took a deep breath.

I pressed my teeth together. "Okay." The bathroom filled with the white noise of rushing water as I turned the faucet on. It splashed when I stuck the washcloth under the flow. I knew Matt remembered. He'd watched, even if all I could remember was feeling the needle. My gut lurched, and I added soap to the washcloth. An image of Matt's red eyes flashed in my mind again, as I washed the scar with the warm soapy water. Touching it stung, kept stinging as I rinsed it. I dried it with a hand towel, and the terrycloth scraped over the bumps. The cold of the alcohol didn't give way to additional burning, which meant, for now, that it was closed up. I knew there was a chance it would burn after the strings were out.

Matt held the scissors in one hand and his phone in the other. I reached for the scissors and he let them go almost absently, as my hand closed on the handle.

"What first?" I asked, and my jaw tightened again, my stomach giving a quick heave.

Matt had his phone out, focusing on something. With an audible gulp, he answered. "You need to cut the first knot."

"Okay." My hands started to tremble. Sweat beaded up on my forehead.

Matt's eyes flicked down. "You you want me to?" He set the phone down and started to wash his hands.

"Not yet." A squeak left my mouth. "Don't leave."

He huffed a laugh, his face cracking into a little bit of a smile. "I won't."

I cut the first knot and tugged gently, and the string came free. My gut tightened. It hadn't hurt all that much, beyond the irritation in my skin.

"You good?" Matt asked, his voice steady.

My face was almost soaked now. "Yeah." My teeth clattered together. "I just need to finish."

Matt's hands rose halfway, but he dropped them, almost awkwardly, his gaze steadily on me.

With a deep breath, I met his eyes, not wanting to touch it myself anymore. It hurt, and that wouldn't be any better if he touched it, but his hands at least looked like they weren't shaking. "Can you?"

"Yes." He leaned over his phone again, studying it. "Just don't move much."

"I won't." Being tensed up wasn't helping the burn of the nerves. A bead of sweat tickled the side of my face as I focused on the shower curtain. The pain increased as Matt snipped the next part, and the hot zing through my side made me flinch. "Sorry."

Matt kept working, his hands much steadier than mine would have been. I studied the pattern of stars on the curtain, my attention caught by how much this really did hurt.

"I'm halfway done," Matt murmured.

"Okay."

His eyes met mine for a moment, worry in them while the rest of his face was set in a frown. The image of that day in Compass Hill returned, and I looked back at the curtain.

With one final tug and a shot of pain, Matt straightened. "I'm done."

The nausea surged up then, as I looked down at what was left of the wound.

"I'm gonna sit down." I plopped onto the toilet lid, my stomach roiling. Wrapping my arms around my middle, I leaned over, willing my stomach to calm down. I heard Matt open the jar of cotton balls, and I felt him approach as he cast a shadow over me.

"I need to clean it again," he said, voice soft.

"I know." It came out as almost a groan, and I pushed up a little straighter and took a breath.

This time, it burned some as he swiped the wet cotton over the scar. Tossing the cotton ball in the trash can with one hand, he grabbed the tube of antibiotic ointment with the other and held it out to me.

"Thanks," I said, taking it and suppressing the nauseated shudder that tried to run through me.

"Do you want to stay here today?" Matt asked.

We'd seen that car at the Dupree house before, and today it had followed me.

"Do you want to have a look at that box of letters?" I hadn't opened it again.

"Sure."

Would it be a good idea to stand up right now? At least with the air conditioning, I was cooling off, since I'd been soaked with sweat.

"We can wait a second," Matt said as I gripped the toilet lid to stand. He leaned against the counter, staring at me.

"Okay." Another deep breath. My lungs filled, and the scar stretched, but without the threads, it was more free. "Do you think it's infected?"

Matt swallowed. "I hope not." Hesitantly, he added, "It's not streaked or anything, so hopefully it's just irritated."

"Hopefully." The floor was cool to my bare feet as I pulled them back to prepare to stand, and put my hand out on the counter, unknotting my t-shirt. Matt leaned forward a little, like he was ready to help, but he didn't reach for me.

My face reddened.

A quiet knock came from downstairs, too low of a sound to be the front door.

I stood, my eyes widening. "That sounds like the back door."

Matt walked to the top of the stairs. "Why the back door?"

"I don't know."

The car had followed me. Were they back? What if they weren't knocking, but trying to get in? My heart started hammering, and my hands, which had steadied, began to shake again. Matt's phone wasn't on the counter, so he must have pocketed it, and I had mine. We could call the police and hide if we needed to.

Matt's phone buzzed once. He fished it out of his pocket, confusion and surprise dawning on his face. "Danny's here." He rushed downstairs.

At first, I was confused. Why was Danny at my house? Slowly, I followed Matt down and into the living room, catching up as he got to the back door and opened it.

Danny stood on the other side of the door, and offered a cautious smile. "Hi."

"Come in," I answered him.

Matt moved back, and Danny stepped into the house, a coat folded over his arm.

Danny looked back and forth between us, his eyes landing on me. "Are you guys okay?"

"Yeah," I answered. "Why are you at my house?"

"No one answered next door," Danny explained. "I figured Matt was over here, since his truck was in his driveway."

"Good guess," Matt said.

Danny eyed me again. "How are you doing?"

"Fine."

His eyes narrowed.

"We just took her stitches out." Matt's tone didn't offer any commentary, at least.

Danny's face slowly creased into a confused frown. "Are you supposed to do that yet?"

"They were in too long," I told him. "They weren't feeling all that great."

Danny's still unsatisfied frown deepened. "Too long?"

"Yeah, over two weeks," Matt said.

Danny's face opened up, and some realization broke up the confusion he'd been showing. "Oh."

"What?" Matt asked.

"Okay, so the time didn't match up again." Danny paused, took in a breath, and let it out. "It's only been four days in Trenavell, so that's why I was a little confused about the stitches."

So it had been longer on Earth than there. "We've been there trying to get into the city. More than once."

"The city's locked up," Danny told us. He cleared his throat. "Can we sit down?"

"Yes, please," I told him. "Can I get you some water or anything?"

"I can get it," Danny said.

Matt and I waited, watching his cousin get water and still holding his coat.

Danny had half-emptied the glass when came back into the living room and made his way to the couch. Matt sat on one of the chairs, and I perched on the edge of the recliner.

Danny finished the rest of his water and set the glass by his feet, then leaned his elbows on his knees before turning to me. "So…you took the stitches out yourself."

"Matt did."

He pressed his lips together. "I'm guessing since you weren't able to get into the city."

Matt and I exchanged a glance. Danny would probably want to know about the brown car, and how it had followed me the way it had.

"Do you know why it's all locked up?" Matt asked.

Danny shook his head. "Wish I did." He stared at the carpet. "I've been sleeping in basically a barracks in the castle, and haven't been able to leave until a little while ago."

"How did you get out?" Did Danny know about the hole in the wall? Had he taken the barriers down?

"Cargan." Danny took a breath in. "He was in a hurry. Meris and Noam are under supervision, and Noam wanted me to try and get you two back to the city, for obvious reasons."

We still needed to get back there. We had to tell them what we'd overheard from Mr. Simpson. But if Danny was let out of the city, in a hurry, by one person, then how were we supposed to get back in? "Should we go there now?"

Danny winced. "When I left, it was dark. I think it was sometime in the early morning."

"So it could be the same time of day when we go back," Matt said.

Looking back and forth between them, I narrowed my eyes. "Y'all can see better in the dark than I can."

Matt's eyes widened as Danny laughed.

"Good point," Danny conceded. "We can." With another pause, his face sobered. "But it might not be a great idea to go back at night."

Matt leaned forward. "So…do you think tomorrow would be better?"

"It might be," Danny answered. "Or we could wait a couple hours."

Matt met my gaze. "We could, but…my mom."

Danny would need to know everything that we'd heard. His mouth set. "Aunt Jen knows stuff."

Matt's eyes hardened. "Yeah."

Danny lifted his chin, his eyes recognizing something. "Did she tell you what she knows when you got back?"

"We overheard something," I told Danny. "Mrs. Dobken hasn't said anything to us directly."

"What did you overhear?" Danny straightened.

Matt had clearly started to get angry. "A conversation about what we did to the gates. A friend of Mom and Dad's came over here really late the night we got back, and they holed up in the dining room, and me and Anya listened in."

Danny glanced at me, alarm spreading over his face.

"Yeah, they apparently didn't know the Dupree gate existed," I told him. "Or, the friend said that him and some other people didn't know about it." *I might as well explain.* "The daughter of the woman who owns Dupree's land knows about this, and apparently sealing the gates was a surprise, but…he told Matt's parents that they should keep a close eye on us."

"Okay." Danny sat back. "I'll…have to see what Mom and Dad have to say about that."

Matt's shoulders dropped, his face calmer. "So if the gates are sealed, how are you getting home?"

Danny's mouth quirked. "Well…there's a gate at home."

My heart sank. We'd sealed the gates because Meris had said we needed to, and we'd trapped Danny in Trenavell. "So…is that one sealed?"

He shook his head. "No, but…" His smile was sheepish.

"You used gates that are sealed now to get around Trenavell," Matt finished.

Danny nodded, not a shred of anger on his face.

"I'm sorry." Why had I listened to Meris?

*Because you wanted to find out more, and you know that.*

"Don't apologize," Danny said. "I'll get home somehow."

"What about ECU?" Matt asked him.

Danny got quiet and solemn again, and his eyes focused on the living room carpet, calculating. "This is supposed to be need-to-know, and I think you guys need to know." He looked up at each of us in turn. "I'm not exactly going to school."

"Gap year?" Matt asked.

A small part of Danny's smile came back. "Guess so. I'll be in the area, and it's gonna look like I'm in school, but I'm supposed to keep an eye on you two."

Matt tilted his head. "Why are you keeping an eye on us?"

"Per my mom," Danny answered. "You two need someone here." He paused. "Mom and Dad are part of a faction separate from the government of Trenavell but loyal to it."

*Then who is Lukas Simpson with?* "Did she know about the gate here?"

"Yes." Danny's face held a little remorse.

Matt's expression was just as puzzled as mine felt like it was. "So who are Lukas Simpson and Rebecca Davis working with?"

"I don't know," Danny answered. "Whenever I can get home, I'll see if Mom does."

Matt would never say anything about his Aunt Della in front of Danny, but I remembered how he'd felt, and the things he'd told me. Despite that, Mrs. Dobken was the one who had been hiding so much from her son. Matt seemed lost.

"What are you going to do tonight?" I asked Danny. "Where are you staying?"

With a shrug, he looked at my back door. "If we don't go back immediately, the Dupree house."

There was no way of knowing what else was in that house, other than the gate. As doubtful as it was that a person was staying there, the Dupree house was basically in the middle of the woods, and might look like a really nice home to an animal. "But…"

Matt frowned at his cousin. "You can't stay in there."

Danny grinned wide. "Why not? It's got a roof. I don't have to think about anything busting out of the ground, and I don't have to evade enemies."

Matt smirked. "What would my mom really say if you stayed here? She's not gonna kick you out."

Danny's eyes narrowed. "I'm not antagonizing Aunt Jen." Amusement took over his voice as he spoke.

"She can't say anything," Matt argued. "Not if she still wants to keep a secret. She might not even show a reaction."

Danny shook his head. “Either way, the Dupree house is the best option.”

Matt looked at me, almost asking for help. The Dupree house couldn’t possibly be comfortable. It was summer, for one thing, and hot with that heavy humidity. I thought of the car, and wasn’t too sure that Danny wouldn’t be evading enemies if he stayed there.

“I don’t think you could stay at my house,” I told Danny, wincing.

And he laughed. “I wouldn’t ask that.” He sobered, his eyes studying me. “Your parents don’t know about this.”

I shook my head. “That was why we were trying to have Noam remove the stitches.”

Eventually, somehow, all of this would be something that my parents would have to know about. I didn’t know when or why I’d ever tell them. The thought of going missing from here because of something that happened in Trenavell didn’t haunt me daily or anything, but it was a distant specter in my mind.

“My parents do have Tim’s old room,” Matt said to his cousin. “You could even hide in there.”

Danny didn’t budge. “They’d hear me walking around, which I’d have to do at some point.”

“It doesn’t seem safe for you to just stay in the woods,” I told him, completely sure that I wasn’t going to convince him at all.

"That's pretty relative," Danny said, his voice kind, but firm. "Now, I can try to get you guys back to Compass Hill, but I don't think we'd be guaranteed free passage."

"Cargan could help," Matt offered.

Danny didn't look sure. "Well, it seemed like the only reason he let me out of the city was because the timing was right for it."

Meris and Noam needed to know about what we'd heard from Lukas Simpson. At some point, we'd have to go to Compass Hill. And the car. We'd seen that car at the house, and it had followed me so menacingly. "Danny, something's going on here, too."

"What?" He frowned fully for the first time.

"There's...a car that followed me from a babysitting job in this neighborhood." That was creepy enough alone. "It's one that ran into the back of Matt's truck a while back, and we've also seen it at the Dupree house."

"When did it follow you?" He glanced back and forth between me and Matt.

"Not too long before you got here."

His eyes went down to the scrape on my leg. "Oh."

"The Dupree house might not be that safe for you," Matt said.

"Noted." Danny leaned back on the couch. "Maybe the sun is up on the other side of the gate now."

That clearly wouldn't mean that Compass Hill was open, but Cargan could still be around. "Let's at least try," I said.

# Chapter 5

We stood at the top of the staircase in the cellar, the golden light dulled just a little by the slowly brightening line around the edge of the door.

Danny smiled, his face hopeful. "Sun's actually coming up, so that's good." He unbarred the door and pushed it open.

The cold air that rushed into the space made it clear that my sweatshirt, the pocket of which held the map in a plastic bag, wasn't really sufficient enough anymore, at least not when it was morning in Trenavell. The goosebumps still moved in a harsh wave on my side, but not as bad as before. It was doing a world of good to have the actual threads out. Hopefully that would be enough.

Danny went first, and Matt waved me through after him.

At least the wind wasn't blowing now. The pink glow of the freshly-risen sun wasn't enough to warm the air, though, and I knew that if we did return here, I'd likely have to bring a coat. It may not have been that long since we'd left, but at some point, autumn would become winter here, and I had no way to know how cold it would be.

"So they're all in the city," I said to Danny, my voice low. "That's why there's no one in the woods."

"Yeah."

"What about Naolon?" Matt asked, confused. "Were they beaten that badly?"

Danny shrugged. "Trenavell did re-take a lot of towns, using the same technique they used here."

The fighting that had randomly broken out. I realized that, other than the three villages I had actually seen, I wasn't sure how many towns and how big of a feat it was to get them back under the control of Trenavell.

Without warning, a memory of the village I'd gone into with Noam came flooding back. The snap of that first gunshot, the screams, hearing Iacomus at the head of the massacre while we ran away. He'd been looking for the four of us, after Meris had shot him. Iacomus had seen us, had attempted to apprehend us, and after Meris had reacted the way she had, he'd started looking for us.

It was a good thing that the guys were mostly quiet as we walked. I couldn't think about that village now. We'd run. They'd wanted the four of us, and in response, they'd murdered people who had nothing to hide. It was likely that most of them beyond that one man hadn't seen us anyway in their own scramble to leave.

Had Trenavell not had a plan in place for that village? A dawning shadow in how I saw Trenavell waited at the edge of my thoughts.

*They're not Naolon.* That was the box I could put Trenavell in right now.

We stepped down onto the main road that led out of the woods and to the city. The sun only touching the very top of it made it even more obvious at how low Compass Hill sat. Its name had never made sense. Why was it called that?

Other than the shadow of an early morning, the line of sight to the city was clear. No dots of travelers moved on the road, coming or going, which made sense considering that the city was tightly locked up.

Mr. Simpson had said that news traveled slower now, since we'd activated Dupree's device. Would other people in Trenavell know that Compass Hill was closed off so readily?

"Whoa," came Danny's voice next, as he stopped.

"What?" Matt asked him.

Danny pointed in the same direction that we had seen the strange shadow exiting the ground so recently. "I think that's a burrow beast."

"Anya calls them dirt whales," Matt said, a smile growing on his face, and directed at me.

Danny laughed loud and grinned. "I think I like that better." He focused on the long creature as it exited the ground in the same way it had the other time we'd seen it, not bursting through the earth, but moving smoothly at an angle.

"We saw one before," I said. "Same place." It crawled fully out of the ground and took off in the same direction it had gone before.

Danny watched the shadow as it brightened in the growing daylight. "That's…an interesting way for it to get to the surface."

"Yeah," Matt said. "We've seen one do it differently before."

After another few seconds, Danny stepped off the road and into the field, his pace a little faster than we'd been going. "Let's go this way."

Matt and I exchanged a glance and caught up with him.

"Why?" Matt asked.

"I want to get a look at what it was coming out of," Danny answered. "I don't think they usually care too much about making the same paths, so there might be one already there."

The city moved out of the shadow as we made our way across the field. "Do they eat people?"

Danny shook his head. "I'm pretty sure they're herbivores." He paused. "They're also big enough to be indifferent to us."

There'd been skulls of ones in enclosures around Skyrren. Someone in Trenavell had once kept them. I didn't know why, unless there was some use they had in construction. But why in an already constructed city? Wouldn't that be dangerous or unpredictable, considering how those things moved around, and considering that they'd left holes in the Skyrren paddocks? "Can you tame them?" I asked.

"There is a strain of domesticated ones," Danny answered. "They're not as big as the one we just saw."

We had gotten halfway to the creature's exit point when dirt popped up from the ground nearby. Without another warning, a yard or two ahead of us, the tip of a pointed head popped out of the dirt. The ground didn't rumble, or shake. The creature emerging out of the dirt wasn't even moving all that fast. With a snort, it threw chunks of dirt out as the rest of its face followed.

We stopped short, watching.

The rest of the body kept exiting the ground, two sets of thick, muscular legs digging gouges into the soil as a third and fourth set pushed the creature into the sunlight. A coating of dirt dulled the scaled, ribbed skin without hiding the dark gray and white stripes along the body. Paws at the end of the legs reminded me of a mole's, but with long claws. As the creature completely left the hole, it turned its bony head towards us, a nose twitching and wiggling at the end of the face, tiny eyes suddenly visible, shining as it opened its eyelids. Ten sets of legs straightened before it bent the back five sets and reached its head to the sky, the eyes disappearing as its body elongated. Then it did the same motion with its five sets of front legs, pushing the back end of its body up before lowering its entire length back down to how it had been when we'd first seen it. It sniffed again, without approaching us.

The head was smaller than the skulls in the Skyrren enclosures, and the body was maybe thirty feet long. Was this one younger?

It turned the way the larger one had gone, clawing some at the ground and sniffing before, a few hundred yards away, it stopped again and started to dig, flinging dirt up.

"I think it's a baby," I said, voice soft.

Matt turned to me. "Why do you think that?"

"It's small and it just followed the big one." With a half-smile, I added, "You know, like a calf. And it has markings on it, and the other one doesn't."

"Good point," Danny said. "Let's see what the bigger one was using."

We proceeded, going slowly. More dirt occasionally flew up into the air in different places, and the pointed tip of a snout poked its way out of the ground, though we didn't see another calf. In the distance, I thought I saw the tail of the juvenile as it made its way back underground.

And then we arrived at where the parent had made its way out of the ground. Hard, cold sunlight illuminated an entrance into the earth, a smooth pathway, maybe a hundred feet wide, leading at gentle angle down into a dark, rectangular tunnel entrance that, by my estimation, was much bigger than the adult burrow beast. The creature could fit comfortably. The entrance yawned somewhat far away, the illusion of closeness resolving as we walked down the slope.

What I didn't expect was the subtle change in the soil as we approached. It didn't look any different, but it was firmer, as though a hard surface was under it.

I scraped it with the toe of my shoe, but that didn't reveal anything visually.

Wc pauscd a fcw yards away from the dark tunnel. I'd been right. It was bigger than the burrow beast, the top of it around twenty feet above our heads and the same width as the pathway. The straight lines showed that someone had carved it.

Danny pulled a flashlight out of his pocket and shined it into the opening. The burrow beast or dirt whale or whatever had disturbed the soil at the edge enough to actually make it give way and show the dark surface underneath.

"So, you've seen it twice," Danny said, puzzled.

"Including today," Matt answered.

Danny's flashlight beam moved around in the space. It was a strong light, but it didn't light up the empty tunnel very far.

*What's down here?* "You said they don't care about making the same paths."

"They usually don't," Danny corrected me. "But if the little one's a baby, then it may have nested down here."

We stood quietly for another minute, still staring.

"Do you think this goes all the way to the city?" I asked.

Danny glanced up to his left, eyeing the edge of the field, clearly thinking. "It might."

"Should we try?" We'd have to get into the city at some point, and there wasn't a reason not to try. We'd gotten the stitches out, but if the city was locked up tight and if Mr. Simpson had shown up at Matt's house a few hours after we'd gotten back, and if the brown car had blatantly followed me, then this all could be urgent.

"Maybe we should." Matt looked at me. "Noam might want to see where the stitches were taken out. He's more likely to be able to spot if it's infected."

"And the car," I argued, almost defensive, irritated, for some reason, at Matt's worry.

*Calm down.*

Matt pulled a small flashlight out of his own pocket. "Danny?"

His cousin nodded. "You guys want to reach the city, and we can't go through the gate, so we need to find a way in there, at least to tell your friends that things are okay." Danny faced the tunnel again. "So shall we?"

Matt and I nodded at him, and Danny moved forward.

The stale chill in the tunnel made my breath fog in the illumination from the flashlights. As we walked away from the sunlight, points of light scattered on the walls brightened. Moss lamps, giving a glow to the inside of this tunnel, followed the two branches of the path: a soft curve to the right and a straight passage that continued forward.

A chill ran over my skin as I recognized something unmistakable on the curving wall: an arrow, or at least what looked like one. That realization caused another one, that there were round shapes on the walls around us, flat and faded from what had once been on them.

"Are those signs?" I asked the guys, stopping.

Both of them paused and turned slowly, shining the beams of their flashlights around at the circles.

"They could be," Danny answered.

More chills. "What was this?"

"It's like a highway tunnel." Matt's voice stayed low.

Was that exactly what it had been? Why? What would the point be? The tunnel sloped down into the ground. It didn't go through a mountain. There was no reason for an underground highway tunnel here. There was a road to Compass Hill; why would anyone have needed to go underground? Were the winters that harsh in Trenavell?

"Let's keep going," Danny said.

We weren't going as fast as we might have on the actual road. There weren't any more of those creatures that showed up down here, and the moss lamps stopped appearing at some point as the tunnel narrowed just a little. It wasn't any warmer, but it wasn't all that much colder, either. The plastic bag around the map crinkled softly as I stuck one hand into the front pocket of my sweatshirt. We passed a door with a round sign on it, unreadable, and I wondered it it was a service entrance.

*But who's using it?* Like Compass Hill's name, this abandoned highway tunnel didn't make sense, even if it did lead to the city. This wasn't a mountain, and there was already a road above us.

We passed a few other doors, and more signs. At another point, the tunnel curved to the left, and the space opened up into a wide expanse with a line of columns marching down the center. In the distance, on the other end, stood two closed doors. The walls on either side of the space had a couple of doors as well, but they were open and dark. I had to wonder where they went, but I didn't particularly want to go through them.

"I think that's how we get in," I said, reluctant.

"Probably," Danny answered.

As we advanced across the empty space, the guys' flashlights caught glimmers on the dark walls, and made dancing shadows from unidentifiable refuse scattered around. The wall above the double doors held another oblong sign, but I still couldn't read the characters on it. They weren't recognizable at all, and I couldn't think of anything they looked like that I had seen before.

Until I remembered that first morning after the scream in the woods.

The copper disc. The carvings on that were similar.

"Matt, do you remember that copper plate in the woods?"

"Yeah." He eyed the sign above the doors as we stopped in front of it.

"Do you see the similarities?" I asked him.

"What plate?" Danny asked.

If only we had showed him that. "Matt and I found this metal thing in the woods, like half-buried, and it had stuff carved around it. Letters, I guess, that looked a lot like the ones on that sign."

Between that and the car, it definitely wasn't safe for Danny to camp out in the Dupree house.

"Oh." Danny frowned, his eyes reflecting the light for a second. "Why was it in the woods behind your house?"

"We're not sure, but we heard someone scream back there the night before we found it," Matt said.

"Interesting." Danny reached for the handle on the door and pulled.

It opened freely, but let out a squeal as it moved, echoing around us.

"Great," Matt said, the sarcasm springing from his mouth, bright enough to drag a laugh out of me as the door stuck open.

Danny went through, letting me follow. Matt pulled the door behind him, with some struggle and another loud squeak.

The space we went into was smaller, though empty. Two closed doors to the right, separate but next to each other, reminded me of bathrooms. Another door in front of us had a window in it, showing off a hallway that led deeper into whatever this was. We crossed to it, and Danny pulled at the door handle.

It, too, opened, but the hinges crunched loudly. The oblong sign above this door had more of those unrecognizable characters, and below them a round emblem that I couldn't quite see. Danny led us through.

The hallway beyond stretched off into the dark, and the flashlights just did light up the doors on either side, showing framed gaps in the walls. Windows.

*What in the world?*

Danny and Matt inspected things solemnly as we edged ahead. Above each door hung signs that reminded me of the copper disc. My foot scuffed softly, the toe of my shoe sweeping across the smooth floor.

*A smooth floor.*

As the guys went ahead, I stopped and crouched, reaching to feel it, frowning as my fingers slid over the dirty but glazed surface that gave off a soft reflection as my fingers moved the dust.

"Y'all?" I said.

Matt turned, alarm on his face. "What's wrong?"

Had I startled him? "Feel the floor."

He approached, his face relaxing, and knelt down, running his fingers over it. "This..."

"It's not rough." I stood. "It's like really smooth concrete." Was there anything even like concrete in Trenavell that we'd seen?

Matt's eyebrows rose. "Interesting."

Danny bent over a few yards away, inspecting the floor. "Yeah."

Ahead of him, a wide window opened into another room. It didn't reflect any light, so if there had been glass there, it was gone, and as we got closer, glass crunched under my feet. Why was the window broken so completely? Another round and unreadable sign hung on the door beside the window. Matt's flashlight illuminated the inside of the room, and the stuff in there. Tables, desks, cabinets along the walls. Round shapes set into the ceiling, reminding me of recessed lighting.

I touched the round sign on the door carefully. It stuck almost flat against the door, its thin surface rough with corrosion.

"What is this?" I whispered, moving to the broken window and setting my hands on it, peering into the room.

"It feels wrong, doesn't it?" Danny asked.

"Yeah," Matt said.

The smooth floor. The doors, broken windows, and signs everywhere. The tunnel that seemed so much like a highway tunnel. What was this? We were probably near the city, but why was there a tunnel and a workplace underneath Compass Hill? What work had it been for?

Danny moved forward again.

The hallway didn't go too much farther ahead, branching off to the left and right, with a metal door right in front of us.

Danny looked back at us. "I would guess that leads to the city, based on how far we went down at first."

"Think it goes to the castle?" Matt asked.

"It could." Danny stared at the door, his mouth working, like he was biting the inside of it. "Do you guys want to see?"

We didn't have supplies, and I didn't want to get stuck in Trenavell. Last time, I'd pressed Matt to come with me because

I'd wanted to go with Noam and Meris, and I'd been prepared, at least emotionally. Still, I wanted to see what was behind the door, and the long passage we'd gone through had gotten us here without, I thought, anyone noticing. "Okay."

"Sure," Matt said. Did he want to know too, or was he just trying to be a bodyguard again?

*At least he'll be here.*

Danny nodded and reached for the door. As Matt and I waited a couple steps behind, Danny tested the doorknob.

It turned with only the sound a normal doorknob made, no crunch of rust or resistance. He tugged, and the door opened, silent on its hinges.

The hair on the back of my neck stood straight up. I'd assumed we hadn't been seen and that the passage was abandoned, but this door was kept in good repair, and that proved the complete wrongness of my assumption.

The featureless room on the other side of the door held a staircase, this one ending at the ceiling.

We stared at it. Why would it end there?

"Sweet, a hatch," Danny said, almost gleefully, as he climbed the steps.

"Really?"

"There's a seam," Matt murmured.

They'd seen it, and I hadn't, which wasn't all that surprising. Matt and Danny's eyes would have let them see the way the hatch opened, even though no light streamed through the crack. Was it supposed to be a secret, or was there a cosmetic reason that they would have hidden it? Maybe it was constructed for safety, to make sure the door didn't slip through the opening if someone was standing on it. With a glance at the door we'd come through, I realized that it and the others in the structure behind us were all metal, corroded like the signs we'd seen in the tunnel. I'd never once seen a metal door in Trenavell.

What was this under the city?

Danny pushed on the hatch, and it moved open easily, filling the space we were in with muted morning sunlight. He advanced slowly, slipping his hand to the edge and keeping it from slamming open on the floor above. He set it down with a soft thump and climbed up, moving away from the opening to let me out.

There wasn't a lot of directional space, because just beside the hatch in the floor was a big rectangular structure. I stood fully as Matt climbed out, and looked around, orienting myself to the layout in the place we'd climbed into.

The large shape wasn't beside the hatch so much as the hatch was behind it. A door and a wide, dirty window across the big room looked out onto a street. Behind us, empty shelves and barrels lined the walls, and a few stools stood in random places around the space. The structure in front of the hatch looked like a counter. I peered down into the cellar below, and my stomach hitched at the drop.

"Why are we in a store?" Matt asked.

Danny made his way to the window and peered out. "This is interesting."

"Where is this?" I asked.

He turned around with a smile. "We're not too far from the castle."

Matt eyed the hatch below. "How much farther do you think we'd have to go to get there?"

The hallways below us would likely lead to the castle. Would we get lost trying to navigate that?

Danny looked through the window again. "I would guess it's about a street over."

It would be easier to just take the route through the streets instead of trying to figurc out how to get around those hallways.

Danny stepped away from the window and glanced around the store with a wry smile, his eyes landing on a point behind me. I turned.

A staircase I hadn't seen before probably led to living quarters above us. "This would be a better place to stay than the Dupree house."

Matt made his way to the bottom and looked up, and I followed him. Windows must have been uncovered upstairs, because the staircase wasn't dark, just in shadow, and light came from somewhere.

Danny pocketed his flashlight. "It probably would." Coming closer, he took a peek up the staircase, and apparently came to the same conclusion I had. "I'd have to cover the windows, though. Looks like the curtains are gone if it's that bright."

Matt walked around the counter, making his own way to the shop windows that looked out onto the street.

"What if there's someone out there?" I asked, as a warning to Matt.

"There's not," Danny told me. "Not a soul."

That was creepy. Compass Hill had been bustling, I thought. Functioning, anyway. There were plenty enough people to go on the offensive against the soldiers patrolling the streets when we'd been here. Where had they all gone? "Should we try to get into the castle from here?"

"How would we figure that out?" Matt asked. "If we're underground?"

Meris and Noam had to know what we did. We had to find a way to tell them. If Cargan hadn't let them out of the city like he had Danny, then the odds of him doing that at all were pretty low. "We know what direction the castle's in."

"True," Matt conceded. "But getting in there undetected and actually finding Noam and Meris might be a little harder."

"Cargan would help," Danny said. "His shifts are in the chapel, which you know the location of."

The chapel. *Don't think about it.* "Yeah…" Slowly, my eye was drawn to the window as a figure, someone not quite across the street, moved out of my line of sight. I jumped, startled.

"What?" Matt's eyes shot to the window.

My reaction was probably too much, and maybe too late. "I saw someone outside in the street."

Danny frowned, rushed to the front of the store, and pressed his face to the glass. "I'm not sure who it is. Young guy. Not dressed like a soldier." He stepped away and turned to us. "So…we found our way into the city."

We'd tried to get here, and we'd succeeded in actually finding our way into Compass Hill. I had no idea what the part we'd come through was, though we'd have to go back through it to get home, unless we found Cargan and he could ferry us to the gate. That I doubted. Now we had to get out. I had a babysitting job to go to on Friday. "Yeah." The sudden hesitation in my own voice frustrated me.

Danny picked up on my tone. "Do you guys want me to find it, and I'll come get you again?"

Meeting Matt's eyes, I tilted my head. "What do you think?" The door downstairs was maintained. If we made too much traffic in whatever was below Compass Hill, we'd eventually get caught.

Matt glanced at the window, toward the counter, and then at me. "We should go ahead and at least figure out where the castle access is, if it exists."

That wasn't something I'd thought of. "They'd probably want to keep it secure." But we could try. "It's worth looking while we're here."

Danny raised his eyebrows. "Okay. Let's go." He took another peek out of the window, then walked to the back of the counter, stepping down into the cellar.

Matt waved me forward, and I followed Danny. As I reached the halfway point, the light started to fade as Matt followed me, his hand pulling the hatch as he descended. As careful as Danny had, Matt set it in its spot with just a soft thump and continued to the floor of the basement.

With two clicks, the guys turned their flashlights on again. Danny opened the door to the hallway and led us into it, but paused.

"What?" I asked.

Danny stared at the ground. "I'm trying to figure out which way we need to be going when we come to a turn."

"What if the next turn goes the wrong direction?" Matt asked.

Danny shrugged. "Eventually it could turn around and go the right way." He started walking.

"What if it takes us a super long time?" I asked. We'd have to institute a time limit. Getting stuck here wasn't something I was ready to do, and what if the time lined up right? That was pretty likely, considering that a longer time had passed on Earth than it had here. It hadn't been a long time at home the last time, but now that was different. I didn't know what hours were stretching out while we explored below Compass Hill.

"If we don't find it," Danny said, his voice slow and patient, "we can come back. I'll take you guys to the entrance we used, and I'll stay above the store. You could return on your own, or I can come get you."

A soft tick came from down the hallway. The sound didn't draw out, at first. We waited.

It grew to soft footsteps in the direction of a closed door ahead of us and on the left.

My heart started to race. We'd been found.

*It's not Naolon. It's fine.*

That sure didn't help. Knowing that the device activation was a surprise to anyone meant I had no idea what was in store if someone from Trenavell who wasn't Cargan or Meris or Noam found us. Maybe we'd get in trouble, or be detained.

*Please don't let us get stuck here.*

The door opened to soft golden lantern glow, illuminating the figure that slipped through the door.

Ira stood there, holding a large jar that swung from a metal handle, the inside of which glowed with specks of silvery-gold light. He stared for a moment before his mouth curled into a sly smile.

"Well, good morning," he said, self-satisfaction bleeding into every syllable. "I thought somebody was in that shop. Good thing it was you all." His gaze met mine, and his expression slipped for a moment before easing back into what it had been.

Were we near Miriam's house? Had we been next door?

"Ira." Danny's greeting was pleasant, if puzzled.

A look at Matt showed me the anger that blazed in his faintly glowing eyes. I nudged him, and he slowly turned to look at me as I shook my head, willing him to calm down. My injury hadn't been Ira's fault at all.

Matt relaxed, barely.

"Danny Henderson," Ira answered. "And Anya McCall, and Matthew Dobken." The smile faded into a more serious expression, though his eyes still held some mischief. "Good thing I caught you."

Danny spoke. "Ira, do you happen to know why the city's locked up tight?"

"Sure don't." His eyes slipped to me and back, and there was an awkwardness there. If he felt bad, I didn't want to add to that.

"What about Meris and Noam?" I asked.

His chin lifted. "Now, I could perhaps get a message to them for you." He hadn't budged from the doorway.

"Can't we talk to them?" Matt asked.

Ira glanced down. "Not right now, no."

"Why?" I asked. "We have something to tell them." It wasn't something I felt like passing along through Ira, but they had to know.

Ira's face sobered in the lantern light. "They're being watched and can't even find time to be alone."

Did they have someone like Mr. Simpson here, who'd told Meris' parents to keep an eye on her and Noam? It would be a little easier for someone to do that here. Whereas Matt and I were alone for a lot of the time, long stretches of hours when our parents worked, Meris and Noam were here, in a city just retaken by soldiers. And Meris was, technically, the princess.

How were we supposed to meet with them? How were we supposed to tell them anything?

"Do we have an option?" Danny asked.

"Could they sneak away?" Matt added.

They'd done that not too long before we'd met them. "There's places to hide here."

"I suppose they could," Ira told us. "I can talk to my sister, and she can get a message to Cargan." He turned to Danny. "Miriam said he got you out of the city."

Danny nodded. "Yeah, he did."

"Cargan would likely be willing to help with what you need," Ira said. "I can get Miriam to start passing along that message. We can agree on a time for you three to return."

"I'll be in the city," Danny replied. "I might leave to get these two."

With a nod, Ira lifted the lantern higher. "What should I tell Miriam?"

What would be good to pass along? "Maybe that Matt, Anya, and Danny need to meet them underground." I had no idea if Meris or Noam knew this was under here. If they had, maybe we would have used it, but we hadn't. Whatever the place underneath Compass Hill was, Meris was someone who would want to make use of it, especially if it meant that she and Noam could escape or at least spend some time away from scrutiny.

"Fair enough," Ira answered. "I'll escort them here myself." He said it firmly, like a promise.

Danny let out a long breath. "So…I guess I should take you guys back." His eyes reflected the light as he turned to us.

"Yeah." Matt said. "When do we need to come back?"

"Five days," Ira answered readily.

"Bear in mind that the time here and the time on Earth won't always match up," Danny said. "If five days pass here, I'll head to Earth." He looked at us. "If you have five days there, then come to the storefront."

Another passage through the creepy liminal space under Compass Hill. "Okay," I said.

Ira backed toward the door he'd come through. "I'll get that message to my sister. Safe travels." He lifted the lantern, the smile inching back onto his face, and disappeared through the door he'd come through.

So the window hadn't been opaque with dirt. But he hadn't known it was us. He'd just seen people and had gone to look. What was Ira up to? Why was that something he'd investigate? Had he been expecting anyone? As far as I could tell, he hadn't been armed, but maybe I just hadn't seen any weapon he had. It also struck me that there was a chance he knew how to get to the castle from here, if there was a way to do so.

Danny turned around and walked past Matt, leading us past the cellar door and back to the strange entrance we'd come through before. "At least the tunnel's not hard to follow."

Our feet shuffled over the smooth, dusty floor. The crunching of the broken window under my shoes made me wonder again why it was broken. Maybe age, or the stress of being underground. Maybe someone had broken it on purpose.

We passed the twin doors in that lobby-like area before Danny led us through the double doors and back out into the large room we'd been in before, and I wondered what it had all been for.

# Chapter 6

As I rode my bike to Miss Whitley's house, I relished the breeze created by my own movement. It was humid enough outside that I wasn't cooled off a whole lot, but it was better than if I'd walked. I could have driven my car, but would waste gas, since Peach Street wasn't all that far. The stitches being out meant that every bump in the road didn't hurt.

My bike hadn't been damaged, thankfully. The wheel had held up to pedaling, even with no air in the tires. I'd check them this time before I left her house. Maybe Miss Whitley had a bike pump, if I needed one.

Pulling up into her driveway, I parked my bike on the sidewalk that led from the driveway to her porch, directly in line of sight to the door. I could watch it and ask if she'd let me put it in her currently closed garage. Before I left, I could stay in the garage while I checked the tires, and maybe have Miss

Whitley out there with me. That was safe. It wouldn't be too dark when I was heading home.

*That brown car probably has working headlights.*

I flinched at the thought. Maybe it had been stupid to ride my bike here.

*Matt has a truck.* The thought swept through me, a calming current that let me take a deep breath. If I got too scared, I could text him to come get me, and my bike could go in the truck bed. It would be inconvenient for him to drive here, but the knowledge that he would warmed me against the chill of fear.

I climbed the steps and rang the doorbell. I'd never babysat for any of my teachers. Hopefully Jimmy was a good kid, though.

The wooden door opened. Miss Whitley smiled at me from the other side of the storm door. She was dressed up, wearing a sundress and sandals.

"Hey, stick your bike in the garage and come on in," she said.

"Okay, sure. Thanks." I hadn't even had to ask. The garage door ground open as I stepped back down to the sidewalk. After pushing my bike back inside, I dashed out, getting halfway back up the sidewalk before it started closing again.

The sound of a car on the quiet street followed me into the house, the hiss of asphalt almost overtaking the relief at the garage being closed so quickly this time. If it was the brown car, they couldn't get to my bike this time. I didn't look.

"Okay," Miss Whitley said, as I walked into the house, "I got one of those big frozen pizzas. It's still in the oven right now, and I've got the timer set. Eat as much as you like. There are some movies in the other room to watch. Jimmy got a new video game, so he might just wind up playing that the whole time."

The sound of the TV made its way to the front of the house. "That's fine."

Miss Whitley smiled. "Let's go find my son and I'll get you introduced."

The TV got louder as we went down the hall, and a light flickered into the dim hallway.

"Sweetie, your baby-sitter's here," she said as she led me into the room. "This is Anya."

The top of Jimmy's short red hair reflected a muted version of the game colors as he paused it and looked away from the screen, offering a shy smile. "Hey."

"Hi," I answered him, trying to sound cheerful.

Miss Whitley gestured for me to go in, so I did, taking a seat at the end of the couch. The doorbell rang.

Miss Whitley took a step back into the hall. "That's Jake. I'll be back a little after eight, okay?"

"Okay," Jimmy answered.

“Thanks again, Anya.” Miss Whitley disappeared into the hallway, and I heard a rumble of voices from the front of the house before the door closed.

I stifled a yawn. “So…you gettin’ hungry?”

Jimmy nodded, eyes fixed on the screen. “Is it okay if the pizza’s got mushrooms?”

“Of course. I like mushrooms.”

A smile inched onto his face. “Good. Megan doesn’t.”

“Who’s Megan?”

“My friend.” He sat on the couch. “She only likes pepperoni, and she says mushrooms are gross.”

“I don’t think mushrooms are gross.”

Jimmy smiled a little bigger.

“I’ll check on the pizza really quick.” I stood up. “If you want to watch a movie, go ahead and pick one and I’ll bring the food back. If you don’t feel like that, we can stick with your game after we eat.”

“Okay.” Jimmy got down off the couch and went to the stack of movies beside the TV.

The oven timer was almost done with its countdown. Miss Whitley had left a couple of paper plates on the counter beside the oven, along with some napkins, an oven mitt, and a tray. Front and center on one of the refrigerator shelves sat two cans of the same store brand cola my mom had at home.

*Easy enough.*

Once everything was ready, I made my way carefully back down the hallway to the other room. Jimmy held up one of the DVD cases as I entered the room.

"Is this one okay?" he asked.

The drink cans wobbled a little as I set the tray on the coffee table. "Your choice."

He grinned again and dove for the DVD player.

***

We finished the movie, and Jimmy had started his game again when I heard the front door being unlocked.

Jimmy paused his game and jumped up. "I'm gonna go say hey to my mom."

"That's fine," I told him. "I'll clean up."

Slowly, I gathered the empty cans and the paper plates and started after Jimmy, keeping my steps measured so the trash didn't fall off the tray.

"Nice to see you again, Jimmy," came a man's loud voice down the hall. I stopped.

His voice rang familiar in my mind, though I didn't know why.

An overwhelming feeling that I really didn't need to go to the front of the house came over me.

"Nice to see you," Jimmy replied as I inched forward.

Why was the man's voice so familiar? Was he another teacher? Where had I heard his voice before? I knew it would be easy to find out and that it would probably even be polite to say hello. As strong as my instinct for courtesy was, I knew I should not go towards the front door.

"I hope we can do this again soon," the man said.

I could peek.

"Of course," Miss Whitley answered. "Goodnight, Jake." He was leaving. Against my gut, I surged forward, a napkin fluttering as an empty can tipped over onto a paper plate.

"Goodnight."

My foot hit the carpet in the front room in time to see teal and khaki and the back of a man's head slip onto the porch, and the front door closed.

Why had I felt like I needed to stay out of sight? Goosebumps rose up on my skin, companions to the frustration and disappointment inside me.

Miss Whitley smiled as I walked fully into the room. "Thanks for getting that," she said. "What did you two do?"

Jimmy opened the refrigerator.

"We watched a movie and Jimmy played some of his game." As I threw away the trash, Miss Whitley got her wallet out and started digging through it before handing over three bills. Two twenties and a ten.

"Here you go," she said. "And if possible, I'd love to have you watch him again, if you can."

"Sure," I said as I took the money.

Miss Whitley smiled. "Thank you again, Anya. The garage is open for you to get your bike."

Hiding the spike of fear at that wasn't too hard. "You're welcome. And thanks," I added, holding up the bills in my hand.

"Of course!" She smiled and saw me to the door.

"'Bye, Anya!" Jimmy called, a bottle of water in his hand.

With a wave at him, I slipped out the door and down the steps. The stillness suspended the neighborhood in the warm, humid air. Smudges of the last bit of sunlight lit the sky. Miss Whitley's date's voice wouldn't get out of my head. Where in the world had I heard it before? He was just my teacher's random date. His voice wasn't all that distinctive, just deeply familiar.

My bike still stood in the garage, close to the wall and leaning on the kickstand. My heart hammered at the memory of being followed, and I wanted to stall, and tried to. The tires were whole and full, the caps still tight. It was too late to text Matt, unless I wanted to stay in the garage until he got here. I'd completely forgotten. But it wouldn't take long to get home. My mouth dried up.

As I wheeled toward the street, the garage door ground shut behind me.

My eyes adjusted to the evening light. The sky still offered some sunlight, but the orange glow of each street light didn't quite meet the others enough to cut through the deep twilight shadows. If the car waited in one of those pockets of night, maybe turned off so I wouldn't be aware of it, I wouldn't know until it cranked up. Nothing idled nearby that I could hear.

Pushing off, I listened. I knew I'd hear a car start and I knew if I did, it would be that brown one. Even if it was summer, it was late, and what other cars, realistically, would be suddenly starting up as I pedaled?

Or maybe it wouldn't have to be hiding close by and off. Maybe it could be waiting far enough away, dark headlights ensuring I wouldn't see it while the streetlights let the driver see me. It had followed me home when I'd left the Tomlinsons' house. The driver would know where in the neighborhood I'd pass by.

Houses blurred past me, the wind in my ears keeping me from actually hearing anything. My heart hammered from exertion and fear together.

Something lit up in the corner of my eye as I sped around the curve onto Willow Drive, fighting to keep control as the quick flash drove home a spike of terror. That had to be headlights turning on, and it had to be the brown car.

As I reached my driveway and braked, a soft rumble of thunder reached my ears.

Relief melted the cold fear I'd worked myself up to. I caught my breath and jogged my bike to the shed. The wind picked up, cool with a hint of rain in it. My street stayed empty.

The car probably hadn't been there at all. I was home. I was fine.

I still ran as fast as I could to the front porch and into my house as the thunder sounded again. The TV was on, nearing the end of the show my parents were watching. The air conditioning highlighted how much I was sweating. I'd had the soft drink with the pizza long enough ago that I was thirsty again, and I made my way to the kitchen.

Mom stood by the open cabinet where we kept the glasses. She smiled as I walked in.

"How was the job?" she asked, walking to the fridge, a glass in her hand.

"Pretty good." I reached up to get a glass of my own. "Miss Whitley had a frozen pizza in the oven when I got there. We just watched a movie, and Jimmy played a game."

"Can I ask how much you made?" Mom sipped from her glass as I filled mine.

"Fifty dollars," I told her.

"Nice." She walked back toward the living room. "What are you planning on for later tonight?"

Gulping down water, I shrugged. "Not sure." It wasn't that late. The thunder rumbled again.

"Are you gonna babysit anymore for Miss Whitley?"

"Yes, but I'm not sure when." Another gulp of water. "Also, I'm watching Mrs. Tomlinson's kids again."

"Melissa told me," Mom said. "The kids thought you were pretty cool."

"That's good." I drained the glass. "They weren't hard to watch. They built a LEGO skyscraper the whole time."

Mom laughed and stepped into the living room. "Well, keep working and saving."

The rain started to rush down on the house as I climbed the stairs, so the storm definitely didn't make it practical to talk to Matt through the window. I thought of the other thing I hadn't taken a look at yet: the box of letters. I still didn't know who had brought them to us, but I guessed I was supposed to have them, for some reason. I had no idea if they'd be helpful at all, or give us any information. Maybe the rest of them weren't from Dupree. The first one we'd had was one he'd written, but the rest of them could be from someone other than him.

I got to my room, closed my door, and went to the dresser. If the letters had any interesting information, I could also take them to Trenavell. The plastic bag with the map peeked up around the edge of the shoebox.

Carefully, I placed the old box on top of my bedspread and sat down cross-legged in front of it, then removed the lid. When Matt and I had first found the letters, they'd spilled out across the floor of the Dupree house. I didn't remember if we'd put them back in any particular order, and doubted that they'd been put in order by whoever had dropped them off at my house. At the very least, they hadn't been removed from their envelopes, or they'd been put back in them. Whoever had that burgundy car had made sure they got back to me, and I didn't know why that was. Who'd taken them in the first place, and cleaned the dirty piano keys? Why'd they even done that?

The first envelope had only "Davies — Ocracoke" just like the first letter that Matt and I had found, the one that mentioned the book. It had been vague, but also had clearly mentioned James Abney, if not by name. Opening the envelope in my hand, I carefully slid the letter from inside and unfolded it.

> "Dear friends,
>
> We have here in this most beautiful state a mountain, some miles far west of Salt's Creek, which has by people before mine borne the name, as I have been told, of Jomeokee, which in our language would be "great guide." It shares its newer name with a town nearby. You will be familiar with this town's like or sibling in name in other places, though these sibling places have only themed names in common.

As notable as the rocky landmarks of my own home may be, it is the sibling town I wish to address, and the virtues thereof, however hidden they may be. Indeed, I believe it best if perhaps some attributes of the place remain accessible to but a few, as not all, I think, are fit. I include among those few your friends T, L, and MA. It was true at one time that the Skyrren library may have contained the best guide to these attributes, but one must today find the right book to obtain that knowledge. My pleasure at keeping some knowledge of good things to a few may seem less than humble, but that is a risk I take willingly.

Maggie sends her love, and a recipe for pie. Both of us again extend an unending invitation for you to journey inland and stay with us. I hope to receive a letter from you soon.

All the best,

Gavin Dupree"

*What…?*

Reading it again, I tried to figure out what in the world he was talking about, other than something in North Carolina. He'd mentioned Skyrren, but not the name of his own home state. What sibling towns was he talking about, and what did that even mean?

Who were the friends he'd listed by their initials?

And he had mentioned a book again.

After folding that one carefully, and sliding it back into the envelope, I reached for the next one.

> "Dear friends,
>
> Maggie is pleased that you enjoyed the pie recipe. She adds that she would love nothing more than for you to share the dessert itself among your church congregation and with neighbors.
>
> You are among those, as well, that I am glad share knowledge of the best attributes of the places mentioned in my last letter. Bar none, the one I have benefited from most is the simple access, and that has gained us all so much that I believe will be fruitful later. Such a web could be seen as a vulnerability, and history agrees with me, but the web may also be a tool. My apologies for the letter sounding so much like a riddle, but you have your own key to it. I should add that the vulnerability of this web is not universal. You both favor the number thirteen,

and that will enlighten you should you find yourself discontent with island life.

As we have welcomed our child, Maggie and I both look forward to the days when we hear of the same from you, and more so when we see the light in your child's eyes.

Before I leave this letter, I must ask this question, which I should have posed in earlier adventures: what is your closest train station?

Best regards,

Gavin Dupree"

It was worse.

What web? He mentioned a riddle and a key, but it couldn't mean the device, not if he told his friends they had their own key to it. What did he have simple access to?

Why would the number thirteen enlighten them?

He'd made reference to the reflective eyes that Matt's family had, and the simple question at the end made sense.

Maybe the next one would be better.

"Friends,

My questions regarding train stations showed how I have forgotten just how far you are from things. I will attempt to procure the information myself, as well. You will find it useful, most especially for visits, which I hope you will be undertaking soon. I would likely be welcoming you at our own home, if possible.

Regarding the place I have mentioned before: T may share the attributes of the place with the man about whom you asked. He can be trusted and I have also gotten the deepest assurances that there will be no official word of it. My humility remains at stake, I fear.

I have undertaken a work of my own recently: a map. I am but an amateur and have not great skill at cartography, but it could be useful, and I am particularly proud of this map. It is not without imperfections. I may draft another for you and ask for any corrections you may offer to me.

Salt's Creek proves itself to be a most interesting town. Though it has, until lately, grown, that seems to have met a plateau. Though I find my fellow citizens overwhelmingly honest and fair after our troubles, I do worry about stagnation. Quiet is desirable, but not absence.

Would the two of you consider a Christmastime visit?

Regards,

Gavin Dupree"

A spike of recognition went through me when I read about the map. It wasn't much, but he at least did say that he was working on one in this letter. But who was "T"? Who was the man that Dupree referred to?

The troubles he referred to in the letter had to mean the trial, and he'd praised the fairness of the people here. They'd acquitted him of murder, though the articles we'd read had suggested that that wouldn't be the case, not with how whoever had written them had assumed that Dupree would be found guilty.

What had Salt's Creek even been like back then? Dupree hadn't wanted it stagnant. A sense of sad, near-reverence for his unfulfilled wish ran through me. He'd wanted the town to keep growing, and it had done the opposite of that. I thought of the empty storefront of the bridal shop, the glass still painted with the name.

"Dearest friends,

We'll be welcoming more of our family soon. Our sweet daughter is such a joy to our hearts. We were glad to meet your young one. She is a delight, and the glow in her eyes was welcome to see. It is the truest shame that our children will not have the luxury of proximity to each other, but be assured that you all are family to us, and we will endeavor to bridge the gap however we may.

You have my thanks for all suggestions and corrections made to the map. I trust that you saw the markings I indicated, and one in particular with which you may be familiar. I would like to know if the placement is confusing, or if my lack of clarity might be of value. I find myself wondering if you might benefit from a similar marking, and if you agree, arrangements can be made.

On the subject of our children, I want to express our hope and optimism that they will live in prosperity. In years far ahead, when my time has passed, I hope that my family takes on this with the satisfaction of readiness. I don't wish to specifically request that of you and yours, all things being considered, only for my family.

I am glad for the times we meet in person.

All the best,

Gavin Dupree"

My ceiling fan chilled me for a moment as I read Dupree's words lamenting that his children and the Davies' weren't close.

And then I started to warm inside. Matt and I were the difference. Whatever his mom had hidden, we'd still grown up together. Whether or not she knew who my family was, and who I was descended from, Matt and I were friends, well over a hundred years after Dupree had expressed his regrets to Jendra and Rynon Davies.

But what had he meant about taking something on with the satisfaction of readiness? What had he hoped for his children?

*They found other skies first.*

A memory of the note on the newspaper came rushing back. How it had sounded like Mrs. Barnes had been trying to tell Elijah Dupree something. Like she'd been trying to convince him.

What had Gavin wanted his children to continue after his time, and why wouldn't he request it of the Davies?

With a glance at the rest of the letters, I grabbed for my phone. I doubted that the rest of the letters were any easier to understand than the few I'd read.

*Hey, I started going through the letters.*

Matt's reply was quick. *What do they say?*

I snorted. *Nothing that makes sense. They're really vague.*

*Do you think the rest are like that?*

*Probably.* I'd have to go through them all, but the near mind-bending sentences wouldn't be all that fun to go through. What was the point? Was it a waste of time to even read these? We didn't have the letters that replied to these, and clearly there had been replies. They'd liked Maggie Dupree's pie recipe.

My phone let out a ding.

*We can go over them together.*

What would a second pair of eyes do?

But we did have time. We had days before Danny would try to find us, or before we had to try and find him.

*Sure. Come over tomorrow.*

Reading the first one again, I focused on the mention of a book. The right book. What did that mean? Did it refer to the one he'd said he'd hidden in Skyrren? The name of that city was also in the letter.

Matt's answering text was fast. *Okay.*

Carefully making sure they were tucked safely into their envelopes, I put the letters away again, hoping that, with Matt's help, something might start to make sense.

The thought that we'd somehow overcome Dupree's lament and were friends warmed me again.

# Chapter 7

A little after nine the next morning, I crept out of my back door and made my way to the trampoline to wait. Matt was going to come over. His truck was still at home, so he didn't have any yards to cut this morning, as far as I knew.

As I climbed on, I waited for the tug in my side to spike into full-on pain, but it didn't. Relaxing, I clambered up onto the trampoline. I'd made the right decision in going ahead and getting the stitches out. Even the bumps there had flattened and faded in the couple days since Matt had removed them.

The humidity had set in already, pairing heavily with the morning's high temperature. I started to sweat, even though I wasn't doing anything.

Goosebumps sprouted over my skin, contrasting with the heat, as I thought about the long highway tunnel we'd walked down, all the way through that and dark hallways to the basement of a storefront somewhere in Compass Hill. Someone had made the tunnels and hallways, at some point, but when? Why hadn't we used it before? Did Meris and Noam even know it existed? And beyond that, I wondered what it actually was originally.

There'd been arrows pointing directions, and round signs on the walls.

Another chill went over my skin like a wave. Humans did live in Trenavell, but it had been clear, the day we'd met Noam and Meris, that humans weren't the only people on the planet. When we'd run to another cave, fleeing villagers, they'd been reluctant to even enter to look for us, in fear of who they'd called the "swamp folk."

Matt's mom's people.

Moon-eyes.

Matt had told me that there were a lot of them lower in the cave system that night, in the big cavern that we'd had a window into. There was no way they all lived underground.

But what was the tunnel?

Another group of people on this planet meant another language.

How close had they been as we'd navigated our way through the tunnel system to Compass Hill?

Matt's back door opened and shut, and I turned to look at him as he walked across the grass to the trampoline.

"Good morning," I said, my voice sounding distant to my own ears.

He set his hands on the edge of the trampoline and tilted his head. "What's wrong?"

"Wrong?"

He climbed on. "You look like you're a million miles away right now."

I couldn't help the joke that popped up. "Maybe more like a million light-years," I said, gesturing towards the woods.

Matt's gaze followed my hand, and he cracked a smile after a couple seconds, letting out a laugh. "Oh." With a narrowing of his eyes, he continued. "Best guess, huh?"

"I think any guess could tie for best as far as that planet is concerned."

"Probably." He lay back on the trampoline, his hands behind his head. "I guess you left the letters inside?"

"Yeah." And now I'd gotten caught up with thinking of the tunnel.

Had Dupree known about the tunnel? He'd been in Compass Hill. He'd put his device there. Surely he'd known about what was underneath the city.

"That's fine," Matt answered.

A soft, warm breeze coursed over us.

"Matt, what do you think that tunnel was?"

"I'm not sure." He stared up at the bough of a pine tree, far above us, in my backyard. The evergreen needles fluttered softly in the breeze, and the movement of the thin clouds above created the illusion that the thick trunk swayed in the wind more than it actually was moving.

"There were arrows." I paused. "And signs, I think. The writing on it looked like the writing on the copper plate."

He nodded.

"Think Meris and Noam know about it?"

Matt's hazel eyes narrowed. "I don't know. Do you think they'd have used it?"

"If they can't get there now, then that might not matter." We sure hadn't used it before.

"Wish they did," Matt said, his tone a little darker. "We could have skipped over that stop at Miriam's."

Pushing down my irritation, I answered. "Yeah, we could have, so…"

He looked at me. "Benefit of the doubt. They don't know about it."

"Guess we can tell them about that, too." He'd wanted to see the letters today. "Want to go inside?"

"In a little bit." He looked away from me and back up to the top of the pine tree. "It's nice out here."

"It's hot."

"Well, yeah, but…" He stopped. "It's nice."

"Okay." Leaning back on my hands, I crossed my legs and watched a bird wheel over the tops of the trees.

***

A while later, as the sun crept higher and the trampoline started to heat up, we went inside to look at the letters.

Matt sat down in my desk chair as I went to get the box of letters out of the dresser.

"How likely is it that anyone in your family has the other side of these?" I asked him as I sat on my bed.

He thought. "I feel like my gramma would have talked about them, because it would be weird, and she likes mysteries and stuff."

Opening the box, I kept my gaze down on the stack of envelopes inside. "Do you think your mom and dad might have them?"

Matt was quiet for a minute as I kept my eyes down. His voice held a sharpness in his answer. "I wouldn't be surprised if they did and hid them or something."

Remembering the meeting with his mom after we'd come through the woods and run into her sent an uncomfortable awkwardness crawling through me. "Um…Matt?" It was hard to meet his eyes as I asked this question.

His eyebrows rose.

"Is your mom…mad at me or something?"

He frowned. "Mad at you?"

My face blazed suddenly. "I mean, I dragged you to Trenavell despite all her efforts to keep this a secret."

"No you didn't." His face smoothed out, his eyes warm. "I followed you."

"Yeah, but…" She'd acted so weird toward me that day. "You didn't have to."

The corner of his mouth lifted. "I did tell you I was sticking with you."

He had.

Swallowing thickly, I pinched one of the letters between two fingers, barely keeping myself from bending the edge of it it back and forth. "She just saw us together that one day and immediately found a bunch of stuff for you to do."

"But she hasn't actually said anything." His voice gained an edge. "And honestly, I doubt she will. She wanted to keep all this a secret." He calmed. "Keeping me busy is her way of doing that since she's probably not going to actually talk about Trenavell."

"She could just say we're spending too much time together," I told him.

"We've always spent a lot of time together," Matt argued. "Imagine randomly keeping us from seeing each other while trying to still stay friends with your parents."

That *would* seem hostile, or rude at the very least. "Yeah."

Matt cleared his throat. "She can't do anything or say anything without revealing the secret."

Nodding, I took a deep breath. "Okay."

He smiled. "We're good."

I warmed inside. "Okay. We're good." As my face cooled, I handed over the first letter I'd read yesterday. "Take a look at this one." Maybe together we'd make sense of it.

Matt carefully took the envelope and slid the letter out. His eyes roved over the words, lids narrowed, a frown at the edges of his mouth. "This *is* really vague."

"Exactly."

"Too bad the pie recipe's not on here," he added, his mouth quirking. "I'll have to see if my gramma has any particularly old recipes that would be this one."

"Tell her to pass it along," I answered.

Matt smiled and read the letter again. "Okay, so 'Jomeokee' I can look up." He pulled his phone out and set it on the bed beside him.

My face pinked. "I didn't even think of that."

He glanced up at me. "It was probably really late when you read them."

"Not that late."

He shook his head. "Whatever. I can look it up, and maybe that can give us a clue as to what these twin towns are supposed to be." He set the letter down, picked up the phone, and tapped out something on the screen, his eyes darting back and forth between letter and phone.

His eyebrows rose, and he looked up at me. "It's Pilot Mountain."

Pilot Mountain. A landmark, and a town near it with the same name. And the town had a sibling, somewhere else, another location with a common theme for the name. He knew the Davies would be familiar with what he was referencing, if they knew the name of a town in North Carolina.

"Compass Hill."

"What?" Matt read over the letter again, his face smoothing as he realized the same thing I did. "The names."

Nodding, I sat forward eagerly. "Yeah, he was trying to tell them something about Compass Hill, or referencing something they maybe already knew."

Matt scanned the letter again. "What do you think the 'hidden virtues' of Compass Hill are?"

I chewed on the inside of my lip. "Secrets. Maybe ones that are useful." But they'd have to have known about the place that Dupree had named. Maybe it was agreed upon. "Do you think they probably knew about Pilot Mountain even existing?"

Matt shrugged. "Yeah. For his message to be understood, they had to have known it was a place at all."

At first, I thought that using the name of a well-known landmark wasn't much of a code. If you knew what Pilot

Mountain had once been called, then you could figure out what place Dupree was talking about.

But, even if you knew that, it didn't make any sense unless you knew about Compass Hill, and I doubted he was informing the Davies of the "hidden virtues" of that city. They knew about them. That sentence just brought up the topic.

Matt handed me the letter. "Let me see the next one."

"That one's even more confusing." I handed it over and read the one he'd been looking at. "He mentions a book and Skyrren, specifically the right book. And he wrote some people's initials."

Matt quietly read the letter I'd given him, his eyes narrowing as he went over the words. "Well…he uses the word 'riddle' in this one."

"I doubt it's the same one." What was their key to whatever it was he was talking about?

Matt frowned. "Access to what? What does thirteen mean?"

"Told you it was more confusing." I wondered who the three people mentioned were. Dupree said they were friends of the Davies, and "T" would show up again in another letter.

Matt snorted. "The 'light' in their kid's eyes." He grinned up at me. "Pretty bold reference."

"Could be an inside joke," I offered.

He handed me that letter. "What did you think of this one?"

"That it's worse than the other one."

He tilted his head. "What do you think the web he was talking about was?"

A web.

The wheel looked like it could be a web.

In a flash of understanding, I blurted out one word. "Network." The gates we'd sealed had to be on a network, and I knew there might be a second one. "Like a gate network."

The excitement in Matt's face bloomed. "And if the vulnerability isn't universal…"

The map. "Then not everyone knows about the web." He'd made the map of what looked like his network. How did that connect to Compass Hill? "He talks about making a map, and he asks for advice about it in this one." I handed the third letter to Matt.

After a minute, Matt spoke. "He asked how far a train station was from Ocracoke Island, which does not have a physical connection to the mainland."

That jerked a laugh out of me. "He did ask that."

With a smile, he looked down at the letter again. "Though he did say he forgot and told them he'd be finding that information for visits."

"Was that necessary if there was a gate network?" I asked.

"Depends on how many gates were being used and how." Matt squinted at the letter. "So whoever 'T' is, he mentions them again, and also a second person, who can be trusted, but Dupree doesn't name him."

"And Dupree's humility was apparently at stake here." What did that even mean? Was he trying to brag?

Going through these letters with Matt was a little easier than just trying to figure them out myself, but they still didn't make any sense, and I was beginning to doubt that having the other half, the letters written in reply, would even help.

Matt leaned back in the desk chair. "This is kind of a reach, but if all this information was secret, and only a few people knew any of it, then that might just be a way of saying that there were only a few people 'good' enough to know."

"Good enough?"

Matt shrugged. "Not in a way that meant they were inferior, but he may have been saying that there were only a few who *should* know."

It was almost as mind-bending as the letters, but not as much of a reach as Matt thought it might be. These letters probably had plenty of stuff between the lines that we wouldn't be able to figure out, just because we weren't the Davies. We were doing well enough making guesses.

"And the man 'T' knew wasn't supposed to make any of this official, which makes me think he was someone in charge of documentation or something." That was a good guess for me. But was it really a guess? Dupree had all but written that exactly, even if we didn't know the identity of "T's" friend.

"Yeah, that's what it looks like." Matt's mouth quirked down. "Kinda sad he saw the decline of Salt's Creek back then."

"I don't think it was permanent then," I told him. "I mean, there was a sign for a bridal shop."

"Could have been waves of growth and decline, then," Matt offered. "He mentioned the trial as 'troubles' in here."

"Yeah." It was another side to the articles I remembered reading in the *Salt's Creek Advance*. Whoever had written the news of Dupree's acquittal hadn't been happy. "Didn't the article say that most of the citizens thought he was guilty?"

"I don't guess they actually did," Matt answered.

Dupree had been sad about this town, and he'd still considered it to be a good place. James Abney had had a hold on a few people, I guessed. People who were in vocal positions, maybe who hadn't liked Gavin Dupree. But plenty of the citizens, at least twelve of them, had made the decision that Dupree couldn't have killed a man. I needed to know more about Dupree as a person. He seemed to have been a good man. I had no idea why he'd have created the riddle device, which had made things difficult for Trenavell, but it probably also hadn't been wartime when he'd made it.

"Think the Davies ever visited at Christmas?" I asked Matt.

"Maybe." He looked up at me. "Or the Dupree's could have gone there."

"Christmas at the beach," I remarked.

We traded the letters, and I handed him the last one I'd read the night before.

As he read it, and took his time going over the words, Dupree's lament about our families and how we'd overcome that came back to my memory. The thought of how our friendship had kept that from happening, how it had kept our families close, warmed me inside, but that warmth extended to my face as I sat with the friend in question.

I knew my face was reddening. Why? Was I embarrassed? Was there some subconscious depth I'd applied to my thoughts, and did those intensify as I sat here with Matt?

And why would they, anyway? He was my friend.

Matt glanced up for a second before looking back down. "You know what?"

"What?"

He kept his eyes on the letter. "I think Dupree would be pretty happy that his descendants are still friends."

With a nod, I tried to get the redness in my face to calm, but that was just making it worse. "Yeah. Probably."

Matt looked up at me again. "You okay?"

"Yes." I scooted backwards on my bed and leaned against the wall. "He says something about a marking on the map, and that the Davies might benefit from a similar one."

Matt glanced at the paper again. "Yeah." Studying the letter, he continued talking. "He talks about his children taking on something."

Dupree had made an effort towards some task. As my face cooled, I thought of the pictures in our attic, of all the photos with the riddle device key on it. Of the newspaper with a note from Mildred Barnes on the page.

*They found other skies first.*

"I guess they were supposed to be part of the whole Trenavell thing, too." I scratched my side as it sent a little itch along the scar. My phone let out a ding.

*Hi Anya, it's Joanna Whitley. Can you watch Jimmy for me next Tuesday evening at 5:00? Would be for a couple hours.*

"Who's that?" Matt asked me.

"Miss Whitley." I sent back a message that I could.

*Thank you so much!*

That was a little earlier in the day. It wouldn't be so dark out when I made my way home, I thought. Or I could drive, which might itself be safer than just taking my bike.

Hopefully we wouldn't somehow get stuck in Trenavell and make me unavailable by virtue of never showing up for the job.

Matt handed the letter to me, and I put it back on the short stack we'd looked at this afternoon.

He shook his head again. "My brain hurts."

I laughed. "It's even worse trying to figure them out without a second person."

Matt rocked in the seat of my desk chair, his face thoughtful. "Do you want to take a break from them?"

There were a lot more letters in this box, but they probably were as hard to figure out as the first four. The fact that Matt had gotten us as far as he had just by looking up one thing in the letters was good. "From the letters, yes."

Dupree had said he'd hoped someone would carry on his work. He'd laid that groundwork with the device key on the sampler in the photographs. He'd helped the Davies settle in North Carolina, though I didn't know why he'd done that. And he'd made the riddle device itself, to seal the gates.

"What?" Matt asked, impatience in his voice.

"I want to know what Dupree was up to."

"Extraterrestrial stuff," Matt said.

Giving him a look, I offered my own thought. "Well, yeah, but more than that." Meris had warned us of the possibility of an invasion to Earth through the gates. It was scary at the time. But was that the whole reason the device existed? Clearly, it had performed its function, but why had Dupree made it at all? "It can't just be that he made the device. He had a reason to make it that didn't really match up with what Meris said, because he didn't use it then. He just left behind the key to it, and then made a map of what looks like a whole other network. Plus there were people who were in the know about all this, but not a lot of people."

Matt leaned forward and sat still, his eyes focused on his hands. "He mentioned Skyrren." He stopped, hesitating. "Maybe we need to…"

"What's wrong?"

"That I don't particularly want to go to Skyrren again."

My stomach heaved at the memories. "Me, either." I took a deep breath in. "I doubt we could. It would take forever."

Matt nodded. "And we kind of found it by accident last time."

After a glance at my dresser, I eyed Matt. "Can't you read a map?"

He fixed me with a flat stare.

Shaking my head, I sighed. "The book's probably gone, anyway." I thought. "Think your gramma has it?"

"I don't know how we'd narrow it down to ask if she has it," Matt answered. "We don't actually know what the book is."

Gavin Dupree had never been clear on what anything was. He'd named Skyrren. The frustration built up, rising in my throat. The letters had never been anything but confusing and cryptic, and it had taken actually being in Trenavell and talking to Meris and Noam to know that the rhyme on the sampler had meant anything at all.

"No. We don't."

Apparently going to Trenavell would always be the key.

# Chapter 8

A day passed, and the late morning found me sitting on my bed, my empty backpack in front of me and my thoughts focused on the letters, the map, and that copper disc under my bed. If nothing else, I could compare the disc to the signs to see if they actually did match, and how closely. Meris and Noam would need to see the map, to compare it to Noam's. The letters could use a few other sets of eyes.

My phone dinged once, a text from Matt.

*Danny's back. He says to meet him at the edge of the woods.*

The hair on my neck stood on end as I replied. *Why the woods?* It hadn't been five days.

*The car's at the house.*

My heart sped up at those words.

Why didn't Danny come all the way to Matt's house?

*I'll meet y'all out there.*

Quickly, I put on jeans and shoes, shoved the map, letters, disc, keys, and a flashlight in my backpack, then grabbed my coat. I had no idea if Danny had anything more for us than information, or if we could even safely get to Trenavell, but I had to be prepared.

Flying down the stairs, I knew I didn't want to see the car, and I didn't want whoever was driving it to potentially see me. Why was I even in a hurry?

*How did Danny get past the car?*

If he'd managed to make it to the edge of the woods, then whoever had driven the car wasn't near the gate. Horror dawned inside me as I thought that maybe they could be in the Dupree house, hiding, listening to Danny. Watching him.

The back door slammed loudly behind me as I shot out of it and down the deck stairs. When I was halfway across the yard, Matt's back door shut. It was already hot outside, and I found myself, however scared I was, looking forward to the chill of Trenavell's autumn weather as I dashed into the brush, followed quickly by Matt.

"Hey," came Danny's whisper, and I jumped, whirling around with a silent Matt to see his cousin.

"Hey," Matt answered.

"You guys can take your time," Danny said. "Catch your breath. I didn't see or hear anyone at the Dupree house yet."

"We should get it over with," Matt said.

I snorted. "I think we all know we're not gonna 'get it over with' any time soon."

Danny glanced at the woods behind him. "We can make our way there."

So it looked like we were going to Trenavell. I pulled my backpack all the way on. "What happened?"

"Ira got in touch with Meris and Noam, and they'll meet us under the store," Danny answered. "How long's it been here?" He started to move through the woods.

"A couple days," Matt answered.

Danny blew out a breath. "It's definitely been five days in Trenavell."

At least we didn't have to wait all that long, and at least the times were close.

Now that we were moving, the temperature seemed to rise. The chill in Trenavell would relieve that. Would it be raining? At least, though I wasn't really prepared for that, much of our way to the city would be underground.

Close to the house, we stopped. A familiar brown shape sat brazenly parked directly in front of the porch.

Without waiting, I grabbed both of the guys by the arms and towed them to the wide tree nearby. Thankfully, it could hide all of us, if we angled the right way against the trunk. I didn't dare peek around.

Matt did lean out for a second. "Looks like they have a license plate now."

Danny's eyebrows went up. "They didn't before?"

"Not when they hit my truck," Matt told him.

I huffed. "Guess that's how they're driving around town and not getting stopped." Part of me wanted to look. There wasn't anyone outside with the car, so maybe it would be okay, just for a moment. Matt had peeked, after all. Before I moved, I strained to hear any reason why I shouldn't.

Then came the sounds of footsteps emerging from the house and crossing the porch, clearly two people.

"...ought to be glad I can try and fix this," came a man's voice. "Still can't believe you." One of the car doors opened with a low-pitched squeal. The second person, whoever it was, hadn't answered. "Get in the car." The second door popped open, then both of them closed within a second of each other, the metallic clash ringing in the woods. The car roared to life, then moved off, leaving just the sound of its tires on the gravel road.

I waited until that sound had gone quiet before pushing myself away from the tree. Dust kicked up by the car's tires floated above the gravel.

"We should've tried to see who that was," I said.

"And they would have seen us," Matt answered.

"Sounds like one of them was in trouble," Danny offered. "With more than just one person, if someone had to 'try and fix' it."

The woods remained otherwise quiet.

Matt stared at the house and through the dark front door. "It's probably empty now."

We needed to hurry. I rushed for the porch steps, though I doubted that the two people would be back. Hopefully they wouldn't. And hopefully they'd actually been in Trenavell and weren't meeting with someone who was still inside.

It was hard to push away the spike of fear that someone else might actually be in the house.

*Maybe we can outrun them.*

As I stepped over the broken door that still lay over the threshold, I heard the guys hurrying after me. I knew my tennis shoes were a little too loud, even if I was trying to be careful. Behind me, the door slid over the wooden floor as someone's foot hit it.

The kitchen wall stood open an inch or so. I rushed down into the cellar and waited as Matt and Danny stepped in, and as Danny carefully pulled the door so it stayed open only a little. My eyes adjusted to the dim golden light, and the chill of the cellar cooled me off.

"I'll let one of y'all go first," I told them, pulling my coat on, wishing my hands would get still.

Danny looked up the long set of stairs. "I'll go first."

As we arrived at the top of the staircase, Matt reached past me and brushed his hand over a cluster of golden lights. A barely-audible buzz sounded. "It's interesting that the moss lamps do pretty well down here."

So long ago, as we'd watched the lights go by a train window, traveling through the night, he'd told me about them. "They don't thrive on Earth."

Danny had his hands on the bar across the door. "I remember Gramma trying to grow them."

"They died." Matt stared at them, his glowing gaze moving to his cousin. "So…the fact that they're here in this gate means…"

"The cellar's not on Earth." Goosebumps rippled over my skin, taking a harsher path across the scar as I said it. "Know anything else?"

Matt shook his head. "Not much. I know my gramma can't keep them alive, even if she does try and feed them…stuff they'd normally eat."

Danny watched us quietly, then poked gently at a moss lamp. It vibrated for a second.

Matt's eyes caught the light as he answered. "She said she tried stuff like eggshells and all that other stuff you compost, but nothing works for that long." I could hear him swallow.

"She said burrow beast skin, like what they shed, is the best." He cracked a smile. "Dirt whale skin."

Danny lifted the bar and pushed the door open, letting in sunlight.

We'd seen them in patches on the ground, and I wondered if those patches were holes that the creatures had made. They probably shed skin when they went through the dirt like that.

Matt let out a huff of a laugh. "Then Mom said that those things were just a story, and Gramma looked kinda confused after that."

Danny set the bar into its place on the wall. "Where would Gramma even get skin from them?"

We stepped out onto the empty road.

Matt shrugged. "I don't guess there's anywhere she can anymore."

"Too bad," Danny said, voice light. "They look pretty cool."

What *had* been her source, if Matt's Gramma was from Earth? What were the other creatures native to this planet like? We'd seen burrow beasts, and those almost-canine animals that had followed us. The latter were venomous, probably just through their teeth. The one that had attacked that day had scratched me without leaving anything more than the claw marks, though it was possible that it just hadn't released venom from its claws.

I stuck my hands into my coat pockets, focusing the memories from that encounter into the effort of clenching my fists.

When we arrived at the top of the slope that went down into the dark tunnel, I could see the bulk of the larger creature far off, and to the side of it, the almost playful flick of dirt clumps into the air from what I'd assumed was its offspring.

Hopefully this wasn't a nesting ground, or a hibernation den, if we kept needing to use this tunnel. Danny had said that the beasts were indifferent, but they were still large enough to hurt us on accident. If we disturbed a nest, they might not be so indifferent, if instinct drove them.

As we walked downward, and the guys turned their flashlights on, I swung my backpack around on one shoulder to grab my light from inside. The three beams together at least showed us more of the inside. More signs. Directional arrows. Tunnels that turned off of this one, and nondescript doors. The last sent chills down my spine even if I knew they'd be practical for sheltering from a burrow beast if we needed to.

When we reached the part of the tunnel that led to the more open space in front of the double doors, my flashlight caught a sign I hadn't noticed before, above the tunnel's exit, stretching across almost the whole wall. The wide, tall markings formed, presumably, another word I couldn't read, but underneath that was a round symbol.

“What do y’all think that means?” I asked the guys, pausing and letting my flashlight beam rest on the shape.

It was a spoked wheel with no border, like the one that Dupree had hidden the device keys in at the bottom of that well. Dupree’s wheel had been on the side of the boats in the river, and an eight-spoked wheel had been the shape of the completed riddle device in the chapel.

The difference in this one was that it had thirteen spokes.

“Looks kinda familiar,” Matt said, voice dry, adding his own beam of light.

“Sorta, but not really,” I told him. With more light, I now noticed that the letters and the symbol were an iridescent white, and set into the wall.

Danny shined his light up there as well. “It looks official.”

That shouldn’t have given me chills. It all looked official down here. There were signs and arrows in this smooth tunnel. There were turnoffs and doors. It shouldn’t have even bothered me at all that Danny was right and that the symbol, stamped on everything, most likely was official.

But why did it look official at all? When had it been put there?

“Have you ever seen it, Danny?” Had it been an old emblem of Trenavell? Maybe it was on their flag, and I’d never noticed.

“No,” Danny answered, his voice distant, mystified.

Slowly, I moved the flashlight down, looking instead across at the double doors at the far end of the space before us. Matt and Danny did the same thing, and this time, I noticed how messy it was, noticing more scraps and junk strewed around on the ground, not directly in the path, but around it. A large spring, ten feet away, made a shadowy illusion that stretched over the floor behind it. A chunk near it looked like molded metal, and an abandoned handle next to that had a broken end.

Another chill ran over my skin as we arrived at the double doors.

At least we'd be under that store soon. That wasn't as bad as whatever this was, because it did go up into a place that actually had windows. This creepy abandoned office building, or whatever it was, held dark hallways and empty doors that would be a good place for something to hide or nest. Clenching one hand in my pocket, I tried again to pour my anxiety into that action, tried to keep my flashlight facing forward, tried not to look into any of the rooms, even when an errant motion of a flashlight reflected *something* back at us. It was probably just glass or metal. No one was down here. No one followed us. If some kind of animal lived down here, we were loud and in a hurry, and probably pretty scary to it, at least at this point. If there were people, they probably had an interest in not being seen at all.

"Do you remember where it was?" I whispered.

Danny laughed quietly. "I've pretty much only been down here. Someone delivered supplies to the store cellar, but otherwise I've been looking around down here."

"Where did you stay at night?" Matt asked.

"I slept behind the store counter." His cheerful face wavered for a second, and I wondered if Danny had seen or heard something down here that had stopped him from staying in the living quarters above the storefront and the desolate hallways underneath the city. He clearly wasn't afraid of moving around down here otherwise.

Finally, Danny led us through a door. The staircase on the other side would take us up to the storefront.

"Do we need to go up?" Matt asked.

Danny shook his head. "Not yet. I think it should be okay if we do, but Ira was going to get Meris and Noam to meet us down here." He peeked out of the door, then closed it most of the way and crouched by the wall.

My backpack wasn't heavy, but the weight did pull on my shoulders. Pocketing my flashlight, I shrugged out of one of the straps and swung the pack around, holding the strap in one hand. It swung a little.

Danny eyed my backpack, nodding at it. "What did you bring?"

"The letters, that copper disc, my keys…" I hadn't told Danny about the map. I'd had it the other day as we'd navigated the underground tunnel, but I hadn't detailed it what it was, or even taken it out of my pocket. "A map."

"Of what?" he asked.

The backpack lurched suddenly as the disc inside shifted. "It looks like a gate map of Trenavell." I grabbed the loop of the pack and shook it to even the weight out. "Gavin Dupree drew it."

Danny straightened, his gaze puzzled. "How'd you get ahold of it?"

"I found it in a garage in New Mexico." Slowly, I became aware of a light growing in the hallway. It was soft, steady, and silvery-gold, accompanied by the shuffle of quiet footsteps.

Danny stood slowly and turned to the door, then peeked out before slipping out into the hall.

"Danny." A familiar female voice greeted Matt's cousin.

Matt and I went after Danny into the hallway, now lit by two of the same type of lantern that Ira had, because Meris held one as well. With the light in the hallway increased, I could see a third door just down the hall past the one Ira had used last time, one that probably led into another cellar. There was likely another one beyond that one, an entrance to a space below a shop or storefront. Or maybe a house. With all the entrances to this underground part of the city, why hadn't anyone seemed to know about it? Cargan hadn't even used it when he'd gotten Danny out of the city. He'd just gone by the gate.

Noam and Meris watched us over the glow of the lantern she held in her hand.

Behind them, Ira moved to put his hand on the next door down the hall. With a half-smile, he lifted the lantern as if in salute and disappeared through the doorway. The glow dimmed.

Meris gave us a nod. "Good to see you all."

An awkward moment stretched out. The nerves along my scar started itching again, and I reached under my coat to scratch my side, being careful, glad it didn't hurt as much as it had.

Noam watched me. "I need to take those out."

Matt snorted. "No you don't."

Shooting Matt a glare, I turned to look at Noam's confused face. "We already did."

Noam's eyebrows rose, then dipped back into a frown. "What?"

I hesitated. Noam being so incredulous was probably for the same reason that Matt had kept urging me to actually go to a doctor to get them out. It wasn't the best idea to remove stitches in my bathroom. "More time passed on Earth than it did here." With a breath, I kept explaining. "They wound up being in too long, and they were starting to hurt, so…" Gesturing at Matt, I finished. "Matt actually was the one that removed them."

Noam blinked, silent.

Meris walked forward. "How long was it on Earth for you?"

"Two weeks," Matt answered. "And that was before we even tried coming back."

Noam cleared his throat. "Tried?" His eyes went down to my side for a second, but the look in them was somehow different than Matt's. There wasn't anger, just an almost clinical appraisal.

There would be a lot to lay out for them. "We actually went through the gate and all the way to the city a few times," I told them. "The gate works fine, but y'all know the city's been locked up." Did they know about the hole in the wall being completely blocked? "We couldn't even get through that one place in the wall. It's boarded and bricked."

Meris' eyes flashed. "Of course it is." She turned to Danny. "And my brother let you out."

He nodded.

Meris eyed the dark hallway around us. "And you haven't been anywhere aboveground here, yet?"

"Just the storefront above us," I told her.

"It's not a bad place to camp out," Danny offered, lightly. "I've been sleeping there."

Noam fixed his gaze on me. "Anya, may I at least look at the scar?"

It was a good thing that the irritation was healing. Maybe that would reassure him.

"Sure." I reached for the door to the store cellar. "Do y'all want to go up into the store?"

"The light's better," Matt added.

Danny's cheerful voice offered another benefit. "There's places to sit, too." He grinned. "Or a least a floor that's not in the dark." The light was enough for me to see the quick shadow that passed over his face.

Matt watched his cousin. Maybe Matt saw the same thing I did, that Danny had seen or heard something down here that had him a little spooked. His eyes flicked to mine. Danny would tell us without us asking. Maybe.

As I led my friends into the cellar space and up the stairs, I lifted my hands to push the hatch in the floor open. It gave little resistance as I guided it to thump softly on the wooden shop floor and moved out of their way.

The windows were as dirty as ever, but it was still bright enough outside that the light was good in here, if soft and muted. As soon as Danny had cleared the hatch and shut it back, Meris took a place behind the counter, back straight and chin high, like she was holding court, and set her lantern on the surface in front of her, leaning her rifle against the edge.

Noam moved toward the window, and I followed.

"We all have flashlights," I told him as I swung my backpack off and set it down. "Would that help?" I held mine out.

Noam appraised the sunlight. "I may not need it, especially if I'm not removing anything." At least, with that sentence, he had let through some amusement. "Just turn your right side toward the window."

"Okay." It was cold in here, and as I took my coat off, the chill raised the hairs on my arms. "Be quick, because it's pretty chilly in here."

He smiled. "I will."

Turning so that the sun gave him as much light as it could, I rolled up the edge of my t-shirt, revealing the still-flattening bumps on each side of the pink scar. It wasn't as angry as it had been before, and it definitely didn't hurt as much.

Noam peered closer. "I see the bumps in the skin."

The other three were way too quiet. "They were worse."

"How did it feel?" Noam's brown eyes looked up into mine.

"Like I said, it hurt." A tickling sensation ran along it again. "It burned, which got worse when I touched it. And it itches, which wasn't fun when it was still that painful before."

Noam's shoulders had dropped, his face relaxing. He nodded. "Just the healing process. And the nerves." Eyeing them once more, he held my gaze. "Is it still irritated?"

Matt wasn't close to me, but his stare held the same sensation as him walking too close behind me.

My face warmed. "Yeah, but not as much."

"I'm going to press the skin," Noam told me. "If that is something you'd be all right with."

"Go ahead."

Noam gave me a nod, his expression focused, and gently and firmly pressed two fingers along the line of the scar, moving along the healed gash. A soft burn followed his fingers, and an itch after that.

He leaned up, pulling his hand away. "It's healing well." He offered a warm smile. "You're keeping it clean?"

"Yes." I rolled my shirt down. Movement behind me told me when Matt turned around and stopped watching. My face heated up again.

Noam stepped away. "It looks like it should keep improving."

As I pulled my coat back on, Matt did turn to look at me. Then his gaze went past me to two dusty stools in front of the window.

Before he could move to bring them over to the counter, I dragged them, putting my backpack on top of one. They weren't that heavy. Danny had perched on the top of a barrel, and Meris had pulled another barrel up closer and sat on it.

Noam climbed onto the counter itself and sat there, facing the center.

"This is a fine meeting space," Meris remarked, satisfaction all over her face and filling her words. She leaned forward on her elbows. "We have not been able to find anything like that so far."

"Who are y'all meeting with?" Matt asked.

"Each other," Meris answered, exasperated.

Noam's gaze lingered on her. "It's been nearly impossible to find anywhere suitable."

"Or any time," Meris added. "So many rooms suddenly become excellent for storage, and often the both of us find that we are, interestingly, required for separate tasks." Acid built in her voice.

Noam's tone was more measured. "Did you think that your father returning to a position of leadership would somehow lead to them thinking it appropriate for us to continue the appearance we were creating?" His eyes, however gentle and placating, held some shadows.

"They're trying to keep us apart," Meris snapped.

Noam's reply remained measured. "Well, for all purposes, you're still their princess."

Meris' eyes flashed as she lifted her chin. Then her expression stilled and evened out, her eyebrows rising, her face calm, but her eyes calculating, as though she had some dawning idea and wasn't going to share it. "This meeting place will need to suffice for now, then."

Noam just gave her a nod. If he'd read whatever she'd said with her eyes, I didn't know if they'd ever share what it was.

Danny put his hands on his knees and leaned forward, the movement businesslike. "So, did you guys have Cargan let me out of the city?"

"Of course," Meris nodded. "Noam was especially concerned about Anya."

"Do you know why Cargan had to?" Matt asked her, drumming his fingers softly on the counter.

Meris' gaze went past us and directly to the dirty window. "I wish I did know more." She turned to Danny. "Considering that you are friend and family to Matt and Anya, their work on the device alone should have guaranteed more hospitality for you."

Well. That was my introduction. "Yeah, about that…" I said, taking in a breath.

Both Meris and Noam put their focus on me immediately.

"About what?" Meris asked.

"The device." Looking at Matt to brace myself, I tried to think of what I wanted to say, of how I wanted to present what we'd found out that night in Matt's house. "Um…someone wanted us to activate the gate sealing device." Frustration flooded through me then as Meris looked confused at the distinct lack of revelation that I'd offered. Of course *someone* wanted it. Meris and Noam had been the ones to try and find the pieces in the first place.

She blinked. "Well…of course."

With a shake of my head, I tried again. "I mean that the night Matt and I got back home, we overheard a conversation in his house, between his parents and a friend of theirs, and it sounded like no one was expecting the device to be activated at all, even though you said Naolon was planning on invading."

"No one in the government of Trenavell expected it," Matt added, clarifying.

"But…" Meris' confusion was evident. "Someone was talking about Naolon."

Noam's quiet reply to her brought another dimension to things. "You overheard someone talking about it."

"Who?" Danny asked.

Meris focused on the jar lantern in front of her. "Cargan was one of them." One of the little lights twitched.

Moss lamps. I stared at them as another one did the same.

"So…he sent you after the pieces?" I asked. He'd helped us. He'd clearly been aware of what we were up to when we'd met him at that fort.

Meris shook her head. "Noam and I departed after sending a message to Barnabas." She tilted her head. "He may have told Cargan."

She'd eavesdropped.

Remembering how we'd bypassed a long land distance in Trenavell just by using the gate to New Mexico, and the one from there in that garage, I knew it was possible. Mr. Simpson had said that news was traveling slower. They used the gate network for delivering messages. "Do your parents know we used the device?"

"I haven't heard your names," Meris said. "They would know you by sight, simply as friends of mine, but as far as I know, they haven't spoken of you."

But it had only been a week and a half. There was a lot to figure out from retaking their country. The king would probably reach the point where he would be considering me and Matt and our role in this, especially if sealing the gates made things harder for their war effort.

Noam crossed his legs and leaned forward over his knees. "So, from what you heard, our government may not have expected or wanted us to activate the device."

"Right."

Meris set her hands flat on the counter in front of her. "Why was my brother talking about the riddle device and Naolon, then?"

Cargan was technically a prince, and served as a chaplain. He was closer to being a part of the Trenavellan government, in any case, than Meris was. But he had helped us. He had wanted to stop Naolon. Wouldn't the riddle device be the way to do that?

A part of Mr. Simpson's words came back to me then. *We'll need to act soon.*

What did that mean? Was he even connected to this? Part of me wondered if Meris had lied about Naolon invading Earth, but I didn't think she had. It was possible that she misunderstood something, but I couldn't figure out what there was to misunderstand. If Naolon wanted to take over a place, then access to it through the gates would guarantee them the chance to try, at the very least.

Why would they want to take over Earth? Why would they bother, or dare? Earth was a big planet, and Naolon was one country, of a size unknown to me, on one of five continents. My heart started to race. Meris' warning about Naolon invading Earth didn't actually make sense. My gaze fell to the little lights in her lantern, and I focused on them. One twitched a little bit, and then another one nearby did the same. If Meris wasn't lying, then maybe she didn't quite understand the size or population of Earth. I'd gone along with her, and dragged Matt. Even if he wouldn't see it as me dragging him to this planet, and across Trenavell, I'd still done that because I'd been scared of what Meris said when it hadn't even made sense.

"Why's Compass Hill all locked up?" Matt asked.

"We're not sure," Noam answered. "They've been keeping us on different tasks. We haven't been required to attend any other strategy meetings." He gestured at the dirty window. "If you'll notice, you've not seen anyone making their way around."

Noam's words chilled me. We'd been here before. The first day we'd come to Compass Hill, it had been a bustling city, and when we returned, it presented the same way until the fighting broke out. "Why did it change?"

Meris shrugged. "We don't know."

"Are there still people here?" I asked.

"In the castle," she answered. "And throughout Compass Hill, in some houses. Miriam is still here, if you ever needed to go to her house."

I tried to keep my face neutral and not show the aversion I had to returning there. "Some houses?" That was interesting. If people were living here, people other than citizens like Miriam who expressly helped, then why would any of the houses be empty at all? "So…did people just leave their homes?" Had the empty houses been occupied at all recently? Compass Hill sure looked like an average city, albeit one under occupation.

How wrong had my perception of Compass Hill as a city actually been?

"I would assume that most people evacuated at one time," she answered.

"And came back?" Matt asked. He was following my line of thought.

Meris blinked, realization spreading over her face, maybe as she remembered the days we'd been in the city. "Oh." She looked down, frowning. "There were a number of people here."

Noam shifted on the counter. "Also, would Naolon have let that many people leave the city if they were occupying it?"

"I doubt they would have," Danny said.

Reaching into my backpack, I grabbed the gallon zip bags in there, one that held the letters and one that held the folded up map. "Also…we have letters that Gavin Dupree sent to Matt's ancestors, and a gate map he drew."

Meris stared at the bags in my hands. "Does Matt's family know you have the letters?"

Was she hoping they would be allies? "No." I opened them and pushed them to the center of the counter. "They were in Dupree's house, and someone took them from there. The day we got back from Trenavell, they were left on the front porch of my house."

Danny straightened up. "Do you know who brought them?"

"Somebody with a burgundy car," I answered.

With a frown, Meris asked the inevitable question. "Why were they in Dupree's house if they were sent to Matt's ancestors?"

"We don't know," Matt told her. "My grandparents live several hours away, on an island that's only accessible by ferry, and that's where my ancestors who got the letters from Dupree lived, too."

Noam pulled the bag of letters toward himself. "Do you think your family has the ones they wrote to Dupree?"

"They could, but that doesn't make a whole lot of sense, either," Matt said. "Why would they trade?"

"Plus, the letters from Dupree have some sort of vague information." I watched Noam pull one out and carefully slide the letter from the envelope.

"Is it helpful and vague?" Meris asked.

"Kinda." I'd have to explain Pilot Mountain, both the landmark and the town. Maybe the other two would have some insight into why Dupree would be writing about a city his friends had to be familiar with. After all, Compass Hill was the capital. The Davies were moon-eyes. They had to have known about this city, and if they'd known Dupree a long time, what was the point of being secretive about a capital? "One of the letters starts off with a reference to a landform in North Carolina that has a town near it. Both the landform and the town are called Pilot Mountain, and based on some of the things he said, he was talking about Compass Hill and some attributes of it in the rest of the letter."

"Interesting," Noam remarked.

"Yeah," I agreed. "Especially if they would have known stuff about their own capital."

Meris lifted her head. "It wasn't the capital then."

Matt and I exchanged a glance before he spoke. "Wait, what was?"

"Skyrren," Meris said simply.

Why hadn't we known that before? "Okay, so…was Compass Hill anything back then?"

"A city," Meris answered. "But it wasn't the capital until the government center was moved here after Skyrren was rendered uninhabitable."

The seat of government was in Compass Hill, and had been thirteen years before when Naolon had taken it over, and Naolon treated Compass Hill like a capital. Not all capitals were the biggest or most populous cities, at least on Earth.

But when Gavin Dupree was alive, when he was assembling his riddle device, Skyrren was the capital, and he hadn't chosen Skyrren as the place it would be activated. The web, the network, had to have been accessible in Skyrren, but Gavin Dupree had chosen Compass Hill to place an extremely important and war-altering device.

Skyrren was supposed to have been unlivable, though I knew it wasn't empty at all, so people were able to go there safely. He could have put the device there. "Why'd he pick here?" I asked, my voice low.

Compass Hill looked like it had been cobbled together, not planned. That wasn't too weird, and actually expected of a place that might have grown. But underneath this somewhat new capital ran a series of passageways, the entrance of which lay far from the wall, big enough for those creatures to traverse without even having to burrow.

Moss lamps. Sprinkled in the darkness, seen through the dirty window of an old train that we'd boarded from a depot in the woods.

Looking up at Meris and Noam, I blurted the question. "Why isn't there a train station here?" If Compass Hill had always been a city, and was major enough to become the capital, then the rails should have run through here, too. We shouldn't have had to trek through the woods at night for Ira to hang a lantern as a signal in the dark.

"You mean the stop should be in Compass Hill," Noam said.

Matt's eyes narrowed. "Yeah, that would make more sense than it being all the way out where it is."

"That it would." Meris toyed with the handle on the jar lantern.

Maybe Compass Hill hadn't been important enough to have a rail station when Dupree made the device. The poisoning of Skyrren, or whatever happened, had only been in 1986, a hundred years after the date on the first letter Matt and I had found.

And pondering the choice of Compass Hill didn't even begin to touch why he'd constructed the device in the first place.

My gaze fell on the plastic bag that held the map. Why would he have made a gate map while also creating a device that would shut down a whole network of them? "Y'all should check out this map." Carefully, I pulled the map out of the plastic bag and unfolded it in the center of the counter.

Meris leaned over it, her eyes flicking around the scattered markings all over the parchment, finally focusing on the bottom right corner, where Gavin Dupree had signed his name. "Where'd this come from?"

"New Mexico."

Danny looked pleasantly surprised, but not confused.

*Does he know about Moon-eye?*

Meris and Noam glanced at each other.

"That gate in the desert," Matt supplied.

Meris' face smoothed out, neutral instead of puzzled. She remembered the desert, and the garage full of junk we'd found.

But I'd discovered something, and I hadn't shared it. Leaning back a little bit, I let my defenses go up, ready to answer if she decided to question me harshly.

Noam slid the map to himself, handling it gently. "It looks very different from mine." He glanced for a moment at the corner with Dupree's name, and then focused on the main part of the map. "No railroad on this one."

"Maybe he forgot it," Matt said.

Meris still hadn't started questioning me. My defenses might not have been great to her, but I did have them ready. It hadn't been too long after finding the desert gates that we'd also found the riddle pieces. We'd been attacked by some creature in the woods that had also been tracking us. I'd had a run-in with an ax, because Ira had been scared. None of those were great explanations as to why I'd hidden the map instead of telling them immediately, but they were things that pulled my attention away from the map. Plus, on top of it all, they'd told me to keep the riddle key to myself. It could have been better for me to be the only one that knew about the map, especially if someone stole it and used it. Briefly, I thought of Gavin Dupree and the words he'd written about keeping information to only a few people.

A soft itch spidered along the scar like a trickle of water, and I reached under my coat, balling up part of my t-shirt and scratching.

As Noam slid the map back to her, Meris relaxed and, after another glance, passed it to me. "Make sure nothing happens to it."

"Can I see it, Anya?" Danny asked.

I nodded and gave it to him.

He perused it. "Interesting that the railroad tracks are missing."

Matt answered his cousin. "It could have been like a paper towns kind of thing."

But who would have wanted to copy it for any reason that might make that necessary? "You may have been right about him forgetting the tracks, too." Dupree's secrets and vagueness when he had offered information might indicate why the map was hidden, but why was its hiding place somewhere so risky?

Meris had picked up one of the letters, and her face took on that same confusion that I know Matt and I had had when we'd read them.

"This makes no sense, even if it is about Compass Hill," she remarked.

*Unless…*

Compass Hill hadn't been the capital in the 1880s. It hadn't even had a train station, despite being a city that had drawn the government here so many years later. I thought of the hallways below us, and the abandoned tunnel with its signs and directional arrows and turnoffs. Compass Hill's secrets, the things that Gavin Dupree had discussed with the Davies, were things he'd kept to himself and only a few others. Whether or not there was actually something in Skyrren that we could figure out, he'd still offered initials, and those had to lead to names.

"So we'll have to figure out Compass Hill," I answered.

There was clearly something here. As empty as the creepy hallways and rooms below were, something hid there.

"And Dupree," Matt added.

That we could try to do at home. I nodded, eager, however pointed Matt's words were.

Meris scanned the letter again. "Skyrren may need to be a destination as well."

That stopped me. How were we supposed to get there? We hadn't meant to find it the last time, and we'd only gotten as far as we had because of the train, which was gone now.

Danny's mouth had set in a firm line. Matt had started to shake his head.

I wouldn't cringe away from this. "Um…Meris…I don't think we can."

Noam watched, his brown eyes intense as I spoke, his focus sliding to Meris.

"Why?"

Matt stiffened beside me, his spine straightening from the slouch it had been in. "We don't know where it is."

"We have a map," Meris said. "Both of which are also gate maps."

*Really?* "Yeah, and they're both pretty useless, because the ones on Noam's map are all sealed, and these aren't exactly labeled." Swallowing, I continued. "Y'all didn't know anything about the Kings Road gate, we found a couple of gates leading to the American Southwest, and the only reason we found Skyrren at all was because the train derailed. We had to walk through a cave to get away from some villagers that chased after us."

All those hours, clinging to Matt's backpack and following the glowing lines smeared on the stone, trying to outrun their rapid fading until we finally reached the gray sunlight in another cavern.

"Then we can find these and try them," Meris suggested, her tone optimistic.

I thought of how the time passed while we were actually here, how unpredictable it was. We'd done okay the last time, but I doubted that would happen again. The days were closer to actually matching up now. "Meris, we can't go on a quest to find Skyrren. We never know how long it's been on Earth when we're here."

"How long passed on Earth when you went with us to find the riddle pieces?" Meris asked.

The answer would not help. "A few hours."

A smug expression grew on her face.

Matt apparently recognized it. "That's pretty atypical, Meris." He paused. "It's been anywhere from no time at all, to several hours. Five days passed here, but only a few at home before we came here today." His irritation gave an edge to his voice. "We can't risk going on a journey that could take a long time, because we'd just go missing at home." His eyes flashed for a second in the illumination from the moss lamps. His parents could guess where we'd gone. My parents wouldn't have any idea, and that in itself scared me.

I imagined Meris was gritting her teeth as she held Matt's stare for a few moments before turning to Noam, as if to ask for his support.

He was calm. "We can't make them go with us, Meris."

Her mouth fell open. "I wasn't going to command them."

Danny hopped off the barrel he'd been sitting on. "But they are right. I can stay in Compass Hill, but they'll need to go home and come back every day."

Matt and I had to hold our ground. "We need to concentrate on figuring out Compass Hill and Gavin Dupree." Even if he had mentioned Skyrren, the letters weren't about that. It was Compass Hill's name that had been written in code, and that had to mean that the biggest secrets were in this city, somewhere underneath us, secrets that people still held today.

Secrets that might even be held at home, in anything we could find about Gavin Dupree.

Meris' eyes hardened as she turned again to Noam. Then she sighed. "Very well." She all but rolled her eyes as she added, "We would need a way to get out of the city, anyway."

"There's a way out of the city," I told her.

Danny propped on the counter. "Yeah, the three of us came through this tunnel that started pretty far from Compass Hill and led all the way here." He smiled a little. "The actual tunnel part, at the beginning, is big enough to fit an adult burrow beast."

Meris' eyes widened.

"And the tunnel changes after a while," Danny continued. "It gets to a big open space with doors at the one end. On the other side of the doors are whatever the hallways below us are. I made use of my time here by learning the route through the hallways, so if you ever absolutely needed to get out of the city, there's a way out."

Meris sat quietly and stared again at the moss lamp lantern in front of her.

Several of the little lights inside twitched gently, and I wondered if they were communicating among themselves, or if the little movements were separate. They could be involuntary responses of a connected network.

"Then…for now…," said Meris, "we perhaps should understand the nature of Compass Hill's secrets."

Danny slid the map over to me, having folded it back closed. Neither Meris nor Noam reached for it. I guessed we were done, for now, with studying it.

"We can try to find out more information about Gavin Dupree." Matt and I would need to go to the library again. What I wasn't so sure about was whether any of the stuff we did find would be useful to us or relevant at all to Trenavell. "We'll plan to come back every day," I added. Looking at Matt and Danny, I thought of the two figures who'd already been in the house when we'd arrived at it, and I realized we'd forgotten to mention that at all, and I frowned.

Noam zeroed in on me. "What?"

Trenavell may not have known about the Kings Road gate, but plenty of people did. "We forgot to tell y'all that there were people in Dupree's house when we got there."

And the car. They'd been driving that car. There was a whole other wave of stuff that we'd have to explain to Meris and Noam.

"Do you know who they were?" Meris asked.

Shaking my head, I kept going. "I do know they were driving a car that's followed me home before." With a deep breath, I gestured at Matt. "And it's the same car that ran into the back of Matt's truck a while back." How familiar were these two with what a car even was? The only vehicle that moved under its own power that I'd ever seen here was the train.

"Followed," Meris said.

Sheepish, I looked up at Noam. "That happened right before I took the stitches out."

He offered a grave half smile.

Meris hopped off the stool and moved it, then slung her rifle on. "We should start investigating Compass Hill." She bent behind the counter as Noam hopped down onto the shop floor, and the hatch made its soft thud as she set it down.

Danny was staying here anyway, but I turned to Matt. "We have time today."

He met my gaze. "We have time here, with no idea what time it will be when we get home."

"It's gonna be like that every time regardless," I told him. "Maybe we should at least all start learning our way around here." The eerie, empty rooms might actually lead to some answers as to what this had been.

"That's true." He didn't look mad or like he wanted to argue all that much.

With a hop off the stool, my tennis shoe soles landed softly on the hard floor, and I grabbed my backpack to put it back on. "Hey, Meris…how did y'all get down here?"

She stood at the edge of the hatch, looking down into the cellar. "The chapel has a similar opening behind the altar."

I had a good guess as to how I'd managed to miss that. "Well…y'all will have to show that to us." It might not be a good idea to go up into the castle itself, but it would be good to know a quick way in, especially if I ever wanted to have a look at the device again.

Part of me wondered if they'd cleaned the floor since the day we'd been there.

Meris took another look at the dark cellar as Noam went down the stairs, but she didn't answer me, just followed him.

Danny, Matt, and I stood behind the counter, waiting for someone to go after the other two.

Matt gestured. "Ladies first?"

"Don't you want to go in front of me?" I asked him.

"They're down there," Matt answered simply.

"Okay," I said, and followed Meris and Noam. Danny brought up the rear, pulling the hatch closed.

Meris cleared her throat, the light from the moss lamp lantern shadowing her face. Even in the lower light, she looked ill at ease. "Can the three of you show us the tunnel?"

Danny pulled out his flashlight. "Sure."

As we made our way back through the hallways underneath Compass Hill, I kept my ears open for any noises that might have been something other than our own echoes. It was pretty easy to understand why someone may have been down here, since it was abandoned. But if there were other animals besides the possibly nesting burrowing creatures, they were hiding. We weren't that loud, but we would be an unknown to any animal here.

Danny led us. No one spoke.

Meris' lantern was a good addition to the three flashlights that we had, even if it wasn't as strong of a light. Ira'd had one too, and I'd never seen one before we'd met Ira the other day. How were they made, and how did they keep the moss lamps alive? How long did they last?

We found our way to the part of the underground structure that opened up into the large room.

"The next part goes to the actual tunnel," Danny whispered. "Do you guys want to go to the end of it?"

"Yes," Meris told him.

Matt and I could head home from there, or go with them back to the city, and the thought that a long time could have passed at home made me want to make sure it hadn't.

Noam spoke as we crossed the wide expanse to the tunnel. "Do you think that the burrow beasts are around?"

Danny shook his head. "No, they were heading away when we were here earlier."

I knew they were indifferent and wouldn't eat us or anything, but the sheer size and speed of them did make me want to avoid them.

The flashlights made moving shadows from the debris scattered around the big open room. Instead of contributing to that, I trained my light on the wall above the tunnel entrance at the sign there. Meris lifted the lantern she held, and the only way to tell she'd done that was by the subtle shifting of the glow behind us.

"Another sign," she said.

"There are a lot of them down here," I told her. "Obviously we can't read what they say, but they're clearly words."

"In the actual tunnel, there are directional arrows." Matt's flashlight beam found one as we entered the passage.

The wider spaces of the tunnel made our footsteps echo, even if we were trying to walk quietly. The nearly complete darkness made me think that the signs down here had to have been reflective at one time, but they weren't at all now. Maybe, since no one knew they were down here and wouldn't be cleaning them, they were too dirty. Otherwise, wouldn't they be protected from the elements and less likely to decay?

As we walked, my shoulders relaxed, tension easing from my whole body in the openness of the tunnel. Both the tunnel and the hallways were dark and empty, though the tunnel's echoes of our footsteps gave the illusion that we weren't alone. On top of that, the tunnel had a nesting ground at one end.

But there was somewhere to go. It wasn't all close rooms and hallways and tight spaces. The tunnel, at least, held a clear and open way out at one end. Watching the dawning light as we approached the end soothed the rest of the tension away in time for us to climb the gentle slope into the empty land.

A quick movement in the distance, more dirt thrown up by the younger creature, drew my eye. I couldn't see the adult. If they were like a lot of animals were, the parent might be close, maybe burrowing itself, neater than its offspring would be.

Switching off my flashlight, I stuck it back in my pocket and turned to face the castle with my friends.

"That's quite a distance," Meris said.

"And a vulnerability," Noam added. "If people know about it."

Whatever the hallways underneath the city had been, it didn't have that use anymore. "The only reason we noticed it was because one of those creatures was using it instead of digging out of the ground." I eyed the woods that would take us back to the gate on the road and looked back down the slope into the tunnel. *A vulnerability.*

Danny had been sleeping behind the shop counter. There wasn't a lot of room back there, and staying hidden all but required that he sleep on top of the hatch. The windows of the living quarters above must not have had any coverings.

What if someone was using the passageways underneath Compass Hill? What if it was Naolon?

Iacomus had seen me and Matt and Noam and Meris. He'd been alone, and we'd gotten away. But he'd seen us for long enough that he'd actively looked for us after that.

My stomach twisted, breaking sweat out on my forehead as I remembered what Noam and I had fled from that day. I knew that Iacomus wasn't in Trenavell when they'd retaken their country, and they'd been unable to find him.

Had Iacomus been behind the wheel of the brown car as it had followed me through my own neighborhood?

Was the aboveground part of Compass Hill safer for us?

Aware of him staring at me, I turned to meet Matt's near-frowning gaze. He raised one eyebrow, and I swallowed hard, trying to calm the racing thoughts and the memories of the village.

"We can use this tunnel to make our way out of the city when we need to," Meris said.

Noam pressed his lips together, exasperation clear in his brown eyes. "When would we need to, Meris?"

"Apparently soon, if we're going to be otherwise trapped," she told him. She sharply turned to me and Matt. "How ready are you two to set out for Skyrren?"

She'd said that we needed to start investigating Compass Hill. What exactly had she meant? Research in Skyrren? "Not at all," I answered. "We can't go on a walking quest to a city we found by accident."

Meris looked at Noam. "Ira can help us catch the train again. It would easier than it was the last time, with the use of this tunnel."

Noam frowned. "The train exploded."

"There could be another one," Meris said, apparently trying really hard to have a logical tone for words that didn't make sense. "Or it may have been repaired in that time."

"But there was just that one guy," Matt said. "How would he be able to do that?"

Meris shook her head. "I'm sure there's more than one man."

That was far from proof, though she could be right. Regardless, even though I did wonder if Compass Hill might be safer for us, there was no way we could go to Skyrren now. "You said we needed to investigate Compass Hill."

Her eyes hardened. "When could the two of you accompany us to Skyrren?"

"Definitely not today or this week," Matt told her. With a glance at me, he added, "We should actually go home now."

Meris played with the strap of her rifle, her eyes focused on the ground, calculating.

"We can come back," Matt said.

"We just can't go to Skyrren right now," I finished. Even as I said that, part of me did think that we needed to be prepared, upon any return we made, to stay in Trenavell. We'd either have to get supplies or be dependent on our friends for them. "But do y'all want us to come back tomorrow?"

Meris finally looked up from the ground. "Tomorrow would be fine." She turned to the slope into the tunnel. "I suppose we should return to the castle."

Danny looked at us. "I can take you guys to the gate," he offered.

Meris and Noam stepped towards the edge.

"It's fine," Matt said. "We can get there."

Danny nodded, his forehead creased in worry, his eyes wide. "I'll see you guys tomorrow. I'll come to Earth first and check in."

Both Matt and I nodded. Danny moved away to lead Meris and Noam through the tunnel, and Matt and I walked back towards the woods, taking the empty road.

I looked back. Compass Hill stood quiet in some weird siege, locked up against enemies who weren't even there.

Without warning, hard memories came rushing back of the busy village in the middle of an evacuation, of the defiance of one man and the gunshots that had followed. More cold sweat broke out on my forehead, and my heart started to beat wildly, my breath not yet matching up with it, my feet wanting to run as we climbed under the trees to the Kings Road gate and the tension that had left me in the tunnel returned.

A gentle grip on my arm made me stop. Relief, weirdly enough, flooded through me, as I looked into Matt's eyes, grateful for a second to breathe. My heart slowed.

"What's wrong?"

The clear, calm words of Iacomus asking if the villagers had seen me and my friends rang through my head. "Do you remember the village that Noam and I went into?"

Matt looked down for a few seconds, then took a deep breath, his gaze moving back up to meet mine. "Yes."

I hadn't talked to him about it at all. He knew it had happened. But he hadn't been there, or seen the desperate scramble of the people. As the stark memory of the first snap of a gunshot and the screams flooded back, I clenched my fists.

"Anya?" Matt's face softened with concern.

*Deep breath.* I let my hands relax. "I didn't actually see anything." At least the only memories were the awful sounds that had echoed through the woods after us.

"That doesn't matter." Matt's voice, calm and gentle, helped. "It was still…"

I didn't have to agree with him, or find a word to finish his sentence. I didn't know a word that fit, that weighed enough or hit hard enough, to fully explain what it was like to hear a massacre. There was no way to explain how I'd managed to not have it with me constantly, beyond the fact that other traumas had followed.

And Trenavell hadn't been able to find Iacomus.

Steeling myself, I took another deep breath and pulled my thoughts away from where the memories had etched themselves. If anyone ever held Iacomus accountable, at least I would have something to offer in that effort. "Matt…I think we need to get some supplies. Food and stuff."

"Okay." He tapped on the back of my arm. "We could go to the grocery store for some food."

"Dry stuff," I told him.

"Yeah."

When we reached the gate, Matt opened the door and ducked into the golden glow. "Do you think Meris will blow up the lock or something to this door if she wants to get through and can't?"

I snorted. "She might would, if she had the right materials."

We were quiet as he put the bar in place, and we stayed quiet as we made our way down into the cellar.

As we went through the hole in the kitchen wall, Matt spoke again. "We need to sharpen your knife."

That sent a wave of nerves through my gut. The dull knife on which someone had left a note from his aunt. "It's under my bed."

"I'll bring my knife sharpener over."

We stopped in the middle of the kitchen. The light stretched longer through the window. The air still hung heavy inside, and would probably be the same way once we stepped onto the porch, but the sun had moved significantly.

I looked at Matt, alarmed. "What time do you think it is?" We hadn't been in Trenavell that long, but it was possibly early evening in Salt's Creek.

Matt pulled his phone out of his pocket. "It's almost six o'clock."

Rushing down the hallway, I eyed the broken-down door, readying to step over it. "How do we explain hanging out in jeans and coats, in the woods, in summer?"

Matt offered an answer I hadn't thought of. "Well, ideally we should be covering up if we're in the woods anyway."

"Why are we in the woods in the first place?"

"I don't have an answer for that."

We hurried for our backyards, loud on the underbrush.

"So…we should go to the store for supplies later." It was evening now. When were we gonna have time?

*Not like the grocery store is a forbidden hangout or anything.*

"And we need to take a couple canteens, which I have," Matt said.

"Cool." We still had to work out going to the store. "So… how about you come back at eight and we can go get the food?"

*Maybe I can make it upstairs without them actually seeing me.*

"What time does the grocery store close?" Matt asked.

"I have no idea."

Matt's eyes narrowed. "Are your mom and dad gonna let you go back out?"

"You know they will." A small surge of guilt emerged as I pulled my backpack off. If they saw me, how would I explain that *and* the coat? Holding the backpack out to Matt by the loop on top, I asked, "Can you take this?"

We reached the front corner of my house, and Matt grabbed one of the straps. We stood looking at each other.

"So, eight o'clock?" Matt asked, the backpack swinging from his hand.

"Is your mom gonna let you go out?"

Matt shrugged. "I don't know." Something in his face hardened. "I could always sneak out."

"Because that would go so well."

"Better to ask forgiveness," he said, an edge in his voice.

"Probably not, actually," I told him.

"Well, if I can't, then I'll let you know and we can try and get stuff early tomorrow."

"Okay." With a glance at my porch, I balled my coat up as small as I could. "Talk later."

As soon as my front door opened, the smell of garlic and tomatoes, with a hint of other seasonings, wafted down the hall. My parents' voices paused briefly when I closed the door behind me.

"Anya?" came my mom's voice.

A pair of footsteps approached the stairs as I got halfway up. The coat would be hard to explain.

I heaved it the rest of the way.

"Where've you been?" Mom asked as the end of a sleeve dropped out of sight.

A shrug. "Hanging out." *On another planet.*

"We're eating soon," she said. "I made spaghetti."

"It smells good," I said. "I'm gonna change into some shorts real quick."

"Can you come set the table afterwards?"

"Sure," I answered.

"Thanks." She went back to the kitchen.

Why was my heart beating so fast? Was I afraid of questions? Clearly my mom didn't care one way or the other that I was in jeans on a hot summer day. She hadn't pressed any further. I'd just been hanging out, and that was good enough, because I was trustworthy.

Not that I was very trustworthy at all anymore.

My coat lay unfurled on the hallway floor. Gathering it up, I hurried to my room as another set of footsteps climbed the stairs. My parents' bedroom door shut.

Matt had my backpack. It would stand out in Trenavell, but I'd learned from wearing jeans and red tennis shoes that that didn't matter too much on that planet, because being from Earth wasn't weird.

Where exactly was I going to get a sheath for the knife?

Once I changed and started to make my way downstairs, my hunger asserted itself. Even though that many hours hadn't passed for me personally, my body must have thought I was past-due for lunch, because I hadn't actually eaten since breakfast.

My stomach let out a loud growl as I walked into the kitchen.

"Wow," Mom remarked, laughing. "Hungry?"

"Very," I answered, going to the cabinet. She'd put the noodles and sauce on the table, along with a bowl of corn on the cob, and a bigger bowl of salad beside a plate of garlic bread. My mouth watered. "It looks really good," I said eagerly, my stomach growling again as I opened the cabinet door and grabbed three dinner plates.

Mom brought over a pitcher of tea as I set the plates on the table, adding utensils, glasses, and salad bowls.

"Do we have napkins?" I asked her.

"Just get some paper towels," she said. "Let me go call your daddy." She walked up the hall to the stairs and called Dad as I tore off three paper towels and placed them on the table, then took my seat to wait.

Mom came back into the kitchen as I was pouring myself some tea, and I could hear my dad's footsteps in the hall. My stomach growled again.

"It looks good," Dad said as he walked in. "Smells good."

Mom smiled. "I don't like heating up the kitchen too much, but I hadn't fixed this in a while and I had a craving."

Once Dad had said a blessing, I reached for some garlic bread and took a bite while my parents served themselves pasta. The sauce splashed a little as I poured it over my noodles, leaving a freckling of red on one side of the corn. My parents had been talking, but I hadn't been listening. My stomach let out a quieter growl.

"So you babysat some future architects the other day?" Dad asked as I chewed on a forkful of spaghetti.

As glad as I was to get food in my stomach, nerves rushed back as I thought of the aftermath of that babysitting job. "Yes. The Tomlinsons. The twins spent the whole time building a skyscraper." The image of the brown car creeping behind me popped up in my head.

"How tall?" Dad asked.

"About as tall as me." I swirled more pasta onto my fork.

"Got anything tomorrow?" Mom asked me.

"Nothing tomorrow."

Mom nodded. "Just keep saving up money." For a second, she looked like she had more to add, but didn't.

"I am." It would be okay to bring up my bike, even if they didn't have to know about the brown car. "I wound up riding my bike to that job and another one, so I didn't use gas." Avoiding thoughts of the car didn't work, so I tried to make it look like my body wasn't reacting to the memory. That I wasn't still shaken. That going to another planet had taken the edge off.

"Not a bad plan," Dad said. "At least if you stay in the neighborhood. You babysitting again soon?"

"Tuesday night. For Miss Whitley." Was she going out with Jake again? Maybe this time I'd actually get to see his face. Maybe his voice just sounded similar to someone else's.

"Good," Mom said. "Anything else you and Matt have going on?"

The mouthful of food I had went down almost without me chewing it. "Not really." The swallow of tea I took made me realize how thirsty I'd been, and I reached for another piece of garlic bread. *They probably notice you stuffing your face, liar.*

Would I want another meal sometime in the middle of the night?

Glad the conversation had turned away from me riding my bike, I tore a piece off the slice of bread in my hand. Would it even be a good idea to tell them I'd been followed by a creepy old car?

*Of course it would be a good idea.*

But I'd have to tell them all the other stuff. I'd have to tell them about the Dupree house, and explain about going to another planet to look for a device that shut off portals to that world. I'd have to tell them what Ira had done, and show them the proof, the scar from the stitches we'd taken out in my bathroom.

I wasn't ready to do that.

# Chapter 9

I waited in my room for Matt. The grocery store was open until nine. Hopefully they'd have what we'd need.

Someone knocked on the door downstairs, and one of my parents went to answer it. We could pack the supplies in my backpack when we got back to my house. Hopefully, he'd put the pack itself into his truck.

Dad pulled the door open as I got to the top of the stairs.

"Hey, Matt," he said.

"I'll be right down," I called, then dashed back to my room to get my wallet. My flip-flops still waited by the door where I'd left them. The twenty dollars in my wallet had to be enough.

When I got to the front hall, Dad looked a little puzzled. "Where are y'all going?"

"Grocery store," I said, keeping my voice light. "For snacks." I wasn't wrong. Granted, it was more like provisions than snacks, but we *were* planning to get food to eat. "We'll be back pretty soon."

"Okay," Dad said, pulling the door wider to let me out. "Drive safe."

"Yes, sir," Matt answered.

"How are we splitting this up?" I asked once we were out in the humid night air.

"Evenly?" Matt offered.

I rolled my eyes. "I meant, who's buying what and how much should we get?" I shrank in reluctance from thinking of blowing twenty dollars on stuff that we might not need.

"We'll just have to see what they have there," Matt said.

"Okay." We reached the truck. "Guess we'll see."

I eyed the price label on the shelf. "I had no idea that jerky was that expensive."

"And that's for the smaller size," Matt said.

I studied it. "How badly do you think we need it?"

Matt shrugged. "I mean, Miriam did give us dried meat last time."

The country music playing over the store's speakers was just loud enough that we could talk above a whisper. An employee pushed a dust mop past the end of the aisle.

"And it is supposed to be backup," Matt added.

We didn't even know if Meris could get supplies this time. I peered at the sign above the aisle. "We could get some boxes of protein bars and some nabs."

Matt looked at me. "You're thinking peanut butter crackers are good enough sustenance?"

"I'm thinking that I hope we don't need them," I retorted.

Matt was quiet. "They are better than nothing." He reached out. "Look, I'll just buy the big bag of jerky and you can get the other stuff."

"Works for me," I said, then stepped away to head for the cracker aisle, leaving Matt with the jerky.

As soon as I stepped onto the other aisle, I was aware of the slight hollowness in my stomach.

*No way I'm hungry again.*

But a box of plain wheat crackers looked really good. My stomach let out a little growl.

*I can't spend all my money on crackers.*

Down the aisle, the boxes of nabs stood on the shelf, the different colors indicating what flavors the store had. I knew the protein bars were on another aisle.

Surging forward, I grabbed three boxes of nabs, each one with ten packs inside. Hopefully they would just be a supplement. I knew the protein bars would cost even more than these, so maybe I would only need to get two boxes of those. Hoping again that we wouldn't need them, I turned around, grabbing a store brand box of wheat crackers, barely looking at it.

Matt walked my way as I emerged from the aisle. His gaze went to the extra crackers in my hand.

My face heated up. "These are for now. I'm hungry." Lifting the three boxes of nabs so he could see them, I stepped past him. "I just need to get the protein bars."

"Okay," he said.

Once I had two boxes of those, we made our way to the one checkout line that was open.

The cashier, an older woman, smiled at us. "Did y'all find everything you need?"

"Yes ma'am," I answered, setting my stuff on the belt.

She scanned one of the boxes of nabs. "Looks like you're stocking up on some snacks."

"Just getting stuff in case...we need it." My face warmed again. Why was I evasive to a random person?

"Well, that'll be $14.78," she said.

I handed over the twenty dollar bill I'd brought and waited for my change.

"Have a good night," she said as I took my change and moved out of Matt's way, plucking the grocery bag from the bagging area on her other side.

As we left the store, I noticed a bulletin board by the door, filled with fliers. In the lower righthand corner was a colorful one, that, in bright colors, advertised the first annual Salt's Creek Fun Fest, on Labor Day weekend, in our downtown.

I blinked. That was new. Matt turned to me as we passed the board, then followed my gaze.

"A fun fest," he said as we stepped out into the parking lot. His truck was one of four vehicles, and I guessed the other three, parked far at the end of a row, were employees. A soft summer night breeze ruffled the dark bushes at the end of the building. Above an empty cart corral, one of the parking lot lights flickered.

"Yeah." I twisted the handle of the grocery bag around my wrist, then let it untwist as we got to the truck. "What vendors would they even have?"

"Whitley's and pizza," Matt answered as he unlocked the doors.

I climbed into the passenger seat, the box of crackers in my lap, and buckled.

Matt closed his door and cranked the ignition. "You gonna rip into them now?"

With a pop of glue and cardboard, I stuck my hand into the box and reached for the plastic bag inside. "Yep." I tore it open, making sure to be loud, and pulled out three of the crackers, stuffing them in my mouth and crunching down. "Yum."

Matt cracked a smile and left the store's parking lot.

I tried to crunch more quietly as I shoved three more crackers in my mouth.

Matt glanced at me. "You're eating those pretty aggressively."

"Okay, one, it's not aggressive, and two, I'm being neat." Pointedly, I ate another cracker.

"That was aggressive," Matt said as he pulled into the driveway and parked. The bags shuffled softly as I unlocked the front door.

"We're back!" I called.

"Okay," Mom answered.

I led Matt upstairs to my bedroom and dropped my bag on the floor. Matt set his own bag beside mine as I crouched by my bed, reaching carefully for the knife underneath.

My hand closed around the hilt. "Did you bring your sharpener?"

"Yeah."

The dull blade slid along the carpet as I pulled it out from under the bed. Carefully, I held it out to Matt.

"Thank you," he said absently, his hand folding around it securely, but his eyes unfocused as he fished the knife sharpener out of his pocket. After letting the knife go and grabbing the gate map, I sat down cross-legged in front of him.

Matt's hazel eyes studied the blade, narrowed. "This isn't just a knife."

"Then what is it?"

"A bayonet." He leaned up. "I mean, now that I've gotten a good look at it, the blade's pretty long." He showed me the hilt, facing the end of it towards me. "See the holes? It would fix on a gun that way."

"Would this be more useful to Meris, then?"

"No." He set it in his lap. "It looks like it's from the first World War."

"Seriously?" Where had Matt's Aunt Della, or whoever had speared the note on the end of the blade, gotten it? "Wow." I reached for the grocery bags and set them between us, then looked at Matt. "Since you didn't bring your backpack, I can just keep this stuff with me."

The sharpener rasped softly. "Okay."

"Cool." I slid them under the bed.

"How early should we go?" Matt asked.

"How early can you get here?"

Matt's eyebrows scrunched down, but his hands still moved steadily and calmly, his eyes focused downward. "Maybe nine o'clock."

"Works for me."

I unfolded the map on the carpet, taking a second to appreciate how small it was, for what it was. Gavin Dupree had made it manageable. He had to have done that for some reason.

"Who was this for?" I asked.

Matt stopped and looked at me, puzzled.

"The map. It's small, so it seems like it was meant for travelers who would need to use it quickly and who probably knew how all these routes worked."

"Still don't know what those routes are," Matt said.

"We'd probably have to go through them one by one to see where they go."

"Not easy."

I shook my head. "Sure isn't, not if they're all across Trenavell."

Matt turned the blade over in his hand. "Getting there." He looked up at me. "Any idea yet what you're gonna put this in?"

"Something that'll let me get to it fast." Not that I'd know what to do. "I really hope I won't need to use it." There wasn't a sheath for it, and I wasn't sure how I was supposed to get one anyway. "That said, I could wrap it in an old t-shirt."

Matt shrugged and bent over again. "Fair enough."

*I really don't want to have to use it.*

"Okay," I said. "Let me find one."

In my third drawer down was the oldest, rattiest t-shirt I had. "How close are you to being done?"

"Pretty close."

A couple minutes later, Matt set the bayonet on the carpet in front of me. "There you go."

"Thanks." I set the blade down on the unfolded t-shirt, carefully wrapping it while letting the hilt stick out, then slipped it into my backpack and reached for the box of crackers, grabbing a handful of them before nudging the box toward Matt. "Please have some."

He picked it up and reached in, the bag crackling. "What do you think we'll find out about Compass Hill?" He paused. "Like, why would Dupree have picked it?"

I shrugged. "I dunno." I crunched for a few moments. "I… kinda hope we find something unexpected and cool." My face warmed.

"Cool?"

"What?" I shot back. "It's interesting."

"When has something unexpected been a good thing in Trenavell?" Matt's glance went for a second to my right side.

I pushed my irritation down. "I don't know, Mr. 'this is New Mexico.'" I took a deep breath in.

Matt's chin lifted, a look of realization growing in his eyes. "That gate went to New Mexico, and so did the one in the garage."

I blinked. "Yeah…just…out in the open with that wheel on them." Goosebumps ran over my skin.

"Do you remember if they were lockable?" Matt asked.

"No." No one had followed us. I knew that.

"So that's two gates that might not be a part of the main network," Matt said. "And they go to Earth."

"Plus the Kings Road gate," I said.

Matt grabbed more crackers. "Do you think those two in New Mexico were sealed when the device was activated?"

"They both had wheels on them, so they could still work." I didn't have a great idea of where those gates were in Trenavell. I knew we'd gone back to the village with the well soon after we'd gone through the garage gate, but I didn't know how to get there again, or to the first one.

But both were marked by that wheel, and one stood beside a highway, far from Salt's Creek, near a sign for a town called "Moon-eye." Another chill ran over me.

It was almost ten when Matt left.

"See ya," I said as he went out into the humid night, reluctant to add on the word "tomorrow."

*It's not like we're criminals. Calm down.*

But he waved and didn't say anything about the next day, either. We were clearly in some unofficial agreement about hiding things.

I padded to the kitchen with the box of crackers to put it in the pantry. Metal clattered on ceramic as Mom entered the kitchen, holding a coffee cup that had a spoon sticking up from it.

"What were y'all up to?" she asked as she went to the sink.

*Interplanetary travel plans.*

I shrugged. "Hanging out." Technically, we had been working on a personal project, but I had no good way to explain an emergency snack run to the grocery store on a summer night, or the newly sharpened bayonet under my bed. We didn't desperately need several boxes of nabs, two boxes of chocolate peanut butter protein bars, and a family size bag of jerky. I hoped I was casual enough. We'd been in somewhat deep discussion, but maybe it'd still appeared like we'd just been hanging out.

"Where'd y'all go?" Mom asked, sounding amused.

"The grocery store," I said. "To get snacks."

She nodded, turned the water on, and rinsed her mug out, then cleared her throat.

My spine tensed with the impression that there might be a line of questioning about to come.

Mom stepped away from the sink and headed back towards the living room. "Well, y'all have fun. Enjoy summer." She disappeared around the doorway.

I relaxed. Was there something off about her last sentence?

*There's not something off about everything you encounter.*

# Chapter 10

*Ding.*

My phone's screen lit up briefly on my nightstand. My alarm clock read 7:54.

I grabbed the phone and read Matt's message.

*I can't go today. I'll explain later.*

With a frown, I set the phone back on the nightstand. A heavier meaning clung to his words. It was odd that being able to go to Trenavell had suddenly become an impossibility in the hours between our trip to the grocery store and now, but why would he need to explain it? He cut people's grass all the time, and that had never needed explanation.

Danny was going to check in. Was he going to make his way to Matt's house, or stay by the Dupree house and send a text? If his phone battery was lasting this long, then he'd probably kept it off when he was in Trenavell.

I picked my phone up again and replied to Matt. *Okay. Let me know when you can do that. Want me to text Danny?*

Maybe I could go through more of the letters to see if Dupree might have given away anything more concerning the nature of Compass Hill.

*Sure.*

*Okay. Talk to you later.*

Pulling up Danny's number, I took a peek at the last time I'd sent him a message. We didn't communicate through text all that much, so it had been a while. November, a couple of years ago, probably after the Thanksgiving weekend that the Hendersons had made the trip down to North Carolina, though it hadn't been the last time I'd seen Danny between that Thanksgiving and when he'd shown up in Trenavell.

*Hey Danny, Matt didn't say if he'd already sent you a message, but he can't go to Trenavell today. Said he'd explain later. Let me know when you get this.*

Matt hadn't specified what later meant, either. Maybe he'd be done by noon. Hopefully. Though I knew it was probably already warm outside now, I also knew that lunchtime was when it would be really hot and humid, as the long afternoons would have started to settle in place by late morning.

A flash of memory from our quest came back, of the pursuing villager who'd seen Matt's glowing eyes and had said something about the "swamp folk," meaning moon-eyes.

I didn't know a lot about Trenavell's planet. I knew that there were non-humans there. Matt had pointed out their silhouettes in the cave, able to see them much better than I could. But at no point had we been in any swamp.

Maybe there'd be a chance to explore Trenavell one day, or maybe more of the planet than just that one country.

My stomach growled softly.

It would probably be good to get breakfast while I waited for Danny to send a message.

After a bowl of cereal, I headed back upstairs. I'd left my phone on the nightstand, and the screen was dark when I went back into the room. I picked it up, pressing the button at the bottom of the screen

Danny had sent a message fifteen minutes before.

*Hey, I'm headed towards your backyard. Can you meet me there? Can't stay long.*

*Sure.*

I slipped my flip-flops on and stuck the phone into my pocket. In all likelihood, I wouldn't have to lock the back door to my house, so I didn't put my keys in my pocket. If I felt like locking it was a good idea, we did have a spare.

The morning sun, though a couple hours old on this summer day, shone fresh and bright through the window above our front door. A car hissed on the road as it drove past, the soft shadow hardly there, a flash of sun on glass brightening the window for a second.

The nerves along my scar prickled in succession down the line of flattening bumps. I scratched it with my t-shirt as I went out onto the back deck.

*Maybe I* should *lock the door.*

Once it was closed behind me, I tested it, and the knob didn't turn. At the edge of my yard, where the brush led up to a thinner line of trees, a figure in a ball cap moved from behind a thick pine tree and waved.

Danny smiled as I reached the trees, but his eyes stayed solemn as he spoke. "I'm guessing you probably don't know any more than you did earlier."

Shaking my head, I took a glance at Matt's house. "No."

"Me either." His gaze went to the street for a second, then the empty driveway of the Dobken's house, his eyebrows drawing down and in as he let out a puff of breath.

"What?"

Slowly, Danny turned back to me. "I did manage to get in touch with my mom, and let her know that I can get from Trenavell to North Carolina fairly easily." His face lit up with amusement. "So I wonder if I should follow my mom's suggestion and show up at Aunt Jen's house randomly."

Would Matt's belief that his mom wouldn't say anything hold true? "I'm guessing you think Matt's mom would be okay with it."

He almost laughed. "I have no idea if that's the case or not, but my mom thinks that Aunt Jen wouldn't react at all, since she's in a lot of denial about this whole moon-eye thing." Danny shook his head.

I'd never been around Danny's mom and Matt's mom together for long enough to see how they actually interacted with each other, but Mrs. Dobken was the one who was actually hiding things, who had randomly found tasks for Matt to work on that one day, and who'd clearly known about all this without telling us. And Danny's mom was trying to get him to randomly show up at her sister's house, with no explanation and no way for him to be in North Carolina that Mrs. Dobken would talk about.

I looked back at Danny and tilted my head. "How is your phone battery not completely dead?"

He snorted. "It's close. Usually I can find places to charge it during crossings, but I keep it off when I'm in Trenavell." He sobered, glancing at the empty driveway again.

"I guess you could tell Meris and Noam that we can't be there today." It was just one day we couldn't go. I still didn't know what Matt felt he had to explain about that.

"Yeah." Danny turned slowly to look back into the woods. "The house is pretty quiet."

"How about the city?" Had he even been able to go up to the surface level?

With a shrug, Danny silently answered my question. "Nothing much different in the last day, from my limited view."

The last day. "So the days are matching up right now."

His eyebrows rose. "Yeah, actually. Huh." Whether it was a pleasant realization or not, it sure looked like it was the first time he was realizing it at all.

It did mean we'd have to be really careful about the time passing when we were there, though it was already obvious that we couldn't just stay or count on only hours passing on Earth the way they had when we'd set off to find the device pieces. "How do you plan to find out anything?"

"I'll try to get up with Ira," he answered. "If I can." After a pause, his eyes narrowed. "Failing that, I can go to Miriam. I would assume that she's still a safe person to contact."

"Safe?" Would we find ourselves needing to go back to her house? Did it also have an entrance into the underground passages in Compass Hill?

He nodded. "Discreet."

What did that mean? Hadn't she been on Trenavell's side? She'd helped us. We'd gotten supplies from her, and she'd known where to send Ira. Ira had been the person Meris was supposed to meet, since he was Miriam's brother. Another dimension of what we'd done opened up. Sealing the gates hadn't been expected. Had it been wanted, even eventually? "Okay."

With another nod, this one a little more determined, Danny took a step backwards. "I'll check back in with you tomorrow morning, if I can." He laughed a little. "If you don't see me, then you can assume that the days may not be matching up again, but I'll text both of you when I can get back."

"That sounds good," I told him as he turned from me and slipped into the brush, almost as quiet as he had been that night by the river.

As I headed to my back door, I wondered why Miriam would need to be discreet, and why Danny would mention that at all. It was a good thing, but who was she hiding from? Were there spies we had to worry about in Trenavell, or were Matt and I not supposed to be welcome? For a second, I thought that maybe we could be wanted by the Trenavellan government, but wouldn't we have been detained when we were so close to the wall? Someone had to have been watching and guarding the city.

*I should have asked Danny.*

***

My phone let out a ding and vibrated once, moving enough to bump the edge of the copper disc on my comforter.

My mom.

*Hey, do you think you can babysit this Saturday night for another one of my coworkers? She has a four-year-old daughter who needs a sitter.*

It wasn't like we'd be able to go to Trenavell on the weekend and hide that we were in the woods. We did have the option of driving to the house from Highway 58, but we also weren't the only ones that had a chance of taking that route. It wouldn't be bad to keep earning money, either.

*Sure.*

*Great, I'll get the info for you.*

I bent down over the disc again and ran my finger carefully around the edge, feeling the symbols that I knew were letters, my hand passing smoothly over the part that had been worked on enough to restore the shine. This was possibly another one of those signs on the tunnel walls.

It was small, though. The size of a dinner plate, and I knew that, in general, at least on Earth, signs tended to be much larger close up than they appeared from a distance. If someone was far away, this had a chance of being nearly nonfunctional. Plus, it was copper. While the corrosion had brightened it to a light green, it would have been too dark to be helpful when it was new unless it was illuminated in some way.

And it was almost a dome. That's what I'd thought it had been when we'd found it.

This couldn't be a sign, not for something in the tunnels. Maybe it had been a sign on something else, or maybe even a button.

I turned it over. The dome effect was partially caused by the fact that it was concave on the back, but not deep. The corrosion on the inside of the disc scraped rough on my fingertip.

My skin caught on something, and I pulled the disc closer to my face to see.

It wasn't just corroded in that spot. The bent, broken metal had a tear, ripped away at some point from something else. Inspecting it closer, I moved inch by inch around the edge. Directly across the circle was another irregularity, but not a tear in the copper. It looked more like it might be somewhere a latch would fit.

This copper disc was a door to something. Someone had broken it off at some point, brought it to Earth, and half-buried it in the woods, leaving one part to shine in the sun.

I thought of the scream the night before we'd found the Dupree house.

Had the disc been brought that recently?

*Why would they have done that?* Was the disc supposed to go to someone, and had the screamer been the courier? And there was no way they hadn't used the Dupree gate, but where had they gone? Why even bring this thing here?

I jumped when the phone let out another ding. It was 3:02 now.

*I'm done. Give me a half-hour to clean up.*

Wondering if he'd stopped for lunch or at least to cool off, I sent an "okay" back to Matt and turned the copper disc to the front side again, then set it back on my bed. I could go downstairs and wait for him.

As I got to the top of the steps, the muffled squeal of the mail truck's brakes sounded as it stopped at our mailbox. The least I could do was bring the mail in for my parents instead of having it be outside in the box all day. The truck had started moving off down the street as I reached the front hall. I hadn't been outside since I'd met Danny. How hot would it be? I pulled the wooden door open and reached for the handle of the glass door.

My heart jumped into my throat as the brown car appeared from my left and drove slowly by my house. I slammed the wooden door, locked the doorknob and the deadbolt, then ran back upstairs and into my bedroom, slamming that closed too.

*What if they park in the driveway?*

What was I supposed to do? I was by myself. I couldn't call my parents and tell them about a random car driving by once, especially if they didn't know the car had followed me before.

*You're assuming it only drove by once.*

There wasn't anything audible from any car up here. I walked to the window in my bedroom, just to check what I could see from there. The angle wasn't good enough for seeing all the way to the front, though. A dark gray SUV passed by in the gap, going the opposite direction that the brown car had.

Climbing onto my bed, I curled my knees up under my chin and eyed my phone.

I so much did not want to be by myself.

The half-hour hadn't passed yet. He was supposed to come over here. Was it even safe for him to do that?

He could run. He was fast.

I grabbed the phone, unlocked, it, and called Matt.

"Hello?" he asked.

"Please come over as soon as you can."

"I am. What's wrong?"

"The car."

"The brown one?"

I nodded before remembering that he couldn't exactly hear that over the phone. "Yeah. I went to get the mail and it drove by right as I opened the door."

"Did you stay inside?" he asked.

"Uh-huh."

"Where are you now?"

"My bedroom." I took a deep breath. "It's really obvious that my car's the only one here, Matt."

"Yeah…" His footsteps came over the phone as he walked quickly through his house. "Um…"

"What?"

"It's still out there."

A strained and terrified half-cry, half-moan came out of my mouth. "Please come over."

"Give me a few more minutes. I'll come to the back door."

"Thank you." Cutting the phone off, I sat back, shaking. Why was the car outside my house? What was the driver waiting for?

What if they were on the front porch?

I waited ten minutes. My phone let out another *ding*.

*I'm here.*

I got up, my knees wobbling, and crept down the hallway, then made my way down the stairs. As quietly as possible, I walked to the back door. A shadow waited on the other side of the closed blinds. I leaned close, trying to see through one of the holes in the blinds that the cords went through.

Matt.

In two quick movements, I yanked the door open and pulled him inside, then slammed the door and made sure every lock on it was locked.

"Come on," I said, grabbing his hand and pulling him up the stairs to my room.

Once we were in there, I locked that door, too, but it was only a button on one side. The other ones had to hold, because all it took to unlock this one was something narrow enough to stick through the little hole on the other side.

We stood together, me trying to listen to find out if the car was going to pull away. With my door closed, listening for that probably wouldn't be all that effective. For how old the car looked, it wasn't being any louder than most other cars.

I swallowed hard, still shaking.

"Do you want to just hide up here?" he asked.

"I don't know." We could stay up here with the door locked until our parents got home, or just before that. We'd still be alone if we parted, but not for as long. "Maybe?"

He eyed the door. "We could also stick the desk chair up under the doorknob."

Considering it, I scanned the chair. "I mean…" It wouldn't really keep a determined person out of this room. My stomach twisted thinking of that.

Matt shrugged. "I was kinda joking."

Staring at my backpack, I nodded absently.

He kept talking. "I'm not leaving."

"Okay."

Leaving.

At some point one of us would need to leave the room for something.

"We could both leave," I suggested.

"Huh?"

The car had appeared so suddenly. "We could go to Trenavell." I twisted one of my hands. Even if the time was matching up, we only had a couple of hours until our parents were home. It took a while to walk from the gate and through the tunnel to the underground part of Compass Hill. But part of me would rather be there than here.

Matt looked at me for a few seconds, his face hesitant. "For now, we could check and see if the car is still out there."

"Should we go if it is?"

"I don't know." He unlocked my bedroom door.

We made our way quietly down the hallway to the stairs. Trying hard not to make anything creak, I made for the front door and looked through the peephole.

My gut flipped when I saw the car parked in front of the house, an indistinct figure in the driver's seat. I groaned.

Matt pulled me back from the door, his eyes focused on me. "So it's still out there?"

"Someone's sitting in the front."

He looked back up my stairs. "Okay, we can go back to your room."

There wasn't time to go to Trenavell. And even if we did run out the back door, whoever was in the car could just chase us through the woods, if they were listening and heard the door slam. Or they could make their way to Highway 58 and just take that route.

Even if there was time to go to Trenavell, we might not be able to get away from the mysterious driver.

"Yeah."

We made our way back upstairs slowly. The stairs creaked softly as we went. If we needed to, we could always call the police, even if it might take them a minute to get to my house.

We stepped into my room, and I locked the door behind us, tempted to stick the desk chair up under my door.

"How long do you think they've been out there?" Matt asked.

Turning to him, I shook my head. "I don't know. That was the first time I opened the front door, so they could have been there for a long time." They could have waited until Matt had come over to actually park the car, or they might have parked several times. I'd mostly been up in my room. "And you didn't see them when you got home?"

"No." He sat in my desk chair. "If they were driving in front of the house, then they could have just reached our street, or they were turning around somewhere else when I got home."

My mattress bounced a little as I plopped onto my bed. "Well...they can't do anything once our parents get home."

"Yeah." Matt's face fell.

I scooted back to lean against the wall. "So you were going to explain something about today."

"Today, and tomorrow, and this weekend, and next week," he answered, his words heavy and his eyes sharp.

"What's going on?"

Matt's gaze fixed on my backpack where it slouched at the foot of my bed, still empty. "Mom somehow found a ton of people who need their grass cut during the week." With his pause came a frown. "It's only every other week for most of them, but tomorrow, and early Friday, and next week, are all tied up, with somehow no jobs on the weekends."

Trying not to jump to conclusions, I leaned forward over my knees. "Well…if they're paying you…" He did cut grass all the time. It was his job in the spring and summers and early fall.

Matt shook his head. "Look, I'm not worried about money or working too hard or whatever. It feels intentional and not in a completely helpful way."

Maybe it was. Mrs. Dobken might have been a nervous person, and what we'd done had probably only made it worse, but the "worried mom" thing had never been over the top. Maybe she had come up with this. "When did she tell you?"

"After I got back home last night."

Could she have called them all in the short timeframe we were at the store? "What about this weekend, though?"

"Oh, we're going to the beach." His sarcastic delivery was followed by a guilty wince. "I mean, we're going to Ocracoke on Friday to stay with my grandparents for a couple days, and we'll be back Sunday night."

"When are you leaving Friday?"

He shrugged. "Probably before lunch."

It wasn't that long that he wouldn't be in town, and the weekends were okay. My parents were home on most Saturdays, and every Sunday. They'd both already had their work weekend this month. I would be alone for the several hours between the Dobkens leaving and my parents getting home.

But I could do the same thing we'd chosen to do today and stay in my room. Mom had asked me to babysit on Saturday night, and I would definitely be driving to that job. "Do you really think your mom has an ulterior motive?"

"Yes."

On that one afternoon when we'd come back home to find his mom, she'd offered me that weird smile, like she knew she had to smile, and didn't want to be rude, but like she also might not have been thrilled to see us leaving the woods together. And we both knew that Matt's mom was completely aware of the gate and that she knew that someone had sealed the gates.

Had Danny relayed that to his mom, and would Mrs. Henderson tell Mrs. Dobken about anything she might not yet know?

Danny hadn't been back to Earth until recently, and that lined up with Mrs. Dobken finding a ton of work for Matt to do, away from me.

But I didn't want to take any of it personally. She was worried about Matt, and I understood. With a sigh, I changed the subject. "I talked to Danny this morning." The memory of how he'd said his mom wanted him to show up at Matt's house drew a smile from me.

Matt raised his eyebrows, amused. "What?"

"His mom suggested that he show up at y'all's house."

Matt laughed. "That would be interesting."

"It would. He'd at least get to charge his phone."

Matt's face sobered. "That's what he needs to do." He reached into his shorts pocket and pulled his phone out, quickly sending a message to Danny for the next time he was on Earth.

I frowned. "I don't think that would help your mom stay calm at all."

Matt shrugged. "She definitely wouldn't turn him away, and he needs somewhere better to stay than an empty shop."

Danny clearly considered the shop a better option than the Dupree house, but he still hadn't said anything about what he might have heard that had made him decide to sleep there instead of underground.

"And he'll have to go home at some point," I told Matt. We'd cut off Danny's route back to his parents by using the riddle device.

Matt set his phone down. "I'll bring both of y'all to to my house tomorrow afternoon."

"Okay." Mrs. Dobken wouldn't likely turn away her nephew, but I decided then that I wouldn't try to stay for supper there.

# Chapter 11

Matt had said that he'd be done around the same time as he had the day before, a little after three o'clock.

With a *ding*, his text arrived to confirm that he was home.

The brown car hadn't shown up again, at least not when I'd looked.

Danny waited at the edge of the woods.

*What next?* I asked Matt.

*I'll clean up and come get y'all. Twenty minutes.*

If I hadn't seen the car yet, it was probably safe to go outside. I could wait on the trampoline, or I could go straight to where Danny waited. Either way, if the car did drive by again, I would be with someone, or not visible at all.

After fifteen minutes, I headed downstairs with my keys and phone, and took a peek through the tiny holes in the blinds.

No brown car.

As I climbed to the center of the trampoline, my scar tugged a little. The temptation rose up in me, for a moment, to jump. Now that the stitches were out, it *would* be better. But I'd already started sweating a little in the humidity. At least the sun wasn't hitting the surface fully right now, though the fabric had probably baked earlier in the day. I crossed my legs and sat, facing away from the woods and towards the back of my house. If someone did park and get out of the car and approach the backyard, I'd see them.

When Matt's door opened, I jumped, not expecting the sudden noise, even as quiet as it was amid the summer sounds of our neighborhood. Behind me, the brush at the trees' edge rustled as Matt pulled the door closed behind him and crossed the grass to me. I hopped down, nerves along the scar sending a zing across my skin. The woods went quiet. I glanced back. Danny made his way across the grass, holding a coat, and the three of us met.

"We're hanging out at my house," Matt said, his tone edging on smug.

Danny held up his phone, smiling a little. "Good. I need to charge my phone."

"Cool." Matt nodded once and turned, leading us to his back porch.

I knew the tone in Matt's voice was because his mom wouldn't be expecting Danny. He hadn't asked his mom about any of this, and we'd only found out anything because we'd eavesdropped on a conversation. It was a good guess that his parents had called their friend to come over after Matt and I had returned that day.

His cousin showing up unexpectedly would be a stressor. If Mrs. Dobken saw our discovery, despite her secrecy, to be a wound, then maybe Matt had found some salt to rub in it.

A couple of hours passed. We'd played a tournament of sorts on Matt's game console, since he only had two controllers. Danny had showered while his phone charged.

Matt hadn't shut his bedroom door, so we could hear the front door make the unmistakable sound of someone unlocking it, then the footsteps in the hall, and, last, the soft closure of the glass door.

"Matt?" His mom called up the stairs, and the cousins looked at each other.

"Hey, Mom!" Matt yelled back, and hopped up, Danny following him a second later.

The controller was slack in my hand as I waited to figure out what I was supposed to do. Mrs. Dobken seeing me might not have the best consequences if Matt was going to spring Danny on her. I looked up at Matt and raised my eyebrows in a silent question.

"Wait here," he murmured as his mom's footsteps started climbing the stairs. Together, the cousins made their way out of the room, down the hall, and to the top of the landing. Their footsteps stopped, and neither the guys nor Mrs. Dobken spoke.

"Danny?" The confusion and shock in Mrs. Dobken's voice were clear.

"Hey, Aunt Jen!" Danny's loud, cheerful greeting would have echoed in a hallway without carpet.

"What in the world are you doing here?" She was trying to sound pleasant, but the confusion was still there, stiffening her words.

"Just a visit," Danny answered.

"Okay…" The climbing resumed, and I froze.

It wasn't against the rules for me to be here, and it never had been. Matt's parents, like mine, made him keep the door open, and we had. She just wouldn't have to go too much farther to see me, and it was still far from clear if she still wanted me to be friends with her son or not.

*Might as well not look like I'm hiding.* I leaned over as the footsteps got louder. Mrs. Dobken climbed onto the landing and accepted a hug from Danny as her eyes turned towards me.

I waved. "Hey, Mrs. Dobken."

She pulled away from her nephew and headed for Matt's bedroom door, the boys trailing after her. Matt's hazel eyes focused on me. As the three of them stepped into the room, all three pairs of eyes flashed briefly in the light, Mrs. Dobken's most brightly.

"Well, what were y'all up to?" she asked, smiling stiffly, her eyes wide just like Matt's, a shade of overwhelmed fear settling in them. He'd inherited that expression.

"Game tournament!" Danny answered, excited, slipping past his aunt and plopping down beside me.

Mrs. Dobken had to have noticed that Danny's dark hair hadn't dried all the way yet, but was a shower all that much more suspicious than him randomly showing up when he was, as far as she knew, in Michigan?

*Unless she knew he wasn't there.*

Maybe her sister had told her where Danny actually was.

Matt stepped around and sat across from me and Danny.

Mrs. Dobken's eyes changed abruptly, forcefully, from overwhelmed to stern, and she turned to Matt. "I guess you finished all the yards for today?"

"Yes ma'am."

"Okay." She glanced at me. "Well, good to see you, Anya. I'm gonna go make a call real quick." She stepped back into the hallway and made her way to the staircase.

Mrs. Dobken had been surprised, clearly, but she hadn't actually said anything about Danny being here. The Dobkens were supposed to leave tomorrow for Ocracoke.

Would she invite him along?

A door closed downstairs.

Matt shot a grin at Danny. "She's probably calling your mom." He jumped up. "Let's go listen."

"Okay." Laughter filled Danny's voice.

We moved quietly, trying to avoid creaks on the stairs. The room that Mrs. Dobken was in, the dining room, didn't have that thick of a door, and I could hear her voice as we reached it. Matt slowly rested his ear against the painted wood.

My hair brushed loud in my ear as I did the same thing, but Mrs. Dobken's voice wasn't obscured at all, once I was in place.

"...not do that, Del?" A pause. "Seriously?"

A voice on the phone was audible, but not intelligible.

"Whatever." A muffled huff. "What am I supposed to do, Del? We're going to see Mama and Daddy tomorrow."

The voice answered.

"Yes, obviously, but what about when we get back? I don't even know what he's doing here."

Another reply.

"Do you want to get a flight for him, then?"

Danny would have to go home at some point, somehow, and however he'd normally go was no longer an option, unless the gates came unsealed for some reason.

"What about school?"

ECU. Allegedly.

"Look, Del, we'll just take him with us this weekend and I can stick him on whatever flight you choose when we get home."

Danny's mouth quirked.

"Is that the best idea? Really, Del?"

Della answered her in a quick string of words I still couldn't understand.

"Fine. Talk to you later."

With that, the three of us scrambled away from where we stood, and Matt lunged for the front door. I shot out first and ran down the front steps. My parents' cars sat in our driveway.

Matt and Danny walked with me to the end of the sidewalk in front of Matt's door as Mr. Dobken parked.

"Guess I'll head home," I told the guys. "I wasn't gonna stay for supper, anyway."

The door of Mr. Dobken's car opened and closed, and he walked toward us from behind Mrs. Dobken's car.

"Well, hey Danny," he said, surprised.

Danny grinned. "Hey, Uncle Johnny."

Matt's dad gave me a nod. "Good to see you, Anya."

"Hi, Mr. Dobken."

He continued toward the front steps and went into the house.

At least the adults hadn't stuck with us. "Are you going to Ocracoke, Danny?"

“Probably.” He sobered. “I’m not sure…you know, about the others.”

With Danny away with Matt’s family, there’d be no one in Trenavell for a couple of days, and no one to take or bring messages.

“I could try and go tomorrow,” I told them, my stomach flipping over. It wouldn’t be fun to venture through the tunnel alone, and I knew the city probably wouldn’t be open. The underground passages might as well be a labyrinth, somewhere I could easily get lost in, without Danny there, and I didn’t want to be both lost and alone. The brown car might be at the house as well.

“Please don’t,” Matt answered, exasperated.

“I won’t.” With a sigh, I stepped into the driveway. “I’ll see y’all Monday, I guess.”

“I’ll text you,” Matt said.

“Okay.” I turned away from my friends and headed for my own front door.

***

Leaning against the wall of the vestibule at church, I waited for my parents as they spoke to another couple that they knew.

Matt had texted me twice, as they left Salt’s Creek on Friday and when they arrived at the ferry that would take them across to Ocracoke Island.

On Saturday, the babysitting job I'd had across town, for a five year old named Olivia, had been pretty quiet. We'd colored in two of Olivia's coloring books the whole time.

The afternoon sun streamed through the glass at the front of the church building, brightening and shifting as people headed out, passing the doors off to the person behind them, or letting them close when there was no one.

"We'll see y'all next week," my dad said, and I pushed away from the wall to catch up to my parents, idly catching part of a conversation somewhere near me.

"And what did you say your name was?" asked an older man.

"Jacob Andrews," answered a voice that I recognized.

I couldn't stop and try to figure out where he was standing. As I moved, the conversation faded. Whoever Jacob Andrews was and whoever he was talking to hadn't been walking.

Had that been where I'd heard the voice? In church? Maybe Jacob Andrews had made announcements once, or spoken about something. A prayer request, maybe. I'd heard his voice somewhere before that one sitting job for Miss Whitley, and there was a possibility it was here.

Quickly, before we reached the doors, I looked around behind me.

Plenty of people still hadn't gone outside yet. Groups of kids clustered in one place. A man faced away from the doors at the other end of the lobby, talking to an older guy, their conversation inaudible from here. A couple with a baby hurried out of the building as the baby started to fuss. It was possible that the two men were the ones I'd heard talking, but my parents were stepping outside now. I caught up with them.

"Y'all wanna go to Whitley's?" Mom asked. "That sounds good to me right now."

"Sure," Dad answered.

"Sounds fine," I told them as we walked to the car. The early afternoon sun warmed the tops of my feet. Whitley's had good milkshakes. Maybe I could get one.

The mystery of the familiar voice settled a little, almost solved.

## Chapter 12

Not a single thing eventful happened the rest of the weekend, and Danny headed back to Trenavell late Monday morning.

That afternoon, I met Matt in my backyard again. We sat across from each other in the middle of the trampoline.

"How are your grandparents?" I asked Matt.

"Good," he answered. He smiled a little. "They said you ought to come with us next time, since they have plenty of room."

"That would probably be fun."

His solemn gaze dropped to the surface of the trampoline, flicking around like he was studying it. "I probably could have asked my grandparents some stuff if my mom hadn't been around all the time." He looked up at me. "I probably could have looked for the letters, too."

"Assuming they have them," I said. "It's weird that Dupree's house had the ones addressed to the Davies, so..." With a shrug, I glanced up at my house. "I mean, we could have them, or my Granny might." The house in the woods still had stuff in it, too. A couch. The piano. "It's possible they're in his own house." The only other person that might have letters from the Davies, if they weren't in the house, was Mildred Barnes.

Matt nodded, his face still troubled. "So my mom filled up my schedule so I couldn't come over here."

A pang rushed through my insides. "Did she actually say that's why?" It would be worse, probably, if she'd done something as direct as forbidding Matt from seeing me. If she'd intended that, then this was a roundabout way to accomplish it.

He hesitated. "It just feels like it." The guilt in his voice came through.

It wouldn't do any good to accuse his mom myself. "When's the next time you have the whole day off?"

"Wednesday," he answered.

"Okay." I would be at Miss Whitley's house the night before that. Maybe I could actually get a look at Jake this time, if he was going out with her, and completely solve that mystery. "Well...maybe we can go that day."

Matt smiled at me. "Okay."

"I didn't tell you about the guy at Miss Whitley's house," I said.

"What guy?"

"Her date." It was him at church. The fact that I'd heard his voice had cemented that. "I heard him talking to her and Jimmy, and he sounded really, really familiar, but I can't figure out who he was, and I didn't get to see him."

Matt scraped his thumbnail across the trampoline surface. "What's his name?"

"His name is Jake. I also heard him at church on Sunday, talking to another man." A breeze picked up. "His whole name is Jacob Andrews."

Matt shook his head. "I can't think of anyone by that name."

"Me either, but I've heard him somewhere." A thin cloud moved across the sun. "He could be a teacher at school that we just don't know. I also think that if he was at church, then I could have heard him there at some point, too, giving announcements or something."

"Possibly." Matt looked up as the sun dimmed a little. "Is Miss Whitley going out with him tomorrow night?"

"I assume she is."

Matt nodded. "He could be another teacher."

"Could be." Leaning back, I spoke. "I hope so. I kinda want to know who he is." Why had I felt so strongly that I shouldn't enter the room he was in? "I just also had this feeling that I wasn't supposed to go see who he was."

Matt frowned. "That's interesting."

"Yeah." The sun dimmed further as a steadier wind blew. Looking up, I caught a flash. The rumble followed about ten seconds later.

Matt got up. "Let's go inside."

"Okay."

The wind rushed through the woods as another almost gentle flash brightened the afternoon for a moment. We hopped off the trampoline and climbed the stairs to my back deck.

***

Miss Whitley's garage was closed up when I pulled in, the driveway empty, so Jake wasn't at her house yet. As much as I wanted to see his face and find out who he was, relief trickled in. Weird, just like when I felt like I shouldn't show myself the other time.

I grabbed my phone and wallet from the passenger seat and turned my car off, glad for what would probably be a calm evening.

Jimmy answered the door when I rang the doorbell. He smiled, his freckled face lifting as he pushed the screen door open.

I stepped back and caught it, pulling it the rest of the way. "Hey, Jimmy."

"Mom got a pizza!" was his answer.

Miss Whitley appeared, wearing a sundress and sandals. "Hey, Anya. I did get you two a pizza from the new place. Might be good to warm it back up in the oven before you eat it. Is pepperoni okay?"

"That's fine. Thanks."

Miss Whitley waved her hand. "Don't worry about it. You're very welcome." She paused. "I do hope this place sticks around. It's really good."

Music reached the front door from the TV room.

"Okay, so, Jimmy's been playing his new game a lot," Miss Whitley told me. "Sounds like he just fired it up. Jake will be here in a few minutes, so you're welcome to go see if Jimmy will go two-player." She smiled, but something else, unreadable, flickered in her eyes.

"Okay."

Her smile widened. Was that relief? *Weird.*

"Awesome. I'll see you two when I get back."

"Yes ma'am." I followed the sounds of the game and took a seat on the couch. Jimmy knelt in front of the TV, his eyes fixed on the screen. At the front of the house, the door opened, and I heard Miss Whitley greet someone. A man's voice replied.

"'Bye, Jimmy!" came her call.

"'Bye, Mom!" Jimmy bellowed. His eyes stayed fixed to the screen.

"So what's this game about?" I asked.

Jimmy stayed focused on the screen as he told me the story. I watched the motion, listening as he explained, for a half hour until he saved it and paused.

"I'm hungry," he said.

"I can go warm the pizza up." I stood.

Jimmy got up and led me to the kitchen, where the pizza box sat on the stove. He lifted the lid to look.

I turned the oven on and set it to what I thought might have been the right temperature. "Can you show me where your mom keeps the pizza pans?"

"Yep!" He bent down and pulled open the drawer under the stove, yanking out a large pan and handing it to me.

"Thanks," I said.

He smiled back and went to the refrigerator. "Do you want a drink?" he asked.

"Yes, please," I answered, carefully sliding the already-cut pizza onto the pan. "This will only take a couple minutes once the oven heats up."

The fridge closed, and two drink cans thunked on the table. A chair scraped on the kitchen floor as Jimmy took a seat. A shushing sound of paper on paper reached my ears, and two napkins fluttered as Jimmy set them on the table.

"Thanks for doing that." The oven beeped, and I slid the pan inside.

"You're welcome."

A few minutes later, I cut the oven off and took the pizza out. It smelled good, and the cheese looked right. Miss Whitley had set a stack of paper plates next to the stove. I grabbed two, set a slice of pizza on each one, and put one of the plates down on the table in front of Jimmy. "You can get however many you want after this one."

He nodded and slurped from his can of cola, then started eating, taking little bites of the pizza between slurps.

It tasted just as good as when my parents had gotten it. I couldn't remember if there'd been a pizza place in Salt's Creek recently, beyond vague memories of some chain that had been gone for years. Whitley's was the only restaurant that had managed to stick around, and it had been here for decades.

*Never really thought about that before.* Plenty of people lived in Salt's Creek, so why did we have so few restaurants that actually stayed?

Jimmy spoke. "You're the funnest babysitter."

"Aww, thank you," I said. "That's really nice of you to say."

Jimmy fidgeted with the crust of his pizza slice. "Mom's been hanging out with Jake a whole lot."

"What do you think about that?" Was my question invasive?

Jimmy shrugged. "He's nice."

"That's good."

"I guess." He took another bite of pizza and chewed quietly, thoughtful. I had to wonder what he was thinking about. Beyond her being my teacher, I didn't know Miss Whitley that well.

"Does your mom like him a lot, you think?" Maybe even asking that was an overstep.

"I think so," Jimmy answered. "I guess that's why she hangs out with him so much."

"Maybe the three of you will go somewhere sometime," I offered. "So you can get to know him better."

A little smile lifted Jimmy's face. "Maybe we'll go see a movie."

"Or eat at Whitley's."

"Yeah, my uncle owns that," he said, bouncing.

"I eat there a lot with my friends." Taking a bite of my pizza, I chewed slowly, savoring it. "They make really good food."

Jimmy lifted out of whatever mood the talk of his mom's relationship with Jake had put him in. He didn't dislike Jake, as far as I could tell, but he also might not have been sure of the guy, which I could understand.

After another slice each of pizza, Jimmy and I cleaned up and headed back to his video game.

"You wanna play too?" he asked, lifting a second controller so I could take it.

"Sure," I said, sitting down next to him. He started a new two-player game.

We wound up playing for the rest of the time Miss Whitley was away. When we heard the front door opening, Jimmy paused the game and rushed out of the room without another word.

Getting to my feet, I listened to the conversation at the door, trying to place Jake's voice. Part of me wanted to go into the room and actually look at his face, to see why the sound of his voice had imprinted itself on my brain.

I also wanted to hang back and not see him, or be seen.

But it would probably be rude if I didn't introduce myself. *Just a peek.*

Slipping into the hallway, and to the front of the house, I focused on the two adults at the door and tried to keep my face polite as the man looked at me.

I went still.

The smiling, friendly man with the familiar voice gave nothing away as he looked at me. "Good evening. You're Anya, right?"

I hoped my face was frozen in politeness, hoped it didn't fall in the fear that shot through me, hoped desperately that it stayed pleasant.

Iacomus, king of Naolon, smiled at me from the front hall of Miss Whitley's home.

I made myself nod. "Yes sir. Anya McCall." The first time I'd seen this man, he'd caught us in that empty village and he'd fallen as Meris' bullet hit his arm. "Nice to meet you." The second time his voice had sounded through a village, he'd committed an atrocity that I'd heard happen. Why in the world had I just given him my last name?

Not a speck of doubt could take root in my mind. It was him. Not in the dress of a soldier from Naolon, but a light green polo shirt and a pair of khakis.

"Same here." He turned to Miss Whitley. "Well, Joanna, I better get going. Let's do this again soon."

She smiled, just as warm. "Sure. 'Bye, Jake."

"Goodnight." He shot me another warm, friendly smile, and my jaw tightened, my stomach almost heaving as my own smile locked in place, staying while he let himself out.

What if he waited for me? How in the world was I going to stall? He couldn't wait that long, but neither could I. An engine started.

Miss Whitley looked up at me. "Thanks so much again, Anya. Did you like the pizza?"

How was I managing to hide my thoughts so they didn't show on my face? "Yes, it was good." I stuck my hands into my shorts pockets and desperately gripped the fabric as the trembling started.

"Good!" She moved toward her pocketbook. "Let me get your money."

I'd have to take my hands out when she got back. They'd still be shaking.

I waited, wanting to leave. This whole time had been nice until I'd decided to satisfy my idiotic curiosity and show my stupid face. Though I listened hard, I still couldn't tell if tires moved over the driveway outside, or the street.

Miss Whitley handed me fifty dollars.

"Thanks," I said, running the bills between my fingers to hide the trembling.

"Of course."

The bills shushed over my skin as I fidgeted with them, trying to stall. "Um…Miss Whitley, do you havc any officc hours at school this summer?"

She nodded. "Starting at the beginning of August, Monday to Friday, noon to three o'clock." She paused. "Did you have something to discuss?"

"No ma'am," I told her. "I just…was wondering. In case I needed to ask anything." Was that the sound of tires on asphalt, or a cicada? Was it even time for those yet? "Thanks again."

"Of course. And thank you. Have a good night, Anya."

"'"Bye, Anya!" Jimmy called out.

"Y'all too. 'Bye, Jimmy!"

I went out onto their small porch and shut the door behind me. My gaze drifted up to the corner, where a quarter-sized wasp nest hung, a single wasp perched on it.

Shuddering, I rushed down the steps and to my car, trying to calm down, wanting to scream and throw up, do something that I logically knew I couldn't do in Miss Whitley's driveway. Jake's car was gone.

As I sped home, part of me expected to see a car following, maybe even that brown car.

In my driveway, I turned the ignition off and gave a quick glance around as I let myself in the house, glad for my mom's vigilance on wasps and their nests, thankful for the cans of wasp and hornet spray that lived inside and outside by the front door in the summer.

Inside, I peeked into the living room. "Hey, y'all." I put the cheer on, boxing up my horror and terror and pasting on a happy face. The air conditioning in my car had cooled the terrified sweat.

"How'd it go?" Dad asked.

"Great," I said. "Jimmy and I played a game, and his mom got us a pizza from that new place."

"Was it as good this time?" Mom asked.

"Yeah, really good." I had to tell Matt.

"Maybe we'll get some more this weekend," Dad said.

“Hopefully that place sticks around.” I glanced into the hall. “I’m gonna head upstairs.”

My mom spoke. “Are you gonna babysit for Miss Whitley regularly?”

“Maybe.” Would Jake be there next time?

“Good steady job,” Mom remarked.

“Definitely,” I said. “‘Night, y’all.”

Matt needed to know. The harsh reality blazed back in. My teacher was dating the king of Naolon. I pressed my teeth together to keep the nausea at bay. He’d seen me, and he knew my name. He’d been at the same church we went to.

Iacomus was in town.

Dating my teacher.

Why was he here?

My scar itched. On my bed, I curled up on my side, unsure if I’d even sleep that night and not knowing when something would eventually be too much for me to handle.

This, I had to stick into a box until morning.

***

It was only ten-thirty, and I started sweating in the minute it took to walk over to Matt’s house. The heat would intensify to blazing this afternoon.

Mrs. Dobken’s car sat in the driveway. Matt didn’t have any yards to cut, but his mom had randomly taken the day off herself. I rang the doorbell and waited a minute, the air thick around me.

The door opened. Mrs. Dobken's face stilled, almost cold, for a second before moving into a pleasant expression.

"Anya," she said, pushing out the glass door. It took a few seconds of quiet to realize it was my turn to speak.

"Hi, Mrs. Dobken," I said. "Matt's here, right?"

She nodded, still smiling. "Come on in." She stepped back, and I ducked into the cool hallway. "He's upstairs."

"Thanks." As I climbed the stairs, I knew her eyes watched me.

Matt sat on the floor in front of his TV, playing a game.

"Hey," I said.

"'Morning," Matt answered. He paused the game and turned to face me as I took a seat across from him.

"How'd the babysitting job go last night?" he asked.

Not saying anything at first, I let just a little bit of the fear out of the box I'd shoved it into. "Miss Whitley's date is Iacomus." If I panicked completely, I'd just be loud.

Matt's face fell. "What?" He grabbed my shoulders. "Did he do anything to you?"

"Wouldn't I have started with that?"

"Did he say anything?"

I shook my head. "Just…the usual 'nice to meet you' stuff." A tremor started deep in my core. "He knows my name now."

Matt's mouth dropped open as he let me go and leaned back.

"Matt, I need you to come cut the grass." His mom's voice from downstairs cut sharply into our conversation.

He frowned. "I…guess I'm doing that now."

"Okay." Starting to stand, I said, "I didn't know you were supposed to be doing that right now."

He shook his head. "I didn't either." He pushed to his feet. "I'll be down in a minute, Mom!"

She didn't answer him.

Matt leveled his gaze on me again. "So…I'll go do that."

My hands shook in earnest. "Okay." I had stuff I could do, but we had to go to Trenavell at some point. Iacomus was in Salt's Creek, and he'd disappeared after the battle.

A strange memory returned, of someone at the meeting we'd all gone to with Meris saying that Iacomus was the same person who'd been king of Naolon over century before.

*No way he's that old.* "Have you heard from Danny?"

"No."

"Matt, please come down here," Mrs. Dobken called again.

With an unsteady smile, I moved toward his bedroom door. "I'll let you go cut the grass."

He grabbed his tennis shoes. "Yeah. Stay inside."

"I will. It's hot." Mrs. Dobken didn't appear again as I headed out the door.

## Chapter 13

The next morning, at eight, I had my backpack on my bed to pack stuff in it for Trenavell. The food we'd bought went in the outer compartment, and I shoved the disc into the larger main one, closest to my back, on top of the folder full of Dupree's letters and the map. I wondered if the food should go in the main compartment. Not that it would be that much more protected. The bayonet, wrapped in the old t-shirt, fit alongside the disc. My keys jingled as I tossed them into the bag. I pocketed a small flashlight.

*What in the world am I going to do with a bayonet?*

Grabbing my phone, I stuck it into my jeans pocket, put the backpack on, and headed downstairs, clutching my coat. Matt was going to meet me at the trampoline. He had nothing to do today, and his mom hadn't taken today off.

My heart started racing as I reached the landing. Why was Iacomus in Salt's Creek? Had he been afraid that Trenavell would keep him prisoner? Was he really as old as he was supposed to be? That sounded like a pretty weird rumor to have spread.

Making sure that both doors were locked, I slipped down the steps and waited by the trampoline, keeping my eyes on the woods.

A shadow moved, and Danny stepped out from the brush just as Matt came out of his back door. I waved at Danny and watched Matt make his way to the trampoline. We took off across the yard and into the trees.

"How are things?" Danny asked.

"Iacomus lives in Salt's Creek," I told him as we hurried for the Dupree house.

"What?" Danny's question snapped out in an almost-yell.

"He's dating one of our teachers," Matt said. "Anya saw him Tuesday night at that teacher's house."

Danny's mouth dropped open in horror. "Did he see you?"

"I…his voice sounded familiar when she went out with him before, and I also heard his voice at church on Sunday, so on Tuesday I actually went out to see who he was."

Danny's face pinched in a frown. "And he's seen you before."

Now that I'd opened that compartment, I wanted to crumble. "When Meris shot him. He saw all of us." And I'd introduced myself. "I told him my whole name, but he already knew my first name."

Danny let out a bitter laugh. "I'm gonna have to live here."

"You could," Matt said. "Aunt Della could see if Mom would do that. That way you're around us enough to watch." Matt's hazel eyes flicked for a moment to me.

The spark of annoyance that didn't have its roots in common sense came back. *Calm down. This actually is dangerous.* We reached the Dupree house. Something fluttered in the window upstairs as Matt stopped at the side of the big tree, and I leaned against it. Danny waited behind us.

"No one's here," Matt said.

Together, we dashed across to the porch and up the steps. Matt led the way down the hall to the kitchen and pulled the wall open, and we rushed down into the cellar. The daylight faded behind us as Danny pulled the wall closed. Matt led us up into the golden light around the Kings Road gate.

The woods teemed with a hard silence as we pulled our coats on, all three of us quiet as we made our way down to where the road left the woods.

As soon as I saw the silhouette, far ahead on the road, I stopped, and the guys came to a stop as well.

The dust cloud behind the figure moving toward us grew.

"They're going pretty fast," Matt said.

We moved right, following Danny as he made his way across the field, his eyes trained on the shadow where the ground dipped down into the tunnel.

I hoped that the burrow beast had left its nest.

We rushed down the ramp into the tunnel as the figure we'd seen clearly resolved into a cart being driven towards the woods.

Wasn't that part of the road supposed to be too dangerous? Meris had said that. The gate was in a weird place because the road was rough.

Where was the cart going?

As we passed fully into the tunnel, all three of us clicked our flashlights on.

We hurried, and I was glad for the smooth floor underneath my feet. There wasn't much to trip over.

As I cleared my throat, an echo bounced around the tunnel. "Do y'all think that Trenavell will want to take Iacomus into custody or anything?"

Matt swept his light smoothly across our path as we moved forward. "How would they get him?"

Danny's flashlight beam lit up one of the unreadable directional signs in the tunnel. "Assuming the gate isn't locked in the Dupree house, then they could come right to Salt's Creek, but they'd also have to know where he lives, and somehow get him to Trenavell without people noticing them doing that."

I flinched at the memory of the crack of a gunshot echoing from the village as Noam and I fled, and nodded quietly. Any attempt to detain Iacomus would probably mean he'd make sure someone noticed.

Was Jake Andrews the driver of the brown car? I hadn't seen his car either time I'd babysat at Miss Whitley's, so it could be him. My heart thudded once as I realized that, if Jake was the driver, it would mean that Iacomus knew where I lived. My jaw tightened, and a cold sweat gathered on my face.

It was a junky brown car. It hadn't even had a license plate the first time we'd seen it, when it had slammed into the back of Matt's truck. With a deep breath, I thought that Jake's polo shirt and khakis didn't match the car, with all its disrepair and the until-recently absent license plate.

But warm, personable manners also didn't go well with the massacre of a village full of people just because they hadn't seen us and couldn't give us up.

My flashlight beam wobbled as we reached the open space that led to the double doors, and my right shoe loosened on my foot. I glanced down and stopped. The strings had come completely out of the knot, and one end trailed behind me.

"My shoe's untied." I crouched to tie it, and the guys paused. Danny watched ahead of us, trailing his flashlight over the large space between us and the doors, looking almost like he was doing it absently. Matt turned, his tennis shoe scuffing softly over the surface and echoing briefly before quieting.

I pulled the loops of my shoestring tight and stood, and the echo of a sound picked up again.

*That's not right.*

Dread washed through me as I met both pairs of reflective eyes, the cousins' alarm clear in their faces. The burrow beast hadn't ever come this far.

The space around us went silent again.

Danny gestured for us to keep going, and we hurried as fast as possible without making too much noise, the shadows of the random refuse dancing as our flashlights passed over their abstract shapes. I didn't welcome the approach of the double doors at the end. At least the tunnel was big and at least it led outside. Everything on the other side of the doors was small and tight and full of hiding places that, as far as we'd been able to tell, didn't contain anyone from Trenavell to at least help us. It was just a creepy empty space.

Danny edged his way in front. Matt and I walked beside each other, following him into the dark hallways. My foot crunched over something, maybe broken glass, and I flinched.

We had almost reached the door to the shop's cellar when a soft thud from somewhere distant sounded once.

Danny's eyes widened, but he didn't stop walking. We all just kept rushing until we reached the hall where we'd been meeting. It was at least a hiding spot. If nothing else, we could actually go outside, onto the street. Trenavell wasn't our enemy.

The glow of a moss lamp lantern met us, appearing to my adrenaline-flooded mind to be floating before the figure behind it resolved into Ira.

"Did you all hear that?" Ira asked, without another greeting, as we drew near him.

Danny looked around at us. "Not the first time I've thought I'd heard it and some other noises." He winced, eyes flicking down for a moment. Had he not wanted to tell us that? Was that why he slept probably on top of the hatch behind the shop's counter?

"Where are the other two?" I asked.

Ira drew in a deep breath and let it out, his face solemn and worried. "The chapel."

"How long are they gonna be there?" Matt's tone wasn't as harsh as it had been with Ira before. Maybe he was letting the other boy off the hook now.

Ira shook his head before speaking. "I don't know. It's been about five hours now. Since before sunrise."

Danny frowned. "What's going on?"

"I don't know." Ira turned away from us. "But I can tell you that you can hear what's going on in the chapel if you're below it."

Meris had said there was a hatch there.

Ira kept speaking. "I'm supposed to be at home."

"I know how to get there," Danny answered.

Relief spread quickly across Ira's face. "Good."

We walked, keeping quiet, aware that something was in this space, making mysterious noises, and that probably meant it was actually someone. Ira slipped away from us and into another passage that would take him home.

Danny led us through the hallways, passing broken windows and doors closed and open, all with unreadable signs, before coming to a stop where two passages intersected, one cut off by a closed door to our left, and one ahead of us. He pointed his flashlight beam down, showing that the passage became a wide staircase. On the edges of the steps, gleaming white stripes caught the light, and a wider doorway at the bottom had an oblong sign above it, unreadable text and a round emblem on it, the latter of which I guessed was that wheel with thirteen spokes. Dark, flat rectangles lined the wall the whole way to the other opening. The chill seeping up from the bottom of the staircase flowed over me, and the hairs on the back of my neck stood up straight.

Matt pointed his flashlight at the nearest rectangle on the wall.

A forest with blue trees lined the bottom of the picture. Mountainous clouds of a thunderstorm stacked up behind the trees, and the bottom of the picture had another word I couldn't read, with the round emblem in the corner. On the one across the passage from it, I could just see a beach, with waves cresting and white foam on the sand. If anything, they reminded me of tourism posters.

What was this place? What was down there?

Danny cleared his throat and spoke, his voice distant and distracted. "We're near the center of the castle." The closed door we'd stopped at had a small sign next to it, and Danny pushed it open.

"What do you think is down there?" Matt asked, voice soft.

"I don't know, but I want to see it," I answered. What were the posters? What was all of this? Why was there a network of tunnels and offices and rooms under the city?

"Me too," Danny answered, leading us a little bit more before he stopped at a heavy-looking door that stood alone in this particular hallway. If what we'd been seeing were signs, this one was covered with them. The unreadable words paired up with sharp symbols that I didn't recognize, the sheer number and harsh shapes suggesting something dangerous beyond the doorway.

Matt reached out and ran a finger over one of the signs. "These look like safety warnings."

Danny nodded. "They probably are." He grabbed the handle. "I don't think they apply anymore." With a pause, and a meaningful look at me and Matt, he kept on. "I think it was safe in the 1880s." He tugged on the handle, and with the softest creak, it opened to a small room where more signs coated the wall. He pointed his flashlight at the far end of the ceiling, highlighting the edges of a large hatch, and pockets in the wall below it that served as a ladder.

"The chapel's above us," Danny whispered. Nothing creaked. I knew that the floor was mostly stone.

None of us spoke as a voice became clearer.

"Who informed you of the existence of the mechanism and the pieces?" It was a man, but I wasn't sure who.

"No one," came Meris' sharp answer, muffled by the hatch.

As I listened, I turned to the wall to the right of the door we'd come in.

"Meris, you must tell us," a woman's voice said.

"No one told me," Meris insisted. "However, I excel at listening."

I stepped closer to a box attached to the stone wall.

"Noam?" It was the man again.

"I can vouch for her highness." Noam's answer wasn't anywhere near as sharp as Meris' had been. He was speaking with respect, and she with familiarity.

*Her parents.* Raising my flashlight higher, I inspected the square box on the wall. Rust covered it. A few straight lines ran away from it on each side. The thickest of the lines ran from the bottom and top of the box, straight towards the ceiling and down to the floor.

"The altar's above us," Danny said.

"Meris." The man's voice was firm, but not quite stern. "Who did you hear it from?"

There was no answer this time.

"Tell us," came a woman's voice, a different one.

"With all respect, Lady Hestia, you were the one who whisked us out of your own office, and you knew we did not have what you thought we might have." A pause. "Were you not involved?"

I reached out and touched the metal box, feeling the roughness of its age, the bolts holding it together. It wasn't humming. There wasn't any noise, other than the ones we made, and the voices from upstairs.

"My assumption was that you were couriers working for the king, not your own selves." Lady Hestia's harsh tone wound up tempered by the surface separating us from the chapel.

I remembered the jolt of something I'd felt when turning the wheel after placing all the keys into the cylinder behind the altar. It hadn't been like a shock, but like I'd activated something, a machine that maybe was only designed to work once. Was this box how the riddle device sealed the gates?

Meris' dad spoke. "Our concern is espionage. All the passages are closed off for the time being. Your friends brought the key here and found the pieces."

Swallowing, I turned to Matt and Danny, my gaze following the straight lines along the other three walls and landing on a round object on the opposite wall from me. My heart dropped a little.

The king continued. "My concern is not the seals, but whose words and what idea got into your head to decide to piece the device together."

Meris answered, still calm. "I excel at listening, but I will not say who I heard speaking of it." She hadn't given a reason why she'd decided to put the thing together.

"According to our man on the inside, Naolon is not pleased by the loss of the gates," the king said. "They are confused, but regrouping, though Iacomus has still not reappeared."

"How much do you know?" the other woman asked. Meris' mom, I guessed.

No one answered, though I also couldn't tell who she'd asked.

The king cleared his throat. “How did your friend find the key to the device?”

“I don’t remember, and I don’t remember if I ever knew.” I could almost hear Meris crossing her arms, and I realized I also couldn’t remember telling them where we’d found the words to the key.

“Where did they have the key?” her mom asked.

“Written on a piece of paper.”

“Was that the only thing on the paper?” Hestia asked.

“Yes. It was handwritten. The paper was wrinkled, but not old.”

My eyes widened. If she kept going, they’d know I’d copied it from somewhere. Would they come looking for the photo album? That didn’t make sense. Maybe if they did, they wouldn’t assume it was in my house. If we told them about Jake being Iacomus, there was a chance they’d come to Earth anyway.

“Daughter.” The king’s voice grew stern this time. “You and the Earth children took the work of Gavin Dupree upon yourselves in retrieving the pieces of this device and activating it.” The king knew something.

My heart started to pound, and my breath sped up.

“What was his work for?” Noam asked.

My eyes went to the box again. That and the elements behind the altar above us had sealed every single gate in

Trenavell, which, whatever that meant, had to have used a lot of power. Why had that been Dupree's work at all?

No one answered for a minute. "For Trenavell's aid," were the words that finally came from the king.

"Then isn't it good that we took this on ourselves?" Meris asked.

She had a point. If it was, then why were they being questioned? Why was it so important to find out who else knew, especially if it was already done?

"For Trenavell's aid" had to mean something deeper than just the war, didn't it? The war was important, but I already knew that Trenavell hadn't been expecting the gates to be sealed.

What was the whole point of Gavin Dupree's work, if it didn't actually help?

My eyes drifted. What was the thing on the other side of the room? I walked past Matt and Danny and towards it. Was it related to the box behind me? As I approached, I studied it, the details clear in the bright beam of my flashlight.

Light green corrosion and a layer of dust coated the surface of the round compartment. If there'd been a cover on it, it was gone now, and the insides were exposed and hard to understand, possibly incomplete. As I leaned closer to the edge of it, I could see where metal had been snapped off, and a latch on the other side of the circle from the break. The interior resolved, not into clean and usable parts, but to a charred mess, and instead of straight lines issuing from this one, crooked rays of burnt stone, like lightning scars, stuck out in all directions in the wall around it, a near representation of a sun.

What had burned the wall?

Turning away, I looked at Danny. "Do you know what this is?"

He shook his head. "No."

I stared up at the hatch. I didn't know exactly what most of it was under. Had the altar been built close enough to keep it from being functional, or were the hatch and the chapel the same age?

Meris and Noam's interrogation had come to the topic of Gavin Dupree, and if the adults were thinking clearly, they'd know that the device key was copied from somewhere. They knew our names, and that we were from Salt's Creek, North Carolina.

We might be next, and my suspicion rose that Trenavell might want to keep us in Compass Hill. According to Ira, Meris and Noam had been in the chapel for five hours.

Maybe I could distract the ones questioning.

Danny had heard things down here, and we definitely had heard noises ourselves. Could I at least startle the adults by making a sudden sound myself?

The pockets in the wall were deep, but it wouldn't be too easy to climb up the ladder, especially as it being part of the wall made the climb a ninety degree angle. The handle of the hatch attached to a band of iron along the length of the door.

Sticking my flashlight in my pocket, I stepped into the first hole in the wall, half my foot getting a good hold as I stepped up into the next one.

"Anya!" Matt hissed.

If I weren't hanging on, I would have waved him off, but I shot him a quelling look before finishing my short climb. As close as I was getting to the hatch, I didn't want to speak.

Carefully, I pulled my left hand out of the space in the wall and reached for the handle, grabbing it firmly. If I slipped, it wasn't too far to fall.

Taking in a deep breath, I shook the handle up and down in its place, careful not to actually open the hatch much, just enough to let it bang into its frame. I thought it might have echoed.

"What was that?" Meris' mom shouted.

"May we go?" Meris asked. Footsteps shuffled across the chapel's floor above us.

I gripped the ladder again and climbed back down. "We should find somewhere to hide."

Danny grinned and led us out of the room, and Matt shut the thick door behind us.

# Chapter 14

My heart raced. "So…do y'all wanna check out that other part we saw?" We could hide there, assuming there weren't other people.

"Why did you do that?" Matt asked me.

"To make a distraction."

Danny laughed and kept leading us, and we all fell silent again as he headed back to the staircase we'd seen with all the posters. The white edges of the steps picked up the flashlight beams as we descended and approached the opening at the other end. Even in the dark, with only our flashlights, the chill and growing echo gave the yawning sense of a wider space beyond. At the bottom of the staircase, a short landing, still part of the passage, held more posters.

Then we stepped through the doorway.

Our flashlight beams passed over the walls, the light reflected by lighter trim around five tall, arched openings that surrounded the central area. The light didn't make it far into the dark passageways.

How far down were we?

"Look at that, guys," Danny said, pointing his flashlight at a symbol on the ceiling.

Above us, at the center of the room, was the emblem we'd seen, the wheel with thirteen spokes. The color matched the trim around the arched doorways, white and faintly pearlescent.

"Why are there thirteen?" I breathed, the fog of my breath streaming out in the calm chill of the underground concourse.

*You both favor the number thirteen….*

What did thirteen mean, though, and why did the spokes of Gavin Dupree's symbol have eight? He could have taken inspiration from this one, but what did either wheel mean?

Danny lowered his flashlight. "No idea."

Matt kept studying it. "It's everywhere."

Like a logo. *For what?*

My eyes had begun to adjust to the darkness down here. A light flickered down one of the wide passages. The guys pointed their flashlights down it while I dug mine out.

It looked so much like an airport or train station down here, something expressly for transit. Was there an electric light somewhere? I took a step forward.

"Anya," Matt said.

"I want to see that light," I told him, walking faster. I passed under the entrance to the passage, noting the round sign up there before my gaze fixed on a steadier glow farther away that was briefly outshone by the harsh strobing. I passed the flickering light, unable to really see what it was in the inconsistent illumination, and walked toward the other glow.

Matt caught up to me, his flashlight illuminating several rows of broken seats in front of the stark bright outline of a wide doorway, the line wider on one side.

"It's open," I said, moving toward it. Where did it end up? Where'd the light come from? The guys followed me, their footsteps an uneven echo on the floor.

"Yeah," Matt said.

The light nearby flashed again.

As I passed the podium next to the door we'd stopped at, my right shoe flopped on my foot, too roomy for the shoestrings to still be securely tied. *I'll tie them in a second.* As I pulled the door fully open, gray light flooded through, showing me a misty landscape, lit by soft sunlight, the air colder than when we'd entered the tunnel by the road.

A gate.

As I walked into the daylight, my shoe loosened further. One end of the shoestring caught under my foot, and I stumbled fully into the bright gray day. Something flickered in the corner of my eye, and with a short, sharp buzz, the space I'd come from vanished behind the solid face of a stone wall with a now impassible doorframe.

I froze, staring at the stone, my gaze dropping down to my shoes.

Both ends of my right shoestring rested on the ground, one end several inches shorter and sliced cleanly off. My pulse sped up.

There was no way back, and if I'd been a second slower….

Lurching at the wall, I beat on it with my fists, the sides of my hands stinging from the impact, but didn't dare make any other noise.

*What's that gonna do?* If the gate had closed completely, then there was a good chance they couldn't hear me anyway.

Was I actually alone? Whirling around, I took in the edge of a forest nearby, and the bluish-green color of the trees. Thin clouds threaded across the sky, muting the sun, except for a pile of that I thought, for a moment, was a building thunderstorm that might pass over soon, catching me outside in it. But, though my mind wouldn't pinpoint the exact problem, *something* in the angle of the clouds didn't resolve into how a thunderstorm should look.

Then the poster in that stairwell came back to mind. That's where I was, somewhere on Trenavell's planet.

I didn't dare turn my back on the woods again, and rubbed my arms, pressing against the wall, the wet chill thick in the air. The living sounds of animals made the forest more noisy than I thought it should be, as cold as it was.

Closer to me, a straight line of stone or brick or something led away along the ground from the wall, ending somewhere in the distance. I leaned away and took a glance at the stone behind me. Lines of mortar held them together. I stood in the ruins of something.

And then, I heard a noise that was decidedly not organic behind me. Another buzz. With no other warning, two hands grabbed my arms and yanked me backwards. I stumbled hard into Matt, my eyes still glued to the foggy landscape, and his arms closed fully around me. We both sat down hard, sliding a foot on the smooth floor.

"Are you okay?" He let go.

"Yeah." The end of my shoestring still lay at the edge of the doorway. "Why…why did it…" My dry throat caught on the words as I leaned forward and reached for the string.

"Trying to figure that out," Danny answered quickly, his flashlight beam traveling slowly around the doorframe. He pushed it almost all the way closed and crouched down closer on the right side. "Ah."

"What?" I asked, taking a deep breath.

"Okay, so there's a bunch of pegs around this," he answered. "This one is made of wood instead of whatever else the others are, and it's cracked."

Sure enough, white circles glimmered in intervals around the doorway. The cracked one must have been a replacement at some point.

Matt glared at the door, anger and horror in his eyes. "That could have taken your leg off."

My core shuddered.

Danny stood straight and winced. "We have to assume that this is a risk with any other ones we find down here."

The other light flashed again.

"We'll have to inspect them," I said.

There was another buzz and a partial flicker as the broken gate I'd gone through blotted out the light around itself. Goosebumps flared up on my skin. *Don't think about it.* My hands shook.

"Are you really okay?" Danny asked.

"I guess." I tied the cut ends of the string back together. At least I wasn't in that evergreen blue place. At least I wasn't trapped, and at least I had all my limbs and fingers.

Matt stood and held his hand down to me, and I grabbed it a little tighter than I normally would have as I stood. I held on and squeezed once, hard, suppressing the terrified shudder wanting to rip through me.

Letting go, I took in a deep breath. "So…I…" My mouth had dried up. "There are more of those, for sure."

The other one, which I now knew was a gate in bad disrepair, strobed again.

Danny walked towards it, leaving us standing by the gate I'd gone through. My knees started to shake as we watched him.

"Anya," Matt said.

I looked up at him."The trees were blue."

His eyes glowed steadily, his face hard and solemn.

"There were ruins." I swallowed. "Or…I mean…there was what was left of a foundation on the ground, and the door was in a wall that was still holding together…" I squeezed the flashlight as my hand shook.

Danny walked back to us. "I don't think we can find out where that one goes." Despite the smile he pushed onto his face, the cheer in his voice had weight. "Do you think Meris and Noam were able to get away?"

"We can go back to the store cellar," I answered. "They need to know about Iacomus." Why couldn't I get my voice to be louder?

"Good idea," Matt said.

I backed away, watching as the broken gate went dark again, then turned, following Danny, Matt beside me.

The hall brightened.

But my eyes couldn't adjust that fast, not enough to illuminate the hall that quickly. As the softest scuff of a footstep reached my ears from behind us, all three of us turned and froze to watch a growing glow in the distant dark. A figure briefly dimmed the light as it stepped into our view and turned a pair of glowing eyes on us.

They didn't speak. We didn't speak. I couldn't even tell much more about them beyond the vague pallor of their skin, which I could probably only see because of the combination of our flashlights and the bright light that streamed into the hall.

Matt tugged my arm and took off running back to the main concourse of the station, and I gladly sped along with him.

We sprinted, my heart hammering, our footsteps echoing and our lights bouncing and all of it too loud and too noticeable and too followable. And with all three of us running, it was impossible to tell if there was a fourth set of footsteps coming after us. Looking backwards would slow me down.

Directionless, we sped across the concourse and into another passage. If the figure behind us was actually in pursuit, then we'd have to hide.

A harsh gate outline glowed down the passage we were in. Skidding to a stop in front of it, I stared at the near-void of the door. The light illuminated a podium beside it, and made shadows from the rows of seats.

Somehow, in stopping, I'd signaled my friends to do so as well. Matt came up beside me. Whoever the other person was, they hadn't caught up yet. As I stood there, trying to catch my breath, my eyes adjusting made the light around the door soften and expand, showing off the wood and metal, and the iridescent pegs around the frame, all of them whole. Just as I reached out for the handle, some sound that I couldn't quite figure out made its way to us, echoing off the stone interior. My heart started beating faster. I yanked the door open, pulled Matt's arm, and lurched through.

Matt and I flew through the doors, my inertia taking me farther than I intended. I tripped. My knee struck the floor and a zing of pain shot up my leg. Danny spilled through the gate and pulled the door shut with a loud snap, and I pushed myself back up. The door closing echoed here, though not as much as it must have on the other side.

We stood inside a room lit only by sunlight. The thick, humid, stale air held no breeze. To my left, a desk guarded the door we'd come through, a chair pushed up against it.

This was a solid building, if an old one. My gaze fell on a round clock sticking out of the wall, the gray paint on it chipped and the hands long stopped. Faded ads from decades past hung on the walls. A cigarette machine, covered in dust, sat beside empty drink and snack machines, the glass fogged by grime on all three. Upholstery on the seats in this room had split, and stuffing peeked out of a bunch of them.

We'd found our way to something that wasn't a ruin, and it wasn't all that old.

Motion at the other end of the building, outside the dirty windows, drew me across the dusty wood floors.

Cars.

The sun flashed, dulled by dirt, off of something, probably a windshield on another car, and I blinked, my eyes finding a house across the street from the station, and the faded sign in the front yard.

*Future Project of the Salt's Creek Restoration Society*.

The Salt's Creek train station, closed and abandoned, held a gate to Trenavell.

Footsteps approached me, quiet on the wooden floors. I turned as Matt stopped beside me, his eyes taking in the house across the street. Another car drove by, and I could just tell that its turn signal flashed. Someone going to Whitley's.

Not a single peg had been missing from that door. My eyes went to the front entrance of the train station. Two wooden doors with glass windows had horizontal rectangular plates, corroded with age, the word "push" stamped into the metal.

A darker part of the station drew my eye, a shadowy corner behind a long counter with stools lined up, cracked upholstery matching the other chairs closer to the gate. Scant letters on the on a board above the space had probably been a menu.

"Danny?" was all I could get my mouth to say as I turned to look at the guys.

He had heard the question that I couldn't voice. "No," he said. "I didn't know."

Matt still stared at the empty house across the street, the house that hadn't once been worked on our whole lives. "There aren't…" He stopped, frowning.

"What?" I asked.

"All the windows are intact here," he answered.

Blinking, I turned to look. There weren't many windows. The station wasn't all that big.

All of them were dirty. Grimy.

But present. No plywood. Glass intact. If there'd ever been broken glass, it had been replaced.

"Do you think…the town knows about the train station?" I asked. Looking again at the gate door, I studied it. On this side was a doorknob and a second lock above it, probably a deadbolt.

Neither side had been locked. I looked again at the entrance to the street, sure that the front doors weren't openable on the other side, maybe secured with a padlock. Trying to open them might draw eyes to the train station.

"Are they the ones that own it?" Danny walked over to the lunch counter, shining his flashlight into the shadows in the back, lighting up an old soft drink fountain.

"Huh," Matt said. "Good point."

The station could have fallen into private hands at some point. Maybe that was who funded any repairs it needed. Kept it somewhat nice. I knew that buildings couldn't get but so run down before they were condemned. This station was solid and safe.

Whoever owned it kept it up. If that was the town….

A sweaty chill shivered over my skin. I stepped away from the street entrance. We were close enough to the windows to be seen. Even if there was someone else waiting in those passageways, the underground chill would be better than the stagnant, humid air in the train station.

I turned to the door we'd come through. Walking the old tunnel back to Kings Road would cool me off. I relished the thought of the near-winter air.

The cavernous chill of the facility waited, the still air cooling my face.

*Salt's Creek….*

Noam and Meris would have to know about it, but maybe no one else.

As we crossed the concourse and climbed the staircase, and saw no more pairs of glowing eyes, thoughts kept flying through my head of what could have happened if I'd been too slow going through that other gate. If I hadn't tripped, and if I'd just strolled. If I'd only peeked my head through.

I flinched.

What if Ira had had any other kind of weapon? What if Matt had been in front of me, what if Ira had swung the axe higher up? What if one of the four of us had been shot while Meris led us through the castle during a battle?

*What if I was slower?* A lump grew in my throat with every scene.

"How do they keep that from happening to other gates?" I blurted. The Salt's Creek gate wasn't broken.

"Maintenance," Danny answered. "I assume. I doubt wood was supposed to be used, if that stone is in there."

What was the white stone?

"Dupree's map…" The gates sprinkled all over the map of Trenavell. There were other passageways, and we hadn't been anywhere near the end of one. If there were more clusters of archways, then there could be even more gates. Was this what the map had been for, to show where these gates went?

*Then why would Salt's Creek be down here?*

We got to the familiar cellar door, another glow visible nearby.

Meris and Noam stepped forward. Noam carried the lantern, and Meris wore her rifle. Both of them also had backpacks.

"You weren't seen?" Meris asked.

"By who?" Matt asked.

Noam answered. "Well, we were under the impression that there were soldiers searching these hallways."

Matt looked at me. "Good thing we ran."

I twisted the flashlight in my hands. "I rattled the hatch in the floor of the chapel."

Meris laughed a little. "Our thanks."

Noam looked down, his face falling for a second, before meeting my eyes. "Where were you since then?"

Danny answered. "Did you guys know that there's a level below this one?"

"No," Meris told him.

"We found a couple gates," I offered. "I um…I wound up going through one." More mental images flooded my mind.

"What was on the other side?" Meris asked, her voice sharp. Noam started to frown.

"Some ruins of something," I said. "And some blueish-green trees. It looked like it was about to storm."

"And it's broken," Matt added.

"Broken?" Meris asked.

Weren't there broken gates on Noam's map? "It's not stable," I said, leaning against the wall, the bulk of my backpack pressing into me. Something crinkled inside it, maybe a protein bar wrapper. "I stumbled through it and it shut behind me for a little bit."

Noam's eyes widened.

"There was another one nearby," I continued. "It was even worse." Hesitating, I considered the gate to Salt's Creek. I didn't have to tell them everything right now. "And a third one worked perfectly."

Meris lifted her chin. "Would you three want to search for another one?"

"Today?" And that word, flying out of my mouth, betrayed the fear I'd desperately tried to box up. Salt's Creek and its train station gate balanced on the edge of the box, and I shoved it in quickly.

Matt glanced at me. "Ummm…"

Noam spoke. "Perhaps not today."

*I want to go home.*

Meris cleared her throat. "Perhaps we can return to the store, and Anya can describe more fully the place where that first gate led."

Maybe explaining it would calm me down. If the landscape I'd observed was what I focused on, then the images in my mind of the might-have-been could possibly stay in a box. Something to work through later.

My scar itched. "Yeah. I can do that. That's fine."

The posters on the wall came to mind again. Tourism posters.

Multiple gates.

It was a travel station.

Gavin Dupree hadn't made a network. One already existed here, and part of it went to my home.

Meris led us back up into the store. Climbing the steps had helped me warm up, and the difference in the autumn air of Trenavell's surface contrasted with still, underground chill of whatever was beneath us.

I set my backpack on the floor and climbed onto a stool. My hands had stopped shaking and my heart had stopped pounding, but another unwelcome sequence of almost-events played out in my head as Matt sat on the stool beside me.

Danny leaned on the counter. "Iacomus is also on Earth. In Salt's Creek."

I'd completely forgotten that we were going to tell Meris and Noam that. "Yeah," I added. "I talked to him."

"What?" Meris yelped.

"Where did you see him?" Noam's wide eyes and calm words didn't quite match.

"My teacher's house." When had he started going to my church? "And at church. He goes by the name Jacob Andrews."

"What was your conversation?" Meris asked.

Gritting my teeth for a second, I trained my eyes on the counter. "I just introduced myself."

"She was being polite," came Matt's voice, defensive.

"Well...then tell us what you saw at the gate," Meris said.

There was no way to know what Meris was going to do with the information about Iacomus, or the second gate to Salt's Creek. Looking up, I met Noam's eyes. "The gate I went through was on the edge of a forest, and the trees were blueish-green, which makes me think it was an evergreen forest."

"Was it cold?" Noam asked.

"Yeah. And wet. A little cloudy, and like I said, it looked like it was about to storm." But there was no way those clouds were close. How were they even visible with the other clouds? Why did it seem like they were in front of them, and not at the horizon? My mind refused to reconcile the odd way the clouds had sat in the sky.

Meris, with a frown, studied the top of the counter, her expression distant. "I don't know of any forests like that in Trenavell."

Matt leaned forward. "One time y'all said there were five continents on this planet. What if that gate went to another one of them?"

Noam raised his eyebrows. "That would be very interesting." He turned to me. "Did you see anyone else?"

I shook my head. "It was ruins. The wall around the actual door was still intact, but I saw the base of another wall near me. I'm pretty sure I heard animals moving around in the woods. When it malfunctioned, there was just solid stone in a doorframe." *I want to go home.*

Meris' eyes were wide now, still trained on the countertop, her nails digging into the rifle strap at her shoulder. "And there was another gate near that one."

"Yeah," Matt snapped.

She looked up, first at Noam, then at the rest of us. "I'm sure that there are more gates than just the three."

"There's a lot of stuff down there," I told her and Noam. "We just went down the two passages, and there could be other hubs than just the one in the center." The posters. "I think whatever is downstairs is like…a train station or something, but with gates." They hadn't asked more about the gate that worked perfectly.

"So one, at least, would go to Skyrren," Meris concluded.

She'd wanted to go. Dupree's letters had mentioned Skyrren, but we may not find anything of use there anymore.

But he'd also written something about a book. I thought back to the first letter Matt and I had ever found. Dupree said he'd hidden a book in Skyrren, and another letter almost echoed that, saying something about the Skyrren library and something about a "right book." If there weren't archives here in Compass Hill, then would Skyrren have them? If the city had been abandoned for almost thirty years, and the people there weren't exactly running it like a city, then the archives would still be in place.

Did Compass Hill's secret live partially in the less than official route to Skyrren that had a chance of existing under our feet?

Had there been an official gate in Compass Hill, even before the device had sealed the gates?

If Skyrren had been believed to be poison by way of a gate to Earth, then Compass Hill wouldn't want to have a gate anymore. The government had fled, and Skyrren was a long way away.

But odds were that there had been one before we'd used the device, even if it was closed off, and a gate to Skyrren likely existed in the facility under Compass Hill. There was probably a gate to any city in Trenavell, though I had no idea what those cities would be. I'd only ever seen Compass Hill, a few villages, and part of Skyrren.

I didn't want to go to Skyrren today. I didn't want to inspect the gates.

We had no idea what the book in Skyrren would even be about, but maybe in going there, something would connect.

The door of the shop opened without warning.

I hopped off the stool and spun around, starting to reach down for my backpack.

Cargan stood in the doorway, and my heart dropped. He was a chaplain for his father's soldiers. Had nothing ever changed in the Trenavellan government, he would have been heir to the throne. I had no idea if he ranked almost as high as his dad, but there was a chance that he had some authority now, and he could try to keep us here.

But he was alone.

Meris scoffed at her brother. "My thanks for your silence in the chapel," she said in greeting.

Cargan approached, glaring. "My thanks to you as well, little sister."

"I didn't give you away."

He shook his head. "And I was not inclined to give myself up as the culprit." He sighed. "Who rattled the door?"

I straightened. "Me."

Cargan didn't look mad. "It's not as though it was a productive session." He walked around the back of the counter and kept his eyes on the shop's front window. The hatch below him made the softest thunk as it shifted under his feet.

"I could have said it was Barney," Meris offered.

Cargan winced and shook his head. "Not productive."

"Why?" Meris asked.

"He's needed."

"Where?"

"I will not be telling you that." Cargan glanced down at his feet. "How far down have you gone?"

Noam answered. "Only to the cellar level, for me and Meris."

Cargan's gaze traveled over me, Matt, and Danny. "Have you been below that?"

So someone did know. "We found a couple of broken gates."

Cargan nodded. "I'm sure there are plenty more broken ones down there."

*Ugh.*

He kept going. "It took Father and his associates a long time to find ones that weren't all broken."

The king. He'd been in Compass Hill the first time I'd been to the city, sitting against a wall across the street from Miriam's house.

Meris studied her brother silently. He had come to a stop, and the long stretch of silence indicated that he wouldn't say anything else. Maybe he trusted us to figure out whatever it was.

The day of the battle, every person we'd seen on the streets had sprung into action, all of them, men and women, starting to fight, and I realized I couldn't remember seeing other kids besides Ira, and no one younger than him. Maybe I had when we'd first been here, because weeks had passed between our leaving Compass Hill and the day that Trenavell retook it. If Naolon's soldiers weren't paying much attention, then the kids could disappear.

Any civilians could leave. Everyone I'd seen had been fighting.

There was more than just one gate network, and Trenavell had used the one on Dupree's map to bring people here, switching civilians with soldiers, gambling and hoping that Naolon wouldn't notice.

Cargan's eyes were on me, and I sure hadn't been hiding my face.

"This is a military base, isn't it?" I asked.

He gave a single nod. "It is now."

Goosebumps coursed over my side, and I scratched again at the scar.

"Is that why it's all locked up?" Matt asked.

What were they guarding? It was easy to get out of the city if you were underground. Why bother locking anything up? The king clearly knew about the facility.

Cargan stared down at the counter. "Good a reason as any."

Naolon hadn't really kept the city locked. The gate hadn't even been closed.

Dupree's mention of a vulnerability in the letter had to mean the facility underground. Why bother with locking Compass Hill up if it could be readily accessed from the facility beneath it?

Meris cleared her throat. "Anya saw Iacomus in Salt's Creek."

Cargan looked up fast. "Where?"

"My teacher's house and at church." Did Iacomus know where I lived?

"Did he see you?" Cargan asked.

"I talked to him." My core shuddered.

Cargan's sharp eyes flicked to the street window. "I'll assume he'll be staying in Salt's Creek." He glanced at Meris' gun. "He knows who the four of you are."

Noam's face fell for a moment. "We know." His brown eyes went to mine.

Cargan straightened. "Danny, it's possible he knows your association with my sister."

Danny shrugged. "That wouldn't surprise me."

"Are y'all gonna come arrest him or something?" I asked.

Cargan narrowed his eyes. "Considering the massacre he participated in, we would have cause to, considering that the village wasn't exactly a battleground."

They knew about the massacre. A lump in my throat grew, and my heart started to race.

*I want to go home.*

Cargan kept talking. "It may be safer for all of you to stay in Compass Hill."

The noises from underground. The thud. Danny sleeping on top of the hatch, well able to flee into the street if he needed to.

The king asking about us. The fact that activating the device was so unexpected.

Matt read something in my expression as I met his.

"Danny's going to be staying in Salt's Creek later this year," Matt answered Cargan.

Danny smiled a little. "I'm trying to figure out getting home first." His pupils lit up as they flicked to me and back to Cargan. "But my aunt's not gonna kick me out."

Cargan tilted his head. "Your aunt?"

Danny clapped Matt on the shoulder. "Matt's mom, Jen Dobken."

Cargan's confusion stayed on his face.

Danny spoke slowly, measured. "My mother is Della Henderson."

Cargan blinked, his face clearing, his eyes sharpening again. "Will the three of you be safe in Salt's Creek?"

Salt's Creek had two gates in it, and one man I knew was an enemy, and who might not dare act. Salt's Creek had police officers. Salt's Creek had my parents.

I flinched at the memory of the stone wall cutting off the gate behind me.

"I think we'll be fine for now." My voice shook. *I want to go home.* A more distant part of me did want to come back, but for now, I did not want to be in Trenavell.

Cargan didn't betray anything in his face or voice. "Very well."

Danny stepped back from the counter. "I'll see them to the gate."

"Good." Cargan stepped back from the counter and bent down, and the hatch thumped onto the floor a couple seconds later. He disappeared into it, Meris and Noam following.

When we were all standing in the dark underground hallway, the other three walked away silently, and Danny led us through the facility.

We didn't say or hear anything else until we stepped out of the larger tunnel and into the field.

Matt cleared his throat, almost cautious. "Are you really okay?"

I glanced down at my shoe. It was still securely tied, the cut shoestring firmly knotted together where I'd fixed it, and that invited another mental image that I didn't want. What would have happened if I'd fully stopped to tie it? I'd half-fallen through the gate, but if I'd just been taking a step, without the momentum of a stumble sending my body safely out of the range of the gate…

"Yeah," I told Matt.

His face was solemn. "Okay."

Danny didn't say anything. Neither one of them had to. As we walked three across towards the woods, I was glad just to have them here. The quiet woods around us held no one.

I shivered.

Matt stopped at the gate and pulled the door open. "See ya, Danny."

"See you guys tomorrow," he answered.

Matt closed the door and set the bar in place, then stepped around me to go down the stairs into the cellar. This time, it was fine with me that he did that.

# Chapter 15

I'd fallen asleep the night before curled on my side, and I stretched out. One of my hands tingled as the nerves woke back up, and the little bit of headache I had complimented the weird, gross fuzziness of my teeth.

The clock said it was a little after eleven in the morning.

My stomach growled.

Matt and I had hung out after coming home, because when we'd gotten here it had still been early in the day. I wasn't sure how long we'd been in Trenavell. Maybe it was the same amount of time that had passed on Earth, or more. I hadn't even gone to bed that late last night.

My backpack sat on the floor by my bed, rigid with the plate inside it.

The plate.

I thought back to the room under the chapel, and the two boxes, at opposite ends of the room. The straight lines that led away from one, and the crooked burns raying out from the other, the charred insides a hint that something hadn't gone the way it was supposed to.

Had Dupree tried sealing all the gates when he was alive?

Why would he have done that? It wasn't even clear why, beyond helping Trenavell, the device would be used. What circumstances could Dupree possibly have planned for? He would have had no way of knowing that there would be a war that meant Trenavell would dubiously benefit from someone activating that device.

There had to be another purpose he'd had in mind.

My stomach growled again.

I sighed and headed downstairs.

As the chocolate cereal clattered into the bowl, I noticed the half pot of coffee left on the counter, cold now. I could heat it up. That sounded good.

A minute-and-a-half later, I added half-and-half and sugar to the reheated coffee and wrapped my hands around the mug.

Immediately, the image of a gruesome "might have" from yesterday came to mind.

*Stop stop stop.* I swallowed hard and went to the kitchen table, sitting down, shoving a spoonful of cereal in my mouth and chewing it robotically, then swallowing, letting the sweet milk cool my throat.

I was okay. I was fine. Not a single what-if had been reality. I still had all my limbs and I still had my life.

I was okay.

Once I'd washed the cereal bowl and the mug and left them in the drainer, I went back upstairs and changed quickly into a t-shirt and shorts, then crouched by my bed, pulling the map out of my backpack.

As far as I knew about maps, this one looked good. The only thing I didn't understand was why the train tracks were missing, when I knew they were supposed to be there. The missing tracks were a big difference between this map and Noam's, other than the gates. What did it mean that Dupree had left them out?

I stared down at the castle, and the Kings Road gate, noting the road that led to Compass Hill, my eyes drifting to the right where we went down into the tunnel.

My gaze caught first on a soft, unclear image by the entrance.

The map hadn't changed, but in the daylight streaming into my bedroom, I caught new details. Faint lines. I took the map to my window and held the paper closer to my eyes.

The difference became more evident.

With the map lit up brighter in the sun, I could tell the gate markings had faded more than the other ink on the map. Much lighter than both of these, remnants of lines in imperfectly erased pencil haunted paths that didn't follow the map's ink, but still matched up with the gate markings. They'd been there and been erased and replaced by the inky roads of Trenavell. I turned it over to see if there were indentations on the paper on the other side, but it was hard to tell. I guessed that, over the years, the paper had smoothed out anything like that.

Flipping it over, I studied the remnants again.

*He could have just reused the paper for this map.*

It had to have been something else before. Why did the ghost lines go well with the gate markings, if so?

Maybe it had been a map of somewhere else, and he'd disguised it. It would have still been useless as a gate map, then, wouldn't it? Still. He'd been working on something, and it had changed at some point during his process.

I grabbed my phone and shot a message to Matt.

*I don't know what time you're done later, but I took a closer look at the map, and I think it was of something else before.*

However I did it, I had to figure out why Dupree made the device, and what this map had been.

***

The slow hiss of a car driving by my house reached me as I waited on the steps of the back deck for Matt to come out of his house. Map in my hands, I faced the woods. I could briefly see the car's movement out of the corner of my eye before the other neighbors' house obscured it, though not enough to see if there was any brown.

The back door of the Dobken's house opened, and Matt walked up, shutting the door firmly behind him before making his way across the yard to my porch and sitting beside me.

His voice was quiet. "So you think the map was something else."

"There's places on it that look like pencil that was on there and erased."

He narrowed his eyes. "What do you think it was before?"

I shrugged. "It could have been a map of somewhere else and he reused the parchment." Had it had something to do with the boxes on the walls below the chapel? Maybe there'd been plans on this parchment, for each device in turn, the failed one and the one I'd used. I handed the map to Matt. "It could have been plans or something."

"For what?"

"The device." I could picture the burned stone in my mind. "Do you think he made two of them?"

Matt frowned. "Where do you think the other one is?"

"I think whatever powered it is across the room from the one we used." If Dupree had made two devices, making a second one after the first one malfunctioned badly, then why had he left clues that might not have been, and weren't, found until over a hundred and thirty years later?

Matt frowned. "Doesn't look like it worked very well, if it was burnt up like that."

"Yeah." The purpose was sealing the gates, but what was the reason he would have done that?

And people knew about it. "Do you think Mr. Simpson is passing information to your mom?"

Matt looked back up at me. "Do you think my mom would actually punish me if he was?"

I snorted. "I think yes, if she wanted to tip her hand, but she didn't say anything to Danny."

Matt looked like he was a little mad. "Okay, but it really seems like, after everything, she still wants to act like we're not space people and we're safe all the time."

I narrowed my eyes.

"So I don't care," he finished.

"Okay, fine. Guess I don't either." A rush of guilt coursed through me. I didn't like hiding this from my parents. They trusted me, and it was worse because of that. I crossed my arms on my legs and rested my chin there. "Never mind. I do."

Matt's voice was soft as he spoke. "If you told your parents the truth, would they believe you?"

I lifted my head. "I doubt it." I sighed. "I mean, maybe if your parents told them about it all."

"Do you think it'll come to that point?" he asked.

I shook my head. "No idea. I don't even know what we're doing all this for." An edge of frustration crept up inside me. "We put that device together, and that maybe wasn't supposed to be done, and now Trenavell might be watching us." Absently, I scratched at the tickle in the scar.

Matt stared at me, anger hardening his face again for a second. "Yeah."

I drummed on the deck steps. "But then again…there's this map and Dupree set it all up for a reason, and we found that whole whatever it is underneath the city. And with the map looking like it was something else, even if we have no idea what that is…I mean, there's something more, right?"

"What?" he asked.

"Something more in all of this." I met Matt's eyes. "It's gotta be more than the device, and now that car keeps showing up, and there's a gate to Compass Hill in the train station downtown."

Matt nodded.

"We should head to Trenavell." It wasn't too late. "I guess I should go get some warm clothes on. Meet you back here?"

"Yeah." Matt pushed up from the step. "See you in a few."

I let myself back in the house. The air conditioning inside wasn't that much of a relief this time. The walk through the woods would warm us up plenty.

Twenty minutes later, we slipped into the Dupree house. The minimal breeze there stopped short as we stepped inside and the stuffy air closed over us.

"Ugh," I said.

Matt laughed quietly. "Agreed."

As we walked down the hallway, I could half-imagine someone hiding upstairs, listening to our footsteps creaking over the old floors and the single words we'd spoken.

Goosebumps ran over my skin. I scratched the scar, wishing my heart would slow down. Even if someone was up there, we were almost to Trenavell. There would maybe be people around, and if not, we were close to the road and close to Compass Hill.

And we could run.

I pulled my coat on as we walked across the cellar to the light spilling down from the top of the staircase. It glowed brighter for some reason.

"Are there more moss lamps?" I asked.

"Huh?'

"It looks brighter up there," I told him as we climbed. The light wasn't as gold or as soft as I knew the moss lamps should be. It shone colder and harsher.

We rounded the staircase.

The door in the side of the mountain stood wide open. My stomach dropped.

Matt turned to me, his eyes flashing in the winter light. "Um…"

I glanced behind me, down the stairs, and turned back to Matt. "Just…go?"

If there was someone in the house, waiting on the stairs wasn't a great idea.

Matt nodded quickly and hurried up the rest of the way.

We slowed a little, stepping quietly out of the side of the mountain. I pulled the door tightly closed behind us. The door frame squeaked from the pressure I put on it.

"I wish we could lock it from this side," I murmured.

Matt's eyes flicked over the door for a second. "Yeah."

The quiet woods and empty road, cheerful under the bright morning sunlight, set off the blue sky, clear and streaked with long, thin clouds. Trenavell echoed late fall days on Earth.

My eyes found a darker shape in the sky, an orange semicircle that poked through the blue like a half-fastened button.

The moon.

Shuddering, I realized that this was the first time I'd ever noticed it during the day. It being out in the day made sense. If so many other things were so similar to Earth, why would the moon here work differently?

"What?" Matt asked, following my gaze to the sky.

"Do you...does the moon here creep you out?" I asked softly.

He stared at it for a second and shrugged. "Not really."

"It's just so dark," I said. "At night."

He looked away from it, a little smile on his face. "It's...not that dark for me."

I blinked. "Oh...yeah." My face warmed. "Yeah, it wouldn't be, would it?" I hadn't even thought about that, that my best friend came from people made to see well at night under a dimmer moon than Earth's.

Matt laughed.

The heavy quiet seethed as we ducked into the tunnel and clicked our flashlights on.

"Where do you think Danny is?" I asked quietly.

Matt's flashlight beam bounced as he shrugged. "In the store or with Meris and Noam. It's morning."

Maybe Danny wasn't up yet, though that was doubtful.

Our footsteps echoed.

"The front of the tunnel was empty," I said. "And I didn't see either of those burrow beasts." My breath fogged in the chill.

"They could have migrated," Matt offered.

We'd seen one breach the ground in front of us, but I wasn't even sure then what direction we'd been headed, let alone where it was headed. But it had been fall. That assumed that burrow beasts migrated exactly like birds going south for the winter on Earth.

Maybe they went to the part of Trenavell that would be less likely to have frozen ground, wherever this country sat on the planet's surface. "They could."

We reached the open area and crossed it quickly. I eyed the chunks of debris along the side, and the pillars, knowing the latter made good hiding places. I thought of the wide tunnel, and the ones that turned off the main one, and the signs. As Matt opened one of the double doors, I looked back at the tunnel.

It was a tunnel, yes, but it was so like a highway tunnel, and the wide, flat space between us and it suddenly resolved into something I knew I recognized, as empty as it was and as stripped as it had been of markings.

A parking lot.

The door squeaked as it shifted in Matt's grasp. "What?" he whispered.

"This is a parking lot." My eyes found the debris again.

Matt looked around. "What parked here?

The most advanced piece of recognizable technology that I had seen in Trenavell had been the train. Every other vehicle hadn't been any more than a horse cart. "I don't know."

The buzz of the gate shutting off behind me echoed in my memory. I could picture the lines that ran through the stone from the box below the device. The wheel, when I turned it, had jolted in my hands, and the round compartment on the other end of the room under the chapel had all those burns in the stone around it.

Trenavell didn't make sense.

Matt pushed the door open wider. "Let's get to the store."

The less open space would have been where people entered the facility. The level we were on now differed strongly from the level with all the gates. While that looked like an airport, this level may have held offices and other workspaces.

"I think people worked up here," I whispered. "Like…this is the corporate side of an airport." Did the first turnoff in the tunnel lead to other parking?

Meris wanted to go to Skyrren, the old capital. The seat of government.

A book that Gavin Dupree had hidden there, somewhere, might actually have information. I didn't know what Dupree had meant when he talked about there only being a few people who were supposed to know certain information. But maybe, if we could get to Skyrren and see any sort of library, the kingdom archives, or a visual puzzle like the one he'd used for the device keys, then things would make sense.

If the underground facility hadn't been so big, I would have wondered, again, why Compass Hill. But the big highway tunnels and the number of passages and gates on the lowest level curbed that. Compass Hill had been something, long before it was a cobbled-together city by itself in a plain surrounded by mountains. And it connected directly to Gavin Dupree's hometown.

"We should find Skyrren." Our flashlights only made the shadows in these offices a little less deep. This time, I didn't hear the noises that we'd heard before, but that just made me think that they were even more out of place.

Matt let out a quiet sigh. "I agree, but it's not a really safe city, even without the radiation."

"Yeah, but we're not soldiers." Meris was always armed, and technically, with the bayonet in my backpack, so was I. The five of us still wouldn't look like a threat to whoever was in Skyrren. They'd for sure watched me and Matt as we'd made our way along the streets on the edge of the city, but only acted when Naolon passed through. The chill from thinking fully through those minutes when we'd hid raced over me. Whoever they were, they hadn't exactly engaged Naolon in a real fight. They'd ambushed them.

It could be that they wouldn't want Naolon or Trenavell to be in Skyrren, but why did the people there want Skyrren at all, if it was supposed to be too dangerous to live in?

"What if there's more than one gate to Skyrren?" Matt asked. "It's a big city."

I tilted my head. "That would be useful." Blinking, I thought about how the deepest level of this facility was structured like an airport. Cities could have more than one of something like that. "I should have brought a notebook or sketchbook or something. We could at least keep track of where we go down there."

We reached the door that led into the cellar under the storefront, and I opened it. The cellar was empty, and the hatch that led to the floor closed.

Matt gestured for me to go first, so I climbed up and pushed.

The hatch met resistance, moving less than a quarter of an inch. A voice upstairs exclaimed, and someone moved along the floor in an awkward shuffle. Once they'd moved, the hatch opened freely.

Danny peered down, and I jumped before fully registering that it was his face. He smiled. "Hey."

The strain in his voice cracked the edge of his greeting, and the skin under his eyes looked shadowed as I climbed up into the shop and crawled away from the opening.

Matt frowned as Danny shut the hatch. "You okay, man?"

Danny smiled again. "I'm good."

What was happening? Had he been going without sleep? "You look really tired." He hadn't been up. I didn't think it was really early morning, so we'd woken him up by opening the hatch.

"I wasn't able to get to sleep last night," he answered. "It's calmed down right now, but I kept hearing some noises from underground, plus there's something going on in the city." He hesitated. "Compass Hill's gates are unlocked and open."

"What else?" Matt asked.

Danny yawned. "Well, the reason I couldn't really sleep anywhere last night was the fact that there were a lot of soldiers that showed up, so I was trying to evade and figure out what was going on." His face settled into a decidedly troubled expression, exacerbated by the dark circles under his eyes.

"Did you?" I asked.

Slowly, Danny shook his head, yawning again.

A soft creak sounded from below us, and the thump of steps up the ladder followed. Something struck the hatch just before it started to open.

The end of a rifle barrel preceded Meris' appearance. As she looked at me and Matt, her eyebrows rose.

"Good morning," she said, and climbed out the rest of the way, Noam behind her. None of us spoke as they closed the hatch and settled into place.

Maybe Meris knew what was going on. "So Danny said Compass Hill's been pretty busy."

Meris nodded. "I passed along the information about Iacomus, so I assume that there may be an upcoming effort to apprehend him, and soldiers have arrived in that effort."

Alarm and confusion rose in turn. The only ways Trenavellan soldiers could possibly get to Salt's Creek was through the Kings Road gate or the train station gate, assuming they even knew about that one. "But…I only told y'all yesterday." If the gate network was sealed, they'd have to come over land for a lot of the way.

"They may have used the gates below the city," Meris offered.

Why would a city fill up with a bunch of soldiers, though? "How many do they think are going to go to Salt's Creek to get Iacomus?"

She shrugged.

Glancing at Noam, I kept talking. "He doesn't really have soldiers guarding him in Salt's Creek, at least as far as I'm aware." It wasn't great that anyone who came after him would have to go through my neighborhood, down Highway 58, or through downtown. And how would they even find him, anyway?

Noam spoke up. "I don't think the soldiers are in Compass Hill so they can get to Earth and detain Iacomus."

Matt rested his head on his hand. "Were they pulled from other towns that were retaken?"

"I would hope not," Noam answered. "They might have pulled only a few from each for that to make sense."

"Do you know what Naolon is up to?" Danny asked, his voice dragging.

"Not much of note," Meris told him. "But it also doesn't make sense for them to not do anything."

"Maybe there aren't that many people from there that can fight," I said. "If Trenavell managed to get back control of this city and other ones, then it's pretty likely they did some damage to Naolon's forces." How had Naolon taken over in the first place, and had they just gotten lazy or something in the years between their takeover of Trenavell and the day I activated the device?

"Meris, wasn't your dad gonna abdicate or something?"

She nodded.

"What kind of government was he going to step aside for?" What had Matt said?

Meris narrowed her eyes. "I…" She looked stumped, maybe like she didn't remember.

"Representative," Noam offered, steadily and surely.

"How far'd he get?" Danny asked, voice cracking.

"Clearly not far," Meris said drily.

Noam added more. "From what I know, the transition was only in the beginning stages. It had been announced and they were planning to summon the governors to discuss the formation of the new government, and Meris' parents were planning to stay in their positions during the transition."

"Governors?" Meris asked, perplexed.

We had governors at home, but the ones in Trenavell seemed like they might be different. "How did that work?"

Noam shrugged. "Regional governors carried out the laws made by the king and queen, who ruled with equal power."

Meris' eyes were wide. "I…truly did not know that there were governors." She paused. "And there aren't any now."

"Why not?" Matt asked.

"Naolon," Meris said. "And…there hasn't been much time since retaking our country to reestablish the previous structure…" She trailed off.

There really hadn't been a lot of time. But the governors had been an extension of the kingdom before, and somehow everything had fallen apart.

Trenavell had handily retaken their country in a very short time, after being under occupation for thirteen years. I wanted to know more about what had happened when Noam and Meris had been kids, but I didn't want to offend them and wind up insinuating that Trenavell had messed up or something.

"Do y'all…know anything else about what happened back then?" I asked.

Meris blinked. "What do you mean?"

I took a deep breath. "Did Trenavell…fall to Naolon really quickly?"

Her face hardened.

*Uh-oh.*

"Yes," Noam answered.

Meris shot him a hard look.

Noam met her gaze. "What is there to be ashamed about?"

She huffed.

It was clear that Trenavell wasn't lacking people to fight, or skill. How had they managed to lose control of their country so completely?

Did the device have anything to do with that part? Why would Cargan have been talking about it?

"We should go to Skyrren," I said.

Meris straightened, her face brightening. "I'm sure that there should be at least one gate that will take us there."

Matt rolled his eyes as I glanced at him. Meris was probably right, but there wasn't a single sign in the facility that any of us could read. Plus, it was huge. We'd have to look everywhere. It would still take time, and we'd have to make sure it was actually Skyrren that we found. The only other gate we'd found that actually went to somewhere on this planet only had ruins, and I'd only seen part of Skyrren last time.

"Meris, it's going to take us a while, and you don't even know what Skyrren looks like," I told her.

She lifted her chin. "I believe I would know what a palace looks like."

"Skyrren is a large city," Noam argued. "Also, when we go, we know it may not necessarily be safe for us."

She swept a hand at me and Matt. "They were safe there."

"Not that safe," I said.

"You lived," she argued.

"We did then," Matt snapped. "Whoever was there was really close to us, and I'm pretty sure they were watching us the whole time." He paused. "There was a guy killed right in the shop we were in, not real long after his group was ambushed."

"The ones watching could be our allies," Meris said.

Danny cleared his throat. "It might be a good idea to reach out to whoever's there."

We were still going to Skyrren, but a thrill of fear shot through me.

"What?" Matt turned to his cousin.

Danny's face stayed calm and solemn, part of that possibly from fatigue. "They ambushed Naolon and left you and Anya alone." He took a deep breath. "Meris might be right."

Meris' smile grew more and more smug.

Danny kept going. "I think we should wait like a day, though."

"Why?" Meris asked.

Danny's mouth quirked. "I'm tired." But as he shot a glance at me and Matt, I could see that wasn't the only reason. He *was* tired. That was obvious. But he had another idea.

Meris let out a deep sigh. "Fine. We'll search tomorrow. We will start as early as possible and look through as many functional gates as possible."

"Sure," I answered her, wondering at the same time what in the world it was that Danny had on his mind. "We'll get here as early as we can."

Which meant, if we went home now, we could go to the library, depending on what time it was when we got home.

And what was Danny up to? He didn't seem too keen to tell Meris and Noam anything, but he did want to tell us something.

"Let's go home, then," Matt told me. "You want to come by my house, Danny?"

Danny hesitated, going still, his eyes calculating. "Sure." His eyes widened just a little bit, offering a deeper meaning. He definitely had more to say.

"Okay," Matt answered.

"So…we could go to the library today," I said.

Matt's eyebrows rose. "Sounds good."

We stood, and Danny opened the hatch as soon as everyone had backed away. Meris led the way down the ladder and into the shop's cellar. Danny pulled the hatch closed, and we walked into the passage.

Meris stopped short at the figure standing in the hallway. My heart started to pound.

"Meris, if you all are going to be sneaking around, you need to be a little quieter." Cargan's voice stayed quiet, but firm.

Meris sighed. "Brother, we are alone."

His long-suffering look steadied on his sister. "No, you weren't, because I was able to find you."

"Why were you looking for us?"

With a deep breath, his eyes unfocused for a moment. "Father and Mother are." His eyes widened as they fixed again on Meris. "It will be up to you if you want to report to them."

Meris drew back. "Are all the soldiers here because of what I told you about Iacomus?"

Cargan smiled a little. "No. They've been on their way."

The device.

Cargan had told me, that one day in the chapel, that the fact that we were here meant that everything was always more complex than a war between two countries. Compass Hill didn't make sense for the location of the device, since it hadn't been the capital when Gavin Dupree was alive. He'd known about the underground facility, which was huge and abandoned, decorated in at least one place with tourism posters.

"What's the lowest level?" I asked. "What was it?"

Cargan's focus turned to me, his face guarded. "We're not entirely sure, beyond its usefulness."

Something in me deflated a little, but could that mean that not too many people knew about the gate that led to Salt's Creek?

Cargan kept going. "We do not need a great number of people finding their way there."

"Why?" Meris asked.

"It's not a safe place to be," Cargan answered.

So he couldn't tell us why it looked so much like a travel facility. At least he wasn't trying to keep us from looking at it.

"Why not?" Meris asked.

Cargan's face closed off. "Broken gates."

Meris stepped forward. "They're not all broken."

"Of course they're not." Her brother picked up the moss lamp lantern at his feet. "But if you want to go to Skyrren, be careful."

"Skyrren's safe?" Noam asked.

Cargan nodded. "I can guarantee that."

Meris turned to us, a smile growing.

Danny yawned.

"I can guarantee it after tomorrow, sister," Cargan continued firmly.

Meris looked around at us, her fingers drumming on her rifle strap, then at Noam, then at her brother. "Very well. How would we get there?"

"I'll be accompanying you there," Cargan answered.

"Surely Father needs you on duty," Meris said.

"I'll. Be. Accompanying. You." Cargan turned. "Again, if you want to report to Father and Mother, that is your decision."

"Would you recommend it?" Noam asked.

Cargan started walking away. "Not yet." He turned a corner somewhere down the hallway.

Meris sighed. "I suppose we'll see you tomorrow, then."

"Sounds good," Danny answered with another yawn.

"Yeah." I stared down the hallway as Meris and Noam followed the path Cargan had taken.

My eyes had adjusted some, enough to see the dark doors and windows, and the turn at the end. Nothing in here was narrow by any means, but not being able to actually see all that far, and with us not fully knowing how to navigate this part of the city…

Danny led us, without a stumble, back to the wide space between the facility and the tunnel. The few pieces of debris stood guard alongside the parking lot. I doubted that a closer inspection would actually reveal what the pieces were from.

"This has to have been a parking lot," I told the guys.

Danny's eyes flashed as he turned his head to me. "For what?"

Not cars, to be sure. "Well…we have seen horse carts before, so…" I pointed my flashlight up to have a look at the ceiling. The beam reflected clusters of dull circles.

"Where're the stables?" Danny asked, his tone contemplative.

With a look back at the double doors we'd come through, I realized he was right. It wasn't practical to lead a horse through that facility. That was office space, settled above a station for travel. The plentiful reflective clusters above us, if they were anything other than a decoration, could have been lights, which meant that this parking lot would have been well-lit when it was being used.

I pointed my flashlight at one of the doors along the wall. "There could have been stables that way." The light caught a piece of debris.

"Could have been," Matt answered as we passed into the tunnel, his voice echoing strangely between the two spaces.

Since there had been sounds and noises and probably activity, conversation wasn't the best idea, and we all stayed quiet until reaching the ramp that would take us up to the field.

A noise to my left drew my attention as soon as we stepped onto the dry grass.

The smaller burrow beast watched us from twenty feet away, its small black eyes intent and shining in the cold sunlight. The front of its face wriggled with a loud snuffling noise, and its head tilted just before the back half of its body wiggled.

A hissing bellow, ending in a high note, came from behind it, and I looked past the creature to see the much larger one, yards past its offspring, but not approaching.

The smaller one responded, turning to its parent and making the same sound in a higher pitch, almost squeaking at the end, then crawled away from us without another look.

Both creatures moved away from us, the younger one kicking up clumps of dirt as it went, almost playfully.

My knees started to shake as they left. Distantly, the thought that the little one was cute popped into my head, a cognitive tension with the relief that they were herbivores that had decided not to retreat into their nest in the tunnel and run over us.

I turned to the guys, trying to keep my knees steady, and let out a shaky sigh. "So…Danny, do you want to go to the library, too?"

Both his eyes and Matt's were wide as they focused on me. "Yeah." He looked at Matt. "Um, I need to borrow some clothes again."

"Sure," Matt answered.

"What's at the library?" Danny asked, yawning.

"I'm not sure," I admitted, as we started to walk towards the road. "But…I want to see if there's anything about Gavin Dupree other than the old microfilm stuff about the murder case." It wasn't Friday. Lukas Simpson would probably be there, unless he had a random day off. "Matt and I found a letter from Gavin Dupree that said he had hidden a book in Skyrren."

"Do you think there would be a copy in Salt's Creek?" Matt asked.

I shook my head. "A book might not be, but information about him writing a book could be." I paused. "And you never know. If he wrote a book and gave a copy to the library, or someone else did, it might be there."

Danny spoke up. "And if they don't have one, they might know about it."

Matt nodded. "Mr. Simpson will probably tell my parents, especially if Danny is with us."

The nearly bare branches rustled in the wind as we reached the Kings Road gate.

I remembered how Danny had looked at us. Had he been communicating anything at all? He wasn't saying anything right now, and maybe that was because he was tired.

We could go to the library first. Maybe he'd find time to tell us.

# Chapter 16

I pulled into an empty parking spot at the library and eyed the front entrance. An employee stood behind one of the doors, wiping it rapidly with a paper towel. A man pulled the other door open and went in.

Danny yawned in the back seat.

"It's weird how we weren't there all that long," I said. I wasn't tired like Danny, but I knew I would be by the end of what would be a longer than normal day. I wouldn't be tired for any reason that would be evident to anyone else but Matt and Danny.

"Not that weird," Matt said. "Not for Trenavell."

"I know, it's just gonna be a really long day." I unbuckled my seatbelt. I couldn't help the nerves that built up in my core. "Especially for Danny."

He shrugged with his easy smile.

Matt grabbed his door handle. “What are you gonna ask Mr. Simpson about if he’s here?”

“Dupree’s book.” Mr. Simpson knew about the gate in the Dupree house. He knew who we were and what we’d done. I didn’t know how to ask things without actually volunteering information, and it might be better to just pretend that we knew nothing. I reached for the little notebook I had and cracked the car door open.

The staircase inside was empty and quiet. As we reached the section of the building where the local history room was, I saw the man who’d been at the front door when we’d arrived, standing in front of one of the big counters and talking to a librarian there. He glanced at us as we went by, then looked way.

We stopped at the door to the local history room and looked in. Mr. Simpson sat at his desk, moving things around. He’d eventually notice us. I pulled the door open.

At the quiet squeak of the hinges, Mr. Simpson looked up at us and smiled. “Good afternoon,” he said.

“Good afternoon,” I answered, my voice cracking a little.

“Good to see you Matt,” Mr. Simpson continued as Matt and I stopped at the desk, Danny behind us. “What can I help you kids with today?”

“Genealogical research,” I answered. “I’m Anya McCall, and I’m wanting to look into some family stuff.”

Mr. Simpson smiled. "Well, y'all can have a seat and I'll see how I can help you."

I nodded and pulled a chair out. Matt sat beside me, and Danny sat to his right.

Mr. Simpson looked at Matt first. "How are your folks doing?"

Matt hesitated for a second. "They're doing all right."

"And who's this guy with you?" he asked. "I see some family resemblance."

Danny sat up. "Danny Henderson. Matt's mom is my aunt."

"Good to meet you," Mr. Simpson answered. "Matt, if you could pass along a hello to your parents for me, I'd sure appreciate that." He opened a notebook on his desk. "So. Genealogy."

I took a breath. "A guy from Salt's Creek, Gavin Dupree, was one of my ancestors, and I want to know a little more about him."

With a nod, Mr. Simpson jotted something down in his notebook. "Do you have a good idea of where to start?"

I grasped for something, and the map came to mind. That was innocuous enough. "I know he was tried for a murder, but as far as his life…was he into cartography?"

Mr. Simpson's face brightened. "He was an amateur cartographer, and we have some of his work that his oldest daughter donated to the library. Maps of Salt's Creek and Sanders County."

Could he have had anything hidden in those? "That sounds pretty interesting." I wouldn't know what to look for that wasn't the wheel.

"It is," Mr. Simpson agreed. "We don't have them on display right now, but I could bring them out if you'd like."

I glanced at the guys. "We might have to take a look at those." I paused, remembering the letter we'd found. "But also…um…we read something about Dupree and a book. Like…maybe he wrote one?"

Mr. Simpson's eyebrows dipped in puzzlement. "Huh. I'm…not sure I've ever heard that he wrote one."

*Maybe it just wasn't published here.* After all, he'd written that to Matt's ancestors. They were moon-eyes. Maybe it was just something he'd passed along.

Matt leaned forward a little. "Do you think there's a manuscript somewhere if he did write one?"

Mr. Simpson shrugged. "There could be. It's possible that if anything like that were donated, we might not have realized what it was."

Why had Dupree hidden a book in Skyrren? The Davies had lived on Ocracoke, and Mrs. Dobken's parents still lived there. Had Matt's ancestors been from Skyrren? That would make sense.

I cleared my throat. "Was Dupree originally from Salt's Creek?"

"He was." Mr. Simpson smiled. "In fact, his family can be traced all the way back to the town's founding in the 1700s."

"Oh," I said. "That's cool."

"Dupree was actually descended from a man named Abraham Saltz. It took a couple generations for the Dupree name to pop up." He eyed Matt and smiled a little. "And your family is more or less new to the area."

"Right," Matt told him. "Dad's from Charlotte, Mom's from Ocracoke."

"NC State?" Mr. Simpson continued.

"Yes, sir."

"Me too, but I was a few years ahead of their time." Mr. Simpson leaned back. "Always makes me wonder how some folks ended up in this little town."

Why had the Dobkens moved here? There was a whole lot more in Raleigh and Charlotte than there was in Salt's Creek. They were connected to the Dupree family, socially if by nothing else, and if his mom had wanted to avoid her heritage so much, why move here?

"And correct me if I'm wrong," Mr. Simpson said to Danny, "but your aunt has told me that her sister lives in Michigan."

Danny nodded. "That's right. We live in Ypsilanti."

"Quite a ways to come visit," Mr. Simpson said casually.

I tried to keep my face neutral. Was Mr. Simpson fishing for information?

"Not too bad on a plane," Danny answered with a smile.

"True," Mr. Simpson agreed. "So Matt, you headed to NC State for college?"

Matt shrugged. "Not sure yet."

We hadn't talked about that kind of stuff. I felt a pang at remembering that.

Mr. Simpson nodded quietly, his face patient and expectant.

I picked at one of my cuticles. "So do you think there are maps that Dupree made other than the ones he donated to the library?"

"You mean in other government buildings?" Mr. Simpson considered, tilting his head. "It's possible, but I don't know if there are many on display. They might just be part of records."

"What else do you know about him?" Matt asked.

Mr. Simpson laughed softly. "I'm not a scholar on his life, but I definitely know the big story."

"The trial," I said. Would he be another person that would assure us that there was no way Gavin Dupree was guilty, that he was a good man, that he was framed?

"You have some familiarity with it." Mr. Simpson's eyebrows rose. "Want to guess why he was acquitted?"

"He was innocent," Matt said, voice dry, almost sarcastic.

"Maybe he was, or not," Mr. Simpson answered. "There was not enough evidence to prove a single thing happened to James Abney. Dupree had an injury to his arm, Abney had been to his house after a public disagreement, after which Abney disappeared, and an arrest and charge were made. Evidence was very circumstantial."

"That's not really fair," I protested, like it hadn't happened well over a hundred years ago.

"No, and I can tell you as well that the acquittal was not popular among the louder folks in town, specifically anyone who was more apt to believe the paper." Mr. Simpson smirked. "Neither was the Dupree family popular after that. But whether Gavin Dupree did it or not, there was little evidence, and it was the 1880s."

"So…was James Abney really popular?" Matt asked.

"Yeah, why would people want Dupree to be convicted so bad?" I added.

Mr. Simpson rocked his desk chair a little. "James Abney was quite wealthy and had a lot of influence in town." He paused. "He gave a lot of money to make sure he had that influence. I wouldn't say by any means that he owned the town, but he had a voice and seemed to have been willing to offer plenty of incentive to make sure that voice was heard loud and clear, and listened to." He glanced down at his desk for a moment. "He was popular amongst certain people, but he didn't win over everyone."

What he was saying sounded like it was colored with his opinion, but Mr. Simpson also came across as pretty neutral regarding Gavin Dupree. "I guess Abney's donations and stuff are all on record."

"Sure are," he answered. "The *Salt's Creek Advance* published plenty of glowing articles, and there are also financial records to back up a good portion of those donations."

I thought for a minute. What if Dupree had been jealous or something? It was petty, but his family had been here from the beginning of the town. What if he didn't like Abney's influence?

"So were they rivals?" Matt asked.

"I doubt it," Mr. Simpson answered. "The Duprees were well-off, and Gavin had his own farm by this time. The one point of conflict was that town meeting before Abney's disappearance."

I'd have to look more into who James Abney had been. "So is there any information on Abney here?"

Mr. Simpson shook his head. "Not much. Articles about his financial contributions. The trial. An obituary."

"Was Abney from here?" Matt asked.

"No. He and his wife came to Salt's Creek two years before his disappearance."

"From where?" I asked.

"We don't know," Mr. Simpson answered. "He may not have said."

Danny shifted in his chair as I looked at him and Matt.

"It's the unfortunate reality of historical records," Mr. Simpson continued. "We don't always have everything."

We weren't likely to find that out, either. "Well…going back to Gavin Dupree…other than the trial, and records and stuff, is there anything here that we could find out more from?" I smiled, trying to joke a little. "I mean, I don't guess there was a biography written about him."

Mr. Simpson laughed. "No, unfortunately there wasn't. Don't I wish, though."

I knew there wasn't going to be an obvious link to Trenavell in anything we found here about Gavin Dupree. The only thing was his amateur cartography, and that was only clear because we had one of his maps. Would there be any land records for when he passed his property on to Mrs. Barnes' parents? Probably. Just because the price for it was odd didn't mean it hadn't been an official transaction.

So much of the information about Dupree centered around the encounter with James Abney, a rich guy from somewhere else who'd gained the favor of Salt's Creek and had maybe died and maybe hadn't and who'd left behind a murder trial that had followed my family. There was no way every single person in town had been a fan of Abney's, so why had he zeroed in on Gavin Dupree enough to show up at his house? Had they known each other in a place that wasn't Salt's Creek?

But I couldn't ask that yet, assuming Mr. Simpson even knew more than he was saying. I knew he talked to Matt's parents. We were watched enough.

I sighed. "Well…I guess all this stuff is definitely something to think about." I looked over at Matt. "We should probably get going, though." Slowly, I stood.

Matt nodded, and he and Danny got up, too.

Mr. Simpson smiled. "Well, y'all feel free to come back any time. I'm not usually in on Fridays, but the room's open even if I'm not here."

"Thank you, Mr. Simpson," I said.

"Yeah, thanks," Matt added.

"Y'all are welcome." Mr. Simpson nodded. "Tell your parents I said hello. Nice to meet you, Anya, Danny."

"Same here," Danny answered.

I gave Mr. Simpson another smile and made my way to the door with Matt. We quietly walked down the stairs and out to my car. I got in, buckled my seatbelt, and turned the car on once the guys were in.

"Matt…we met when we were four, right?"

"Yeah," Matt answered. "Why?"

I started thinking. "Did y'all move to town right when we met?"

Matt blinked. "I think so." He looked back at Danny.

"I don't remember," Danny answered. "We already lived in Michigan by then."

A figure moved behind my car, visible in the rearview mirror, and I registered that it was the same guy we'd seen entering the library and talking to the librarian upstairs.

"Matt…if your mom was aware of all this stuff, why would she live here if she didn't also want to be up front with her ancestry?"

Matt exchanged a glance with his cousin and looked down. "Good question."

"Also, I think there's no way possible that James Abney was some random dude who didn't like Gavin Dupree."

"Do you think Abney was from Trenavell?" Danny asked.

"Maybe," I said. "We still don't know if Dupree was a killer."

"It kinda sounds like he wasn't," Matt told me.

"But why would Abney try to ruin Dupree's life?" I asked, backing out of the parking space.

"I think it would take figuring out James Abney, but no one knows where he was from," Matt said.

I let out a heavy sigh. "This is frustrating." I paused. "There's no way that Trenavell has nothing about Dupree."

"That stuff's gotta be in Skyrren," Danny said as I backed out of the space.

I tried not to look too closely for brown cars on the way home.

When we arrived at my house, Danny had his phone out, tapping on the screen.

"Checking in with my mom," he said. "I'm gonna see if she can send a picture of moon-eye letters, with pronunciations, so we can see if they match the stuff down in the facility."

I hadn't thought about that. "Do y'all speak that?"

Danny pocketed his phone. "I don't. I can understand some of it, can't really read it, but if there are some similarities in the letters, I can compare them, assuming it's the same language."

"Do you think it might be?" Matt asked.

"It does look familiar," Danny answered.

My memory went immediately to the day we'd found the copper disc in the woods. Matt had looked at it before telling me that the writing on it looked familiar. My eyes snapped to his.

"Matt…the copper disc…"

He nodded slowly. "Yeah. Familiar."

My theory about the burned stone being from a first attempt at the device was probably wrong. Dupree could have copied it, but if there was a degree of familiarity in more than one source, if both Matt and Danny had seen things that they recognized other than the disc, then whatever the compartment surrounded by burnt stone was predated Dupree, and so did the rest of the facility. Meris and Noam had never even said anything much about the facility, which was fair enough, since they hadn't lived there for most of their lives. The noises could be Trenavellans moving around, and all those soldiers had shown up at the city. But most of the gates we'd seen were broken, except for the Salt's Creek gate, and Cargan had even said that it had taken a long time for his dad and his dad's associates to find ones that did work. They'd known about it, and planned around it.

The facility had been integral to retaking the city, and, nearly a hundred and thirty years ago, it had been the setting and the foundation of Dupree's work to seal all the gates.

"Good idea, Danny," I said softly.

He yawned. "Thanks." He grinned. "Think I should hide from Aunt Jen this time?"

"How would you do that?" I asked.

Danny shrugged. "It wouldn't be all that hard, not if we're heading back to Trenavell tomorrow."My phone let out a ding, and I pulled it out of my pocket.

*Hey, Anya, it's Joanna Whitley. Are you free next Friday night, at six-thirty?*

The stark letters on the screen sent my pulse spiking. Friday at seven meant she was probably going out with someone. It was probably Jake Andrews.

Iacomus.

Sweat broke out at my hairline, and the nerves shot from my core up into my teeth.

"What?" Matt asked.

"Miss Whitley." I couldn't blink.

Matt's eyes roved over my face, his expression dead serious. "She needs you to babysit."

"Yeah. Possibly a date with Jake."

Danny stepped closer. "So Iacomus is still in town."

I let out a shaking laugh full of fear and dread. "I don't think he's going anywhere."

Matt glanced down at my phone and back up at me. "Should you go?"

*No.* "I need the money."

He frowned. "Do you?"

"I also need to get information." Would Jake say anything else to me?

"What do you think he'd tell you?" Matt's voice rose.

"I don't know." Looking down at my phone again, I unlocked it and read the message. Maybe Miss Whitley wouldn't be going out with Jake, but I couldn't ask.

*Sure, that would be fine.*

Thirty seconds later, a "thanks, see you then" came through, and I replied "you're welcome" before looking up at Matt.

Danny pulled his phone back out. "Mom sent them."

Matt and I both turned to his cousin.

"Where does she even keep stuff like that?" I asked.

Danny shrugged. "Probably her and Dad's office."

"Is it a book?" Matt asked.

Danny studied his phone screen. "Nah, what she sent me looks like she took pictures of some computer printouts." He held the screen out to me and Matt and slowly scrolled through the three of them.

The white papers on the screen had creased corners and worn holes punched on the sides. One of the pages was dog-eared. Hand-drawn letters joined basic typed words, and I could see speckles here and there on the pages.

Had Mrs. Henderson made this, or had someone sent it to her? Was this passed around to different people? "Where'd she get it?"

A flash of movement in the corner of my eye made all my nerves come alive, and a dark blue SUV drove by.

Danny put his phone away again. "I don't know." He yawned. "Once I get home, I can ask her."

We'd never really fully understood why Danny was in Trenavell. What he'd been up to. Why he kept appearing during our long journey in Trenavell, though I knew he'd used the gate network that I'd sealed.

"Danny..." I started.

"I don't know enough to tell you more yet." His reply came before I could even think of how to structure my sentence.

I swallowed hard.

"Still planning on being here in the fall?" Matt asked.

"Yeah." Danny smirked. "Let's go inside."

Quietly, I followed the guys into Matt's house. I remembered Danny telling us about the third faction that his mom and dad worked with. He didn't know anything about Rebecca Davis and Lukas Simpson, but Matt's parents did. Was this even the same puzzle? The only link between Danny's family and these two people that were here in Salt's Creek was Matt's mom.

Was she part of it? She couldn't be. She'd actively avoided her own heritage, but that didn't explain why she and Mr. Dobken even spoke at all to Mr. Simpson. He'd come to their house, so late at night, after we'd sealed the gates. Was Mrs. Dobken just trying to keep tabs, maybe to assert some sort of control over all of this?

Matt unlocked the front door of his house and led us into the starkly different climate. His parents kept their house cool, too. I shuffled behind the other two, trying to think. All three of us had spoken to Mr. Simpson at the library. We'd asked questions about Gavin Dupree, and I knew he'd pass the information along to Matt's parents, should he meet with them sometime soon. I didn't know what Mrs. Dobken would do with that information. She hadn't done all that much with what she'd been told already, the extent of her reaction being booking Matt for a bunch of lawn mowing jobs and going to Ocracoke for a weekend, and I wasn't even sure she'd been trying to separate us then. She hadn't even, in front of us anyway, reacted to her nephew suddenly showing up with no apparent way to get to her house. She'd welcomed him, and let him stay, and taken him to see his grandparents. Maybe Mrs. Dobken was trying not to react, and hoping that we wouldn't do anything more than we'd already done. Danny showing up had to have dashed that hope for her.

Matt and I sat on the Dobken's couch, and Danny slouched into one of the armchairs that sat on either side of it. We were all barely facing each other, so I moved, setting my back against the armrest and facing both of them.

Matt glanced at me, then at the tan carpet, and turned fully to Danny, who was solemn, his face slack with exhaustion. "Is there anything you can tell us about the other faction?" Matt asked his cousin.

Danny nodded slowly. "It's a moon-eye and human coalition, to benefit Trenavell." He frowned. "I was about five when Naolon's occupation started." With a quirk of his mouth, he added, "That's like, my second clear memory. Hearing about it."

"What's the first one?" I asked.

Danny's smile widened. "Eating pizza and watching a Christmas special on TV."

Something nice and warm in that memory helped me relax as Danny kept talking.

"I remember my mom saying that Naolon had taken over Trenavell. At some point after that, we talked about being moon-eye, but I don't think it was the first time, and I'm pretty sure that it had just…been a thing for my whole life. Mom had some moon-eye storybooks she'd read to us, but they were in English. I'm pretty sure Dad has a Bible in the dialect, but he always uses an English one for church. I remember hearing Gavin Dupree's name, and I used to go with Dad on trips through the gates and around different parts of Trenavell until I knew the route really well." He yawned again. "I don't know every inner working of the coalition, and I don't even know how long it's been around."

Matt tilted his head. "If we're all from Earth, then why are your parents involved with Trenavell at all?"

"Naolon has historically been much less friendly to moon-eyes than Trenavell." Danny's smile had faded. "The Davies actually came to North Carolina for that reason."

I blinked. "Wait…the Davies?"

Matt frowned. "Yeah."

Danny straightened. "Oh yeah. Rynon was from Naolon, originally."

Matt and I met eyes. So he hadn't known that, and I'd had no reason to. A hardness came over his face. His mom hadn't ever told him this, but did she even know it? She knew something, for sure, but she'd ignored family history, and her sister hadn't.

Danny leaned forward over his knees and focused on Matt. "Your mom didn't tell you everything."

What feelings toward Danny's mom were changing for Matt now?

Matt huffed out a ghost of a bitter laugh. "Yeah, she didn't." It took a second for his eyes to flick to me and back down. "I um…I kinda always thought Aunt Della was just… weird."

Danny smiled again. "She's…definitely very much into being moon-eye."

Matt sat quietly for a minute. "I avoided her at family stuff." His jaw hardened, pulsing a little as he ground his teeth. "I wonder how much my mom had to do with that."

"Aunt Jen's probably just scared," Danny said.

Matt nodded.

We sat quietly. The air conditioning turned on with a rush.

The Davies had gone to Ocracoke, assisted by Gavin Dupree. Had the generations after them felt that they owed Dupree anything, if he'd helped them? If Danny had heard Gavin Dupree's name, then I was sure that Matt's mom had also known the name of my ancestor.

Why had Matt's mom and dad moved here, right next door to my parents?

It wouldn't be impossible to do genealogy research. It was a little easier now, but had they traced Gavin Dupree's line right to my dad?

"Anya?" Matt poked my arm.

"Did y'all move to your house before or after we did?" I asked.

"I don't know."

Fair enough. We had only been four. I remembered our first encounter, but not the time-blurred events after.

Had someone planned this, our families being next-door neighbors? Why would they have done that? Jen Dobken didn't want to be involved.

But that was wrong. She was involved, for whatever reason. She and Matt's dad had their meetings with Lukas Simpson. It didn't really match up too well with how she was acting now, but Matt's mom was involved, and willingly.

Matt kept his eyes on me.

"Your mom acts like she doesn't want to be part of any of this, and doesn't want you to, and yet she and your dad are." I didn't want Matt to think in any way that I was leveling accusations against his family.

"Yeah." Matt's resigned face told me that he'd taken my words as the observation I'd meant.

We fell silent again for a few minutes. Danny shifted in the chair, moving around enough to tell me he was trying not to fall asleep.

"What do we do tomorrow?" I asked.

Danny sat up. "I'm going to head to Trenavell early tomorrow morning. You guys can meet me at the shop later." He let out a long breath. "As for right now…" He hesitated, combining a wince and a sheepish smile. "I want to get some sleep."

"Go ahead," Matt told him.

Danny got up from the chair. "See you guys later." He left the living room, and his footsteps moved up the stairs slowly, clearly trudging. A door closed.

"Are you cutting grass tomorrow?" Regardless of when Danny went, Matt and I would have to wait until our parents were gone.

Matt shook his head.

Danny had the guide his mom had sent him. Cargan was going to accompany us to Skyrren. Maybe that would give me something close to an answer about Gavin Dupree, and his map, and the device.

# Chapter 17

I stood beside my dad, drying the supper dishes as he washed them. The vacuum droned in the living room.

Dad set a clean plate in the drainer. "Triple check that one for me. The barbecue sauce was hard to get off."

Mom had baked chicken tenders and fries, and we'd eaten a salad with it.

I looked closely as I dried it. "This one's fine."

"Good," he said, sounding pleased. "How was your day?"

"Kinda boring." I tried to put a sheepish smile on my face. "I went to the library."

"Cool."

My family might not have made a habit of talking about Gavin Dupree, but maybe Dad would. "Hey, do you know anything about Gavin Dupree?"

He looked thoughtful and set another plate in the drainer. "A little bit."

I inspected the plate before drying it. "Do you really think he killed a man?"

Dad tilted his head and washed a glass. "There wasn't a body, but that doesn't always mean someone will be acquitted if there's evidence enough that something actually went down." Dad paused. "Then again, he was acquitted, which means there were plenty who held some doubt that he did anything."

"But James Abney disappeared," I finished.

"Right." He shook his head. "My mama didn't really talk too much about Gavin, but she did love her grandfather, so her view is pretty favorable."

"Makes sense." She wasn't alone.

Dad nodded and scrubbed a fork. "He might have been seen as a criminal by some people, even if he loved his family. My grandfather didn't seem to care all that much for his dad's eccentricities. Family is complicated like that."

Dad's position was the most neutral I'd ever heard.

"So...what's your real opinion?"

He shrugged and stuck the fork over in the drainer basket. "I think, with this disappearance, you'd almost have to be there to know what actually happened, lacking a confession, or witnesses, or remains, but I don't think Gavin Dupree killed

James Abney. I don't really even believe James Abney died that night."

A dark thought, that Dupree could have buried James Abney in Trenavell, crossed my mind. No one would have found Abney. And if the body had been buried on the property, then selling it to Mrs. Barnes' parents for a promise made sense. It was a guarantee that the property would never leave the hands of either trusted people or family.

"Sounds like that trial was a pretty big deal."

"Oh, definitely," Dad answered. "A town this quiet? Big murder trial with a popular victim? Definitely a big deal." He handed me a glass. "I did a history project in high school on it. The newspaper was incredibly biased."

I raised my eyebrows. "Do you think Dupree was innocent because of that?"

Dad shook his head and stuck a salad bowl in the water. "Not really. The paper may have truly believed that Dupree was guilty, and while that shouldn't have been so obvious in their writing, there was definitely a lack of physical evidence and witnesses."

"Wasn't Dupree's wife at home?"

"According to her, she never went outside." Dad was smiling, fully in his element. "So her testimony only agreed that Abney had showed up at the house."

"So who were the other witnesses?" I took the salad bowl from Dad's hand and dried it.

"For the prosecution?" Did Dad almost look smug? "People who'd been at the town meeting."

"Then they never saw him actually come here."

With a slow nod, Dad kept going. "Maggie Dupree testifying that Abney had come to the house, I think, was something that may have helped the jury to make the choice they did."

"Because she was honest."

"Yep." Dad handed me another fork. "She also testified that she helped her husband clean and dress a deep wound on his own arm."

"That's pretty transparent." How stressful had that been for her? If I was remembering the first letter right, then Gavin and Maggie had been expecting their first child then.

"Both of them were very honest about what happened." Dad paused. "Gavin Dupree had a sword that he admitted to taking outside with him, and that Abney had one of his own."

I frowned. "So they had a sword fight?"

Dad shrugged. "Or were going to, but Dupree told the court that Abney wounded him and fled."

"Wow." Why hadn't I ever asked more about the story before finding the letter? Dad was clearly telling me stuff, so something had changed.

We also weren't at Thanksgiving or Christmas dinner.

"How'd you get interested in Gavin Dupree?" Dad asked.

My stomach dropped. "Um…his name came up and… Matt and I just started looking for stuff about him."

"That's cool," Dad said.

He didn't pry any more. My answer must have been good enough. Wasn't that how people got interested in stuff sometimes? Randomly learning something, and diving deeper?

But Dad not pressing, and just accepting my explanation, was good. He and Mom didn't know anything about Trenavell, and they didn't need to know. Guilt started to creep over me, and I tried to school my face into something neutral, or at least pleasant. There wasn't a thing I could explain about Trenavell to them, not yet. My only real evidence, that wouldn't look fake, was the alarming scar stretched across my right side. Would they even believe Matt if he tried to back me up?

"It's an interesting case," I said.

"It definitely is," Dad agreed.

The vacuum cut off, and I could hear whatever show was on TV, indistinct and barely audible over the intermittent rush of the kitchen faucet. The last dish thunked into the drainer, and I put the glass I was drying away.

Dupree's secrets might be outlined as just regular work, if we found evidence of him in Skyrren. That could be the book his letter talked about, like a biography spread out across years and volumes. Maybe that would resolve the things I didn't know.

***

The next morning, I stood in my room with my full backpack, to which I'd added a sketchbook and some pencils.

As I picked up my coat and draped it over my right arm, the doorbell rang. I froze. I could get out the back door, but could I outrun whoever that was once they figured out what I was doing?

I set my stuff on the floor, and crept down the hall to the steps, slowly making my way up to the point where I knew I'd be able to see who was standing there.

A girl with blonde hair in a ponytail stood on the porch, a couple feet away from the door. She looked around toward the street, and I saw her face. It was Sara.

What was Brandon's girlfriend doing here? I mean, we were friendly, but not close friends. The doorbell rang again. I relaxed and stepped back down to the front door, opening it wide and trying to look welcoming as I pushed the glass door out.

"Hey, Sara," I said.

She smiled, apologetic, her face tinged with worry. "I'm sorry to just come by like this, but I didn't have your number."

I shrugged. "That's fine." I paused. "Want to come in?"

She winced. "I don't have a lot of time, but I wanted to ask again if you'd heard from Brandon at all."

I shook my head.

Sara's face fell. "I was really hoping that he was hanging out with y'all or something. He still hasn't texted me back or answered the phone in forever, and neither have his parents. I even called their house phone." She wrung her hands. "His cousin didn't know, either. None of his family will answer or text back."

That was pretty weird. "Have you been over there?" I asked, cringing inwardly. Was that question rude?

She nodded. "They didn't answer the door, and they're there. Their cars are there, and I heard them talking." Her voice cracked a little. "I definitely heard his mom's voice, and MeeMaw said that the lights are on at night and stuff, so they're home."

"I'm sorry. I haven't seen him." I thought of Brandon in those green clothes, running through the castle in Compass Hill, locking eyes with me. He was secretive, for sure, but why would his whole family act like that to his girlfriend? It was weird, but it was also rude.

*His whole family....*

"Um...have they ever done anything like this before?" *His whole family.* My heart started to race.

Sara shook her head. "That's why it's so weird. I thought they liked me, and I like them."

"I'm really sorry." Where was Brandon? Sara and I had different reasons to wonder about him, but for him to effectively disappear and for his entire family to ignore his girlfriend, even when she knocked on the door, wasn't normal.

Especially the family part.

She nodded. "That's okay. I just thought I'd check, since y'all are friends." She backed away. "Thanks anyway."

"I really hope you find him." I paused. "If I see him at all, I can let you know or pass along a message."

Sara's face lit up a little. "That would be great." She pulled her phone out of her pocket. "What's your number? I'll send you a text."

I gave it to her. "My phone's upstairs, but I'll check it."

"Cool." She walked down the steps. "I have a volunteer thing I need to get to, but thanks again, Anya."

"Sure. You're welcome."

She smiled and made her way to the green car in the driveway.

I closed the door and went upstairs to get my phone. I saw Sara's text, sent back a quick "got it" and picked my stuff back up to head next door.

# Chapter 18

A minute after I knocked, Matt opened his back door, his eyes wide in surprise. "You usually wait for me."

"Right, but I don't feel like being outside by myself."

"Okay." He stepped away. "Come on in. I was about to put my shoes on."

I walked into the Dobken's kitchen. Matt sat down at the table and slid his tennis shoes on, tying the laces quickly.

"Did Danny get away okay?" I asked.

"Yeah." He leaned up.

"Did your parents know he was here?"

Matt shrugged. "Probably. Mom never said anything, though." He stood. "You still got all the stuff?"

"Plus a sketchbook." I pushed my chair back under the table. "I need a better way to mark the gates we find in the facility. We need to have a guide to where they go."

Matt nodded. "Good idea."

We headed out the back door. It was early enough that heat didn't add onto the uncomfortable summer humidity, but I still sweated a little as we headed through the woods. We didn't talk for most of the way.

"I asked my dad about Dupree," I told Matt. "Apparently he did a project on him in high school."

"So what does he think about guilt versus innocence?" Matt asked.

We paused at the big tree. Matt peeked around, checking for the car.

"Dad's pretty sure that Dupree was innocent."

Matt turned back to me. "Same reason? No evidence?"

"Kinda." We slipped around the tree. "Dad did a whole lot more research than we have. Apparently Dupree's wife testified that Abney had been at the house, and that she had dressed a wound on Gavin's arm, and Gavin admitted to taking a sword with him outside just before Abney disappeared."

Matt frowned as we walked to the porch. "So did Abney challenge him to a duel?"

The too-new boards of the porch steps squeaked as I stepped up onto them. "Apparently they were going to fight." I stared down the dirt road that stretched to the highway. "Dad thinks Gavin and Maggie being transparent turned the jury in Gavin's favor."

These were the fields that Dupree had worked, where he'd raised his family, before passing them along to Mrs. Barnes' parents. This land had been where Dupree's life had changed. It had been where James Abney had vanished.

As we ducked into the dim house, I let Matt move ahead. "Do you think Abney's remains are somewhere on this property?" I asked. "I mean, why pass it along to only his friends and require it to go back to my family otherwise?"

Matt looked back at me as we headed to the kitchen. "They're not here if Abney didn't die."

"Then where would he have gone?" He couldn't have used the gate in the house. Downtown was a long way to walk.

"There're plenty of woods," Matt answered.

"True." Disappearing into the trees would have been a lot easier for Abney, and if he'd injured Dupree, then he'd have had time to get away, maybe even walk to the train station, if that had even existed at the time. He could have hid so that no one saw him.

The cool cellar made putting on my coat more comfortable. The moss lamps gave us plenty of light, especially since my eyes had adjusted inside the house. A bright line around the door at the top of the stairs made it obvious that it was daylight, so that was good, at least for now. We'd find out whether it was morning or afternoon.

Matt pushed the door open, and I followed him out onto the mountain road. The sun was pretty high, and the sky was clear with only a few long, thin clouds stretched across the vivid blue. The cold wind made me think it was closer to winter than I thought it had been. Maybe it was already winter.

As we aimed for the tunnel entrance, I wondered what Compass Hill was like before the nation fell. Meris had never talked about it, and I doubted if she remembered it. I could barely remember being four years old. Meeting Matt stuck with me because he'd pulled my hair ribbon out, and it had hurt when he'd taken pieces of hair with it.

At the same time that the two of us had been moving into new houses and becoming friends, Meris and Noam had been fleeing to the refugee camp they'd grown up in. It was a little weird to think about.

And it brought something else to mind.

"So…what plans for college do you have?"

Matt blinked. "I'm not really sure."

"NC State?" I offered.

He shrugged. "Maybe."

"Seriously."

"I am being serious. I haven't narrowed it down yet."

"Oh." I paused. "I…I mean, you probably have more choice than I do."

"Why?" Matt narrowed his eyes.

"I'm pretty sure I'm going to a community college for the first couple of years." I cleared my throat. "I mean...if we make it through all this."

Saying that was the first time I'd voiced that fear.

Matt's eyes widened. "Do you think we're gonna die or something?"

I didn't like the way he said it, and it didn't sound exactly right. "Well, this is all a lot to deal with, so I can't really see past it right now."

"Makes sense." A smile inched onto his face. "Same here."

We could have died at any point. I didn't think that Ira's misguided attack had brought me that close, but it wasn't the only danger we'd faced.

The burrow beasts didn't show themselves as we made our way to the tunnel, and I wondered if they had just left the nesting ground for the day, or if the season changing truly did send them to a different climate.

And then, just as we got to the edge of the ramp that would go down into the tunnel, the city itself caught my eye. We stopped.

The dusty cloud rising from Compass Hill didn't look like it was from an actively smoking fire. It drifted a little in the sunlight, but there was a steady source of it, from somewhere opposite of where the wall faced the tunnel entrance. A distant crumbling sound traveled to us, a sharp report ending the rumble. I couldn't hear anything else.

We rushed down the ramp together.

"It sounded like a wall fell," I said.

"Yeah."

The sounds of whatever was going on in Compass Hill weren't reaching the tunnel entrance yet, and for a hundred yards or so, the quiet darkness that we'd always encountered in the tunnel remained. The reflective signs lit up with their soft, colorful flashes, and the tunnel made a gentle curve.

That was when I noticed the light.

Though it was soft, this light wasn't from moss lamps. It flickered, far down in one of the turnoffs from the main tunnel, but not far enough to hide around the curve. Fear spiked, and I barely stopped myself from letting out the startled yelp that threatened. I made a wild gesture at the light, but Matt had already seen, and he took off, giving my arm a brief tug as we started to run. As dark as it was, and as uneven as our flashlights made things, running was the only safe thing we could do.

My breath echoed, loud and ragged, as we reached the end of the tunnel and sprinted into the open area that I had figured was a parking lot. As desperately as I wanted to breathe a little more quietly, the dread of the closed-in passages ahead overtook the caution.

I'd seen mysterious underground lights before, below Hestia's manor, as a glow in a floor grate. Danny had said it was another exit, and it was underground. There had been tunnels we'd taken, though they'd been nowhere as deep as the ones under Compass Hill. And in the cave where we'd hidden that one night, I'd looked down into an open cavern and seen the shadows there, people that Matt could see more clearly than I could.

Matt pulled one of the doors open, and we shot into what I now thought was a lobby. My eyes had adjusted completely. I couldn't yet see any lights in the space ahead of us.

We still ran, sprinting as fast as we could, through the shorter hallways and sharp turns slowed us down.

I knew the door to the shop cellar, and I slowed, trailing behind Matt as he rushed to open it. Danny wasn't down here. My breath came in gasps, as did Matt's.

Matt ducked in with me close on his heels, and came to an abrupt stop at the light shining from above us.

The hatch was open.

Maybe Danny wanted to make it easier.

I quieted my breaths, which just had the affect of increasing my hunger for air.

"Someone was in this storefront earlier," came a man's voice. "That cellar door is open."

"I doubt they're still down there," a woman replied. "Go look."

Matt nearly shoved me back into the hallway and quietly shut the cellar door, not letting it meet the doorframe all the way. He pulled at my arm again and took off.

Where was Danny? Was he hurt? Were Noam and Meris okay?

As I followed, wild fear coursed through me. Except for the time we'd been in Skyrren, Matt and I had never been without our friends in Trenavell. And any other time, it wasn't like we'd been in hostile territory. The utter quiet beyond our breaths and slowing, stumbling footsteps meant we probably weren't going to get caught yet, that no one was down here, and that they wouldn't catch us. Whatever was going on aboveground, no tension of battle existed down here.

With an abrupt inhale, Matt caught his breath and moved so he was walking in front of me. "Do you want to go to the concourse?"

I gulped and nodded. "But I don't know if I want you to go in front of me or not." My scar itched from the exertion and the sweat that had built up under my clothes, and I quickly reached down to scratch it, lifting the bottom edge of my coat up.

Matt glanced back at me, his face falling before he steeled himself. "I wish I had gone in front of you that time."

My breathing slowed. I didn't have a reply for him; at that point, I couldn't even be irritated with him and his guilt. The only thing I could do was nod as he turned around.

It wasn't too far to the door that would take us down to the center of the facility. We stopped at it. Matt shined his flashlight down into the dark, and I inspected the poster we'd passed, the one that showed the trees and clouds on the other side of the broken gate.

"Maybe while we're down here, we can look around at the gates," I suggested. "What if we found Skyrren?"

Matt straightened. "We'd need to go through the gates to figure out which one would lead there." His eyes reflected the beam of light. "We have to make sure they're safe."

My stomach dropped at the thought of losing something worse than the end of my shoestring next time. "At least we know what to look for."

He looked down again. "I wish we could read the signs."

We locked eyes. There had been a chance we could have gotten close, if Danny was with us.

"No convenient English down here."

Matt huffed a laugh. "Well, Skyrren was the capital, right?" he said. "So, if it was the capital whenever that was built, then it was a major city and it might be obvious." He narrowed his eyes. "Or, well, maybe not obvious but we might still be able to tell, especially if there aren't other cities that big in Trenavell."

And people had lived there less than thirty years before. "Skyrren will at least have readable signs once we get there, since it was officially inhabited as recently as 1986." It wouldn't be a ruin.

Matt slipped ahead of me and led the way down the stairs to the branching concourse. When we reached the bottom, I pointed my flashlight up to study the symbol on the ceiling, still struck by its near-resemblance to the wheel. It had to mean something.

"It's really dark in here," I said.

"Good observation," Matt answered.

"Hush," I told him, fighting a smile. "How would anyone have seen anything down here?"

Matt cleared his throat. "They could have had lanterns or torches." He stared up at the wheel on the ceiling. "There could even be old gas lines down here for lamps."

A little wave of dread coursed through me. If there were gas lines down here, and a wall had fallen aboveground, there would be a huge risk. "I hope they don't have gas lines."

Matt sobered. "Yeah."

It sounded stable down here, though. Rumbling would travel. Maybe it hadn't been a wall that fell, or anything foundational. We were under the castle now. If something was wrong with it, then it might be obvious.

"Do you think the gates are why this whole thing is underground?" I asked.

"Possibly, if that made them more stable." He paused. "Stable for the most part."

Five hallways branched off of the space we stood in, each with an unreadable sign above it. A light flashed down one passage.

I swung my backpack around to get the sketchbook and pencil out. "I guess we better start here." I made an "X" on the page for where we stood.

Matt leaned over the paper, his eyes narrowing as he glanced up at the ceiling. "Where should we start?"

In the flashlight's glow, I saw the thing we'd thought was a directory. "Maybe there," I joked.

We approached it together. I cast a glance behind us as we got to the sign, then turned to study the sign, seeing two round shapes at the bottom. One was a smooth, stylized wheel with thirteen spokes, flat and sleek, and the other was one with eight, this one rougher, carved-looking. As I looked longer at it, I could see the other instances of the wheel that pockmarked the sign itself, gouged beside a bunch of words we couldn't read.

Matt touched one of the wheel carvings. "I think we could start here."

Someone had done this. I guessed Dupree. The directory sign had five columns of words, the one at the top of each column larger than the others.

"That looks like the heading of a list." I traced one of the larger words, noting the wheel beside it.

Matt turned, moving his flashlight slowly around to each of the archways, shining his light on the sign above it.

Each sign matched one of the column headings.

"Do you think this is his version of breadcrumbs on a trail?" Matt asked.

"It could be." As Matt slowly moved around, looking again at each of the signs above the archways, I copied the list of names as best I could, adding the wheels. It didn't look great, but it was something I could look at and match against. If we found Danny, having this might give us a head start on looking for Skyrren.

Matt's flashlight beam rested for a moment on the very first passageway we'd gone through. A light flashed, eerie in the darkness. Past that was the other broken gate.

The quiet broke as sounds echoed from the upper level of the facility. As indistinct as the noises were, they brought with them the fresh terror that had pushed us earlier. "Let's go," I hissed.

The passage's arched ceiling was barely shorter than the center of the concourse. My flashlight beam swung as we ran, showing the lighter iridescent pieces that flecked the dark stone. As we passed the broken gates and rounded a soft curve that took us out of sight of the center, the space opened up. Counters stood in front of signs behind them. Goosebumps rippled over me. The counters were nothing short of long-abandoned restaurants or coffee shops or snack bars in this weird twist on an airport. My scar itched in response to the chills in my skin.

To our right, the wall opened up to another space, almost like a waiting room. Beyond the broken-looking benches, and the chairs here and there, a big podium stood by the wall. Beside that, the edge of a wide door glowed softly with what had to be daylight. White circles, whole and all present, shone a little in the doorframe.

I approached it, peering for a moment onto the podium. "There's paper here."

Remains of what I guessed had been documents, now in pieces, littered the podium, scraps with the same unreadable letters on the signs around us. I didn't dare touch them, reaching instead to open the door, expecting a crunchy resistance.

But it came open easily, almost silent. The light on the other side spilled out into the room, not as bright as I thought outside light should have been.

*Why was it so easy to open?*

Matt stared at the doorway, his eyes reflecting the light. "What's on the other side?"

I let my eyes adjust and peered through.

"Ruins." With that word, I stepped forward into what was left of the building on the other side of the door. Broken columns stretched, at their highest, twenty feet into the air above us, smooth gray stone with vertical stripes of the white stone I'd seen set in the floor and around the passageways. Part of a roof still perched around the top of a column, but it was the only piece, a jagged round section from which the rest had broken away. In the woods beyond rested a single dark gray stone bench, the thirteen-spoked wheel in iridescent white on the side.

Like the broken gate I'd gone through, this place was older than the facility. Whatever this was, it had fallen apart a long time ago.

Matt walked past me to the middle of the space, and I caught up to him, trying to keep my feet quiet on the brush and leaves and other stuff that coated the floor. "Stay behind me," he said, almost pleading.

"Okay." Looking down, I moved some of the leaves away with my toe. The gray stone tiles had a blue tint and white flecks. Whatever that lighter stone was, there was a lot of it, or had been. I couldn't remember having seen anything like it anywhere else in Trenavell.

"This isn't Skyrren," I said.

"But where is it?"

I knew Matt didn't expect an answer. I pulled the sketchbook out again and looked down at it, tapping the pencil lightly on the page. How far had we gone in the station? Maybe a few hundred yards? I wasn't sure how to scale things on the diagram I was making. I drew a line a couple inches long and added a small oval, then scrawled "ruins." A soft breeze, ice at its edges, dragged the already cold air past the point of comfort. I shuddered.

Matt turned in a circle, frowning.

My gaze moved to a point even farther than the bench. A dark straight line cut across the ground, like at the broken gate, but stopped twenty feet away, leaving its shadow in the trench of absent bricks beyond the abrupt end of the wall remnant. I glanced at Matt and moved toward it.

"What do you see?" he asked, following quickly and walking beside me.

"I don't know. Probably part of a wall?" I stopped at the bench. From where we'd entered the space, I hadn't been able to see the dead vines on the other side of it. I wondered if the wheel was on that side too, and started to reach down.

"Wait," Matt said.

I stared at the dead vines, remembering the purple flames from the fire Matt had started outside Skyrren that night, and leaned back up. The other vines hadn't hurt him, but they weren't necessarily the same, and there could be something hiding in these.

I backed away from the bench. "Maybe this was a train station connected to gates."

"I don't see any tracks," Matt answered. "Or the rest of this building, either."

"They could have taken the tracks up if they needed the materials."

A voice came through the woods. I couldn't see anyone or tell where the speaker was. A deeper voice answered, the sounds of both making it clear that we were hearing a conversation.

But the words weren't in English.

One of the voices called out louder. *Maybe they didn't see us.* I knew they had to have heard us.

Matt turned and rushed back to the gate we'd come through, tugging me after him. The dry plant matter crunched loud under our feet. As soon as we'd gotten back into the dark interior in Compass Hill, Matt slammed the gate hard.

"I'm sure they heard that," I told him.

Matt was already pushing on the podium. "And I don't really want them investigating further."

I tugged on the other side of the podium. The sides of it looked like wood, and I expected the danger of splinters, but not the weight, much greater than I'd thought it would be.

We lifted it an inch off the ground, enough for us to struggle it into place.

"Is there a lock?" I asked, breathless, scanning the gate.

"Here," Matt answered, twisting a handle at the edge of the door. We probably hadn't really needed to push anything in front of the gate.

I stared at the podium."What in the world is that made of?"

Matt shook his head. "I think we ought to be discussing who those people were."

"We don't even know where those ruins were at, so it was probably people who lived nearby," I told him. "What if they get through? I mean, we blocked it and it's locked and stuff, but…"

I didn't like that they'd clearly heard us. Were they headed our way when we ran?

We stood quietly and watched the locked door for a minute, but no one attempted to get through.

"You know…we didn't check this one against the list." I pulled my sketchbook out, went to the edge of the waiting area, and compared my not-so-great copies to the sign.

My stomach flipped. There was a wheel beside this one on my list. The door had been well-kept up, the hinges not even rusted. Cargan had said that his dad and others had worked to find operating gates down here. Had they built on what Gavin Dupree had left behind?

Dupree had used these gates. That's why he'd chosen to put the device in Compass Hill. It was a central location that led to others.

Matt stared up at the sign. "Do you still want to try and find Skyrren?"

"Probably whoever's in Skyrren speaks English, at least."

Matt barked a laugh, drawing a smile out of me, even if his laugh did echo.

Who in the world were those people we'd locked the door to?

We kept going the same direction we'd been walking, passing more restaurants or shops from when this functioned as a transit station. In one spot, two doors stood side by side with small signs next to them. They could have been restrooms, but there wasn't plumbing in Trenavell.

If the wheel was the thirteen that Dupree referred to, then did he help Rynon and Jendra Davies get to Ocracoke? I could believe that Iacomus was someone who would have visited some brutal cruelties on the moon-eyed people. How had he managed to live so long?

He couldn't have. That was not possible. Iacomus lived when photography was already a thing. Whoever was claiming to be him must look enough like an old photograph or even a painting of the other Iacomus. That happened plenty on Earth. All it would take would be a close enough resemblance, and the illusion of immortality might offer the current Iacomus plenty of power.

We rounded a corner. Bright lines in the shapes of doors, illuminating more seating areas, made it clear this was a bank of gates. A wide hallway led off in a different direction.

"Hang on," I told Matt. The sketchbook and pencil were still in my hands.

"Oh yeah," Matt said.

I marked them as fast as I could in the sketchbook and lifted the pencil away, staring at the gates. The configuration I'd drawn looked familiar, but I didn't immediately know from where.

Matt paced around slowly, lifting his flashlight to inspect each gate before coming back to me.

He tapped the sketchbook. "What do you think?"

"That the way they're situated looks familiar," I blurted. But why did it?

"Familiar?"

"Yeah." I softly touched the ones I'd just drawn. "It's just these few, so I'm not sure what I think I'm seeing." None of them in this bank of gates coordinated with the list.

"Maybe you'll figure it out if you add more," Matt offered. "Or it might wind up being nothing."

"We'd have to explore more of this place for me to add any." We'd gone quite a ways into this station, and we'd heard those noises, which had to be people. *Why do these gates still mostly work?*

At that moment, I realized the possible reason why the drawing I'd made looked familiar. "Um…"

Matt saw something in my face. "What?"

I edged toward the passageway nearby. "Can we look for another one of these hallways?"

His eyes narrowed. "Why?"

"I want to draw it." It might take only one more to prove what I thought I might see. My eyes had adjusted, I thought, enough to see that light shone somewhere down there, just a soft glow, maybe of daylight leaking through a gate. I turned to Matt. "Do you see light down there?"

"Yes."

"Okay, come on," I told him, and we made our way, flashlights lighting the hallway. We passed another lone gate, which I marked quickly, and a short passage through which I caught a glimpse of stairs in the distance. *Where do they go?*

After we rounded a curve to find another bank of gates, I scribbled in rough marks to represent them, and added lines for the possible other grouping of hallways. *We can check that and make sure that's what I saw.*

Since I couldn't scale the drawings, I ran the risk of messing them up and being unable to prove what I was thinking. "Hey Matt, can you get the map out of my backpack?"

"Yeah," he said. I tried to hold myself steady to finish this part of the drawing as he grabbed the folder with the map inside its plastic zip bag.

Matt moved around to face me and unfolded the map as I finished drawing. He held it flat, his glowing eyes darting back and forth between the old map and my sketchbook. "Oh."

I looked at my incomplete copy. "The map isn't a gate map of Trenavell."

# Chapter 19

What I'd tried to draw was nowhere near as extensive as the map, but I'd drawn enough to see how similar the few gates in my sketchbook were to the larger number of gates on the map. That was the reason it had looked like stuff had been erased from Dupree's map. He'd made a diagram of this facility, and the gates, and had to hide it somehow. He'd erased it and made it look like a copy of the map that Noam had.

"The gates sure look like they've always been here." The station wasn't a new discovery. Gavin Dupree had known about it, and he'd had some sort of plan for it. "The Kings Road gate being on there doesn't make sense, though."

Matt studied the map and my diagram. "Think he may have repaired the unstable gates?"

"Maybe." It still didn't make the riddle device's placement in Compass Hill make any sense or offer a clue as to why he'd made it in the first place. Maybe the Kings Road gate was supposed to throw someone off, even though it was a real gate. Was it the same age as the ones down here?

"Who made the other network that we sealed?" Matt asked suddenly.

"I don't have any way of knowing." The map held tons of gate markings, which meant this station was huge. Who'd made the gates here?

Matt narrowed his eyes. "So...the device was supposed to mess things up."

"But...why that at all, and why wasn't the device in Skyrren if it was all networked?" What was the draw of Compass Hill? "Why wouldn't the device be there?"

"Why *would* it be there?" Matt asked.

I thought, trying to make sense of my racing ideas. "Okay, so right now we're under Trenavell's capital, and the other part of the device is here, and the keys were elsewhere."

Matt waited.

Compass Hill was small, I thought, to be the capital of a nation. I understood leaving Skyrren, and I didn't know Trenavell's true size. State capitals at home weren't necessarily big cities, not always. When we'd gone after the riddle pieces, we'd stuck to mostly wilderness, at least as far as I knew, only barely seeing people.

The device had been placed here. The device was important. So why not in Skyrren?

"Compass Hill wasn't always the capital of Trenavell." Some semblance of a shape of an idea formed in my head. Something was here. Gavin Dupree had picked it, and he had picked it for a reason.

Matt posed the next question. "Do you think they picked Compass Hill to be the capital because of the station?"

"Couldn't have been official," I said. "But there's a castle. It's really defensible." I couldn't quite corral the ideas I was having into something easy to say. "But Gavin Dupree was in Trenavell when Skyrren was the capital, and Skyrren would have made more sense for the placement of the riddle device." I paused, finally getting a grasp on the edge of something. "He picked Compass Hill for a reason when it wasn't anything, right?"

A voice came out of nowhere. "I wouldn't say it was nothing."

I jumped before it sunk in that the person speaking was Meris, and watched her and Noam and Danny walk up. Meris held one of those moss-lamp lanterns.

Noam answered her. "I don't think she meant any offense, Meris."

"Y'all are quiet." Matt pointed the flashlight at them.

"I don't imagine you could hear us over your conversation," Meris retorted.

"Why are you guys all the way down here?" Danny asked.

I held the sketchbook up. "I was making a drawing of the gates." A delayed dread washed through me, and with a lot of reluctance, I kept going. "What I've drawn matches the map."

Had we told Danny about the pencil remnants I'd found on it?

Matt spoke. "And it looks like it was something else before it was a map."

Danny's eyes caught the light. "So it's a diagram of this station."

I held the map and the sketchbook out. "I think so."

Noam stepped forward and took them from me.

"Y'all, I wasn't trying to insult Compass Hill," I assured them. "It's just that your family picked Compass Hill as a refuge to relocate to, but what was it before that?" We sure hadn't quieted down, and my heart raced a little faster at the memory of the lights we'd seen in the tunnel. I'd have to find out where Danny and Noam and Meris had been.

"A small town," Meris answered, impatiently, tapping her fingers on her rifle strap.

Frustration blazed through me. "Okay, but geographically, where are we right now? Are we anywhere centrally located or strategically amazing, other than in a shallow valley?" It wasn't a hill. Compass Hill's name had never fit.

Meris and Noam exchanged a glance.

"Not particularly," Noam answered.

My ideas clicked into place. "Okay. Then how in the world was Gavin Dupree able to create a device that would, from here, shut down everything?"

I looked at Matt and Danny as they realized what I was saying.

Meris frowned. "If his purpose was to hide the intention of the device, then it was a good idea to hide it here."

I shook my head. "No, I said how." I couldn't hear any sounds coming our way. "I get the secrecy. Sealing every gate in this nation was a pretty big thing to do, and clearly it wasn't something that was particularly appreciated when Matt and I activated the device." Sourness rose up, like I'd bled for nothing, even though I knew I hadn't. "But…Gavin Dupree wasn't moon-eye, so he had to have had accomplices, and there had to be a structure there already for him to be able to make one little crank wheel that shut everything down." I took a deep breath. "So what was Compass Hill to him?" Had he made or rerouted a gate to Salt's Creek?

I could see the realization dawn in both sets of eyes.

Danny looked at the map and sketchbook, still in Noam's hands. "There's no way this city or town or fort or whatever was a blank slate before that."

Meris nodded slowly. "This facility is certainly proof."

"How old is Compass Hill, actually?" Matt asked.

"Ancient," Noam answered simply.

"Okay, but what does ancient mean here?" I swallowed. "At home it's like…before fifteen hundred years ago, so how do y'all count something as being ancient?"

Meris, hesitant, answered. "I'm…not sure." She glanced at Noam, as if asking him to help.

Noam tilted his head. "Compass Hill has been inhabited for millennia, but…" He trailed off, sounding frustrated, embarrassment at not having an answer coloring his face.

I backed off. "Okay…well…" My voice offered a little echo, and I paused, but no sound followed the echo's fading. "Someone was planning to use the device, and we beat them to it, which means someone that isn't y'all's government might know something about this." I took a breath. "We don't have a clue who that is, so…yeah."

Danny crossed his arms. "I've been doing stuff for Trenavell for a while, with my parents' help and prompting."

Meris' gaze leveled on Danny, her eyes sharp. "Does your mother know about this facility?"

"Yeah." Danny pulled his phone out of his pocket. "She sent me some pictures of stuff that might help us at least sound out the words on the signs down here."

Meris straightened. "How?"

"A possibly similar dialect to the one my mom speaks," Danny answered.

Matt's eyes flicked to my backpack. "I think my mom probably speaks it, too, which means my grandparents do."

And, probably, their parents, and all the generations of what had been the Davies family that went back to their arrival here on Earth, and long before that. They'd escaped something, with the help of my ancestor, a man who left a blatant and obvious mark on so many things.

Stepping closer to Noam, I studied the eight-spoked wheel that Dupree had drawn there. "The wheel there was on the letters I have and it's on a directory down here."

Meris looked down at it. "We have seen it in other places."

The ships on the river. The well, and the lights at the bottom of it. The device itself. "It's breadcrumbs," I said.

Noam looked up, tilting his head. "What?"

*I should bring them some books.* I flipped to the page where I'd copied the names on the directory. "Someone, maybe Dupree, left the wheel carved into the sign in that first big room. I think it's a trail."

"It could lead to Skyrren," Meris said.

I glanced at Matt. "Skyrren was evacuated because of the poison..." I frowned. Logically, unless there were multiple huge, open gates leading into Skyrren from a single town in Ukraine, it didn't make sense for them to have done that.

"Yes," Meris said. "Skyrren was emptied quickly, so any records would only date to when they left the city."

"So it's not even thirty years for here." If Trenavell had even kept them at all.

"No."

"Who would keep records?" Matt asked.

Noam and Meris looked at each other. "We don't know," Noam answered.

Meris played with her rifle's strap. "I can, if necessary, ask my father about Skyrren. It's well known history."

And the king would know his own nation's history, even if Meris didn't. "Wait, so could you ask him about Gavin Dupree?"

Meris' expression shifted into hesitancy. "I can." But there was discomfort in the set of her face. She didn't want to.

"But?" Why was she so unsure at all?

She stood there, her gaze moving from Danny to Matt to me, and back around in the same order, for a long few seconds.

"Something's happening in Compass Hill," Meris said. "Part of the wall was damaged just today."

So we had heard that.

She kept going. "I have not been able to locate my brother, and if he was supposed to guide us to Skyrren and ensure our safety there…"

Though I'd cooled off and caught my breath, and we weren't being pursued, the leftovers of the sweat on my forehead jolted me into realizing that Matt and I hadn't told them the whole reason as to why we'd come this far down. "Um…Matt and I saw lights in the tunnel."

Noam, Meris, and Danny stared at me.

"Probably people with lights," Matt clarified. "So we ran to the shop."

"Y'all weren't there, and we heard other people up in the store who were gonna check the cellar, because the hatch was open, so we came down here," I finished. "But before we even went in the tunnel, we heard something fall, and we saw dust or smoke coming up from the city." I took in a breath. "We decided to look around down here, and we went through one gate that's functioning pretty well, and there was another ruined building on the other side of it, and we heard people talking and I think they heard us."

"What were they talking about?" Meris asked.

If they'd heard me and Matt, then they were probably talking about us. "I don't know. It wasn't English."

Danny's eyes glowed. "Do you think it was a human language or moon-eye?"

Matt shrugged. "We blocked the door with a podium, though."

Was that one of the gates that Meris' dad had found? Were they using it, and had it been one used to switch out soldiers and civilians when Trenavell had retaken the city? I didn't think we'd messed up anything for Trenavell by putting something in front of the door. If anyone was still using the gate, they could just move the podium.

*The lights. The wall.* "Do y'all think that the damage to the city wall has anything to do with people in the tunnels?" How far did the highway tunnels go, and where were the other entrances? As big as the facility was, it clearly had more than one entrance. It was possible that one of the other tunnels had compromised the wall.

Noam answered. "It buckled enough to bow inwards, but it's the newest part of the structure."

Meris abruptly turned to Noam. "How do you know that?"

He gazed back, calm. "It's well known, but Cargan told me. It was damaged thirteen years ago and rebuilt by Naolon."

Meris frowned, fighting a look of embarrassment and squeezing the strap of her rifle. "It could be coincidental. We didn't hear anything before it crumbled, but we also weren't close to it." Her expression cleared. "It's possible that Naolon didn't repair it well."

"Could be," I answered. "But why were there people in the shop when Matt and I got there?"

It didn't sound like there'd been some attack on the city. The wall collapse could have been coincidental, but why were there people searching the shops, and where was Cargan?

And now the wall of Compass Hill, so recently retaken, was vulnerable.

Meris straightened. "We should find Skyrren."

Danny eyed me and Matt. It was possible to find some gate there. We could use the directory, if the information that Danny's mom had sent would be helpful at all.

Skyrren had been the capital, and if it had also been that when this station was in use, then we would find a gate somewhere.

Meris kept going. "Skyrren could be a refuge."

My stomach dropped. "How?"

"Cargan."

"We can't find him, Meris." Noam's voice was low and almost sharp.

Meris smiled. "But I took his promise to mean that whoever is there knows his name."

# Chapter 20

I turned my gaze to the door further up from the one we'd left. "How 'bout we keep going until we get tired?" The edge of frustration in my voice was audible. The five of us had been meticulously checking signs for two hours, and I'd kept drawing. I was nowhere near in possession of a full copy of the map, but we'd gone deep into the facility, staying in the same passage, and my drawing had started to resemble a section of Dupree's map more and more. Other than the lines I'd drawn to represent passageways, the section I had looked nearly identical, though the scale was clumsy. If I could find tracing paper at an office store, then I might be able to make my own copy that was more exact.

None of the gates we'd gone through led to anything recognizable. Half of what we'd found were more ruins, those truly abandoned, and some didn't work at all.

Matt and I stood in front of a door that gave off no flashes and showed no alien sunlight. Dark holes surrounded the frame, empty where the others had pegs.

I pulled the door open and stared at the stone wall on the other side, a chill going over my skin before I marked it on my sketchbook. "Wonder where the pegs went."

Matt traced his hand over the stone. "That white stone could be valuable."

"Yeah." I scrawled "nonworking" on the sketch paper.

Danny let out a deep sigh as he opened one more door and stopped. "Uh…guys." His voice was urgent as he hurried away from the open gate and past the seating area, then looked up at the sign above it, hastily opening his phone.

I pointed my flashlight at the sign, then turned to the page where I'd copied names from the directory.

It matched.

Danny had his phone out, looking back and forth between it and the sign, moving his finger along the screen. His smile widened. "Your highness," he said to Meris, "please take a look."

"What is it?" Matt asked.

Danny looked pretty pleased with himself as he stood back, holding the door open and ushering us through.

Meris hurried through the door, and her footsteps sped up as she rushed into the structure on the other side. We followed.

My eyes adjusted to the muted sunlight, and I began to see more of what was around me. This wasn't ruins; this was whole, if dingy. Dirty windows stretched two stories or more above us. Under the dust, I could see that the hard floor had a sheen to it, like marble or tile. There were benches in the center, counters along the wall, and one really big set of windows at the far end of the structure, with glass doors below it. An empty street showed through the haze of dirt.

Meris looked back at us, clearly excited. "This is Skyrren."

She moved toward the doors. My nerves ramped up as I remembered the ambush.

*You and Matt were fine last time. Chill.*

But there'd been two of us then, and we probably looked pretty lost. I could still imagine the thunk of the man's body falling on the truck I'd hid myself in. His group had been larger.

*None of you are Naolon's soldiers. None of you are a threat.*

As we walked slowly toward the doors to the street, we passed rows of counters with doors behind them, all closed. Were those like the other gate stations?

I stepped away and approached a door. A muted outline of light surrounded it. The other one down the line also had a glowing outline, but softer. Curious, I pulled the door near me open.

The soft light shone through a filter that blurred the field on the other side. The surface wasn't dirty, more like it lay behind distorted glass. The green grass in the field beyond the door bent over in a gust that I could neither hear nor feel, and the sunlight dimmed.

Matt walked up beside me as I leaned back to see if there was a sign or anything above the door, but neither the wall nor the counters had anything like that. At one time, I was sure they had.

"This is a gate," Matt said.

I nodded, staring at the distortion between me and the outdoor scene on the other side. Dread began to soak through as I considered confirming the suspicion I had of what exactly would keep us from stepping into that field.

As I reached out, the memory of the gate shutting behind me, and all the might-have-beens from that, rushed through my head.

My hand met the barrier. An instant of give in a gel-like surface led to something harder, solid. This was a gate, looking out onto a summer day. Lightning flashed on the other side. Thunder never rumbled. We probably looked out onto somewhere on Earth.

And the window that kept the field so quiet came from the device.

I'd done this.

I backed away, trying not to see the horrible things going through my head, stuff I hadn't even witnessed, things I just imagined. A barrier like this coming suddenly into existence as someone walked through it.

Noam and Meris' footsteps had stopped.

Matt and I had activated Dupree's device. I'd pushed for it that day, when Matt had been focused on my injury, and bleeding or not, I should have listened to him.

Because if it didn't matter all that much that Matt and I wore obvious Earth clothing, then it meant people passed between our planets all the time. People used these gates, and our element of surprise meant that there likely were people using it when I'd turned the wheel.

The image of my cut shoestring flashed in my mind once more.

"Anya." Matt's voice, low and quiet. No one else spoke.

I watched another flash of lightning, breathing faster. "This is a gate seal." I turned to him, letting my face break a little.

He watched as rain started to fall on the other side, then reached out himself to touch the window before his eye went down for a moment to my knotted together shoestring.

Solemn, he stepped in front of me and put his hands on my shoulders, gently pushing me away from the door. Danny moved behind him to shut it, his face just as grave as Matt's.

No wonder Trenavell hadn't expected us to activate the device. We shouldn't have.

I turned toward where Meris and Noam watched us from. The confusion cleared from their faces the second after I faced them, Noam understanding first. I did not know what to say, though I guessed they'd heard me. I'd told them about the broken gate that I'd gotten stuck behind. They had to be understanding now.

I stood every chance of having hurt someone by activating that device. Did Dupree know that risk?

With two deep breaths, I moved away from Matt and kept walking in the direction we'd been going before. Even if no one was hurt, how many people had gotten trapped in worse situations than Danny's?

Desperate, I pushed the image of the strange window into another mental box. Tendrils of anger tried to trail out from the image. This silent city was not the place to lose whatever composure I had.

"Do y'all want to keep going?" I asked, holding my voice steady, warding off the strike of snake-like irritation. Neither Meris nor Noam had wanted to see the key. They'd left all of that on me and Matt.

Meris silently turned and kept walking toward the station doors. When we reached them, she set her hands on the bar across one of them, then pushed gently. It swung open silently, sending a chill racing up my spine and goosebumps rising all over my skin.

*They probably grease the hinges.*

Meris rushed outside.

"Meris!" Noam shouted as he ran ahead.

"Shhh!" I hissed, without thinking and just about as loud as he had been. But what was the hurry? What was always the hurry?

*Stop. Stay calm.*

Matt's eyes went wide. I knew he remembered the ambush, too. I didn't know if we had the advantage of looking lost, not with Meris' confidence that Cargan being her brother would help. Worry passed over Danny's face for a second.

*Oh well.* "We have to go with them." I scribbled "Skyrren" on my drawing and made my way after Noam and Meris, swinging my backpack around to put the sketchbook away as I walked.

Meris stood in the middle of the street, facing the station, studying it. "We're near the city's center, I think." Her voice echoed off the buildings around us.

I stared at her, trying to communicate that she needed to be quiet, trying to push down more of the anger, because Noam wasn't helping. Meris apparently had no real idea of the risk here, or of what Matt and I had seen, even though we'd told her.

"How do you know?" Danny asked evenly, in a regular tone of voice.

*Not him, too.*

Meris answered. "Compass Hill took its structural inspiration from Skyrren. It looks old here, and I don't see any trace of the wall that I know surrounds this city." She pointed at the building we'd just come from. "That gate station, I'm sure, is the main one."

The windows we'd seen inside didn't even go to the top of the building, and there were more of them above that, the same height. It was built of stone, mortared together, and in the center of the windows above the station's doors was that thirteen-spoked wheel. The rest of the building blended with the city around it, ending somewhere in the distance, and I started to take notice of the other buildings, as plenty towered over the roof of the gate station.

Meris kept speaking. "And if that is the main gate station, as old as it may be, then the palace is going to be at the center."

Noam eyed the tall buildings around us. "Then we should go there and take shelter, and look for the archives."

*What if there are people in there, too?*

Meris grinned, smug. Not like she was excited to see her ancestral home, but like she was just excited to be right, to have someone side with her.

“Maybe we could not walk right in the middle of the street, though?” I snapped.

After a second, Meris sobered. “Indeed.”

*I know why she bugs Matt so much.*

We walked, moving a couple of blocks before Skyrren proved Meris right.

A fence stood around the palace, the gate of it wide open. Beyond that, the building was big, and grand, but not like anything that defied physics. Grasping for something I could compare it to, I thought of Versailles, and cathedrals, and old government buildings. I could hold those things up against this one and see similarities, but at the same time, wide differences. The palace just made me think of them, with its blend of elegance and stateliness. Though the construction was a mix of dark and light stone, the predominant lighter parts shimmered, iridescent in the sun. What stone even was that, in that amount? Above the doors, like a window on a Gothic cathedral, was that wheel again, stylized, but without the smooth edges, almost a glitching image.

Meris sighed. “I might have grown up in this palace if it weren’t for the poisoning of the city.” She glanced back at us. “Let’s go in.”

As we got closer, the palace changed. It was still pretty and iridescent. But the broken windows toward the first floor of the building made sharp glimmers edged by the void of the dim interior. The wide gray staircase that led up into the open front doors had been broken apart at some point. Vines grew around a nearly perfect circular hole and trailed down the steps, joining with the foliage around other similar holes that spotted the grounds and marred the foundation in places.

"Um…" I said. Most of the staircase was intact.

"Oh," Meris said.

Danny approached it. "Burrow-beast." He smiled a little. "Or dirt whale."

"Think the foundation's okay?" I asked.

Meris eyed the stairs. "Perhaps." She kept walking towards them, Noam following her. Anger began to simmer under my skin. What thing were we on the way to ruin now?

Maybe the burrow beasts hadn't been able to get through much more than what we were seeing and were long gone now. I thought of the one that had nested with its young in the entrance to the tunnel near Compass Hill. Skyrren was farther north than Compass Hill, so if those animals did migrate, they were likely gone, especially if the vines were still here, with little obvious damage.

The steps held solid as we stepped up and climbed to the doors. The wheel on the front of the palace came into better focus and stopped looking like a glitch. There'd been darker stone making the details of the wheel, and some of that stone had been chipped away. Maybe it had value, as well, or maybe thirty years of no maintenance damaged it slowly.

Meris opened the door and led us in, her lantern held in front.

The ceiling stretched high above us still, supported by wide columns leading off into the gentle twilight of indoors. Arched doorways led to other rooms beyond. It was brighter here, but the row of windows on each side of the room had a dingy layer, hard to see through, except for the few broken panes in the glass. Shapes took form in the dim, angular and circular ghosts holding still in soft swirls of dust.

Fountains, each one a different design. I stared at the farthest wall, taking in how massive the hall was, to hold all these fountains with all the space between each one. Water didn't run through them, but I wondered what it would have looked like when it had.

"Fountain hall," Meris said, barely louder than a whisper.

"The conceit of Trenavell," were the next words I heard, from Danny.

Matt and I turned to him.

"What?" I asked.

Danny blinked, brow furrowed. "Fountain hall, conceit of Trenavell, pride and ruin." He paused. "I read that somewhere, but I can't remember where."

"Maybe in your mom and dad's stuff," Matt offered.

Meris frowned, too, but not in puzzlement. "Conceit, indeed. It was supposed to have been a wonder." She gazed at the wide staircase on one side of the room.

"Not so much now," Matt said.

Noam cleared his throat. "The palace was the seat of government, so there should be archives here."

Meris grinned, almost wild. "This is my ancestral home. More than information is here." She walked ahead of our little cluster, but slowly, as if in reverence.

"Stuff about Dupree," I said to Matt.

"Probably," he agreed, his eyes tightening as he looked at me.

Noam spoke up. "I'm going to follow Meris. Do we need to meet back here?"

A harsh laugh came to my throat. "I'm not splitting up in someone's old house."

"It's my family's old house," Meris called back, her voice echoing. "But we should stay together."

Part of me wanted to get the bayonet out of my backpack and have it handy.

Not that I'd know what to do with it.

As we moved through the room, I let myself study the fountains. The emptiness of this palace made me expect to see them cracked and falling apart, but I remembered that they'd only been abandoned for less than thirty years, though I had no idea how old they were in the first place. Meris and Noam might know. I didn't particularly want to ask them, so I stuck with Matt and Danny.

Multicolored tiles, alongside the iridescent white ones, made mosaic designs in the dry bases of some fountains, while others seemed to have star fields at the bottom, solid dark stone inlaid with lighter colors. I stepped back from one design and let it resolve more into a bright image of a spiraling whirlpool set against the dark gray stone at the bottom. I leaned over, seeing the camouflaged tracks within the spiral, small shovel-like shapes at intervals inside. It had been meant to do something, maybe to create the illusion of the whirlpool moving inside. Dry, it was a galaxy.

I caught up to Matt where he stood beside one fountain. On the inside of it, orange and red tile, with not a speck of white, made an image of this planet's moon. Goosebumps rolled over my skin as I thought about Matt's glowing eyes. He'd been made to see under the light of that moon.

Ahead of us, Meris and Noam had reached the other end of the room, and stood at a set of double doors, of which one was ajar. Noam turned to the three of us.

I took a glance back at the rest of the room and took in the fountains and their inherent spookiness. They'd run with water once, and now they were abandoned.

Meris pulled the door open wider as we arrived.

"I believe the thrones are this way," she said as she stuck her head through the opening. "There are doors open at the end of this hall."

"How big is this place?" Matt asked.

Even Meris shrank, distinctly overwhelmed, if I could judge by her unsure posture. "I don't know." She stepped through the door, Noam close behind.

"What do you think she's looking for?" Matt asked.

"I mean, I guess it's like a scenic tour of her family's life," I answered. The brief tour of the fountains had built up a little calm inside me. I could not lose it here.

"We could give her a little more time," Danny said.

"I really want to find something here, though." I turned to the door. "Maybe she can see the thrones, and then we look for…anything about Gavin Dupree." I slipped into the hall behind them. Should I be saying his name out loud?

Meris and Noam had already made it to the end with the other doors. Dim sunlight lit the whole space we were in, illuminating more accents of that iridescent tile.

"This place is huge," Matt said, almost in a whisper.

"Imagine the rest of the city," Danny answered. "Skyrren's really old."

And Gavin Dupree was a friend of Trenavell. He'd been to this planet. He'd been known by this country. The good kind of goosebumps rose up on my skin, of connections and understanding.

Beyond the doors, an aisle led up to two thrones. The throne room in Compass Hill had been an attempt to reflect this one, I guessed.

"What are those things on the seats?" I asked.

We were a few feet away before it became clear what rested on the thrones. Bouquets, long dead and brown, lay in them, one in each seat.

Meris spoke. "My grandfather was the last in his line to sit here."

"What happened to him?" Matt asked.

Her face reddened. "I regret I don't know the story." Her eyes fixed on the dusty brown stems and dried flowers. "But he died before the city was emptied." She turned away from he thrones. "I want to see the royal quarters."

"You don't know where they are," Noam answered.

"I can figure out where they are," Meris told him.

"We all need to go together," Danny said.

At least the palace seemed empty, but how long until we wound up like those soldiers had when Matt and I had been here? Sweat broke out on my forehead as we reached the staircase landing. Across from where we stood, another staircase led up to another floor.

Meris made a beeline for that one, almost towing Noam.

Without wanting to, I remembered the hasty way they'd both handed me back the paper I'd copied the key onto. Rational Noam still did just about everything Meris told him to do. Or, at the very least, he spent time trying to make up for her and her actions.

At least we could just follow them from a distance in here. Maybe I could stay calm that way.

At the top of the stairs, a dark hallway on one end led to a set of grand carved doors, probably ten feet tall. On the other end, to my left, the door-lined hallway stretched on into the dark.

Meris went to the set of doors to our right and pulled one of them open. It squeaked. Soft light poured into the space where we stood.

Tall, arched windows took up one wall, across the hall from several partly-open doors, which had copies of the carvings on the larger set we'd come through. The sectioning off of this end of the hallway indicated just where we had found ourselves. These rooms were probably the royal family's bedrooms.

Even with all the dirt of nearly thirty years, it was pretty up here, and the windows didn't have as much grime. I stepped closer to one and peered through, looking over the tops of the buildings in Skyrren. They stood taller, the boundaries stretching much farther, than I'd figured. Far on the horizon, a mottled shadow suggested the very tops of clouds, distant from here.

We hadn't traversed a lot of the outer part of it, but Skyrren's size made sense as a capital. Wherever Matt and I had found ourselves was probably just a different neighborhood, maybe a newer one. The paddocks of skulls outside the walls, with the wide tunnels heading underground, outlined a purpose. An industry in burrow beasts.

And somewhere here, Skyrren connected to an abandoned city on Earth, and had emptied because of the radiation they feared.

I blinked and thought again that Skyrren being empty because of radiation didn't make sense unless there were multiple huge gates going to one Earth city.

Plus, the gates could be closed off completely. I knew what it looked like to seal a gate, and I'd seen one snap closed behind me, and the station had even had one with none of the white pegs, leaving behind a door to a solid wall.

Though I pushed down the threads of horror that threatened from those memories, I did frown.

Matt came up beside me. "What?"

One of the bedroom doors squealed. Meris disappeared through it, Noam just behind her. Danny stood in the middle of the hall.

I pushed away from the window. "The Prypiat thing doesn't make sense if the gates can be cut off and completely closed."

Matt and Danny glanced at each other.

"You're right," Danny said.

I edged away from them, following Meris and Noam into the room they'd entered. "So why is Skyrren really empty?" I slipped through the door.

Meris stood at a dresser, rifling through an open drawer. Noam faced out one of the room's windows. Meris had already taken a couple of things out of the drawer. They looked like handkerchiefs, but one was a tiny knitted hat.

I picked up one of the handkerchiefs. The name "Merynda," embroidered in deep blue thread, stretched across the corner of the white fabric, matching the same name in yarn on the baby hat.

"Who's Merynda?" I asked, setting the handkerchief down and looking around.

Meris shrugged. "I don't know. Maybe a maid."

I took in the big room. The high ceilings. The tall windows, and the long seat under three of them, padded with a faded blue velvet cushion. Dust covered the blue and purple quilt on the bed, but a hint of the fabric's sheen remained visible, and the bed itself was huge. I reached for the wardrobe and pulled a door open. The hems of several dresses, a couple of them clearly ballgowns, slowly peeked out with a soft rustle.

"I doubt a maid lived here," I told Meris.

She eyed the lace hem on one of the nicer dresses, and I stepped back.

"Someone royal lived in this room," Matt said, reinforcing me.

Noam moved to stand by a chair that faced the windows, a ball of sky blue yarn in his hand. "Meris, do you have an aunt?"

Meris' eyebrows rose, and she tilted her head. "I…wasn't aware of one."

Danny touched the baby hat gently. "Merynda would probably be your aunt, right?"

I reached forward and lifted a lace hem, pulling the skirt out enough to show its length. "This also isn't a little kid's dress."

Meris' gaze dropped slowly down to the hat, the confusion clear all over her face. "I don't know." She looked at the bedroom door. "My father's room should be on this hall." And with that, she rushed through the door.

Noam didn't go after her this time. *For once*, I thought. He set the ball of yarn down on the dresser and picked up the hat, inspecting the name there.

"Do you know who Merynda might be?" I asked him.

"I don't." He set it back down and looked up at me. "I have no idea why Meris wouldn't, either."

I softened as his brown eyes met mine. Noam remained difficult to be mad at.

"Think Cargan would know?" Danny asked.

Noam took a few steps toward the bedroom door. "He is older than Meris, but if no one ever told him about their aunt…" He slipped out.

"Wonder what happened to her." Matt looked back at the wardrobe.

The royal family had been scared enough to leave everything, but they shouldn't have been. Skyrren should have still been the capital. I knew firsthand how completely the gates could be cut off, and how that would have protected the city.

I closed the wardrobe door. "What if she died?"

"Why not pack up everything?" Matt asked.

"Someone left bouquets on the thrones. They might not have wanted to pack her stuff up." Unless the death was related to Skyrren being empty. "Or they didn't have time." I moved to the hallway.

Meris stood with Noam down the hall, holding something in her hand. As Matt, Danny, and I approached, she lifted it to show us.

A tiny blue horse gleamed in the dusty light.

Meris smiled a little. "This was on the table beside the bed. I'll take it to my father."

It was probably safe for her to do that. If there'd ever been a gate in this city that had led to Prypiat, there wasn't a doubt in my mind anymore that they'd closed it off completely.

Meris turned to the carved doors. "Let's find the archives."

She led us back into the hallway and down the wide staircase to the landing below. Our footsteps were audible, the soft scuffing of our shoes on marble making a quiet echo.

We reached the fountain hall again, kicking up dust as Meris aimed for an archway that held two more tall doors, both of them shut completely. We kept quiet, following Meris toward the doors, which did look important. If the archives weren't on the other side, maybe it was something else related to the royal family. It might not be anything more than a ballroom.

When we reached them, Noam tugged on one of the handles. The door moved, but stuck at eighteen inches open. We could get through it.

"I don't think we can oil this one the rest of the way open," Noam said, looking up at the highest hinge, twice his height above him. The door tilted ever so slightly, leaning away from the broken hinge.

No wonder it had gotten stuck. I shuddered as I imagined it falling like the front door of the Dupree house had. Meris stepped in front of Noam and disappeared inside without a word. We followed her lead into the bright room beyond. For a few seconds, I let my eyes adjust. The sunlight dimmed, probably from a cloud.

Rows and rows of bookshelves extended to each twilit end of the room. Tables every few yards would have given people places to pore over records, or write them in the first place. A single large desk stood in the center. I imagined that, at one time, there might have been a chair or stool behind it. More shelves to my left extended all the way into shadow, the soft suggestion of sunlight glowing at one end.

And every single shelf in this room stood empty.

Meris turned to us, her mouth open. "I…believed they were here."

It wasn't the first time in Trenavell that something wasn't where it was supposed to be. But rumors about the riddle device pieces were one thing. This room had held the archives of a kingdom, and it was huge. There had to have been centuries' worth of records here.

"How?" I asked.

"They've had almost thirty years to walk away, if no one's been living here," Matt answered.

"Yeah, but who'd they walk away with?" Why in the world would anyone have taken all the records?

Meris stepped forward. "The signs are still on the shelves." The signs had recognizable letters on them, though not whole words, and three groups of numbers on each.

"Okay." I swallowed hard. "Someone took them, but why?"

"Meris, are you sure they're not in Compass Hill?" Danny asked.

"I *was* sure," she answered, her voice quiet.

She'd been sure about the gates needing to be sealed, too, even if she and Noam wouldn't take on that burden.

*Stop.*

I stared at a row of shelves to my left that had "EY: A.D. 1982" on the round sign at the end, with two other numbers underneath that one. I edged forward. "EY" could stand for "Earth year." What did the other two numbers mean? They were much higher than 1982, but what were they counting from? I swung my backpack around again, took out the sketchbook, and copied the sign into it.

"What now?" I asked. Nothing was here.

A sound, soft and quick, almost like some cross between bushes rustling and footsteps, came from the far end of the room.

Matt turned to face the ancient record shelves behind him.

With no books to dampen them, every sound in this empty room traveled. Something moved in the distant shadows. Close to the floor, a head, dark and angular, peeked out from behind a shelf, then drew back and disappeared.

"There's an animal in here," Matt said, voice low.

"Yeah." *Calm down.* Maybe it was shy and would leave us alone.

"Looks like it's afraid of people," Danny said.

Meris moved ahead of us, rifle up.

A nearly inaudible thump, like a door closing, echoed through the room.

Meris relaxed, lowering the rifle. "I believe it left."

Noam shook his head. "It's still inside the palace."

Meris kept her eyes on that end of the room. "But not here with us." She lowered her gun and turned to Noam. "We should inspect the other end of the shelves."

I focused on the shadows ahead. What years would the signs on those first shelves say? "Maybe we should."

Meris didn't look at me, but her eyebrows rose as she held Noam's gaze, her face hopeful.

He blinked. "You rank above me."

Her face lit up and she turned away from Noam, slinging her rifle onto her back. His brown eyes met mine, and he looked down, following her as she made her way to the other end of the room.

I hesitated, fighting down my reaction to Noam just going along with Meris.

"We probably don't need to split up," Matt suggested, poking my arm as he stood beside me.

"If it got in here before…" I didn't know exactly what the creature in this room had been.

"You've got a bayonet," Matt said, his tone reluctant.

"I would seriously rather not have any large animal from this planet all that close to me again." I'd had the bayonet then, too.

Matt pressed his lips together. "Oh. Yeah. Sorry." His ears turned pink. "That's not my worst memory of last time."

Matt's solemn expression made me think too suddenly of seeing his hazel eyes rimmed in red. My face warmed.

Danny frowned. "What did you get close to and why?"

"One of those big dog-looking animals pounced on me once." I slipped the sketchbook back into my backpack. How close had it come to actually biting me?

Danny's mouth fell open.

Matt watched our other two friends as they got farther away. "Meris shot that one."

Danny snorted. "Then she wouldn't hesitate to do that again."

I'd been apart from the others that time, and it wasn't like she'd done more than wounded it. "Let's not stay split up." We were officially going to leave Skyrren with more questions than we'd come with, but if the signs were still on the shelves, I could at least have an idea of how old Trenavell was.

# Chapter 21

Danny, Matt, and I caught up with Noam and Meris. Meris didn't say anything to us. If something alive still lurked nearby, I didn't want to make it even more curious, nor did I want to run the risk of making a lot of noise by losing my temper and yelling at her or Noam.

The room ended at an arched entrance to another dim space beyond. Empty shelves ran along the wall on each side of the doorway. The nearest sign read "EY 3,000 B.C." That long ago, there wouldn't have been books here. Had they copied into books from other things, or left the old artifacts in place?

How long had crossing between the two planets been going on?

Meris took off through the door. Noam rushed after her. No answer, just action. *As usual.*

A quiet sound came from the far end of the room we'd come through. A soft, ruffly growl echoed in the air, sounding like a dog for a second.

I dared to turn and look.

Like a big cat, it stalked our way. Matt whipped his flashlight up at it.

It took me just a second, as it vocalized in reaction to the light, to realize it was one of those creatures that had stalked us in the night and attacked me. They'd gotten ahold of people in Compass Hill the day the city was retaken, and there had been deaths. The creatures were venomous and vicious.

And Meris had run out of the room with her gun.

The creature in front of us sniffed, then bared its teeth without moving forward.

Without warning, Matt aimed a quick, wordless shout at it.

It jumped, ears laying flat to its skull as it scooted backwards. I grabbed Matt's arm and yanked him in the same direction that Meris and Noam had gone, hoping they hadn't gone far, that maybe there was somewhere to hide.

We just about ran into the both of them as they stood staring into the room beyond. Whoever had emptied the other shelves had done the same thing here.

"Where'd it all go?" I asked.

"Think they took it all to Earth?" Danny asked.

“But where?” Matt eyed a tall, dirt-covered window as the sun dimmed again.

Danny shrugged. “Earth’s a big planet, and so is this one.”

I heard snuffling again, somewhere behind us, and whirled around. The creature’s back end was briefly visible as it passed the doorway we’d come through.

Meris’ footsteps echoed off the hard surface as she made her way to the other end of the room. Somewhere behind me, the soft shuffling and the click of claws faded as the creature went off somewhere else.

It had growled at us, but it had also reacted to Matt trying to scare it. My heart started to pound. Was it habituated to people?

*There are people in Skyrren. It’s seen people before.*

“Where do y’all think it’s going?” I asked softly.

Before Matt could answer, I heard something that sounded like a voice. It didn’t echo, and it wasn’t nearby. But someone had spoken.

I turned to Matt and raised my eyebrows. We weren’t alone.

“There’s someone else in this part of the palace,” I said. At least the creature had walked off. At least it wasn’t actively going after us, but that didn’t worry me. The fact that there was a possibility it was trained, and that its handler was nearby, did. My stomach roiled with nerves, the sensation creeping up into my teeth, the feeling of eyes on us strong as we left the archives and found the fountain hall again.

A sound traveled through the hall. Quiet footsteps and clacking nails, along with a soft snuffle.

Meris came to a stop.

Could we hide in or behind the fountains? If the creature was sniffing, then it didn't have to see us. Was the palace overrun with them? Had it gone to get others of its kind and tell them that there was food?

The footsteps got louder as two figures resolved. One was the creature approaching us at a trot.

Behind it, a man stepped into the sunlight of the fountain hall and made his way to us, lagging behind the creature by twenty feet or so.

The animal reached us, stopped ten feet away, and let out a different kind of growl than I'd heard before, and not one directed at us. It swung its head to look at the man, who stopped to stand beside it.

Cargan.

He placed his hand on its head and hissed something, scratching behind one of its ears. His face set as he stared at Meris.

"You were here?" Meris asked, anger and confusion on her face.

“I told you I would guide you, Meris.” His face was quiet and calm, but the harsh edge in his voice exhibited something else.

“I didn’t know you were here,” Meris snapped. “We proceeded through the gate station in Compass Hill because we couldn’t find you, and we came upon Matt and Anya.”

Cargan zeroed in on me. “Were you two already in Skyrren?”

We both shook our heads.

“How did you find the city?” Cargan turned to Meris again. “You’ve never been here by the station route.”

“Danny assisted us,” Meris answered, almost haughty. Proud, maybe, that she had friends that would help her get somewhere when her brother hadn’t.

Danny spoke up. “Um, no, I have a pronunciation guide from my mom. We…just kinda looked for a sign that would roughly match how Skyrren’s pronounced.”

Cargan stared at Danny, eyes calculating, then slowly looked down at the floor. “You have to stay here.”

“Why?” Meris asked.

Cargan’s steady expression broke into an exasperated glare. “Because you can’t go back to Compass Hill.”

The noises that Danny had heard. The lights we’d seen. The soldiers, and the people inspecting the storefront. The wall.

Noam tilted his head. "What's happening there?"

Cargan's eyes flicked to me for a second.

Fear shot to every nerve in my body as I pictured the silent thunderstorm and remembered the seal's strange surface.

Cargan looked at Noam. "It is empty enough in this palace that sound travels." A stiff, unamused smile flashed on his face. "We weren't sure that someone had entered the palace, but the five of you aren't terribly quiet."

*So I did hear someone talking.*

The creature settled down beside Cargan, huffing a breath out of its mouth, eyeing us with an intelligent gaze that reflected the soft sunlight. I knew it wasn't a dog, but it sort of behaved like one. And this one was at least tame, if not domesticated.

Did Cargan's "we" mean him and the creature? Had the voice been his, giving it a command? Or were there other people?

*You can't go back to Compass Hill…*

Compass Hill had been closed up tight until, according to Danny, more soldiers had shown up. Matt and I had seen those lights in the tunnels, and there were noises. We hadn't been able to find Meris and Noam at first, or Danny, and a group had been inspecting the shop, one of them heading down into the cellar.

I'd activated the device, and something had begun to happen.

Sound traveled here in the palace. Cargan couldn't tell us what was going on while we were out here, and he'd looked at me. Had he meant to?

It wasn't like putting the device together had actually ended the war, and it hadn't been expected or wanted at all, not specifically by Trenavell, even if people like Mr. Simpson and Rebecca were eager to see that done.

Something powerful had gone through the device, strong enough to seal all the gates at one time. The anger I'd tried to contain was bursting at the edges of the box I'd put it in.

Whatever was happening in Compass Hill, Trenavell wasn't making it happen. They were preparing. Reacting.

Cargan snapped his fingers, and the creature beside him got to its feet. He said something again that I couldn't understand, and it left the hall.

But Danny's eyes snapped to Cargan, just for a second.

"How long do we need to stay here?" Noam asked.

Cargan turned halfway away from us. "It may be several days."

Matt and I looked at each other. We'd stayed here longer than that before. Weeks in Trenavell had passed in hours at home, but that was not a standard I could count on. If we stayed here overnight, then it could also be a whole night at home, or longer.

Meris and Noam could stay in Trenavell. Matt and I couldn't stay here, and Danny couldn't either.

The three of us could get home. Matt and I had run through a lot of the station. The upper level, with its tighter hallways, wasn't as easy, but once we navigated through that, we might even outrun anyone who might be in the tunnels. No one had been at the Kings Road gate lately.

We didn't move.

"Where would you be able to tell us?" Meris asked her brother.

Cargan turned back around. "There's a chamber that once served for the rulers to meet with the council of governors."

An image flashed in my head, of a painted and cracked sign in front of a house on Salt's Creek's main street.

If we could get to that gate, that would be a much faster way home.

Cargan was alone right now. He could maybe catch one of us, but not all of us, and if Matt and Danny and I just ran…

I moved closer to Matt, making sure that I was pretty centered behind Noam and Meris, and tapped Matt's arm. Slowly, he turned his head to me, and I looked up into his eyes, then at the palace entrance. Danny's gaze caught mine, following it, and he nodded once.

Noam and Meris would be okay here, and them not coming with us meant that I wouldn't unload on them, that I could possibly cool off.

I took one step back, preparing to turn, putting my weight on my left foot.

Once more, I tapped Matt's arm, then took off, both him and Danny behind me.

"Stop!" Cargan yelled.

His yell was going to travel. Whoever else was with him could reinforce him. They could catch the three of us. I surged as hard as I could, gaining speed, desperate.

Fear that he'd send the creature with him after us swirled up, but he didn't. It didn't strike me as a creature used to attack, anyway. It was docile. All it had done was track us.

Cargan could either chase us alone, fetch his reinforcements, or wait for them. The realization that the three of us had time hit me as soon as we burst out of the palace doors.

And with that, I heard the two additional sets of footsteps following me and Matt and Danny.

It would only slow me down to look back, but I took a glance anyway.

For some reason, Meris and Noam had followed us.

Frustration burned as we dashed across the street and back to the Skyrren station. They didn't know where we were going.

Did she think we were trying to return to Compass Hill? I hadn't even told Matt and Danny, but they'd be much more ready to wind up in Salt's Creek than Meris and Noam were.

We made it to the station. No one had caught up to us yet. I remembered where we'd come from, and I aimed for that gate, my breath coming in gasps as I tried to push myself to be faster.

We had time, though. No one had caught up. Cargan couldn't apprehend us alone, and the creature, if anything, would just be tracking us. I didn't want it in Salt's Creek, but I didn't hear it yet, either.

We ran to the gate that would take us back to the Compass Hill station. It still stood open. The five of us dashed through it, and I heard it close with a loud thud. Matt and Danny got out flashlights.

I slowed to a jog and then to a walk. I couldn't push myself to run anymore, not right then. I couldn't really even talk all that well. We walked, as quietly as we could, all of us breathless, through the facility.

My breath still came in gasps, and we'd almost gotten to the end of the passage, when the a door opened behind us, slamming against the wall.

"Meris!" Cargan's voice echoed in the station, and I took off again. Did he have reinforcements now? Would he dare chase us? A hissed word, maybe a command, followed, but our footsteps on the stone floor drowned it out as we crossed into the main concourse.

My gaze fell on the doorway that led to the upper level, and I knew which passageway we would need to go down. I didn't dare say aloud where I was taking them.

We'd left the door closed, and I knew which one it was, the one with all the intact pegs around the threshold. If it had ever needed repairing, someone had done so correctly.

My foot slid as I stopped in front of the door and grabbed the handle. It opened easily, and I slipped through, trusting my friends to close and lock it behind me.

The heavy air descended on me as I passed into the Salt's Creek train station. I was sweating already from the run, but I knew this humidity wasn't going to let me cool off. My entire body shook with the effort of running here without being able to fully catch my breath.

One of my friends shut the gate and locked it.

On the other side of the door into the Compass Hill gate station, something thumped.

I turned to Meris and Noam, silent, the anger boiling up as the words tore out of me on a wheeze. "What are y'all gonna do?"

They looked at each other, hesitant. Neither of them had the lantern. Where had they left it?

The train station had become oppressive. Jake Andrews' face flashed in my mind. Iacomus was in my town.

"Meris," I snapped again, my voice breaking.

The gate door jerked once, then rattled.

Meris' hand moved, slowly, as if if she was going to grab her rifle.

"Meris, don't," Noam breathed.

Slowly, she stopped and dropped her hand.

What was she thinking? We couldn't see who it was, she couldn't aim, and she was one person.

So was I. A bayonet wouldn't do all that much good either.

Dread filled me, doubling the anger as the door rattled more. We'd locked it, but whoever was there could break the lock. Was there a way to destabilize the gate on this side? Nothing obvious glimmered in the doorframe.

"Meris." A firm voice spoke from the other side of the door. Cargan.

My jaw tightened, heart pounding faster and faster.

After a second of uncertainty, Meris' face hardened. Noam just gave her a nod.

We would have to walk home. We'd have to figure out how Danny would get home, but that was sure easier than figuring out what we were going to do with Meris and Noam. Mrs. Dobken might be almost comically ignoring how weird it was that Danny was on Earth, but neither Matt's parents nor mine would be able to ignore Meris and Noam, and I didn't know how to explain them.

Without another word, I went to the cigarette machine and started to drag it. It barely moved before Danny and Matt came along beside me. With their help, it lifted from the floor a couple inches, and we moved it into place against the door. Its weight quieted the rattling, though there remained a desperate effort on the other side.

Noam and Meris were in Salt's Creek, with no obvious intention of leaving.

Iacomus had seen them before. Even beyond that, Meris had been the one that shot him, and that was why he'd come after us, why he'd carried out a massacre in that village while we were on a quest that we shouldn't have been on.

I had no idea where Jake Andrews even was. He lived here, somewhere. He probably had a house, and maybe at least a cover story of a job. I'd seen him twice at my teacher's house, and once at church.

I couldn't let him see my friends, regardless of how mad I was. If the train station was open, then there was no way they could stay here.

My skin prickled, the air heavy on it, a sharp reminder of our location as I realized how damp my face had gotten. I dropped my backpack on the floor, and it kicked up a little puff of dust. Almost panicked, I quickly wrangled my coat off as Matt and Danny did the same.

Though their movements were calmer than mine, I imagined the overwhelmed looks in their eyes probably reflected my own, if I wasn't more frantic. I'd been the one, after all, to see Iacomus here, to speak to him as Jake Andrews.

Once my coat was off, I caught my breath with one deep inhale, then rounded on Noam and Meris again. "What are we supposed to do with y'all?" The near-frenzied edge in my voice made it come out almost as a yell.

Matt set a hand on my shoulder.

*I can't be too loud in here.*

Noam and Meris drew back a little. Noam took a breath as Meris' expression slipped into one less determined and harsh.

"We could wait here," Meris offered.

Noam frowned. "What would we be waiting for, Meris?"

Slowly, she looked down, and I knew she'd had no plan other than locking the door to her brother.

I shook my head. "Y'all can't. I'm pretty sure someone is still using this gate." With a deep breath, I kept going, "And Iacomus is here, in town. I told y'all that."

Noam lifted his head. "Where can we stay?"

"Not my house," I answered.

Meris' gaze shot to me. "We've been hospitable to you and Matt when you've been in Trenavell."

Noam came to my defense. "They stayed because of her stitches, Meris."

I tensed.

Matt jumped in, his voice and logical argument diffusing the frustration I was about to let out. "Both of us each just live in a regular house."

"And I don't have siblings," I added. "It's just me and my parents. Danny has stayed with Matt because they're cousins." I looked out to the street. "I don't have a good explanation for why y'all would be here for however long you are, and I frankly don't know how to hide you."

The tension in my body rose again and the irritation of not knowing what to do made the heavy air almost perceptibly thicker as we stood in the dusty room. An itch crawled across my scar, and I clawed at it through my t-shirt.

Matt's eyes flicked to my hand. Meris spoke.

"How far is Gavin Dupree's house from yours?" she asked me.

"Not that far," I told her. "Through the woods." I didn't know how we'd get food for them. I could give them the supplies that Matt and I had bought.

Meris, and probably Noam, could hunt, and it might not even sound out of place in the country. Both of them could survive. I didn't know everything, but I did know that they'd done it before, when they'd traveled from the refugee camp to the caves near where we'd met them.

"Very well," Meris answered. "We can stay there and use the Kings Road gate should we need to return quickly to Trenavell."

"How far do you live from here?" Noam asked.

Lifting my backpack, I looked at Danny and Matt, then winced. "It's a few miles. It'll take a while to get there." I knew that walking wouldn't be hard for them, though I didn't know what kind of heat and humidity they were used to.

Danny cleared his throat. "Should we all be seen walking together?"

Matt looked at me. "We could walk home and drive back for Meris and Noam."

"I can stay with them," Danny offered.

The angle of the sunlight outside wasn't clear enough for me to be able to tell what time it it might be. "What if you have to wait all night?" If we got back home really late, we'd be in trouble. If it wasn't too late, then maybe we could go back out, under another pretense.

Danny just shrugged.

Hopefully there wasn't anyone watching this train station too closely.

"We'll be back, then," I told them, and Matt and I walked to the door. We hadn't tried it yet.

It opened, not secured or boarded up, and we let ourselves out into the humid summer day.

# Chapter 22

"Think we'll get home before our parents do?" I asked, noting the height of the sun.

Matt's foot scuffed over a rough patch of broken concrete. "Probably, but it might be close."

As we walked down the sidewalk, I wished pointlessly that we could have gotten to Dupree's house.

"It's hot," I complained, and a tired laugh snuck out.

"Yeah."

Our feet crunched on the cracked sidewalk as we reached the edge of the Whitley's restaurant driveway. A burgundy car signaled left to turn in. It pulled all the way into the restaurant's parking lot and stopped there.

The passenger side window rolled down. "Do y'all need a ride?" It was a girl's voice, almost a yell.

I stepped a little closer to peer down into the window.

Samantha from school looked out, concern on her face. She wore her uniform for Whitley's. It would be so much better to ride in an air conditioned car. Ten times better. And we'd get back to our friends faster.

"Um…" I glanced back at Matt. He looked hesitant and annoyed. "Aren't you going to work?"

She shrugged. "Yeah, but Mr. Whitley's cool, and I'm early, so…"

A flicker of air conditioning reached me where I stood. "Well…okay." I popped the door open and sat inside, folding my arms around my coat and backpack. Matt slid into the backseat, and I didn't dare look at him.

Samantha turned around in the parking lot and headed back onto the street. "I'm not trying to be weird or anything, promise." She rolled the passenger window back up from her side. "I mean, I was like, 'oh hey, I know them from school' and 'oh wait, they're friends with my cousin' and I don't know where y'all were at with coats and stuff, but it's way too hot to walk far today."

"Cousin?" Matt asked.

Samantha shook her head, rolled her eyes, and smirked. "Okay, so Brandon never mentioned me." She scoffed. "Idiot. Love him, though."

"I'm sorry, he really never did," I said. "And we've never been around his family." Logically, it was likely for him to have cousins. I'd just had no idea that one of them was Samantha.

"It's fine, I'm seriously not mad." Her face went unreadable for a second. "Well, okay, nice to meet you, I'm Samantha Evans, Brandon White's cousin."

She was nice. Cheerfully sarcastic, almost, and bubbly. "Nice to meet you." Matt had tried to avoid her, and she was a nice person. Maybe he'd misread her. I still resisted the urge to look at him, but I did relax. Unless Samantha was super good at acting, she wasn't a threat. She was truly being kind and giving us a ride home. "Um…do you need directions?"

She shook her head. "No, I know where y'all live."

Any sort of caution or fear or anything like common sense waited until right then to kick in. I tried to hide it. "Oh. Okay."

She laughed a little. "I mean, y'all are friends with my cousin, so…like why wouldn't I know, right?"

"Yeah." Did that even make sense?

A burgundy car had left the letters on my porch. This burgundy car.

*I can't say anything.*

It didn't take long to get to our neighborhood. Samantha pulled into the end of my driveway.

"Thanks," I said.

"Yeah, thanks," Matt echoed.

"Y'all are welcome," she answered.

I got out of the car. "See you later, I guess." Matt joined me, standing close.

""Bye!" Samantha answered. I closed the car door and she backed out of the driveway, heading down the street.

Slowly, I turned to look at Matt. "She really is nice."

He gave me a dry look.

I waited a second before saying more, feeling something off and wrong in my words, even as I spoke. "I mean…you could…since she seems to like you…"

"I'm not interested in her," Matt answered, his tone final, his eyes looking directly into mine.

I held up my hands, my coat still draped over my right arm. "Okay, fine." I went to my car. "Let's head back to the train station, then."

Matt gave me a nod and got in.

We sat. I cranked the ignition and turned the air conditioning all the way up. I'd cooled off in Samantha's car, but the other three would probably need it. The icy air set my core shuddering as it relieved the heat that had built up. A strand of my hair caught in the stream, blown around by the artificial wind, and I remembered the seal, flinching this time.

"What?" Matt asked.

"The seal in Skyrren," I told him, looking up.

He kept watching me steadily.

"What if I hurt someone?" I asked. "I didn't have to listen to Meris. I could have just left the poem with them. I didn't have to drag you to to Trenavell or activate that device."

"You didn't drag me," Matt said.

I swallowed the lump that had swollen in the back of my throat.

***

Meris and Noam stood a few yards in front of us, looking up at the Dupree house.

Noam turned to me. "We can hide here."

Approaching them, I kept my eyes on the summer-thickened vines. "Yeah, the front door's broken, but I'm pretty sure there's bedrooms and stuff upstairs."

"Do you know how active it is?" Meris asked.

I shook my head. "We've used it plenty. The only other car I've seen here that didn't belong to a friend of ours was that brown one I told you about." This gate hadn't been common knowledge in Trenavell, either, not when Matt and I had first gone there. "If you see that one, just hide."

"I doubt anyone's staying here, though," Matt added.

Meris frowned and faced me. "What about your friend?"

A pang went through me. "I don't know where he is, but I don't think he'd go upstairs."

Meris and Noam exchanged a glance.

“Then we’ll see you tomorrow,” Noam said. They climbed the steps together and disappeared into the shadows of the house.

Matt and Danny and I made our way to my backyard and stopped by the trampoline. I had not one shred of a plan for what to do next. We’d given Noam and Meris food, and they’d filled up the water bottles they had on them. That could get them through tonight, but I couldn’t fund provisions for them, and I wasn’t sure if it was a good option to give them food from our pantry. My parents would notice that. Either of them could hunt.

I knew nothing about Trenavellan game animals. What had they even hunted on their own planet?

With a sigh, I looked up at the guys. “Y’all want to come in?”

Matt just watched me.

Danny smiled a little. “I think I probably better get cleaned up and see about the flight my mom is getting me.”

What time was it now? The sun stood high, but not centered. Mid-afternoon, I guessed. “Okay.” Holding onto the warm metal ring of the trampoline, I leaned back. “Guess I’ll go figure out whatever it is we’re supposed to do with the other two.” I pushed away. “Maybe I’ll see you before you leave, Danny.”

“We’ll come back by,” Matt answered.

I gave both of them a less than confident smile and made my way up the steps to my back door.

# Chapter 23

Matt stood beside my car as I readied myself to get in and drive to Miss Whitley's house. Even though the light would still be good when I was heading home, using my bike would leave me vulnerable.

"I'll be out here when you get back," Matt answered.

My heart racing, I slipped into the driver's side of my car and started it up. My stomach jerked hard. In all likelihood, I couldn't avoid Jake Andrews, but if Jimmy was already absorbed in a movie or game, I could avoid talking to the adults at all, at least until Miss Whitley got home.

Matt and I locked eyes, and I backed out of my driveway.

It wouldn't take me long to get there, and as I drove to Peach Street, I dreaded seeing a car in the driveway, though I didn't know what Jake's looked like.

When Miss Whitley's house came into view, with her garage door closed, my hands relaxed on the steering wheel, loosening tension I hadn't realized was there. I pulled up beside her car and sighed, hoping that Jimmy already had a game going.

As I stood on the porch and rang the doorbell, I remembered the wasp nest that had been growing on her porch, and tensed again as I turned to peek at the corner.

It had grown. Two wasps perched there now, one crawling around as I watched, its legs working, wings flared and ready to take off, or still in that position from landing. Had Miss Whitley not noticed it?

Miss Whitley's door opened then. "Hey, Anya!" she said. I turned to face her, and her gaze drifted up in the direction mine had been as she pushed the glass door open. "Oh, ugh, I forgot that was up there. Please come in."

I entered the front hall and Miss Whitley shut the door behind me. The familiar music from Jimmy's game made it to me.

"Frozen pizza okay?" she asked.

"Yes, ma'am."

She went to the oven and set it to preheat. "Jimmy's probably still gonna be playing that game the whole time," she said.

"That's fine." I'd be glad to join him, as soon as possible, if only to watch.

She smiled. "Just a warning, somebody's aunt just put a pool in, and the aforementioned someone is sharing some characteristics with a tomato today."

"Ouch," I answered, wincing, my ears open for the sound of a car.

"It's not too bad," she said. "I think my sister was a few minutes late with the sunscreen. Let's go back there."

My body let go of more tension. I could hide from Jake Andrews. From Iacomus. Would he come in the house? Would he want to see Jimmy?

"Honey, Anya's here," Miss Whitley called as we approached the room.

"Hey," Jimmy answered, distracted as we entered. He knelt on the floor in front of the TV. A pink stripe cut across the bridge of his nose. I settled behind him on the couch. Watching him play the game would be fine.

"The oven should be done pre-heating soon," Miss Whitley said. "I'll be back around eight."

The doorbell rang. I managed not to jump, but I did tense, and tried to hide it with the eager nod I gave Miss Whitley. "Okay."

"See y'all then!" Miss Whitley said, and disappeared into the hallway.

Would Jake just drop Miss Whitley off when he returned? I didn't know what reason I could give to hide in the TV room.

There wouldn't be much to clean up, especially if we ate at the kitchen table.

But it wasn't like there was anything Jake Andrews could do here, and Matt would be waiting for me.

***

When Miss Whitley's keys sounded in the door two hours later, I tensed again. Jimmy paused his game and dashed out of the room without a word.

Jake Andrews' voice replied to something Miss Whitley said.

He couldn't do anything to me here. Matt was waiting.

I stood, my eyes staring, unfocused, at the colorful screen Jimmy had paused the game on. Turning away, I gripped my phone in my pocket, nudging the keys below it, and headed for the front of the house.

Jake's head turned to me slightly as I went into the room, his eyes fixed on Miss Whitley before shooting to me.

Miss Whitley stepped away. "Let me go get your money, Anya." She disappeared down the hall.

"It's Anya McCall, right?" Iacomus' smile grew, warm and reaching almost to his eyes. But above the smile, the cold, calculating ice stuck out this time.

"Yes, sir," I answered, anger that I'd ever told him my name sending a buzz along my nerves.

The smile slipped a little, a trace of it remaining as it became a thoughtful expression. His eyes narrowed, still good-natured at the perimeters, and hard at the center. "Is your family from this area?"

As fast as my heart started to beat with that question, it was a normal question to ask. I nodded, silent.

He smiled again. "I just thought you looked so familiar." He lifted his chin, a practiced realization spreading over his face. "I think maybe I saw you at church."

I swallowed, trying not to gulp loudly and obviously.

Miss Whitley bustled back into the room. "All right," she said, holding three bills out to me. "Is fifty okay?"

"Um, yes ma'am." My voice spilled out of my mouth.

"I better get going, Joanna," Iacomus said, opening the door. The cold eyes with their pleasant edges landed on me again. "See you around, Anya."

My jaw tightened. He slipped out, and I hesitated. I didn't want to find myself alone in the driveway with Iacomus, king of Naolon. He couldn't do anything in Miss Whitley's house, but there was no telling what he'd try outside.

Miss Whitley waved at him through the glass. A car started, and I thought I might cry in relief.

Hard, quick footsteps preceded Jimmy's appearance in the front hall. "'Bye, Anya!"

His grinning face, as he waved and tore back to the TV room, calmed me a little. From what I could see through the door, Jake had driven away.

My hand jerking as I tried to control the trembling, I waved the bills once and tried to smile. "I'll head on home now. Thanks."

"No, thank you," Miss Whitley answered. "Have a good night, Anya." Her smile actually held warmth through and through.

My steps weren't smooth as I walked onto the porch. It was closing in on darkness outside, and a third wasp had joined the other two on the nest. I grasped my keys and hurried for my car as the wooden door shut behind me. An abstract thought that now was the best time to spray that nest flitted through my brain as I wrenched my car door open, threw myself in as fast as I could, and cranked the ignition. The gust of air conditioning dried the sweat on my face as my jaw tightened, and I desperately tried to loosen it and not give in to the nausea. Going too fast, I backed out of the driveway, hoping Miss Whitley would think I was being reckless instead of terrified.

No other cars made their way through the neighborhood, though it was after eight on a Friday. I could speed home. The dark hadn't set in yet, though the streetlights began to turn on, slowly brightening. Pedestrians had gone in for the night, thankfully. It might not be a good idea for me to be seen driving like this if my parents saw me blazing into our driveway.

As I pulled in, I saw Matt. Black hair, red summer camp t-shirt, and black shorts, visible as he waited on the front steps of his house. With a press of the brake, I brought my car to a stop, put it in park, and turned it off. The air conditioning had been cool, but I didn't think that it had been cold enough to leave me shaking this hard, my whole core keeping up a steady tremble. At least I was home now.

The humid air closed in on me as I got out of the car. Making sure it was locked, I made my way around the front bumper and rushed across the grass to the Dobken's front porch.

As he watched me approach, his eyebrows drawing together, Matt's eyes didn't reflect anything.

He waited half a minute after I'd sat down before talking.

"Was he there?" Matt's voice stayed low.

I laced my fingers together and clenched them, squeezing as they shook, and nodded. A dry spot in my throat grew.

"Did you talk to him?"

Another nod as my core shuddered. My breath wobbled with my single deep inhale. "He remembered my name from last time, asked if my family was from here." My gut roiled. "He thought I looked familiar, and he thinks he saw me at church." I curled my toes up, pushing the tops of my feet against the leather straps of my flip-flops. "And he said he'd see me around." Finally, I looked up at Matt.

His troubled, angry eyes reflected the porch light.

*Hold it together.* "It would all sound like pleasantries, wouldn't it?" Another breath. "Like a regular conversation." Miss Whitley had to have heard him talking, and she hadn't been disturbed by what he'd said.

*She also didn't see him.*

"Do you think he actually remembers where he's seen you other than church?" Matt asked.

With a jerky nod, I answered. "Yes." The cold in his eyes, even though the smile had reached them. I could imagine the same ice there, but unsmiling, as he carried out his crime in the village. The way that his "oh, yeah" face was so smoothly practiced that I was sure that it was only me already knowing that Jake Andrews was Iacomus that let me see through his mask.

My mind began to build bridges. If he knew my name, and knew I was one of Miss Whitley's students, and he knew where she worked, then he could find me. It was a shorter bridge.

The longer one was worse.

He could introduce himself to my parents at church, under the guise of the new guy in town making connections and meeting people. If he drove the brown car, and if he knew where I lived, he could go to the Dupree house, where Noam and Meris hid.

And I didn't know what I could do. I knew he'd led a massacre, but it was on another planet, and I couldn't tell a soul about it who'd believe me.

Noam and Meris would have been safer in Trenavell, whatever was going on there.

"Anya."

I looked at Matt again. *Hold it together.* "We don't know why he was looking for the four of us."

Matt snorted. "Because Meris shot him."

"Well, yeah, but what was he gonna do if he caught us?"

After a second, Matt shook his head. "No idea, but…he can't do much here."

An echo of what I'd thought, though in Matt's words. It rang as true as it had in Miss Whitley's front hall.

At night, we'd be in our houses, our parents there, and truth be told, if I had to, I could hide Noam and Meris in my house. I could find somewhere safer for them. Danny would be here in a few weeks, more permanently, masquerading as a student. Even with gaps, none of us would truly ever be alone.

A lightning bug flashed nearby.

The shaking eased. Whatever Iacomus wanted, the good likelihood that he couldn't get it stood strong.

We would not be alone, and that was our strength.

# About the Author

Amanda Cale lives in Eastern North Carolina with her husband and dog. Find her at the social media listed below!

Instagram: @Amanda_Cale_Author
TikTok: @AmandaBCale
Facebook: Riddle Book Series
Blog: WorldOfRiddle.Wordpress.com

www.ingramcontent.com/pod-product-compliance
Lightning Source LLC
Chambersburg PA
CBHW030550310726
48979CB00011B/2098/J

* 9 7 8 0 9 8 9 5 2 1 1 3 0 *